What Others Are Saying

"The world needs another Star Wars. This is it!"
Norman Wright - Lockheed Martin

"A fabulous book. Very timely in regards to the current trends happening in the bio-medical fields today."
Jennifer Miele, WDBJ - TV 7 Roanoke, Virginia

"Not just for science fiction fans. Anyone who loves adventure stories will love this book!"
G. Runner - Central Transport, Baltimore

"Once I started reading it, I couldn't put it down, even though I'm not an avid sci-fi reader."
Eric Park - Education Coordinator, Pittsburgh

"Don't let this one slip by on your must read list."
Rodger Marjama, Speedwing.net

"This book does have the space opera type of flavor to it and should appeal to most Star Wars fans."
Blue-Zero, The Ezine

"Steven C. Macon has got a Christian Star Wars on his hands..."
A Frank Review

"Top notch and riveting."
Jeff Ovall - author of Chronicles of the HEdge

"A must read for all Star Wars fans!"
Yellow30 Sci-Fi

"The character interaction in this book makes it a strong read."
Gary Costello -Virginia Tech

"The neat thing the story went from a Clancy-ish read to a sci-fi read - drawing in readers who may not normally read science fiction."
author Jeff Ovall

"Steven C. Macon's *Descent into Darkness*, the first book in the *Children of the Dark Millennium* series, tests the accepted version of how life on earth began with a look at a society and star system infiltrated at every level of government and military by clones, replicants and replacements. In a world foreign yet familiar good versus evil as darkness spreads across the galaxy."
Sharon Vander Meer - Editor Happenstance magazine

DESCENT

INTO

DARKNESS

Books by Steven C. Macon

Non-Fiction
What Color Is Your Wallpaper?

Fiction
Children of the Dark Millennium Series
Descent into Darkness
*The Hunted**
*ShadowChild**

**forthcoming*

Poetry
Buffaloes, Beads and Indians
House of the Wind

Editor
The Unknown
Alien Alerts Magazine
Yellow30 Sci-Fi Review

Writing as Steven Fivecats
Poetry
Buffaloes, Beads and Indians
Tea Room Musician
Deep Dark Winter So Cold

Fiction
The Relic and The Curse

Descent into Darkness

Children of the Dark Millennium - Book One

STEVEN C. MACON

A Compass-Signal Book

A Compass-Signal Book

Author Contact
livingtree.entertainment@gmail.com

ISBN 10: 0-615-68255-3
ISBN 13: 978-0-615-68255-6

Revised Second Edition

Portions of this book formerly published as *The Relic and The Curse* under the Steven Fivecats pen-name

Printed in the United States of America

In Memory of

Charles Clinton Macon
1926 to 1990

and

Mark Randell Macon
1960 to 1995

Author's Note

Children of the Dark Millennium began simply as a short story conceived the summer of 1979 while I was working construction in Florida. It had a different title back then. It would also blossom from short story to a multi-volume series of books. The series and the first book would progress through a series of title changes before it was finally completed and published as *The Ancient* in July 2001. Another decade would pass before another version of the book would surface. Yet the original *author's note* will always capture the spirit behind the books in this series....

There is much to be said about vision. "Without a vision the people perish." *This book has been a vision in my life for a long time. It has gone through many stages of revisions and grown into a story kept alive by a simple fact:* vision. *I've believed in this book when others didn't think it had a prayer. I kept my vision and my belief in the simple fact that a good story is hard to kill.*

If you have a vision keep to it. Persistence pays off. If you try and fail, at least you have the satisfaction of doing something. A true vision, burning bright in your heart, will not allow you to give up.

In keeping with what Aslan said in *Prince Caspian*, *Descent into Darkness* is the tale of things that transpired before the fateful events of chapter one first published in *The Ancient*. With the retelling of the story, the reader needs to know that *things never happen the same way twice.* If you have read the first tale, *The Ancient*, then be prepared - things have definitely changed!

No author stands alone. Without our friends where would we be?

For authors pounding the keys on a daily basis, it helps to have people who believe in you. They can be a source of encouragement in tough times when you simply want to throw the manuscript in the trash and forget writing. I've had plenty of days like that!

There are a number of people who stood by and supported me all these decades of working on this project. Yes, this has been a work that has spanned several decades and two centuries. Almost science fiction in that fact alone. I think it is very encouraging when family members and friends believe in your dream. First and foremost is my wife, Debra, who has been the strong anchor in my life and my writing. I think without her this would have never seen the light of print. My mother and brother, Joe, have always been a support. My friends in Florida have been very supportive as well. Bob Dempsey has loved this book even from the first rough drafts. Yes, Bob, I know you don't won't to hear this, but there are other books to follow! Rodger Marjama and Bob Hazen made valuable comments in the early stages. Bill and Debbie Griggs, the book connoisseurs, are another part of my support staff.

I will always remember what my good friend Norman Wright once said, *"The world needs this book."* Norman has since gone home to be with the Lord. In the course of time others came into my life after the first publication of *The Ancient.* Paul Dellinger, newspaper reporter, reconnected me to old time pulp science fiction and became a sounding board for thoughts and ideas. We attended a few sci-fi conventions and even served on a few panels. It was fun! Gary Costello inspired me to keep on when I seriously thought about giving up once and for all. Gary has a big vision for this book. Lastly, I must not forget Frank Creed and Jeff Ovall, good writer friends who really touched my heart with their love and kindness and gave their own pearls of wisdom for this project. Thanks guys!

Writers do write alone, but it's those times of connecting with family and friends that inspire us to keep at it. I will always be grateful for my friends and family. I hope they know that their part in this book is very much appreciated. Without it, this book would have never come to the final form it is today. Again, to all of you — Thank you from the bottom of my heart!

Steven C. Macon
Southwestern Virginia

O.W.L.

Prologue

"Whom the gods would destroy, they first make mad with power. The mills of God grind slowly, but they grind exceedingly small."
– Charles A. Beard

"Power tends to corrupt; absolute power corrupts absolutely."
– Lord Acton

April 16, 2023
Position: 16-S 68-W
O.W.L. Survey One
1435 Zulu

As light came to the high Andes, it was going to prove to be a spectacular morning in more ways than one. Perched some two hundred miles high above the snowy peaks of the Cordillera Real, OWL was watching and absorbing. Only forty-eight hours ago, an earthquake of 7.6 magnitude on the Richter scale had rattled villages and cities for several hundred miles in the high Andes. A number of villages had simply disappeared under tons of rock torn loose from the convulsing mountains. The Observation Water and Land survey satellite was on its initial mapping sequence of the southern hemisphere when the earthquake struck and was ordered to a new orbit to photograph the area of destruction. It was on this new mission that the glimmer first caught the attention of OWL's sensitive cameras. Multi-purpose tasking computers went to work immediately, translating the camera images into signals that would be sent back to Lawrence Bakersfield Laboratories at Livermore, California. It was to be the spark that would ignite a large forest fire of wild rumors and speculations for decades to come.

Mike Murphy, an MIT top three graduate and transfer from NASA's Kennedy Space Center, had just poured himself a cup of coffee and was in the middle of trying to shake the cobwebs out of his brain. He was about to take his first sip of the day when the glimmer caught his eye. He choked, spewing hot coffee all over his desk! "What the . . . ?" OWL's first high intensity images began dancing across his display at LBL.

"What you got?" came the question from his console sidekick, Alex Jenkins.

"OWL's got a contact!" Reflexes and years of experience went into play as Mike attacked the computer keyboard in front of him. In less than five minutes a scurry of activity began to take place in the otherwise humdrum monitoring station of Bravo Lab Niner. Because of the odd glimmer on the film, OWL was ordered into a geosynchronous orbit that would intensify camera operations for the next twelve hours.

By midmorning, it had been ascertained that the satellite did indeed have something unusual. Exquisitely sharp high-resolution photographs were spit out of a high speed photo processor as fast as it could receive the digital data from the orbiting satellite. OWL's sophisticated bank of cameras could photograph an object the size of a bee with such clarity of detail that it was sometimes taken for granted that the images were shot from two hundred miles overhead. The glossy photographs being passed around Bravo Lab certainly created more questions than answers. Just what was it that OWL had spotted?

"I'd say about a mile and a half of the mountain slid toward the bottom of the slope," came a matter of fact comment from Paul Tillis, chief satellite engineer. His bald head reflected the florescent lighting of the room.

"Look at the photos again, Paul," Mike said pointedly, becoming more agitated. He had spotted something and felt it should be obvious to everyone else. "Look at photos number One and number Forty-five."

Paul shuffled through the stack until he found the photos designated numbers One and Forty-five. "Okay, what should I be looking at?"

"Ugh!" Mike rolled his eyes toward the ceiling. "Look at the enhancement on Forty-five."

"I see what looks like pieces of metal." Paul answered.

"Precisely!" Mike exclaimed. "What kind of metal?"

"Looks like wreckage to me!" Brenda Mayfield remarked as she pushed back in her chair.

"That's it, wreckage!" Mike threw in. "It's obvious the earthquake caused the rock slide, but what are all these metal objects mixed in with it? There are no villages in that area."

"Anyone lose a plane recently?" Alex threw out. He had a habit of making wise cracks about almost everything at the lab.

Everyone obliged Alex with a laugh and went back to studying the photos.

AFSPC-Air Force Space Command
Delta Five Comm Station
Falcon AFB
1435 Zulu

LBL's observation hadn't gone unnoticed by the military. Computer displays danced with the exact images Livermore was seeing. Personnel at Delta Five Comm Station were also scurrying to retrieve data.

"Sir, " a vigilant E-5 alerted. "Spy Twelve has something on screen!"

Captain Ben Greene looked at the image for only a few seconds before realizing Spy Twelve, alias OWL, had something significant. "Put the Ghost in the air and get me a commitment from Look Down Tango." He reached for a phone. "Get me General Dalton, pronto!" Ben Greene had an eye for detail that far surpassed his constituents.

OWL was doing double duty as a spy satellite for the military. Its high-resolution cameras were a necessity in the global game of peace-keeper being played out by the United States around the world. Most of the funding for OWL had come straight from NASA and the US Geological Survey; however, the military had paid for the expensive optics aboard the bird and paybacks meant the war machine had dibs on all information filtered down by the satellite.

Bravo Lab Niner
Lawrence Bakersfield Laboratories
2045 Zulu

In less than six hours, top brass from the Pentagon were storming their way down the hallways of Bravo Lab Niner. Their intrusion wasn't a welcomed one and sent a few techs scurrying for the privacy of their offices.

General R. B. Dalton, with two full bird attachés, blazed past the lab assistant at operations central without so much as a "We're here to see..." Dalton pushed open the closed office door and stood across the desk from Dr. Jeremiah Tanner, chief of operations for Lawrence Bakersfield.

Tanner ignored the intrusion for as long as possible until one of Dalton's aides cleared his throat and shuffled his feet.

"Well, General?" Dr. Tanner slowly looked up from the satellite readouts he'd been given by the lab. He removed his reading glasses and leaned back in his chair. He didn't smile.

"Don't get all formal with me, Jerry. I want to know what you've got!" Dalton's tenseness was hard to ignore. His toadies were doing their best to remain militarily cool for the moment, but Tanner had an expression that could crack glass if need be.

"Got your jock strap a little tight, Robert?" Tanner was annoyed by these unannounced guests and their intrusion into his private little world. Robert Dalton and Jeremiah Tanner had been good friends for twenty years, but Dalton's young attachés were nothing more than yes-men. "Do you need your sidekicks?"

Dalton glanced at his aides and nodded. They left the room under silent protest. "That better, Jerry?"

"Much better, thank you!"

"Let's have it then." Dalton was like a kid in a candy store waiting for a special promised treat. The anticipation was killing him.

Tanner slowly got to his feet. "I would have thought you'd already had the jump on this thing. Probably had that spook jet of yours there and back by now." He smiled devilishly. "I know your bunch has its hooks in OWL."

"Tell me something I don't know!" Dalton snapped.

"I've got my team on its way."

"Is Garret really that good?"

"Jack Garret's the best at this kind of stuff. Whatever's down there, we'll know in short order." Tanner paused and walked over to his coffee maker. "You guys didn't loose something you don't want found, did you, Robert?"

Dalton turned a light shade of red and tried to ignore the dig. "Look, Jerry," he glanced around the room and leaned over the desk, "let's just say we're more than a little interested in whatever's down there. Understand my meaning?"

"That's what I thought, Robert." Tanner didn't smile. "That's what I thought."

April 17th
Bolivia
Cordillera Real
2216 Zulu

The exact location of OWL's glimmer was half way up Nevado Illimani in Bolivia. Getting there was not the problem. Garret's team of scientists were flown in via NASA's C-17D to an airbase at La Paz, which was already buzzing with relief flights for the earthquake victims. From there two high-altitude RHA-67 Raven choppers took the team to the snowy slopes of the mountain. In less than thirty-six hours after the sighting, Garret and his team closed in on the discovery.

Despite a moderate headwind, it was a picture perfect day with a clear blue sky to welcome them. The two choppers circled the avalanche on the southern face of the mountain for five minutes while onboard cameras recorded all the events. Satisfied that the slide area was reasonably safe, the choppers landed within three hundred and forty feet of the rock slide. Twisted pieces of aluminum-like metal were embedded among the boulders and jagged rocks, littering a three thousand foot section of the tumbled terrain. One piece, seventy-five feet in length, jutted up from the rocks like a thrown javelin. The metal was radiantly silver against the dark gray granite of the mountain. Reflective sunlight flashed from a hundred thousand points along the slide area. It was like being in a photo session with a thousand frantic photographers vying for a prized cover shot.

Garret exited the chopper, pushed back his goggles, and carefully took in the whole scene. "Good night, Agnes! What have we got here?" He was breathing hard, not just because of the altitude but because of the sight of the twisted metal glaring in the sunlight. Garret stared at the site for a full minute as his team scrambled out of the choppers and huddled around him. More than a few of the team members had awestruck expressions etched on their faces. OWL had indeed found something incredible.

For several days Garret's team slowly combed through the rocks and debris. In this high altitude the work progressed slowly and the cold added many frustrating moments as sensitive instruments froze up. There were occasional tremors, but so far the mountain gave no indication of convulsing again or sliding further down the valley. Pieces of metal, from mere splinters to whole chunks two to six feet in length, were all marked in place and ready to be extracted after proper documentation. At 2230 Zulu hours the next afternoon, another chapter in the book of astonishing discoveries was about to be written.

"Got something, sir!" Avery Hollis shouted as her brush strokes quickened, revealing a solid black plate under the earth where she had been assigned to search for fragments.

Garret and his team quickly surrounded the young redhead and waited as more earth was painstakingly brushed away. Fifteen minutes later the black box was isolated from the wreckage. Two silver insignias blazed brightly against the black metal. Wide-eyed with mouths agape, every eye was fixed on this new find. A few gloved fingers were pointed at the silver emblems.

"What do you think it is, sir?" Avery asked, staring incredulously.

Garret wanted to respond, but his mind was racing far beyond the moment. He was transfixed by the black box and the silver insignias. He slowly removed his right glove and touched them. The emblems were smooth, as if inlaid into the box itself, not painted on or decaled. He knew this was a key piece of the puzzle. Quickly replacing his glove he looked up at those standing around.

"Let's get this thing back to Livermore." Garret swallowed hard and turned to Avery Hollis. In a deep-throated whisper he said to her, "There's gotta be something in there; I'll stake my life on it!" What was in the box would prove to be a more earth-shaking element in the years to come than he could have ever imagined.

April 22nd
Radisson Hotel
San Francisco, California
0930 Zulu

The phone was ringing! And ringing! And ringing! Dr. Thomas Farraday fumbled in the dark for a full minute before he located the screaming machine. He hated hotels. They always put their phones in different places. Why couldn't they be consistent?

"Yeah, what do you want?" Farraday's voice was a step deeper than it usually was. His senses were dulled from the deep sleep. It had been a long day.

"Thomas, this is Jerry Tanner."

Recognition? Where was it? Did he know this intruder on the other end of the line?

"Thomas, are you there?" A pause. "It's Jerry Tanner, Thomas."

Finally, through the haze of slumber a recognizable name. "Jerry?" Farraday turned to the clock on the night stand. *2:30 AM* looked ominously stark. "Do you realize what time it is?"

"Thomas, I don't care what time it is! I've found something you have got to see." Tanner certainly sounded agitated. "Can you come down to Livermore in the morning?"

"I've got a lecture to conduct, Jerry." Farraday was beginning to come out of his sleepy state. "I can't cancel it now. I've got two sessions and I won't be free until about three o'clock." He was irritated.

"Thomas, this is important. I don't care about the lecture. Just get down here!" Tanner was nearly screaming now.

"What's that important?"

"Just get down here, Thomas!" Click!

For the next hour Thomas Farraday couldn't sleep. What was so important that he had to cancel his lecture and fly down to Livermore? *Ah! Tell Tanner to stuff himself! I have a lecture to finish.* For another ten minutes Farraday continued to wrestle with the puzzling call from his close friend. Tanner certainly wouldn't call in the dead of night if it wasn't important. This had better be good!

* * *

When Thomas Farraday arrived at Lawrence Bakersfield he was instantly aware of the buzz of military security. LBL was a top security site, but today security was even tighter. He was ushered through the security check and driven to the lab's main entrance where he was met by Jerry Tanner.

"What did you dig up this time, Jerry?" Farraday grinned as he shook hands with his old friend. "I haven't seen this many uniforms at LBL since your China Sea incident."

Tanner smiled, glancing around as the MPs strolled by. "Never a dull moment around here. Come on, Thomas, you've got to see this!"

"You've got my full attention."

Tanner ushered his friend past more security guards, receptionists, lab techs, and the like, to Second Clearing Lab Twelve. Two fully armed guards checked Farraday's security clearance and then stepped back to their station. When the doors sprang open Farraday and Tanner were greeted by Jack Garret, Mike Murphy, Ben Sauders, a metallurgy expert, and General Dalton.

"This is your man?" Dalton scowled.

"Dr. Thomas Farraday," Tanner motioned with his hands, "this is General Robert Dalton. General, Dr. Thomas Farraday."

"General." Farraday nodded quizzically and shook hands with the man. "What's this all about?"

"Let's cut to the chase, shall we gentlemen?" Tanner carefully studied each face. Anticipation hung in the air as each man cautiously gauged Thomas Farraday's every move. The men had been shielding a table from the professor when he came in. They guardedly stepped away. The black box Garret's team had brought back from the mountain was illuminated by several overhead lamps and sat dead center of the table. "This, Thomas, is why you're here." Tanner pointed to the box.

Cautiously, Farraday approached the table, took a pair of glasses from his coat pocket, slipped them on, and examined the box. It was solid black, measuring roughly twelve by six by eight inches, and appeared to be made of a high-sheen black metal. There was evidence of a tiny seam running completely around the box about three quarters of an inch from the top. A piece of white paper was positioned on top of the box. Farraday pulled himself erect and then turned to Tanner. "And?"

Tanner smiled. "Look at this, Thomas." Tanner carefully, and nervously, removed the piece of paper. Two foreign insignias were inscribed on the box in solid silver. Farraday's mouth fell open. The insignias were actually two letters of an alphabet that was strikingly similar to a group of languages well known to him. "Where did this come from?" He stared wide eyed at his friend.

"South America!" Tanner replied.

General Dalton coughed a warning. Tanner ignored him.

"South America?" Farraday was skeptical.

"South America, Doctor." Dalton interjected. "That's all you need to know right now. I want to know the meaning of those symbols, Dr. Farraday."

"What language? What era?" Ben Sauders asked.

Farraday removed his glasses and looked at each man carefully. "Well, gentlemen, I don't know where you got this box, but those two symbols are actually letters which are strikingly similar to several early forms of ancient Middle East languages: Phoenician, Babylonian, possibly even Hebrew."

"Hebrew?" Dalton questioned.

"Yes, General, Hebrew." Farraday was definitely curious. Perhaps it was indeed worth the canceled lecture. "Now, would someone be so kind as to tell me what this is all about?"

"In due time, Doctor, in due time." General Dalton remarked.

Thomas Farraday gave the general a hard stare.

"I think you should see what's inside." Dalton nodded his head at the box.

Tanner and the rest of the group eyed the box and then Farraday.

"You already opened this thing?" There was concern on Farraday's face. "I hope you didn't damage the contents."

Tanner came over and placed a hand on Farraday's shoulder. "We took every precaution, Thomas." He gave him a weak smile. "Go ahead, open it."

Very carefully Farraday examined the box, feeling along the top seam. Gingerly, he placed his hands on the top portion and pulled up. With just the slightest resistance the top of the box pulled away, allowing Farraday to peek inside. He gave a glance at the men standing around him.

"What do you think, Dr. Farraday?" General Dalton leaned forward.

Farraday glanced back at the box. Inside, were five blue eight-sided triangle-shaped crystals roughly three inches long. The crystals were positioned point down in pre-cut slots on a black tray in the middle of the box. Slowly he reached for the closest crystal and removed it, holding to the light.

"What do you think?" Tanner asked, eying his friend rather closely.

"Interesting shape," Farraday remarked as he turned the crystal around and around in his hand. The crystal reflected the light causing rainbows to flash on the walls. "A little large for jewelry, I would think."

The others glanced at Dalton and then back to Farraday.

"That's what we thought too," Tanner smiled rather devilishly.

"Have an idea what their purpose might be?" Mike Murphy asked, leaning back on his heels.

For a long moment, Farraday kept turning the crystal to the light, turning it one way and then another. After a while he returned his attention to the men in the room. "Have you done any tests yet on these things?"

"We've been waiting for you first, Doctor." Dalton remarked.

"Well, Thomas?" Tanner folded his arms across his chest and stared at his friend. "What do you think they're for?"

Farraday smiled, palmed the crystal and then held it up to the light again. "You ever get a gut feeling about something?"

The others just stared back at Farraday.

Shaking his head, Farraday held the crystal up to the light again. "I got a hunch about this thing. Remember any of those old science fiction television shows in the middle 1990s?"

Again, they all just looked at him with blank expressions etched on their faces.

"One in particular," Farraday smiled. "*Babylon Five.*"

"What are you talking about?" Dalton looked perplexed.

Farraday held the crystal up to the general. "On this science fiction show they had what was referred to as data crystals." He shook it at Dalton. "This general, could very well be something of that nature. After all, we're nearly there ourselves with information storage."

"If that's true, can you retrieve what's on it?" Dalton looked a little skeptical.

"I'm sure Wanda can." Farraday smiled.

"Wanda?" Dalton asked.

"My translation computer." Farraday grinned devilishly. "I designed her myself. Might take a little time."

Dalton came over, glanced at the crystals and then to Farraday. "I'm assembling a team to work on this. The first of them should be arriving tomorrow. Bring your Wanda and we'll see if she's any match for Derrick Parks and his machine."

Tanner and Farraday exchanged looks.

"You game, Doctor?" Dalton challenged with an icy look.

"I'm game, General." Farraday replied, giving his friend, Jerry Tanner, a wink.

"Good!"

June 23, 2023
Lawrence Bakersfield Laboratories
Clearing Lab Twelve
1934 Zulu

LBL had continued to be a caldron of whispered speculations for months. Security was stricter than any other time in previous history. Staff members raised more than a few eyebrows when the arrival of a select group of scientists showed up with super secret clearance. A half dozen large black boxes only added to the wild rumors floating among staff members. Only those in Clearing Lab Twelve knew that these mysterious boxes contained the latest in deciphering computers. There were a lot more military brass walking the hallways these days. More fuel for the rumor mills. Those with the proper clearances knew about the archaeological discovery of a crashed space vehicle on Nevado Illimani in Bolivia. This information was not to be discussed outside Clearing Lab Twelve or Five. Despite objections from General Dalton, who wanted to sequester the wreckage to Area 64 at the AFSPC's Utah Complex, Dr. Tanner and his staff were able to retain marginal control of the discovery. Tanner had assured the general that Lawrence Bakersfield was just as mysterious and hard to get to as his infamous "Dreamland" area of Utah. Dalton made sure of it. He still maintained top security over the project, and was, at times, ruthless in his dealings with the staff and scientists called upon to research the find. Despite trying to wrest complete control over the project, General Dalton realized that he still needed Tanner and his team at LBL. And Dr. Jeremiah Tanner had had to do some digging to find the best qualified experts to do the job.

The Berkley Technological Institute had reluctantly agreed to loan Dr. Thomas Farraday to LBL for an undisclosed amount of time. Berkley president, Gyles Nielburg, had quizzed Tanner for hours as to why he should give up his valued instructor. Tanner had simply stated that Farraday was to head up a team of cryptographers to investigate a recent discovery. This only added to Nielburg's curiosity. Nielburg knew not to press further and gave in to Tanner's request.

Initial tests had determined that the crystals were indeed data storage mechanisms. Tanner was confident that his friend, Thomas, would be very valuable in deciphering the data from the crystals. Farraday, after all, was a top ranked linguist in ancient written language forms. He had been instrumental in translating several ancient tablets found in Mexico and Africa in the latter half of the nineteen nineties. He was also a reputed expert in several ancient dialects. Hebrew and early Middle East languages were his strong points. He ranked as one of the five top Egyptologists in the world.

The first two months had been a nightmare. Personalities had clashed and tempers had flared over the procedures to be used in the decoding process. Time, energy, and frustration had weeded out virtually everyone else. Several of the scientists had their pet processes and wouldn't budge or bend to accommodate any new approaches presented by the other team members. Egos were at stake here, not to mention several reputations.

August 22, 2023
Lawrence Bakersfield Laboratories
Clearing Lab Twelve
2017 Zulu

Programs were written and discarded at a rate of three and four a day. Since the base language appeared so rudimentary at first, Sir Patrick Keller of the British Historical Society and Dr. Allen Douglas of Yale were expecting a quick fix and an easy out. But soon Keller and Douglas joined the ranks of the disillusioned as the decoding task became more complex. In the third month tempers began to flare up over the translating computers being used.

"That machine of yours is pretty fancy," Johnson Beeks of Cornell pointed a boney finger at the ICC R475 translating computer in the far corner of the room, "but come on, Parks, get the key codes right for a change. That's the only way your machine's going to work properly and get us past this grid lock in section four hundred seventy-nine! How many times do I have to keep pointing this obvious flaw out to you?"

"You think yours is better?" snarled Derrick Parks as he glared like a maniac at Beeks' MAC P5000, sitting in the opposite corner. "It's still stumbling over the interlock keys in the subroutines back in section five eighty-three."

"My God, man!" Beeks nearly screamed. "Are you now an expert on my machine? My machine? If we had to wait on *your* machine to finish anything we'd be in a retirement home some place."

Thomas Farraday rolled his eyes and let out a heavy sigh. He removed his glasses and glanced over to where Beeks and Parks stood squabbling like a couple of preschoolers. "Gentlemen, please, let's keep our voices down, shall we?" Thomas keyed instructions into his machine. He could feel another fight brewing here. *Just a matter of time and these geeks are going to kill each other.* He smiled to himself. *Might not be such a bad thing.*

"What?" Parks erupted. "This joker here thinks his machine can do the job and it hasn't gotten to first base yet. He's simply ignoring the key codes."

"He's still stumbling over the inner lock keys!" Beeks pointed a finger in Parks' direction.

Farraday shook his head as he continued to input information into his machine. "This is all going to take a little time, gentlemen."

Parks walked over and glanced over Farraday's shoulder. "Think your machine can do a better job with the inner lock keys than our machines?" There was a smugness in his tone.

"*Information loaded, Thomas.*" A smooth female voice responded after Farraday hit the enter key.

Beeks came over to join them. Parks was eyeing the machine with cold contempt. "Wanda is it?"

"*Yes sir, that is my name.*" Farraday's computer replied.

Parks glance at Farraday. "Voice recognition is a nice touch. But can it do the job?"

Farraday didn't say a word.

"What does W.A.N.D.A. stand for?" Beeks cocked his head to one side. "What kind of acronym is that?"

Farraday smiled to himself and then glanced at Beeks. "It's just Wanda. It doesn't stand for anything."

Both Beeks and Parks frowned at Farraday.

"It's my sister's name and voice." Farraday grinned back at them. "A familiar voice when I'm working on hard stuff. Keeps me focused."

"Whatever!" Beeks and Parks returned to their respective computers and continued to feed them information. But in a matter of time the two men were again engaged in their incessant bickering. They continued in this state for the next few months. Finally one day, Parks and Beeks punched each other out and were quickly terminated from the project. Keller, Douglas and cryptographer Drew Issenhaur dropped out a month after Beeks and Parks little brawl. The sheer frustration and tension of the project had caused them to throw in the towel. The five scientists were kept at Area 51 for several months as General Dalton's security team worked on their cover stories to return them to their former lives.

Dr. Farraday and the remaining four were left with the chore, but differences still plagued the team. Of the final four, an ostentatious German was fired because of continual head butting and blatant disregard for authority. Dalton had put up with the German as best he could, but in the end the hammer fell and Dalton savored every moment of it. Security was once again intensified around Lawrence Bakersfield. After the cryptographer's debriefing stay at Area 51, Dalton took the added precaution and put a full time tail on the scientist. She didn't go anywhere without him first knowing about it. In the end it all came down to Farraday, who because of the intrigue surrounding this discovery kept at it. Jerry Tanner knew his friend well: that he, in the end, would be the one standing when all the others had gone home.

October 12, 2024
Lawrence Bakersfield Laboratories
Clearing Lab Twelve
0647 Zulu

Farraday sat mesmerized for over an hour as the encrypted images flashed across his computer screen.

"*Translation is complete. Downloading hard copy to printer.*" Wanda replied as lights flashed across her many hard drives. "*Program results and run data ported out first.*"

"It's done?" Dr. Jeremiah Tanner looked at his friend.

Farraday winked back at him. "Wanda did good! Too bad Beeks and Parks weren't here to see this." He grinned wickedly at his friend Jerry Tanner.

Tanner winked back and nodded his head as a smile settle across his face. "Satisfaction indeed!"

Farraday could feel prickly heat all over his body. "Display last key images, Wanda."

"*Displaying images, Thomas.*"

Two crude form letters appeared on the computer display.

"There's no question that what we're dealing with is a language which has several base derivatives similar to the major languages that comprised the Middle East at the very beginning of our recorded history. However, the major symbols in the language are astonishingly closer to Hebrew than any other, gentlemen." All Dr. Farraday could do was stare at the screen.

Next to him sat Jerry Tanner, Mike Murphy, and a haggard looking General Dalton.

"Hebrew?" Tanner was as transfixed as Farraday, perhaps even more so. "Why Hebrew?"

"Good question." Murphy replied.

"Why not Hebrew?" Farraday shot back. "After all, the oldest languages known to man originated in the Middle East."

"This was found in South America, Thomas," Dr. Tanner quickly pointed out.

"There could have been survivors, Jerry," Farraday fired back.

They all just stared at the professor. Survivors. No one really wanted to think about it. This type of evidence would only add more fuel to an already building theory of seeding planets by extraterrestrial visitors. But the evidence was hard to ignore.

"You realize it's been a little over a year now?" Dalton pushed out of his seat and navigated toward the coffee table a few paces away. He wanted to change subjects and get down to something a little more concrete; like hard, tangible evidence.

The translation had taken a good year of Farraday's life. It had consumed him. He'd pressed on where others had given up. And with the help of Mike Murphy, computer junkie and hacker, he had overcome several thousand obstacles along the way. He paused, rubbed his eyes, and sighed heavily. His arms were prickly with goose bumps and every fiber in his body was electrified with anticipation. "I wonder if this is what it was like for the cryptographers who worked on the Rosetta Stone?" He glanced at Murphy and Tanner.

"Perhaps," Murphy replied with a yawn. "But they didn't have a computer like Wanda." Murphy's grin turned into a full blow smile. He, too, had spent the better part of a year cataloging the metal pieces brought down from the mountain. He had helped Ben Sauders in his metallurgy research and logged in a few thousand computer hours running analysis. It had been a challenging diversion from the structured routine OWL had imposed on his life.

Several binders stuffed with notes lay sprawled across a large desk where note pads and measuring instruments littered the perimeter. The chair creaked as Farraday sat back, running a hand through his reddish brown hair. He stared at the protective glass box on the table across from the desk. The program results were nearly complete. Farraday sighed and stared at the tray. The translation would be tagging at the end of the run results. The four remaining blue crystals were inside the glass box on protective tempered plastic stands.

"It's funny," he said, taking in the bright shiny crystals, "they came across a billion miles of space to end up here."

Dr. Tanner glanced at the box. Yes, those sparkling objects certainly had put a reverse spin on his life. "Well, probably more like several trillion miles, Thomas." He smiled and shook his head.

Thomas Farraday grinned in reply. "You always liked near to exact measurements, Jerry."

"I guess that's one of my quirks, Thomas." Tanner reached for his cup of coffee. "Those crystals are close to a million years old! I just can't believe it!" An uncontrollable shiver ran up his spine.

General Dalton placed his coffee cup under the spout and refilled it for the fourth time. He took a long sip and eased back against the table. "It amazes me to no end!" He pointed a finger at the box. "Your scientists place the dating of those things somewhere between seven hundred and twenty-five thousand and five hundred and fifty thousand years before Christ. That's hard to fathom!"

Farraday pulled a file from one of the binders and flipped through it. It was too bad that the black box was the only intact piece brought back by Jack Garret's team. Garret had returned to the crash site numerous times in hopes of uncovering more of the wreckage. So far the box and the crystals it contained were the only clues to another era, another civilization, another world.

"This is probably the most important discovery since the Dead Sea Scrolls," Mike Murphy interjected.

"Are you kidding," Dalton laughed. "This is the most important discovery in the entire history of the planet!"

Murphy just nodded his head. Fatigue was pulling at every muscle in his body. His eyes were begging for rest. "You realize that this discovery changes the historical perspective of man's origins?"

They all just looked at the young man from MIT.

"Well, gentlemen," Dalton put his cup back on the table. The coffee was bitter. He checked his watch. "These run results, Dr. Farraday, why do they come out first?"

"Just the basic break down of number of sentences, characters, paragraphs, things of that nature. Gives me a basic idea of how long this document or documents is."

Dalton closed his eyes and heaved out a sigh. "How much more time on the run results?"

"*Run results will be finalized in three hours, forty-seven minutes, General.*" Wanda replied.

Dalton eyed the computer for a long moment and then shrugged his shoulders. "Tests!" He sounded disgusted and exhausted at the same time as he headed toward the door. "It's almost midnight and I need some rest. When that thing is done I want to see the complete print out."

"Very well," Tanner remarked. He watched as Dalton exited the room. He then turned to Thomas. "Well, my dear Dr. Farraday, it would seem you've cracked the surface."

Farraday smiled weakly. "It was Wanda who did all the work."

Tanner glanced at the machine as it continued to buzz in its work routine. "Still a little unnerving that that thing has sort of its own personality."

"Just my sister's voice, Jerry." Farraday grinned. "Wanda did the work, but I did have help," he winked at Murphy.

Tanner yawned and replaced his coffee mug on the table. "I think the General has the right idea. Let's all get some sleep and hit this running in the morning."

"Yeah," Mike stifled a yawn and rose from his chair. "I need some sleep."

"I think we're all overdue for some R and R." Farraday remarked.

"It's been a long day and a long year, professor," Tanner replied. They all left the lab.

October 13, 2024
Lawrence Bakersfield Laboratories
Clearing Lab Twelve
0815 Zulu

Farraday couldn't sleep. He was wound tighter than a spring, and no matter how hard he tried sleep eluded him. Only one thing to do, go back to the lab.

"Didn't you just leave here, Doc?" the sergeant at the security check point asked.

"Yes, I did!" Farraday replied. "This thing just keeps me up nights, Mitch."

Sergeant Mitch Stalls could only smile. He knew, all too well, Farraday's fixation with decoding these mysterious crystals. "Want me to heat you up a fresh batch of coffee?"

"That would be great, Mitch. Much appreciated."

Thomas Farraday eased back into the deserted lab and took his place, once again, at the computer console. He knew beyond any doubt that the data swirling on the screen would send a tremor throughout the scientific world. An ancient manuscript encrypted on a data crystal in a language similar to the earliest known form of Hebrew. It was incredible. He had to be the first to read the translation. A sensor on the computer console lit up.

"Thomas, I did not expect you to return for several more hours."

"Couldn't sleep, Wanda." Thomas grinned at the computer. "So, what's new?"

"*Run results all downloaded, Thomas.*" Wanda replied. "*Main translation is being dumped now. Dump rate is twenty pages a minute. Sorry, Thomas, this is the only speed possible at this time.*"

"Twenty pages a minute is not so bad."

"I am working to increase efficiency to possibly thirty-five pages a minute," the computer replied.

"That would be good." When he stared at the paper tray he couldn't believe his eyes. The run result had been finished nearly forty-five minutes ago.

"You were a bit off on your estimate to the General, Wanda." Thomas grinned.

"I readjusted my main flow stream which enabled me to use five core processors at the same time. Hence, run time was decreased and finished forty-five minutes ago. I thought you'd like to be the first to read it."

"You're a marvel, Wanda." His hands were shaking as he reached for the printout.

"*Continuing with translation dump, Thomas.*"

"Very good, Wanda. Thank you."

He stared at the first line and gasped, his watering eyes widened. He gathered a handful of pages from the printer, took up his pipe, and read. Before him, one unbelievable word after another tumbled off the pages. They told of a time in history that, heretofore, would have been thought purely fictional. Dr. Thomas Farraday's jaw dropped open. His eyes narrowed. He adjusted the half glasses seated on his pronounced nose and traveled back through the portals of time.

Crystal: PCS - One
ID: 1000-0001

PART ONE
Dreams and Shadows

FINAL ENTRY

"In the beginning God created the heavens and the earth. And the earth was without form, and void; and darkness was upon the face of the deep.

"Such was the tragedy that befell the Solarian Federation when the stars exploded and fell from the sky, erasing a once great empire. In time, the struggle would be resurrected when man once more crawled out of the darkness to take up his chariots of fire, thrusting him back across the black velvet of night; perchance to meet his old rivalry, the TeMari, whose Corporate also fled when the stars descended on Terrus.

"Before there was darkness there was the planet Terrus, the Solarian Federation, and the TeMari Corporate." — Jyn, of the House of Hon, Historian to Captain Raven Shadowhand

27 Nollenbre 4988 ADK
Federation Primus / Sol Star System
VRS-Silverwind VSS 23434
Orbital Level 5
Planet: Terrus

PERSONAL LOG: These may be my last words. The ship is crippled beyond repair and Captain Shadowhand is in a sullen mood. Why she chose to venture to Terrus is beyond me. The system was destroyed nearly two centuries ago. Reportedly every Solarian wiped out. From the reports I've read, if there had been any remaining survivors that survival would have lead to a cruel death in itself. But Raven ignored those reports and insisted on going to Terrus, hoping to find her father. Her obsession has proven fatal for all of us. Although we have destroyed the two pirate vessels that ambushed us at Terrus' moon, we sustained damage beyond our ability to repair. Perhaps the wound she received in the battle only intensified her mood the more, though the physician says it was not life threatening. For a remarkably beautiful and slender woman, she fights like seven men possessed. If I hadn't seen her take down the four Brogarian pirates myself, I would not have thought it possible. She has survived more dangers and death than half the crew of the *Silverwind*. This ship is dying and I fear we are all dead men. Our only hope is to land on Terrus. The captain is a good pilot and her second in command is as skilled as well. Still, I don't hold out much hope that we will survive the landing. If we do then Aidioni will have answered our prayers. If we perish then I am ready. Either way, I have secured the family history. If we don't make it, at least our story will live on. The story of a terrible war and the terrible men that tried to snuff out the lives of Captain Raven Shadowhand and her family. I must go now. We are preparing for the landing. Almighty Aidioni, have mercy on us all. Jyn, the ship's historian, signing off.

1

"Behold, I stood at the Door of Heaven, and saw before me the beginning and the end of all creation. I beheld the sacrifice of the Chosen One, the Hand of the Lord. And I trembled as I saw a multitude of people spread before me like a vast sea. I turned to the seraphim that had taken me up. 'Who are these people who look like a vast sea?' *The seraphim replied,* 'These are those who inhabit the creation from the beginning to the end. Ages that have been and ages to come.' *I, Stevann, stood as a man void of speech, unable to comprehend the vision of the Almighty."*—The Vision of Stevann 1:4-9, *The Talbah Canon*

"The threads of conspiracy twisted into a web of knots."— Morgas Sartis, *Seeds of Destiny*

11 Thronbre 4758 ADK
Jeulonza Range / TeMar Star System
Darracura District
Maggermoss
Planet: TeMar

The night was filled with a deep darkness, a blackness so dense that it seemed to have extinguished all available light. A blast of thunder rattled Jerrid Flakkinbarr's teeth as the rain hammered the ground in torrential sheets, driving hard and laced with a bone deep chill. Flakkinbarr stumbled like a blind man through the tangled underbrush. The canopy of branches overhead screeched and moaned like a banshee. Panic had long ago gripped his soul as he desperately tried to put distance between himself and the demon-dargs in hot pursuit. His three piece suit clung to his body like a lead weight, hampering every effort to maintain a steady pace. But nothing was heavier than the weight pressed tight against his stomach. Unconsciously, he placed his hand inside his rain soaked jacket, touching the leather bound book. With each step, the book seemed to weigh heavier and heavier, not only on his gut but also on his conscience. His pace was sickeningly slow as he tore through the forest looking for safe haven. Weaving through spindly trees and dodging thickets, Jerrid continued to push himself harder and harder. Every fiber of his being screamed for a halt to the madness. It took only a moment for the unseen vine to stop him dead in his tracks. He hit the ground so hard that it knocked the wind out of him. The leather book poked his gut, as if to remind him it was still there. The added burst of pain only amplified his misery. For precious seconds he lay there, gasping for breath as another roll of thunder echoed through the dense forest like a cannon shot. He pulled himself into a squatting position and leaned against the hard bark of a tall tree, sucking in air and wishing this night would end. A blinding flash! A deafening pop of thunder, oh so close. Suddenly, a foreboding presence gripped him and made the chill of the rain colder still. He wiped the water out of his eyes, the hair on the back of his neck rising. His whole body stiffened and shook uncontrollably. Just then the rain stopped, switched off as if by magic. The thunder abated and a stillness came over the forest that only unnerved Jerrid Flakkinbarr the more. The book inside his jacket now felt like a penetrating worm, eating its way into his gut, sucking out his strength as it devoured his soul little by little. A crack of a branch drew his eyes toward the right. From only fifty yarrs away he caught the menacing glare of two sets of eerie white eyes. A weird illumination suddenly rippled into the shape of his pursuers, the two demon-dargs. Their eyes were vicious. Eyes that were uncharacteristically mechanical looking. Jerrid's breath came in quick paced gasps. He had to slow his breathing and control himself or his heart would explode.

Between the two dargs a shadow twisted into existence, a shadow blacker than the night. It pulsated and swirled as it fashioned itself into the shape of a man. The demon-dargs snarled, revealing razor sharp teeth as the shadow man hissed a command, "Attack!" Jerrid Flakkinbarr screamed and ran for his life! The book shot out from under his jacket. His heart pounded like a wild drum. Blood flashed white hot, causing another gasp to escape from his lips as he looked around.

For what seemed like an eternity he just stared at the room. The recollection finally dawned. Gone was the rain soaked forest and the hard tree at his back. He was standing in front of his favorite chair in his own study and the warm glow of the lamp next to the easy chair cast soft shadows across the polished hardwood floor. A brown and tan plaited mat lay nearby for accent. It was a spacious room, airy, with a high vaulted ceiling and a row of windows to the right of the chair that ended abruptly at the lavish bookcase filled with digital volumes. A desk was situated just beyond the bookcase at the far end of the study. It was still piled high with work. He stood there for a long moment, taking everything in and waiting for his heart to slow down and his blood pressure to return to normal.

"That brakkin' dream!" he said through clinched teeth, his jaw sore from the effort. Yes, it had been that dream again, the one that had been haunting him for months now. It filled his thoughts with such evil and terror that it made him physically sick. He fought down the nausea as it rose in his throat. He gagged. Dropping back into the chair he placed his head between his legs and took shallow breaths. The bile settled, but the foreboding lingered at the edge of his senses. The dreaded dream. The same exact dream. Nothing changed. Nothing missing. The rain, the night and those evil eyes. The shifting shadow shape of an evil man.

A glance at the lighted cityscape just beyond the windows told him it was late. Most of the skyscrapers had gone dark. The clock to the right of the desk confirmed it was nearly midnight. Easing himself into his chair, he continued to stare at the clock. He had been asleep for almost two hours. The last time he'd looked at the clock it had only been a quarter to ten. He ran a hand through his thick gray hair as his eyes hesitantly glanced at the book on the floor. It must have fallen out of his lap when he awakened from his nightmare. A trembling hand slowly reached out toward the book, as if it were a serpent ready to strike.

You have no reason to fear serpents.

He dismissed the thought and carefully picked up the book. He knew that it was only an inanimate object, but to him it felt as if it were indeed a poisonous viper. For the longest moment he just stared. The thick leather binding was still in immaculate shape, the gilded edging bright and shiny. He tried to convince himself that this was not the evil tome in his nightmare. He heaved out a sigh of relief. It was a copy of the *Talbah Canon*, the Edruian Edition, and to his knowledge one of the last printed volumes available. Jerrid unconsciously glanced at the wall hanging to the right of the clock, *The Varia Tree* design by Patha Grebon. Behind it was his wall safe and in it the book that had come to haunt his dreams. That accursed weight in his gut!

Pulling the tome back to his lap he flipped it open to the bookmark.

Be not afraid of dragons or serpents, for you have power over them. And fear not the Shadow, which is the deceiver of men, for I have given you power to overcome the enemy of your soul. He had been reading from *The Vision of Stevann,* one of the last prophetical books of the *Talbah Canon.*

"Dragons, serpents, shadows," he whispered to the room. *Dragons*, yes he'd faced those terrible dragons on the Tribunal floor. Those stiff necked tribunes who spat fire at every proposal he'd tried to sponsor in the last three years. The chief dragon of them all was Tribune Rez Verlmon of the PaFor Lyxx Range. Verlmon was a calculating dragon who was bent on serving his radical agenda. A smooth talker. He laughed and stared again at the passage. *Serpents*, yes those snakes in the Political Ministry who had been snooping around several of his new hired aides. Those vipers needed to be put back into their pit before they became really dangerous. *Shadows*, these were a bit more tricky. Obscure images and ideas that were certainly creeping around the Tribunal itself and motherworld as a whole. But his friend, Vennie, said the shadows were of the spirit world and deserving of caution. "I have faced them all. And I fear I have yet to face the true Shadow." Flakkinbarr shook his head. The book had been a gift, nearly four years ago, from his best friend, Scribe Vennie Suun, an old university dormmate. Unlike his friend, he hadn't had the opportunity to see any real demons. But he was sure they manifested in the bodies of flesh and blood and probably some of the people he dealt with. Perhaps even Tribune Verlmon.

The Talbah *will give you peace in troubled times, my friend*, Vennie had said.

Jerrid Flakkinbarr heaved out a sigh. "These are troubling times, Vennie, troubling times indeed. And I truly wished I had the peace you so assuredly said I would find." Peace had somehow become illusive for Jerrid.

The peace I give to you is not of this world; let not your heart be troubled.

Jerrid smiled to himself. Yes that was from the fourteenth chapter of Partin, verse twenty seven. It had been one of the first verses he'd memorized when he converted to the Yushannan faith. Vennie had been instrumental in his introduction to Yushann and his teachings. Now though, that once cherished peace was overshadowed by uneasiness. Jerrid knew the TeMari Corporate was in trouble. A person would have to be blind not to see the demise. It certainly didn't take a prophet to see what was happening to the TeMari civilization. The protracted war with the Solarian Federation had given rise to dissension everywhere. Most troubling of all was the unfathomable intentions of a monster hovering to take control. A monster he and every voting citizen had elected to rule them. An evil Shadow had fallen upon the TeMari Corporate. It was his job to see to it that this Shadow was destroyed.

A knock at the door drew him out of his deep, depressing thoughts. "Enter!"

A tall, deeply tanned man stepped into the study. His coal black curly hair accented his strong handsome face. A goatee of similar color added flair. Dark eyes sparkled in the room light. "Sir, I saw your light and thought I would see if you needed anything before I retire."

Jerrid smiled, "No, Vars, I don't need anything. I was just doing some last minute reading."

Vars caught sight of the book, and his eyes sparkled as he recognized it. He looked back at his employer. A slight scowl etched across his face. "You have to catch the early flight out for your meeting tomorrow morning, sir. I think a good night's rest is in order. Mistress Alleis retired long ago."

Jerrid rose to his feet and placed the book in the chair and then stretched. "Very well, I'll turn in now. There's no need for Zoe to fix breakfast; I'll get something to eat on the flight out."

"Are you sure, sir?" Vars raised an eyebrow at this. "It would be no trouble."

Jerrid smiled. "Please, Vars, you and Zoe don't need to get up. I can get myself out the door and to the terminal very nicely."

Vars sighed and then finally smiled. "Very good. May your dreams be peaceful, sir."

"I hope so, Vars, I hope so."

Vars bowed slightly then turned and left the room. A heavy sigh escaped from Jerrid's lips as he turned to a panel by the windows. The dream was fading. Good. The glass darkened as he switched the tint controls to full. He felt something brush up against his leg.

"Tazz," he reached down and patted the gray and black stripped kibbercat. "I thought you were in bed with momma!" Since they had no children, it was a term he used affectionately for Alleis since she was kind of a surrogate mother for the cat. The long haired cat was a yarr long from nose to tail and weighed in at nine and a half kefs. Alleis had found him fifteen years ago on a cold, rainy day huddled up in a corner just outside their building. The poor thing was soaking wet and meowing pitifully. None of the passers-by took notice. Alleis could not abandon the pitiful little creature, so she scooped him up and placed him in her tote. Once they were in the penthouse, she dried him off and placed the fur ball in a cozy warm basket Vars had brought up from storage. At first Jerrid was against having a cat in the house, but Alleis would not be denied. Zoe even came to the small cat's defense and threatened to take a job downtown unless Jerrid reconsidered the issue. Vars only rolled his eyes. He didn't want to take sides. For quite a number of months having the small rambunctious cat was like living with a whirlwind. Amazingly, nothing of value was broken. Drapes survived intact and furniture was left untouched. Time and the persistent amusing antics of the fur ball had allowed the cat to worm his way into his heart. He couldn't recall exactly when Tazz began to sit by his desk and watch him work, but eventually it became a ritual to have the cat sitting on the edge of the desk dozing or just watching. A short time after that, he'd find the cat sleeping on his feet during the night. At first it was annoying and he would nudge Tazz away. The cat was persistent and crept back sometime during the night. Eventually, Tazz secured his place at his feet. Despite the annoyance, all this just confirmed how attached he really was to this special kibbercat. On those long, tiring days at the Tribunal, the one thing Jerrid looked forward to when he got home was a much needed nap. When he stirred from his thirty or forty minute slumber, Jerrid would find Tazz snuggled up against him on the bed. For a cat, Tazz brought a lot of peace to his soul. That was kind of hard to explain, but whenever the cat was around Jerrid felt relaxed and peaceful. When he mentioned it to either Alleis or Vennie they would just smile and come back with, *"Isn't Aidioni good?"* Oh well, he just loved that cat and that was all there was to it; plain and simple. Fifteen years was a long time and Tazz was definitely showing his age. His chin was noticeably more pronounced and his neatly striped coat had begun to lose its sheen. The tufts of hair that stuck out behind his ears had thinned and nearly disappeared. Still, despite a slight arthritic limp, Tazz did well. He wasn't as quick as he used to be, but he could still get up on the bed or into a window perch. Nowadays, he liked his cushion in the sunroom or his special tree out in the garden.

The cat took another turn around Jerrid's legs and then limped over to the door, sat down and curled its bushy tail around its front feet. Tazz's big green eyes fixed themselves on Jerrid's. The cat then gave a silent meow as if to say it was time for bed..

"All right, Mr. Tazz, I'll carry you up!" Jerrid chuckled as he walked over and picked up the heavy ball of fur. Tazz relaxed in his arms and began to purr. "You're just a big baby! Off to bed now!" Jerrid switched off the room light with his elbow and proceeded up the stairway, carrying the cat like a small child.

Transition Corridor Grid
Marker 4 by 1 / Green Grid Sector
BRS-Red Star 412
Destination: Bethleea

On this particular morning there was quite a crowd in the main dining lounge aboard the *Red Star* Shuttle. Waiters and waitresses were buzzing about like bees in spring time. Apparently a large number of passengers had decided on in-flight breakfasts. Flakkinbarr had taken a table at one of the observation portals so he wouldn't miss Bethleea's magnificent view upon approach. It was quite a sight, and he thoroughly looked forward to visiting motherworld's single moon. Bethleea was such a scenic change from the tangled cityscapes of Maggermoss. He'd like to spend more time here if he could, especially in Gernarn, but this visit was not for sight-seeing.

The breakfast fare was quite good by shuttle standards and the steamy cup of kaufee was just to his liking. Not many commercial liners could get it right, but apparently the *Red Star's* chef had the knack. The toast and eggs were also to his liking, but the fish was a little on the dry side. All in all, not bad for shuttle food; but Zoe definitely had no worries. She was an extraordinary chef whose culinary talents were sought out, with a vengeance, by at least a dozen of Maggermoss' upscale restaurants. There was no way the Flakkinbarrs were going to let their prized chef escape. They were fortunate that money was not an issue in light of some of the exorbitant salaries offered her. Of course, Zoe had known Alleis since they were children. That helped seal the deal. Yes, sir! He was sure they had the best chef in the quadrant. Another sip from his cup brought a smile to his face. As he scanned the crowd he noticed an attractive woman dressed in a stylish tan traveling suit, a dark brown tote slung over her shoulder, working her way through the maze of tables. She was tall, with deep olive brown skin and dark eyes set in a beautiful face. Her hair was jet black and cut in a style that added elegance to her bearing. She walked with a purpose, a picture of perfect posture, eyes fixed forward. She walked straight up to his table.

"Tribune Flakkinbarr?" she asked, giving a nod and a hint of a smile. "I am Tribune Kritecca Arronsta. I represent the Akbar Zelok Range."

Flakkinbarr got to his feet and held out his hand. "Tribune Arronsta. Would you join me, please?"

The smile became more pronounced and she nodded. "I was hoping you'd ask." She sat gracefully in the chair opposite him. A waitress quickly appeared to take her order.

"Just kaufee, plain." she replied.

"Very well." the waitress hurried off.

"I've already eaten," she replied before Jerrid could ask. "I won't take a lot of your time. I'll get right to the point."

"By all means!" Jerrid replied, raising an eyebrow.

"I know you are aware of Prop Twelve Seventeen." Her eyes were fixed on him, stern, hard and focused.

"Tribune Verlmon's proposal." Jerrid replied.

"Rez Verlmon is a sadist!" Arronsta spit out the words as her dark eyes flashed.

Jerrid almost choked on his kaufee as he stared at the young tribune. She didn't smile but continued looking intensely at him. "Tribune Arronsta, I know a lot of people have an intense dislike for Tribune Verlmon, but a sadist?"

"Please, Tribune Flakkinbarr," she held up her hands in reply, "Rez Verlmon makes his feelings well known, especially in *regard* to the Solarians, and even more so with those inside TeMari space. I have some serious concerns about Prop Twelve Seventeen."

Jerrid looked down at his plate and then back to the attractive lady tribune. "Please, call me Jerrid. We can dispense with Tribunal protocol for the moment."

She offered a half smile. "Jerrid."

He almost laughed.

"Kritecca," she offered, "you can call me, Kritecca."

"Good."

The waitress came back with her cup of kaufee. "Anything else, madam?"

"No, thank you."

The waitress freshened Jerrid's cup and went to check on her other tables.

"So, tell me, Kritecca," Jerrid began, "what are your misgivings about Prop Twelve Seventeen?"

Kritecca sighed heavily and took a sip from her cup. After a moment she looked back at Flakkinbarr. "If Prop Twelve Seventeen is approved, every Solarian in the Core Systems, and the entire Near Corporate Rim for that matter, will flee to the Far Frontier. Those TeMari with strong Solarian ancestral ties will not be far behind them. We must vote it down, Jerrid!"

Yes, Prop 1217 was definitely something that had been of serious concern to Jerrid Flakkinbarr from the first time he read it. He took a long, slow sip from his cup. Prop 1217, dubbed the Verlmon Act, called for every Solarian within Corporate space to register with the government. It didn't matter if a person had been born on TeMar or not. If you were a Solarian you had to register. No excuses. But the Verlmon Act went further than that. Every TeMari citizen, with even the slightest trace of Solarian ancestry, was to register. Verlmon had stated on several occasions, that because of the war Solarians living inside TeMari space must prove their loyalty. In private circles, Rez Verlmon was hunting for Solarian terrorists he could place before the executioner. Rumors had it that several Solarian terrorists groups were operating deep within TeMari space. He was also looking for ways to strike back at the Atheran-Hoth Separatists. If the Verlmon Act passed, it would only swell the ranks of the Separatist movement.

Kritecca eyed him once more. "Jerrid, I understand there is no love lost between you and Tribune Verlmon. We can't allow Prop Twelve Seventeen to be approved. If we can get enough votes, we'll defeat this bill. It has to die at voting time or the Corporate will only become more divided and more unstable than it is already. More systems will align themselves with the Atheran-Hoth Alliance and the Separatists will gain a stronger foothold." The expression on her face told him how determined she was. He could see it in her eyes. "Can I count on your support at voting time? We must not allow this bill to become law, Jerrid! It will only give the Political Ministry and the SPG more power. They have enough power already. We must stop this!" Realizing she was letting herself get too upset, she took a sip from her cup to calm down.

Jerrid leaned back in his chair and looked at the attractive young woman for a long moment. He had a few colleagues who were willing to join him and vote this bill down, but he wondered how many Tribune Arronsta had lined up? "Do you have enough in your court to see it gets killed?"

She took another sip from her cup before replying. "My last count puts it awfully close. Close enough that if anyone changes their mind, it will tip the scales, one way or the other. Verlmon wields a lot of power. I'm afraid some of those that I've talked to will succumb to that power."

Yes, Rez Verlmon was an influential and powerful tribune. The PaFor Lyxx Range was Verlmon territory and it was seeded with many of the most wealthy and influential citizens of the Corporate. Jerrid sighed as he leaned against the table. "You can count on me, Kritecca. I'll see if I can garner more support."

A bright smile flashed across her face. "Thank you, Jerrid, thank you."

He could see a visible calm come over her. "I hope we get the support we need."

"Me, too," she sighed. Fishing in her tote, she pulled out a farn and placed it on the table.

He pushed the money back to her. "I'll take care of your drink, Kritecca. We need to get a re-count of those who are on our side before the bill goes before the whole Tribunal."

Kritecca got to her feet and slipped her tote over her shoulder. "I agree. Thank you, Jerrid. We're going up against a tough old dragon, and Verlmon almost always gets what he wants. Let's hope we have enough votes." With that she turned and made her way out of the dining lounge. Jerrid stared after her for quite some time.

"A tough old dragon indeed, my lady!" Jerrid said to himself.

Be not afraid of dragons or serpents.

Dragons and serpents. Perhaps there was more credence to the *Talbah's* words than he previously believed. Could it be that the two were in league with one another, Verlmon and the Political Ministry? If it was true, then only heaven could help the Corporate now. "I fear the dragons are just now starting to come out from their dens," Jerrid mused. He paid for his meal and Tribune Arronsta's drink. He gave one quick glance out the portal and then went back to his seat to review his plan before the shuttle landed.

Gernarn Rail Station Seven

The meeting had gone rather well, Jerrid mused as he stuffed his travel bag into the overhead compartment and took his seat by the window. Other passengers hurried into the monorail as the loud speaker blared out departure time. Yes, he was quite pleased. The meeting had netted his Tribunal defense committee a lucrative deal for the new *Vorra* class destroyers. Hunneen's Vargan Company was one of the three final bidders on this particular program. As committee head, Jerrid had come to Bethleea to award the contract to the Hunneen group. He had convinced his fellow delegates of Hunneen's outstanding reputation in development and delivery of all their past military contracts. He wanted the new class of destroyers built by the best. Jerrid could only keep smiling. He had dealt with numerous defense contractors. Most were sickeningly polite when awarded a lucrative contract, but they failed miserably on the follow through. The one thing Jerrid found remarkable was the genuine sincerity he had felt from Cirin Hunneen when he first greeted him. Cirin Hunneen had not turned out to be the stiff necked overseer so many of his colleagues had insisted he was. Quite the contrary. Hunneen made him feel like a long lost friend and took great pains to show him around his vast complex. It wasn't for show or pretense. It was real! After the signing of the contracts Cirin had insisted on lunch at the swanky *Vodsad Kerra Café* in downtown Gernarn. A wonderful experience. The food was far more exquisite than the reports he'd heard, and if any chef could best Zoe, it was the chef at the *Vodsad Kerra Café*. Now he knew he and Alleis had the second best chef in the quadrant, but he wasn't about to offend Zoe. Cirin suggested that on the return visit, when Jerrid came to retrieve the final drawings, that he should come out to his estate for dinner. This was something he would definitely look forward to, dinner at the largest mansion on the entire moon. Cirin even suggested he bring Alleis.

"Tressa would love to meet your wife," Cirin had said as he finished off his meal.

Yes, it had been a good morning indeed.

Jerrid settled into his seat and tried to ignore the noise of the other passengers as they boarded, but his gut began to tighten. There was another meeting coming up that he was not looking forward to. The more his thoughts rambled about this approaching meeting, the more anxious he became. *You're letting this get to you!* He shook it off and sighed heavily. This next meeting was about those missing supply shipments to Geasbok. His contact said he had some startling answers. Hopefully, those answers would provide the location of those missing shipments. But a nagging dread still plagued him. He felt that something was going to happen, something that would change the course of his life and everyone's around him.

Jerrid had changed clothes at the rail station just before boarding. He was now attired in a worn, plain brown shirt and tattered black pants. From all appearances, he was just another local worker headed home. He wanted to blend into the common sea of humanity around him; one of the masses, nothing more. His hair was pulled back and tucked under a dingy cap with a Firecat scramball team logo embroidered on the front. Mingling with the common people at street level afforded him a view of the world that most of his colleagues chose to ignore.

People scrambled for seats as doors hissed shut. A handsome young Fleet officer took the seat next to Flakkinbarr and smiled, placing his carry on under the seat in front of him. The young man filled out his dress uniform rather nicely. Jet black hair and brown eyes sparkled with a glint of recognition that made Jerrid wince. The young man had a strong jaw line and a deep tan.

Do I know this man? He shook off the thought and turned his attention to the window and watched Gernarn slip by as the monorail began to pick up speed. As the monorail slipped out of the station towering buildings quickly gave way to vast areas of green forest, rolling hills, and steadily rising slopes that eventually turned into towering mountains in the far distance. Quite a contrast from the city canyons of Maggermoss, a hundred mycron wide city of monstrous skyscrapers and multi-level twisting highway corridors. Bethleea's countryside brought a sense of peace and tranquility that was sorely missing in Maggermoss. Jerrid sighed and watched the terrain as it began to fade into a blur of browns and greens. Out on one of the rolling hills he spied a large flock of barlas. They looked like white puff balls against the luscious green grass.

It was mid afternoon when the monorail whizzed pass Varia. The small city was not on the stop schedule; the rail had barely slowed its approach speed. It would be just before sunset when the monorail would pull into Pavarondi. There would be plenty of time to meet his contact, obtain the information, and take the return rail back to Gernarn. He'd be back on motherworld by early morning. Hopefully, there would be no snags along the way. Alleis would be busy with her viao practice. He wanted to be refreshed enough to hear her perform with her little quartet at the *Vison Mill Café* at nine. She was becoming quite good at the viao. He smiled, remembering her awkward years. The screeching strings had sent Tazz into hissing frenzies for weeks. After a time, he and the cat had gotten used to it; but he vividly remembered the day the sweetest music came from the study. Alleis had conquered her musical nemesis and won the battle. Now she played with her quartet every Versday. Over the past two years the little group had entertained several dignitaries and performed at some of the formal Tribunal functions. Alleis loved playing. It also gave her an excuse to get out of some of the political functions the wife of a tribune was forced to endure.

Jerrid turned his gaze back to the Fleet officer. From the rank pins on his collar he was a lieutenant, First Order. Campaign ribbons decorated his left breast pocket and the gold Fleet flight insignia was pinned just above them. He was staring straight ahead, seemingly unaware of the surrounding conversations taking place.

"Are you returning from the front?" Jerrid asked out of curiosity.

The young man turned and smiled briefly. His eyes had a deep, knowing look, the look of a soldier who had seen a lot of action; yet there was something more. It was hard to put a finger on it, but whatever it was sent a chill up his spine. Despite this man's youthful appearance, Jerrid had the strangest feeling that those eyes held a thousand years of wisdom. He shuddered, remembering that same look in Cirin Hunneen's deep blue eyes. Jerrid tried to shake off the chill, but it clung like a thin coat.

"Yes," the young man replied, his voice strong, determined.

"I see," Jerrid fidgeted uncomfortably for a moment and turned his gaze to the view out the window. Looking into those eyes was unnerving.

"Going far, sir?" the Fleet officer asked after a while.

"To Pavarondi." Flakkinbarr replied. "And you?"

"Othyn Dresmon." he replied.

Jerrid nodded and glanced back out the window. The strange chill still surrounded him. It sent shivers up his spine, but not as troubling now. He stole another quick glance at the young Fleet officer. *Do I know this person? Should I?* He couldn't shake the feeling that there was something strangely familiar about this young officer, but he knew it was impossible. Totally impossible!

"I'm Lt. Jad Arie'el, sir." the young man extended a hand.

Now that he had a name, he knew that he had never before met this young Lt. Arie'el. Odd, still there was that persistent knowing at the edge of his consciousness. He avoided his eyes for the moment as he shook the young man's hand. Arie'el had a firm grip. "Jubal Dros, Lieutenant." The alias nearly stuck on his tongue. It felt awkward. He hoped the lieutenant hadn't seen him at some formal Fleet function he had endured in his role as tribune.

"Mr. Dros!" Lt. Arie'el smiled. There was a glint in his dark brown eyes. A sparkle of recognition. "I'm glad to make your acquaintance."

Jerrid shifted uncomfortably in his seat. "So you're from Othyn Dresmon?"

"Not exactly, sir." Arie'el smiled. "I'm just visiting a friend's family."

"I understand." Probably the family of a fallen comrade. Jerrid glanced back out the window. "Are you going to be sent back to the War Zone anytime soon?"

"Yes, sir." Arie'el nodded. "I've been reassigned."

"Oh!" Jerrid understood how Fleet operated. "A different part of the front, I take it?"

"You might say that!" Arie'el looked away for a moment.

For a time they rode on in silence as Jerrid watched the passing scenery. After some time Lt. Arie'el took out a digital reader from his carry on and began to immerse himself in its content. A quick glance told him the lieutenant was reading the *Talbah Canon.* A lot of soldiers had gotten 'religion' out on the front. It would appear Lt. Arie'el was among them. Jerrid gave a few awkward glances his way and then returned to watching the passing countryside. He didn't understand it, but somehow, someway, this Lt. Arie'el was familiar. It gnawed at him for myrcons as the monorail sped along.

"Attention passengers. Approaching Othyn Dresmon station." The loud speaker barked.

Lt. Arie'el closed his reader and placed it back in his bag.

"Do I know you, Lt. Arie'el?" Jerrid finally asked, staring at the young man.

"I don't think so, sir." Arie'el replied with that gleam in his eye.

"There's just something about you, son."

"Perhaps I just remind you of someone, sir." Arie'el smiled a little. "Do you have a son in the military?"

"My wife and I have never had children, Lieutenant," Jerrid noted.

"I see," Arie'el nodded.

"I see more and more young people in uniform these days, Lieutenant. Young people going off to war. Some of them will never return home to their families and friends. A war that most of them haven't a clue as to why we're fighting it in the first place." Jerrid sighed deep and glanced back out the window. "Sometimes I wonder that myself. This war with the Solarians has become quite troubling for some of us."

"Yes, sir, I guess it has."

They said nothing as the monorail began to slow its pace into the station, which was still several mycrons away.

Lt. Arie'el turned and fixed his eyes on Jerrid Flakkinbarr. "Sir, we all have a destiny. Each and everyone of us has been born in a specific time and place for a specific plan and purpose."

Where had he heard that before? Jerrid just stared at the young man, not knowing how to respond.

"You have a destiny, Mr. Dros!" Arie'el said it with such passion that Jerrid felt the chill run up his spine again. A cold stirring. A knowing! "There's a course set before you that only you can accomplish. Choose well the path you take from this point on, sir. It will set in motion a chain of events that will shape the destiny of others. People you know and people you don't. The path you are about to put your feet on will lead you into great danger. Be warned! Remember these words. Do not fear the darkness, but embrace the light. And be not afraid of the dragons, but be mindful of the Shadow."

Stunned, Jerrid just sat there as the monorail slid into the station and came to a stop.

"Othyn Dresmon station!" The loud speaker called. Lt. Arie'el pulled out his carry on from under the seat in front of him and got to his feet.

"Good day, Mr. Dros, you are in Aidioni's hand. Peace be with you." He stepped out into the isle way. Pausing, he turned back to Flakkinbarr. "Don't be afraid of the rain, Mr. Dros. It will be your salvation." With that, the lieutenant joined the rest of the passengers debarking at Othyn Dresmon. Jerrid Flakkinbarr could only stare at the backs of the crowd as they exited. The young lieutenant was swallowed up by the people leaving the coach.

In stunned silence Jerrid continued to stare. *Don't be afraid of the rain.* For some strange reason he felt like Lt. Arie'el somehow knew about his dream. It was a crazy notion. How could he? It must have been the wine from lunch. Had to be.

"Be not afraid of the dragons, but be mindful of the Shadow!"

Dragons and shadows! He was being plagued by them in his dreams. "What does it all mean? What does it all mean?"

For the next several mycrons, Jerrid mulled over those words as the monorail sped on toward Pavarondi. *Choose well the path you take from this point on.* The words of the lieutenant continued to echo in his mind as he stared out the window.

2

"The shadows of the past were still clinging to the fabric of the Corporate. What was once thought as forgotten suddenly turned up to be part of the equation."—Monsini Verstusos, *The Tale of Tales*

"Others will bind your hands and lead you where you do not want to go, but I will prevail. Remember I am with you always."
—Second Jadd 1:3, *The Talbah Canon*

Pavarondi
Moon: Bethleea

He'd been stunned by Lt. Arie'el's words and was still pondering them as the monorail slid into Pavarondi station. When Jerrid finally realized that passengers were debarking, he retrieved his travel bag and joined the crowd. He ambled along with the crowd for a while and then turned into a locker room where he found a deserted stall. Securing the door, he pulled another set of clothes from his travel bag and quickly changed. Dressed now in a stylish dark green business suit, he headed toward a locked compartment at the far end of the locker room where he stuffed his bag inside. A quick glance at a mirror on the side of his locker caused him to press back his unruly hair. Jerrid palmed the compartment key and heaved a sigh. *I'm certainly building a spider's web.* He flagged down a taxi just outside the station.

"Where to?" the driver asked.

"The Mysterian Resort." Jerrid replied, the haunting words of the young lieutenant still lingering like a soft mist. *Do not fear the darkness, but embrace the light.* Vennie had said the same thing to him several years back when the Tribunal had restructured the government and elected Dameon Klea as the new Director of the Corporate. It had been tumultuous times for everyone, common citizens and governmental officials alike. With the election of this brash new leader, some had feared darker times were coming to the Corporate. Their fears were rewarded with a deadly war. Others simply saw him as the savior of the troubled star system. At first, even he had admired Dameon Klea for his skillful abilities in feeding starving nations and jump starting a stagnating economy, but over the years the changes in governmental policies had been frightening.

"Yes, sir, the Mysterian Resort is one nice place!" the driver smiled and merged into traffic. "Probably one of the better resorts in the whole area. Now, if you like Solarian architecture, that place has it. Mind you, those Solarians are crafty devils and their designs are a little strange, but it's a nice place all the same. From what I've been told, it's six thousand rooms of posh decadence!" He smiled. "That place has it all. They expanded their casino a few months ago. Makes the *Tagu Ru* on motherworld look like a child's game room. Yes, sir. Got some of the best tellavid games this side of Dora Kerra. And you've gotta see that *Varrus* game. Mean son of a braraka."

"Great!" Jerrid really wasn't in the mood for conversation.

"You like the games or the tables?" the driver kept looking up into the rearview mirror.

"Neither!" Jerrid replied dryly. He wasn't a gambler, at least not in the sense the driver was indicating.

"Come for the shows then," the driver didn't seem to be deterred. "Hey, if you like music you gotta see *Vantrax Complex*. They're a new band and their show is outstanding! Bet those guys are going to be famous one of these days. Mark my words, real famous."

Jerrid chose to ignore him and stared at the passing scenery.

The Mysterian Resort was everything the driver said it was. A fanciful multi-story complex with buildings built of red and white marble. Bright, expansive, and towering. An impressive complex some eight hundred floors high. The resort was built around a large lagoon with easy access to the Tradventaa Sea, one of the largest bodies of water on Bethleea. It was a resort that catered to the rich and famous of the Core Systems. While he might see some con-stars in passing, Jerrid had more important things on his mind. No, he was here to meet Ra'Phaak Piin, his contact in the missing shipments case. Why Piin chose this lavish resort area of Bethleea for their meeting baffled him. The last meeting had been on motherworld several months back in the Vegli District, a far cry from the lavish surroundings here in Pavarondi. That was his first contact with Ra'Phaak Piin. He and another tribune, Gerrius Tuposh, met him at a pre-arranged spot which was nothing more than a seedy café. Piin was a smuggler, a dealer in black market goods to the highest bidder. Goods of the military variety. And Ra'Phaak Piin had links well beyond the Corporate. Rumor had it he was deeply invested in Miranrian trade as well. The Mir war machine was impressive and Mir items usually found their way to the highest bidder on the black market.

It was not normal to find a Shuuto dealing in arms. For the most part Shuutos were mysterious religious zealots few people knew anything about. They were said to have come from a system just beyond the Great Void. Nobody knew for certain. The Director, Dameon Klea, had his own personal Shuuto Priest that accompanied him virtually everywhere. Another disturbing thought that made Jerrid's gut twist into knots.

Jerrid stopped at the front desk and asked if there were any messages for Jubal Dros. The desk clerk retrieved a gold colored envelope from a slot by a key pad.

"Here you are, Mr. Dros." Her enunciation had a lilt to it.

He thanked her and walked to the edge of the circular fountain that dominated nearly the entire main lobby. He tore open the envelope and read the note.

Jubal Dros...
Come to the marina.
Ship: Black Zaar
.... *Piin*

Jerrid smiled to himself as he folded the note and placed it back in the envelope. Piin was never one for flowery words. *To the point as always!* He tucked the envelope into his pocket and headed out to find the *Black Zaar.*

Once he was down on the dock the ship wasn't hard to find. It was the only three masted sailing vessel in the whole place. From bow to stern the ship was nearly 100 yarrs in length, with a black hull of high varnished paint that revealed neither hint of wood nor metal. Accents along the hull were trimmed in gold, and glittered in the bright daylight. Black sails were secured to mast with gold plated connections. Several members of the crew moved about the deck checking the rigging. A bare chested Neccian in white sailor pants stood at the end of the gang plank, arms folded across his massive deep bronzed chest. An imposing figure to be sure. His bald head glistened like a ripe brown melon.

Jerrid pulled up short of the Neccian. "I'm here to see Mr. Piin."

The Neccian eyed him for a long moment. "Your name?"

"Jubal Dros."

"Follow me!" The Neccian turned and started up the gang plank. Jerrid hesitated a moment but then followed as he was escorted to the stern and down into the captain's cabin. The cabin was large, paneled in a white exotic hardwood, with black trimmed edging. As Jerrid surveyed the surroundings he noticed gold knobs, gold comlinks, and gold trays. *There's a fortune in gold in just this one room!* Jerrid thought to himself. Ra'Phaak Piin was seated on a large satin yellow sofa, sipping something from a long slender glass. A black suit of an expensive Desermerian weave covered Piin's thin yellow skinned frame. He sported a long, black drooping mustache. The hair on the Shuuto's head was thick and pulled back tight in a braided ponytail that disappeared somewhere behind his back. Gold rings were on every finger and three gold earrings hung from his left earlobe.

Piin lowered his drink. His almond shaped eyes pierced Jerrid for a moment but then brightened with recognition. "Ah! Mr. Dros, please come in." His voice had a somewhat musical tone to it. "Please, have a seat." He indicated a chair to his left. The Neccian waited by the door.

"Care for anything to drink, my friend?"

"No, thanks," Jerrid replied, as he dropped into the chair.

"Brez, you may go." Piin nodded toward the Neccian.

"Yes, sir." Brez disappeared through the door.

"I trust your trip to Bethleea was enjoyable." Piin smiled.

"A pleasant one." Jerrid gazed around the room. He marveled at the amount of gold in one place.

"I see you like my ship." Piin's smile grew wider. "A trifle thing I keep when I need to relax. The Tradventaa Sea is a great place to sail such a vessel as this one. A magnificent body of water with a number of serene places that offer rest from the wearisome worlds around us. Quite a different challenge to sail on water as opposed to hurling through hyper." Piin took a slow slip from his glass. "Are you certain you wouldn't like something to drink?"

Jerrid shook his head. "No, I'm fine, thank you."

Piin nodded. "Very well, but if you change your mind let me know."

All Jerrid could do was nod.

"I suppose you want to get right down to business, eh, Mr. Dros?" Piin flashed a devilish grin.

"That's why I'm here."

Piin straightened up. For a long moment he focused on Jerrid, measuring his face. "Your friend, Tribune Tuposh, seems very worried about these missing shipments to Geasbok, Mr. Dros."

There are ways to take care of your problems. Jerrid shook his head. Where had that thought come from? He focused on Piin. "He has good reason to be concerned about the missing shipments. The committee he chairs has oversight in military funding. The supply shipments to the Geasbok penal colony have suddenly become very expensive."

"Yes, so it would seem." Piin pushed up to the edge of the sofa.

"Only two out of six supply ships ever reach Geasbok. What's happening to the other four? This has been going on for two months now."

"You may not want to know where your shipments are disappearing to." He smiled again, staring hard at his guest.

There are ways to take care of your problems. The thought slammed into

Jerrid's mind. It was powerfully persuasive. *What ways are we taking about here?* he asked himself. *And what problems?*

Piin eased back and laughed. "Ah, Mr. Dros, so serious. You and your friend, Tribune Tuposh, pay me good money to find these things out for you. Please, don't be so concerned."

Jerrid almost laughed. "Concerned? Mr. Piin, we're talking about millions of ruuls in defense funds disappearing into thin air. I think that's a pretty big concern."

Piin reached for his glass and took a long sip before he spoke. "Your missing shipments are being diverted to the Vi'Kiin star system."

Jerrid's mouth dropped open.

Piin smiled. "I see this is troubling news."

Troubling news. Vi'Kiin was a Miranrian system three parsecs from the border of the Sazaadar Range out in the Far Frontier. "Vi'Kiin is a Mir system."

"Yes it is, Mr. Dros. And there is a rather large Miranrian military base there as well." Pinn smiled, fixing a steady gaze on Flakkinbarr.

Jerrid swallowed hard. "Then we're not talking about pirates, are we?"

"I know quite a few pirates, Mr. Dros. Some are, shall we say, my very dear friends, but no one I've talked to is willing to admit to hijacking these ships. I did some snooping around, as you would say, on Vi'Kiin and found your supply ships there."

"Were you able to verify their identification?"

"Quite easily, my friend." Piin smiled. "I know several customs agents on Vi'Kiin, Mr. Dros. Shall we say we had an exchange of ideas." Piin laughed. "I was able to get a copy of the ship's log, ID tags and crew manifest. Not too expensive, mind you." The Shuuto took another sip from his glass. "I even tracked down one of the crew members. An interesting character for sure."

Jerrid was puzzled. "What do you mean?"

Piin pushed forward. "These supply ships of yours were crewed by replicants."

"Replicants?"

Piin just shook his head. "Does this surprise you, Mr. Dros?"

"Yes it does." Jerrid knew, all too well, about the replicants. Bio engineered warriors created nearly a millennium ago to fight off the Solarians. "But no one is manufacturing replicants anymore."

"That's where you're wrong, Mr. Dros." Piin got to his feet and began to pace. "You see, someone is manufacturing replicants again. I tracked down this crew member and I had him analyzed."

Jerrid waited for him to continue.

"My men are very good. They found out that your replicants are being manufactured on Geasbok."

"Geasbok?" Jerrid almost bolted from his seat. "It's a penal colony, some state criminals and some prisoners of war."

Piin continued pacing. "My men retrieved the data from the replicant's brain. It provided all the details. These replicants have been replacing the ships human crew as they off load on Geasbok. Over the course of five trips the entire human crew is replaced. It's a very clever plan."

Jerrid didn't say a word.

"The replicants have been programmed to commandeer the ship once it's loaded with supplies and then report to Vi'Kiin. Once there, they become the property of one Voka'Simral, the Red Eye Guild Master. He deals heavily in Mir weapons bound for the black market."

Neither man said a word for a long time. Jerrid chewed over the information. Replicants were once again being manufactured on Geasbok and supply ships were disappearing into the Miranrian Federation.

"There is something else you should know, Mr. Dros." Piin's facial expression became hard. "Not only are replicants being manufactured on Geasbok, but clones as well. Thousands of clones."

All Jerrid could do was stare. Who was making clones and what was really going on? "You're certain?"

Piin erupted with laughter. "I didn't have enough time to find out specific details. Security is getting tighter and tighter out there. What I do know is that the SPG have been brought in to handle some of the facilities."

"SPG?" Jerrid just shook his head.

"Word has reached my ears that someone with powerful influence within the government is requisitioning heavy armament out of the Miranrian Federation." Piin smiled. "Very heavy armament, my friend. Expensive armament. Very, very expensive stuff."

Jerrid just sat there.

"Your defense funding for Geasbok is being funneled to Voka'Simral inside the Mir Federation to purchase a considerable amount of expensive weaponry. The rumor is that these weapons are headed to Corporate space very soon."

"For what purpose?"

Piin smiled. "It's obvious, isn't it?"

"To start a bloody war with the Miranrians?"

"I'd be willing to place a wager on that!" Piin stepped to the end table and retrieved his drink. He took a long sip as he focused on Jerrid.

There are ways to take care of your problems. Jerrid seemed bolted to the chair. His mind swirling. *Your problem is Klea. There are ways to eliminate this problem.* Jerrid blinked. The thoughts were troubling, but it really made sense. Yes, Klea was the problem; he was the Shadow. Jerrid shook his head. His mouth suddenly felt like cotton. "I think I'll take that drink now."

Piin smiled and turned to a large wine cabinet. "I have an excellent *Avon Perier*. Has been aged a long time. I think you will find it to your liking." He turned to his guest.

Jerrid nodded. It sounded good.

As Piin poured the wine he glanced back toward his guest. "A war with the Miranrian Federation will only prolong things. Perhaps it's time to consider other options to remedy this situation." Piin offered the slender glass of wine to Flakkinbarr.

Jerrid took a long sip and savored the wine. "This is good stuff."

"I'm glad you like it."

Klea is your problem. His elimination would best suit the whole Corporate. Jerrid blinked. Eliminate the Director of the Corporate? That was crazy! How had those thoughts invaded his mind? It had to be that cursed book! Ever since it came into his possession he'd had nothing but troubling thoughts, particularly where Dameon Klea was concerned.

Piin sipped his wine and stared long and hard at Jerrid. "You are a man of means, Mr. Dros. A person in your position could finance a quick fix to make sure this war comes to a much needed end."

A man of means. For the most part, Ra'Phaak Piin knew only that Jubal Dros was a wealthy overseer with deep pocket connections to several tribunes and a few defense contractors. Piin had been employed by his "little group" to find out things. He was a well placed snoop. "I am a man of means, Mr. Piin, but exactly what are we talking about here?" Jerrid asked.

There was a long drawn out silence as Piin focused his eyes intently upon Jerrid Flakkinbarr.

The solution to your problem is simple.

Piin smiled to himself, eyes narrowing.

The solution to your problem is simple. Jerrid blinked. *How simple?*

"There is really only one solution to the problem, Mr. Dros." Pinn grinned. *Kill Klea!* It was a simple seed, planted well, planted deep.

Kill Klea! Jerrid's head jerked back as the thought hammered his mind again. Kill the Director of the Corporate. *How?* He certainly couldn't. But it seemed like the only solution to the problem.

Piin smiled wickedly. "You have a dilemma, my friend - Geasbok shrouded in mystery. We have replicants and clones being manufactured there, but we don't know why. I would say it's a cause for alarm." He sipped his wine and continued to smile. *Assassinate Klea. It can be arranged.* Piin threw the mind probe again. He could tell he was getting deeper. Good!

Jerrid sat there for the longest time. Finally he looked up at Piin. "It seems I have a bigger problem than I thought."

"One that can be easily eliminated, Mr. Dros." The glazed look on Jerrid's face told him his mind probe was working.

"I see no other alternative than to kill Klea." Killing Klea was the only thing Jerrid had on his mind. A quick solution to the shadow that had been troubling the Corporate for years.

Piin smiled. "Then that is your solution, Mr. Dros. Kill Klea!"

The voice sounded hollow, but it seemed right.

"I can't do it!" was all Jerrid could mumble out of the fog that encompassed his thoughts.

"There are professionals who handle such delicate matters, Mr. Dros." Piin replied. "I have such a man in my service. He would serve you well. His fees will be expensive for a high profile job such as this. Mind you, I would be getting a percentage of the funds."

The long neck glass was made of a rose colored material that gave the red wine a deep blood color. *Blood, yes, and I will have it on my hands. But it must be done! Must be done!* Jerrid swirled the wine around for a time and then took a long sip. *Kill the Director of the Corporate.* He couldn't believe he was actually plotting something this macabre, but his mind kept telling him that was what really needed to happen. With Klea out of the way, it was highly probable a treaty could be reached with the Solarians and the war ended. If not, then the Mirs would certainly get involved and eventually the war would spiral out of control. The Separatists involvement only made matters worse. Yes, Klea had to be taken out. He finally looked at Piin. "How much are we talking about here?"

Piin pursed his lips. "About seventy five million ruuls."

"Seventy five million?" Jerrid almost choked.

"We are talking about Klea, my friend." Piin glared at Flakkinbarr. *You have the money, spend it. Get rid of your problem!* Piin didn't mind lining his pockets with a good size sum. He had other motives for wanting Klea out of the picture, personal ones at that.

Seventy five million would just about clear out a sizable chunk of his funds, but Jerrid couldn't shake the fact that it had to be done. He took a long sip from his glass and then looked back at Piin. "You have a man that will do the job and not talk?"

"Oh, yes!" Piin grinned. "He's a professional. He's done this more times than you really want to know, Mr. Dros."

"I'm sure."

"Brez!" Piin yelled.

The Neccian came back into the cabin. "Yes, sir?"

"Send in Serpa."

"Yes, sir!" Brez disappeared again.

A short time later Brez reappeared with another bronzed skin man in tow. He was more ominous looking than Brez and was dressed completely in black.

Piin waved a hand at the man. "Serpa, please come in."

The man called Serpa stepped from behind the Neccian and came to the center of the room. He glanced at Jerrid and then back to Piin. Jerrid stiffened as an uncontrolled chill ran up his spine.

"Mr. Dros, this is Serpa, the best there is for this type of job." Piin was all smiles again.

"Mr. Dros." Serpa nodded, but didn't shake hands.

"Serpa, Mr. Dros has a very profitable assignment for you." Piin grinned and gave a wink Jerrid's way. "An extremely profitable job, Serpa, but a very dangerous one as well. I have assured Mr. Dros you can handle the situation in spite of the danger."

Serpa eyed Piin for a moment and then Jerrid. "Whatever the job, Mr. Dros, I can handle it to your satisfaction."

"Mr. Dros and I will work out the details, Serpa." Piin remarked turning back to his wine. "You and Brez may go now."

"Very well," Serpa replied. He and Brez left the cabin.

"It will take some time to arrange the financing, Mr. Piin." Jerrid replied.

"I'm sure it will, Mr. Dros. Serpa and I will be contacting you as our plans come together." Piin reached again for his wine glass and tilted it toward his guest. "To success, Mr. Dros. Success!"

Jerrid tilted his glass and downed it. Success! Somehow, someway, he felt he'd been pulled into the spider's web with no way of escape.

Do not fear the darkness, but embrace the light.

The light he was suppose to be embracing seemed to be fading. All he could feel was the darkness closing in around him.

3

"When pushed into a corner with no way out, even the smallest verrea will become an enraged beast." — Tosaar Julink, *The Vanishing Act*

9 Sakbar
High Tribunal Assembly Hall
Maggermoss

The sun was glaring as Jerrid stepped out of the cool Tribunal Assembly Hall and headed toward the parking area. The white marble steps descended one hundred yarrs to the street below and reflected the bright light back into his eyes every step of the way. The only thing on Jerrid's mind was the defeat he had left behind in the Assembly Hall. The air was thick and still. He'd lost proposals before by slight margins, but this defeat hung heavy on his shoulders and slowed his pace. Not only was it a personal defeat, but it was a defeat that was going to change the face of the Corporate for years, if not decades, to come. He had halfway expected dark ominous clouds to be gathering overhead when he emerged from the Tribunal Hall. Instead, the bright sunlight seemed to be mocking him. *Aidioni, what do I do now?* Jerrid was looking for some glimmer of hope in all this.

Do not fear the darkness, but embrace the light.

"Embrace the light!" Fumbling for sunshades, he squinted against the glaring sunlight as he continued on down the steps. Finally, he slipped the shades over his eyes and stared toward the street. *Despite the light, Lord, I can only feel the darkness is gaining. Show me the way.*

"Tribune Flakkinbarr! Tribune Flakkinbarr!" He heard someone shout above the crowd of aides and other tribunes as they were leaving. Jerrid stopped, turning this way and that, trying to determine who the female voice belonged to. After several minutes, Tribune Arronsta pushed her way past a clump of chattering aides. She stopped, took in a few deep breaths and then stood looking at him for another long moment. Kriteeca had on a lovely white business dress with pearl earrings that bobbed when she moved her head and a sleek pair of white trimmed sunshades. "I'm sorry, Jerrid. I had no idea Tribune Hallenn would cave in."

Jerrid gave her a half smile as the crowd thinned out and they were left standing alone near the top of the steps. "I don't think we were ever too sure about Ceysseur or Monsoka."

Kriteeca just shook her head. "I was hoping it would be closer than it was. A tie vote would have been better."

"It would have just postponed the inevitable, Kriteeca." Jerrid didn't smile. "Tribune Serruus is as smooth a talker as Verlmon, and his influence definitely contributed to our demise." He looked at her with determined eyes. "I am going to find out why Juyin Hallenn betrayed us. He expressly told me he would vote in our favor and Monsoka always follows Hallenn's lead. Hallenn betrayed us; that's a given. His vote, along with Monsoka and Ceysseur tipped the scale in Verlmon's favor."

"Betrayed is right." she replied.

"This is a dark day for the Corporate, Kriteeca, a dark day indeed."

They stood there lost in thought as aides and other colleagues continued to exit the building. It seemed everyone was in a hurry to leave the battlefield and forget the voting carnage that had taken place moments ago. Most passed them by without so much as a glance but a few looked his way. Even though they couldn't see his eyes for the sunshades, Jerrid stared back.

"What's going to happen now?" Kriteeca asked.

What could he say? The Verlmon Act had passed, the Tribunal was now preparing to face the consequences of that passage. More laws would be ram-rodded through and Jerrid knew that the Tribunal itself might face a purging. "I fear a long dark night is ahead of us. For decades the hatred of Solarians has been a festering cancer ready to explode. The general populace may take arms against the Solarians within our borders. Those who hate them now have a weapon to drive them out of the Core Systems and into the Far Frontier. Soon, there may be no safe haven for any of them."

Kriteeca drew in a breath. "Or for those who stood up for them."

That was a sobering thought. He nodded, "You're right, absolutely right."

Tribune Arronsta just nodded and hung her head as she started down the steps. Jerrid watched her leave. He steeled himself and started toward the parking area with determined steps. He knew precisely where to look for Tribune Hallenn.

The Third Eye

After any major vote on a big proposal, every bar and pub within sight of the High Tribunal Hall and Administrative Complex would be packed with tribunes and their aides, celebrating the victory or bemoaning the loss. Bar owners were certainly glad for the business and hoped more big proposals were planned. Jerrid Flakkinbarr knew exactly where Tribune Juyin Hallenn would be. *The Third Eye* was a swanky little bar on Vineland Street just three blocks from the Administrative Complex. It was Hallenn's favorite haunt.

The Eye was basement level with the main entrance on Vineland and a secondary entrance on Georngin Avenue. Its lavish decor consisted of dark knotted wood trimmed in black ironwood and lighted with smoky glass lanterns throughout. Red and black velvet cushioned booths dominated most of the interior with a circular bar that ran the full length of the building. *The Eye* was packed. It took a few minutes for Jerrid to locate Juyin, hunkered over a tall glass of Bivorian brandy in a back corner. The pudgy tribune didn't even look up as Jerrid slid into the seat opposite him.

A waitress appeared almost from nowhere. "What would you like, sir?"

"Bilden tea, please," Jerrid stated without taking his eyes off Juyin.

She smiled and punched it into her comlink. "Anything to eat?"

Jerrid shook his head, "No!"

She disappeared into the crowd.

Silence.

Tribune Juyin Hallenn sat there staring at his drink. Juyin always wore dark blue suits, and this one was now wrinkled and stained under the armpits. His face was flushed and he was breathing hard. Flakkinbarr knew he hadn't wasted any time in getting here. His transplanted hair piece was the only thing that wasn't drooping.

"I don't hear the sound of blasters clicking." Juyin finally said, still not looking up. He meant it as a joke, but didn't laugh.

"Fortunately I didn't bring one today!" Jerrid tried to keep himself from snarling. *Otherwise there would be a hole in that brainless head of yours!*

"You want an answer, don't you." Juyin finally looked up. His pudgy face filled with remorse.

"That would be a start."

Juyin took a long slow sip from his glass. "I'm being pressured, Jerrid."

"By whom?" Jerrid cut him a hard glance.

"I am sorry that I told you I would vote against the Verlmon Act." Juyin blinked. "I'm sorry, I really am."

"Being sorry doesn't cut it, Juyin." Jerrid snapped back.

"Look." Juyin glared back. "I don't like Solarians, period. I really wanted to vote your way. But you see, I have three groups of lobbyists who decided, at the last minute, they wanted the bill passed. So they put the pressure on. Why the last minute change, I don't know, but these *deep pockets* are used to getting their way."

The waitress reappeared with Flakkinbarr's tea. "Will there be anything else, sir?"

"No." Jerrid replied. "This will be all."

"Very good." She turned and vanished into the crowd again.

They sat in stony silence for a long time. Juyin stared into his glass while Jerrid sipped his tea. "We were counting on you, Juyin." Flakkinbarr stated. "If you had voted against the bill, Monsoka would have done the same. It would have given us the edge we needed."

"Jerrid," Juyin eyed him with hard dark eyes. "The Solarians are an arrogant and prideful people. They got what they deserved. My father was swindled three times by Solarian traders from the Consortium Rim. He was gracious in spite of it and eventually recovered his loss, but I have never forgotten how they swindled him. I hate them." Juyin paused and took a sip from his glass. "I'm not the only one who wants to see them out of the Corporate. There's something much larger at work behind the scenes, considering the fact that up until today, the *deep pockets* didn't care whether the Solarians stayed or went."

Yes, Jerrid had heard all about Juyin's father and his misfortune with traders from the Consortium Rim. He knew, all too well, the people who disdained the Solarians. The hatred was becoming a cancer that was infesting the Corporate. "Who's pressuring you, Juyin?"

Juyin took another long sip from his glass before he answered. Then, leaning across the table, "You don't want to know, Jerrid. They wanted favors in the past, which at the time seemed rather harmless. They pumped a lot of money into some of my campaigns in order to get a few items passed through the Tribunal. The proposals they backed were good ones. Now, though, they've called in some of their markers. My political future is at stake here. I may loose the next election unless I start making their interest a priority."

Special interest groups were starting to pop up every where. Many carried considerable power and leverage. Enough leverage to end a tribune's career. "At least give me a name, Juyin."

"Look, Jerrid. You're my friend. They saw myself, Monsoka, Ceysseur and Serruus as the most likely influence for the swing vote. They put the pressure on. I'm sorry, but I did what I had to do to save my career." Juyin stared at the table again.

Who are these mysterious lobbyists anyway? The power they wielded had spooked his friend.

"How much sniffing around have these people been doing, my friend?"

Tribune Hallenn eyed him for a moment. "I don't know." Juyin shook his head. "I've got a lot of projects on my docket right now. Several of them are of key interest to these people."

There was another troubling question that surfaced. "Do you think they suspect your involvement in the missing shipments investigation?"

Tribune Hallenn sat there, staring at his glass. "I never mentioned that to anyone. The only time that is discussed is when our little group is together. And only then, no where else. I don't think they are aware. These people want the Solarians out of the Core and out of the Corporate, and that seems to be their focus."

Piin had said it appeared the government was behind the missing shipments. *Could these mysterious lobbyists Juyin refused to name be the ones?* Jerrid leaned over the table and stared hard at him. "You best keep it that way, Juyin. If this leaks out before our investigation is complete, all of our careers could be in jeopardy. Not to mention our lives! If your lobbyist friends start to snoop around too much, we may have to take steps to eliminate that threat. You best be careful, Juyin. A lot is riding on this."

Juyin nodded. "I understand, Jerrid, I certainly do."

"Do you?" Jerrid looked at him hard. "Remember, Piin said someone of influence within the government is purchasing heavy armament out of the Miranrian Federation." Jerrid kept his voice to a whisper. "If these lobbyists are the ones, this could become very deadly, Juyin, very deadly indeed."

Juyin pushed back his seat, stared at his friend, then emptied the glass in one gulp. Jerrid casually sipped his tea, never taking an eye off Juyin. "I really don't like the turn this whole thing is taking, Jerrid." The panic in his voice and the fear in his eyes did not go unnoticed.

"Just keep your cool, Juyin," Jerrid whispered. He began to wonder about Juyin's loyalties and what would happen to them if Juyin was pressured, or threatened for that matter. "Once we get to the bottom of this, we can all breathe a little easier."

Juyin pushed up from his seat with visible difficulty. "I hope you're right, Jerrid. I hope you're right." He dropped six farns on the table and left without even glancing back.

The waitress came and retrieved the money Juyin had left and then glanced at Flakkinbarr. "Anything else, sir?"

Jerrid pushed his tea away, handing her three farns.

"Thank you, sir!" She smiled, collecting the empty glass and cup.

"You're welcome." Jerrid politely smiled and watched her melt back into the crowd. He got to his feet and exited before any of his rivals decided to gloat about the victory.

4

"Friendship binds us together... Soul to soul... We share a common cup... The cup of Life... And we consider the roads we must travel... Though we part, we will know... Our friendship lasts beyond this distance...You are my friend..." — from the poetry of Gandhi Caisson, *The Long Road Home*

25 Sakbar
Darracura District
Flakkinbarr Penthouse
Maggermoss

It was late afternoon. A cool breeze was filtering through the tall red zebin trees that made up the great wall divide between the Flakkinbarr's penthouse garden and the garden of Yanni Sarratiss. The gardens were one hundred and thirty stories above street level, and today there was a slight chill in the air. Jerrid fastened the light jacket he was wearing. The padded cushion in the wicker chair was comfortable. He sat watching Tazz nap under the large yellow zebin tree. Most of the garden's eight yarr tall trees were zebins, red or gray leafed. Vars had selected the broader leaf yellow zebin to dominate the center garden spot and it had become Tazz's outdoor haunt. It was referred to as Tazz's special tree. The tree's broad leaves turned into a dazzling yellowish blaze in the fall. Accented against the red zebins it was a breathtaking display. Alleis loved the tree. *It's a reminder of Aidioni's fire in his creation*, she'd said numerous times. In his younger days, Tazz would perch on the lower branches as he spied out birds. These days, Tazz had to settle for just relaxing at the base.

There were a few clouds on the horizon, but they didn't appear to be threatening. To his left, the taller structures of the Darracura District etched a harsher line across the horizon. Tazz was curled up on the neatly manicured grass that surrounded the tree, sleeping peacefully with his tail curled up around his face. A half yarr wide terraced wall ran along the edge of the top deck from the tree wall for one hundred and fifty yarrs, the full length of the garden. Interspersed between lookouts were small bluewood shrubs. A gray marble walkway wound its way around the entire edge of the penthouse garden. Smaller ironwood trees, palms and clover pike plants were interspersed to accent the taller zebins. Colorful flower beds added additional splashes of brightness. An assortment of other green leafy vegetation was artistically planted around the upper levels surrounding several alcoves. These open spaces were tiled in a darker shade of the gray marble. It was still a paradox to think of Vars as a gardener and servant instead of a highly skilled physician from Zys Vion. When Vars had married Zoe, he'd given it all up to be with his beloved. Vars had insisted on the working arrangements. Jerrid smiled to himself and glanced around the garden area again. Yes indeed, Vars had certainly done an excellent job of planning this garden and of maintaining it for the past ten years. He had successfully turned a ramshackle top deck into a lush ecosphere. But it was more than that. It was their haven, the place where he and Alleis could come and just forget about the problems plaguing the Corporate, even if it was just for an hour or two. Vars had also constructed this little peace of heaven so that there was an alcove for entertaining and for the quiet moments when he and Alleis could come and kick off their shoes and snuggle together, barefoot, as they watched the setting sun. Of course, Tazz would take up his favorite spot under the tree. Jerrid was going to miss this place.

"It's getting close to the time when I'm going to have to send Alleis away, Tazz."

The tip of the cat's tail twitched and his ears pivoted in Jerrid's direction.

"This whole situation is becoming too dangerous. I've got to get her safely out of the system before there's any backlash." He reached for a tall glass of bilden tea on the end table next to his chair. A pitcher of tea and two more empty glasses were on a service tray that Zoe had brought out earlier. Taking a slow sip, he eyed the kibbercat again. "Of course, you'll go with her." He smiled as the cat's tail twitched several more times, eyes still closed, ears perked forward. "I can count on you to make her feel at home where she's going. I think you'll like it, too. Lots of lawn space in a very quiet setting."

The cat raised his head, opened his eyes and stared at Jerrid.

"You might even find a mouse or two." He grinned at the cat. "Are you too old to chase mice, Tazz?"

The cat looked at him and gave a little squeak.

Jerrid laughed. "I thought so!"

He knew by this time Tres Dulor must be well underway with the renovations to the old Zha Trade Headquarters. Zha had abandoned it for a more spacious structure on the southern continent of Tau Kerus Four. Alleis liked space and had always longed for a home away from the tangled mess of the city. She was finally going to get her wish. Alleis would be safe on Tau Kerus Four. The planet was in the Auroya Range out on the Far Frontier Rim, toward the galactic center. It was a backwater star system. Not too many people cared about Tau Kerus Four; it had no attractions, offered no hope of wealth, no resources, no intriguing setting for the adventurous traveler. Tau Kerus Four was just plain and simple—boring. A perfect place to hide and getaway from the sordid affairs plaguing the Corporate. Tres Dulor had undertaken many jobs for Dros Enterprises defense projects. He was trustworthy and discreet. As far as Dulor knew, the conversion of the Zha Trade Headquarters was simply a summer get-away for the head overseer of DME. Most overseers had getaway places throughout the Core Systems. His would be just a little farther out. Dulor would do a good job; he always had.

"Tazz, what have I gotten myself into?" He looked at the cat for a long moment as the cat stared back. He regretted the day he took that trip to Jeezli. *They should have sent Beslock.* "I should have never bought that book. Never. It's been a curse since the day I got it. Nothing has gone right since then." He took another sip of tea and contemplated all the troubles that seemed to follow him since he came into possession of the accursed journal. Nearly every proposal he'd submitted for legislation had been defeated. No, that wasn't entirely true, he had to remind himself. It just appeared that way. Out of seventy five bills of legislation, only those with military content were defeated. This was strange and he could never remember having this problem before. He chaired a subcommittee with strong military appropriations connections. Now that he thought more about it, only the bills involving the war directly had been defeated. Why? Perhaps it was his stance that the war needed to end and a peaceful solution brokered. A lot of people hated the war; a lot of tribunes hated the war. No, his troubles were not totally with the Tribunal and his colleagues. The real problem was the contents of the book. He feared this thousand year old mysterious journal was implicated in what might be transpiring on Geasbok. And if it was, then it would be just a matter of time before the cancer spread and destroyed the whole Corporate. He couldn't let that happen. No! He had to stop it. He and his friends.

"What am I to do, Tazz?" Jerrid sighed and leaned back into his chair. Tazz got up, stretched and eased down from his napping area. Hobbling to the wicker chair, Tazz climbed up in Jerrid's lap and settled himself down, purring loudly. For a long time Jerrid stroked the cat and gazed off into the distance. The soft feel of Tazz's fur and the sound of his purring was like soothing music. "You knew exactly what I needed, Tazz."

Forty more minutes passed as Jerrid sat stroking the cat and gazing out at the dwindling light of the afternoon. Alleis was at viao practice with her quartet and wouldn't be home until around nine. *I've failed you, Aidioni. Lord, I pray you will forgive me. But Dameon Klea cannot remain in power. He is the Shadow that will destroy the Corporate. I fear I cannot undo what has already been set in motion.* He could not look for any real peace; what was he thinking? Had God abandoned him? No, Aidioni would never abandon him. He promised. But he had abandoned Aidioni and took measures into his own hands. Surely, he had fallen for this trick of the Deceiver.

This Shadow has to be eliminated! That thought would not leave him alone. *It must be done.* There really was no way out. His beloved Corporate would be laid waste by the savage monster now in power. Even if he wanted to back out, he couldn't. He must follow this to the end, no matter what the circumstances. He scratched behind the cat's left ear and the purring grew louder. "You've become my little shadow over the past few months, Tazz." He'd never really thought much of it until recently. He couldn't pin point the exact day, but in the last several months whenever he came home Tazz was there to greet him. The cat would then follow him wherever he ventured in the house. The sunroom, the cat was there, his study, the cat was there. Always at his side, hobbling along. When he would curl up next to Alleis in the evenings, the cat was either at his feet or perched in a spot close at hand. Jerrid smiled and continued to stroke Tazz behind his ear. "I'll see if Averson at Tribunal Security can get you an ID and I'll take you to work with me one of these days." Jerrid chuckled as the cat turned and looked at him, eyes narrowing. "Course, Averson might find it hard to get you security clearance."

Tazz turned his head, got up and went over to the closest bluewood bush, climbed into the short shrub and then proceeded to walk along the wide railing that marked the edge of the garden. Despite his age and arthritic limp, Tazz still had a grace about him when he walked. It was a long drop to the street below.

"You be careful there, Tazz!" Jerrid quickly got to his feet and went over to where the cat was perched, looking out over the vast cityscape and the bay just beyond. The cat sat on the wide railing as he surveyed the structure below. Jerrid followed the cat's eyes.

Some sixty-five stories below them the faint hum of worker droids could be heard as they labored to raise the Sagga building. The droids worked around the clock at a staggering pace that rivaled their human counterpart. The structure steadily climbed toward the sky. Jerrid frowned as he gazed at the work in progress. "That thing's coming up faster than they thought it would. Who would have thought droids could work that fast? I've heard rumors that it's going to go one hundred and fifty floors. If it goes that high, Tazz, it will block our view of the bay completely. Alleis will be sadly disappointed."

The cat gave a low chirp as he got down from the railing. Jerrid watched him return to his spot by the yellow zebin. He followed and settled into his chair.

For a long time Jerrid watched the cat, sipped his tea, and occasionally glanced at the distant horizon.

"Yerrid! Yerrid!" He heard a voice call from the garden gate at the dividing wall. Tazz raised his head. Jerrid got up and went over to the ornately decorated red zebin wood gate and opened it. Yanni Sarratiss smiled at him as he opened the gate.

Yanni was a chunky little man with thick white hair and a deeply tanned complexion. He wore bushy sideburns that gave his face a full rounded look. He had an infectious smile and deeply set dark eyes that sparkled with a constant joy. But this evening that joy seemed to be dimmed.

"I vas hoping you vus out on zis nice evenink, Yerrid." Yanni's accent was thick. He was from Eloisinia, the large island nation in the South Zarras. It was a wonderful accent, full of character.

"A very nice evening, Yanni." Jerrid motioned to his place. "Please come in and sit for a while."

"Zank you, my friend." As Yanni walked to the alcove he spied the cat. "Tazz my old fuzzy friend, how you be feeling today?"

Tazz gave Yanni the silent meow and laid his head back down on his front paws.

"Such a lazy you are Tazz." Yanni laughed and sat down in Alleis' chair.

"Would you like some tea, Yanni?" Jerrid pointed to the pitcher on the table.

"Yah, zank you." Yanni smiled.

Jerrid poured him a glass.

Yanni sipped it and smiled. "Fantastic! Zoe makes best tea I tasted in a long time."

Jerrid returned the smile as he settled himself back into his chair.

Yanni was an Exchange Broker, probably the best in Maggermoss. He and the Flakkinbarrs had become quite close since Vars had constructed the penthouse garden. Yanni had greatly admired Vars' work and had hired him to do his own garden. A common gate at the dividing wall allowed easy access to both gardens. There had been numerous parties given in both gardens over the years, but since Yanni's wife, Erriana, had passed away several years ago those parties had nearly ceased.

"I transverred your funds as you requested, Yerrid." Yanni took another slow sip from his glass. He reached into his pocket and withdrew a small comlink and passed it to Jerrid. "As you requested, ze funds are untraceable." He frowned a little. "Please, I don't vant to be a snoop, but zat vas a large sum to put in sealed account."

Jerrid slowly lifted his glass to his lips and took a long sip before looking at his friend. "Yanni, I need those funds for a special project, and I don't want anyone to know where they came from. I can't say anymore than that." He felt his gut tighten. The slow gut wrenching feeling was returning. An image of the ancient journal flashed through his mind. *The darkness will descend and men's hearts will fail them.*

Yanni eyed him. "Somezing troubling you, my friend?"

He shook his head. "No, Yanni. Just something I ate, I believe."

Yanni laughed. "Too much of Zoe's cooking I take it."

"You might say that."

His guest became very quiet for a time as he sipped his tea and glanced around the garden. "You know Yerrid, zis new law zat vas passed. I fear it dangerous von, wery dangerous. Zere's a lot of talk I hear."

"What kind of talk?"

Yanni leaned forward in his chair. "Zere are several good brokers in my office. Wery good men, Yerrid. Wery good Solarian men."

Jerrid just nodded.

"Zey're leavink." He took another sip from his glass. "Zey're going to ze Far Frontier. A lot more vill follow zem, Yerrid, a lot more."

What could he say? It was probably just the beginning of a large exodus out of the Core Systems.

"You not Solarian, are you, Yerrid?" Yanni eyed him. "Ze reason for zose untraceable funds?"

Jerrid laughed. "No, Yanni, I'm not Solarian."

Yanni looked relieved, but the worry in his eyes still remained. "I'm glad, Yerrid." He looked around the garden and then leaned forward in his chair. His voice barely above a whisper. "I'm Solarian, Yerrid, and I'm gettink out of ze system before zings start happenink."

The confession startled him. Jerrid's jaw dropped open as he looked dumbfounded at his friend. "I had no idea you were Solarian, Yanni. No idea."

Yanni waved a beefy hand. "Long line of Solarians in my family, Yerrid. I'm afraid zings vill get out of hand and ve vill loose everyzing, no matter who's ve are."

Jerrid said nothing. Could he reassure his friend that things weren't as bad as they appeared? No, he'd just be perpetrating a lie. Really, what could he say?

Waving his hand in Jerrid's face, Yanni's eyes narrowed and he focused hard. "Look, ve've been friends long time, Yerrid, long time. I'm no prophet but I know zis is no good zing ve been forced to accept. Zis man, our Director, I not like him from ze first day he become ze leader of zis Corporate. No sir! He's a dangerous man, Yerrid, wery dangerous. Ze only vay zings vill change is if Klea dies or someone kills him. Only vay."

"Yanni!"

"It's true, Yerrid!" Yanni's joyfulness had long vanished. Deep despair was etched across his face. His eyes burned with a haunting look. "I'm leavink the system. I'm selling my place, getting out. I just hope ze new buyers you vill like. I hope zey honor the garden Vars has worked so diligently to keep."

Jerrid leaned back in his chair and just looked at his guest. Here was a man he'd known for ten years. A good man. A wealthy man and an astute businessman. He sighed heavily. "You've made the right decision, Yanni. As you said, things will only get worse. Much worse, I'm afraid. You'd better go to the Far Frontier. Hopefully, you'll be safe there."

Yanni waved his hand. "You can't help vay zings turn out, Yerrid. But I vanted to let you know zat without Erriana, life is not as meaningful. My children have zeir own lives. I told zem zey better leave." He shook his head. "Don't know if zey vill listen, but I tried. Troubles coming, Yerrid, big trouble and I's leavink." Yanni placed his glass of tea back on the table and pushed up from his chair. "I be selling soon. I'll let you know who ze new owners vill be. Perhaps zey vill be good neighbors, my friend." He gave a weak smile and walked toward the gate.

Jerrid just sat there watching him.

Yanni paused at the gate, waved his hand and closed the gate behind him.

"Oh Tazz, what's going to happen next?"

The cat eyed him for a long moment and then gave a silent meow.

"Ze only way zings vill change if Klea dies or someone kills him. Only vay."

Indeed, that was the solution to the problem. Piin's man had better be good. Yes, he'd better be good. All the while, Jerrid continued to wonder why he was getting deeper and deeper into plotting Klea's elimination when he knew he should be running as well.

5

"Life and history are seemingly the same river and we are the individual streams that feed this great flow. Some streams are greater than others, impacting the river with force and sudden calamity. Still others are small trickles that join the flow with not a pause or an uproar. Yet each adds to the greatness of this mighty river." — Borgan Sarfi, *The Twist of Fate*

27 Sakbar
Hunneen Mansion
Moon: Bethleea

Alleis was standing in the middle of the bedroom suite transfixed by the sheer elegance of the decor. Expensive Far Margoon rugs of deep tans, reds, and yellows spread like a vast sea of tight designs that stretched fifteen yarrs in a perfect square. At the edge of the bright colorful rugs was cream colored marble tile. The walls were painted off white and the combination of the colors had a cooling affect on the room. The ceiling was about seven yarrs high, a best guess, and sculpted in a grand display of painstaking craftsmanship. The detail was dazzling. At the very center, a four yarr wide chandelier of exquisite cut crystal added to enhance the elegance. A fireplace, two and a half yarrs tall, made up of light gray stone dominated the wall opposite the bed. Three red velvet upholstered high back chairs were placed to the right of the fireplace as a loveseat of the same red velvet was positioned directly in front facing the hearth. A third chair and table were to the left of the loveseat.

"I cannot get over this place, Jerrid!" She whirled around one more time, her long light yellow evening dress flowing out like the unfolding of a gorgeous flower. "This is the grandest thing I've ever seen." The radiant glow on her deeply tanned face took his breath away.

She's still as lovely as the day I married her, Jerrid thought. She paused long enough for her light auburn hair to settle on her bare shoulders and her gown to fold in around her legs. Her thin frame and small size made her appear younger than her forty-four years. Alleis was the energetic and adventurous one. She had a drive that often went way beyond his.

They had met at the university. He was a second year law student; she was a freshman. They quickly married against all good sense and counsel from both sets of parents. The only blessing they had gotten was from his dormmate, Vennie Suun, Alleis' first cousin. Having no children themselves, he wondered if all parents had such a difficult time as theirs did when their only children married young.

Jerrid and Alleis were happily married. She was the jewel of his life, and he did everything possible to see to it that she was comfortable. When he became a tribune, their life took on a whole new dimension. Life became much easier. Alleis took to the new role with charm and enthusiasm, as if she had always been meant for greater things.

She liked being the wife of a tribune. It afforded her the opportunity to mingle with important people, travel to exotic places, dress in expensive designer clothes, and live in a posh penthouse high above Maggermoss. She had made the most of it and also had made her husband proud. Alleis was the eye of the party, performing with such social grace and charms at the many official functions a tribune was forced to endure. She was well liked by his colleagues and their wives. Alleis was a rare jewel, and life with her was rich. Since the reconfiguration of the government five years ago, and the ascent to power by Dameon Klea, the atmosphere in the Corporate had become oppressive and foreboding. Jerrid and Alleis watched as their lives went from happiness to disillusionment. *You must not let these thoughts spoil your evening.* Alleis would not be pleased if his mood became dour. Even though it had been a business trip to view the final blueprints for the new destroyers, they were here to enjoy themselves at this grand mansion. Jerrid pushed the foreboding thoughts out of his mind as he pulled on his dark blue dinner jacket. He shoved the annoying ID bracelet up under his shirt sleeve..

"Should we build one like it?" Jerrid grinned at her.

Alleis moved across the rug like a silent breeze as she stood before him and straightened his left lapel. Her silver ID bracelet sparkled in the light as she smoothed the material down. "You certainly do look handsome tonight!" She gave him a bright smile. "And no, as much as I like this massive three hundred and twenty five room mansion, it's a little too large for me."

"A little too large!"

Alleis giggled. "I think Vars would have a stroke trying to take care of it."

"I don't see how the Hunneen's do it with just seventy five servants." Jerrid remarked. "Of course there are the droids."

"It's massive, Jerrid, pure and simple." The radiant glow remained on her face. "I've thoroughly enjoyed our time here. I'm glad you asked me along. Tressa is such a wonderful hostess. Those children of hers are so adorable and well mannered."

"That little Mira is certainly precocious. There's just something unique about her." Jerrid relaxed his arms and fastened his jacket. "I have a feeling, though, that all the Hunneen children are very special. Probably comes from their good genes."

Alleis laughed and nodded. "They are three very beautiful children, although I don't think Master Sar would appreciate the word beautiful at his age."

Jerrid agreed. "From what his father tells me I think Sar has his eyes set on entering the Watchman Academy."

There was a knock. Jerrid walked over and pulled open the massive white six panel door. A tall young man with olive complexion and large features was standing on the other side. His tailored white suit enhanced his large frame.

"Tribune Flakkinbarr," he bowed slightly. "Dinner is prepared. If you will accompany me, I will escort you and Lady Flakkinbarr to the dining room."

"Jink, isn't it?" Jerrid nodded, remembering hearing the young Ovian's name mentioned when they first arrived.

"Yes, sir!" Jink's smile grew larger.

Jerrid returned the smile as Allies came up behind him.

"Chef Jorn has prepared a grand dinner this evening in your honor." Jink was bubbling with enthusiasm. "Chef Jorn is the best chef in the whole quadrant."

Jerrid eyed Alleis for a moment and then glanced back at the young Ovian. "The best chef in the quadrant you say?" He winked at his wife.

"No one can best Chef Jorn, sir." Jink threw out his chest with confidence. "Chef Jorn is simply the best!"

"Lead the way, Jink." He gave Alleis another wink. "I'm certainly looking forward to a dinner from the best chef in the whole quadrant."

"You will not be disappointed, sir, madame." Jink turned and proceeded down the four yarr wide hallway with the Flakkinbarrs close behind.

The smile on Jerrid's face continued to grow as he gave his wife another wink. Alleis suppressed a giggle.

"Another dinner guest will be joining you this evening." Jink turned slightly to his left as they proceeded down the long hallway. "Marshal Vandermern from Watchman Command just arrived within the half hour."

"Vandermern!" Jerrid's face brighten the more. "I've been wanting to meet the new head of Watchman Command. Looks like this evening is full of pleasant surprises."

* * *

"That was an excellent dinner." Alleis commented as she followed the tall slender blonde woman through the double doors to the portico just off the dining room. Tressa Hunneen was dressed in a long mauve colored sleeveless evening gown. Alleis followed her across the marble porch to a bench tucked between two large red zebin trees. The night was calm and filled with the scent of blooming flowers. With a wave of her hand

Tressa motioned for Alleis to have a seat on the finely sculpted ironwood bench. With a slight smile, Alleis sighed and settled on the bench. Tressa then gracefully sat down next to her.

"Jorn is such a great chef," Tressa remarked. "We are fortunate to have him; he has been with us for a long time and is like family to us."

"A remarkable talent." Alleis replied, gazing at Tressa's sparkling blue eyes. The woman had a presence about her that spoke of strength and determination. "We have a wonderful chef in Zoe, but I do believe that Jorn's dinner topped it all. The piria peas and sauce was an incredible dish."

Footsteps sounded on the marble floor and they turned to find Tressa's daughter, Lexra, slipping up to the bench. She was the near image of her mother. At fourteen years old she moved with all the poise of someone older. Dressed in a light blue short-sleeved gown she certainly looked like a first year undergraduate. She paused, smiled at Alleis and then nodded to her mother. "With your permission, Mother, I would like to have Hon take me to Talsah's so we can study for exams."

"Oh, I had forgotten that exams were this week." Tressa responded. "Yes, tell Hon you have my permission. But don't stay too late."

"I won't, Mother." Lexra turned and bolted toward the double doors.

"She's a striking young lady." Alleis remarked, catching the slight frown on her hostess' face.

"That she is," Tressa nodded, eyebrows still close together as she stared at the double doors. "Although, I think we have spoiled her."

They both laughed.

"This is her first year at Edmond Academy and it has been trying for Lexra. Thankfully, she made a friend who's helped her to adjust." Tressa relaxed and spoke of her children and some of the funny things they all had done over the course of time. Alleis told her of the difficulty she had in learning to play the viao and what it meant to finally become accomplished enough to play it the way it was meant to be played. Her dream was finally realized when she was asked to become a member of a string quartet whose members were also part of the Grand Maggermoss Symphony.

"Oh, I love the Grand Symphony!" Tressa exclaimed.

Alleis then elaborated on some of the functions the quartet had been invited to play. Tressa and Alleis talked well into the night.

* * *

No more than thirty yarrs from where Alleis and Tressa were discussing children, cats, and musical instruments, Jerrid, Cirin, and Marshal Vandermern were on another portico seated around a glass table sipping tofi brandy Chef Naru had brought out.

"So how does it feel to be in command of all the Watchmen, Marshal?" Jerrid asked, fixing his gaze on the man seated opposite him at the table. Vandermern was a large framed man well over two and a half yarrs tall. His hair was similar to Jerrid's, steel gray, but it had a few accents of dark gray peppered throughout. A thick gray mustache accented his upper lip. The marshal had piercing green eyes that took in every detail.

"Too early to tell, Tribune," replied the marshal. "I'm sure if you were to ask me that question again six months from now I could give you a more accurate answer."

Jerrid nodded and sipped his brandy. "Even then, Marshal, it may not necessarily be an accurate one."

Vandermern nodded and tipped his brandy glass to his lips.

The sound of footsteps drew everyone's attention to the lower terrace. Sar Hunneen and Jink, the servant, with purpose in their stride, bounded up from the lower level. Sar stood nearly as tall as the Ovian, built similarly to his father, but having blond hair instead of black. Bright blue eyes sparkled with a youthful spirit. Both youths paused and then looked at each other. Jink nodded, and Sar pulled out a comlink from behind his back. "Pardon the intrusion, sirs." Sar spoke and looked at his father. "Father, Jink and I would like to make formal request to apply for admission to the Watchman Academy." He handed the comlink to the marshal.

Vandermern took it and keyed the entry. The screen's glow illuminated the marshal's face in a soft green light. He carefully read through the application. After a few moments he looked up and winked at Cirin.

Cirin, who was dressed in a satin white shirt with bellowed sleeves, leaned across the table, winked back at the marshal, and then fixed his son with a determined gaze. "You two are going to need sponsors. Have you approached anyone on that regard?"

Sar glanced down at the marble tiles and then at the marshal. "I was hoping Marshal Vandermern would sponsor both of us, sir."

Marshal Vandermern leaned forward and rested his elbows on the table top. "As the new head of Watchman Command, I really can't sponsor anyone."

Sar and Jink both looked devastated. Apparently they hadn't thought about the marshal's new position.

Jerrid was amused as both young men looked at each other, trying to figure out their next move. From its inception, Watchman Academy recruits had to have sponsorship from some government or military authority. It was one branch of the military that did not recruit off the streets. One had to be chosen, selected by the Watchman Board of Inquiry to attend. It was a prestigious assignment, an elite group. Most sponsorships were handed out by high ranking officers to sons, daughters, or relatives. Only the top percentage of Primary Level Education graduates were ever sponsored, good grades and personal recommendation the key playing factors. Here were two young men trying to get sponsorship. They were determined, he could tell. He cleared his throat. All eyes turned his way. "The Marshal may not be able to sponsor you two young men, but I can."

The light brightened in their eyes.

Jerrid fixed the younger Hunneen with his gaze. "I understand, Master Sar, you will be finished with your Primary Level Education by the end of the year."

"Yes, sir." Sar replied with enthusiasm.

"And you, Master Jink." Jerrid glanced at the young servant. Most people would not have used the term, master, with a servant lad, but Jerrid felt it important to show respect. "Have you completed your Primary Level Education?"

The smile on the young Ovian's face told everyone that he was honored to be counted as an equal. "Yes, sir. Last year, sir."

Jerrid winked at Cirin. "Then, gentlemen, once I receive your files at my office, and your grades are within the acceptable range, I'll send a formal declaration of sponsorship straight to the Watchman Academy."

"Thank you, sir!" they both said at once.

Cirin smiled and nodded to Jerrid. "Well, I think you two have your answer."

"Thank you, Tribune, sir." Sar and Jink exclaimed again.

Jerrid and Vandermern laughed.

"If you will excuse us, sirs," Sar nudged Jink in the ribs, "I want to help Jink clear the dinner table."

Cirin laughed, "You may go."

The young men bolted from the portico.

"There go some fine young men." Vandermern said.

"Yes, indeed." Jerrid replied.

"Thank you for sponsoring them, Jerrid." Cirin replied. "This is an important step for them. I know Jink's father has some reservations about him joining the Watchmen, but I think he's capable."

"And your son?" Jerrid asked.

"Sar is a strong, determined young man." Cirin noted. "Much like I was at one time. He will do well."

"Like his father before him." Vandermern added.

Jerrid gave a sideways glance to Cirin. "You were a Watchman?"

Cirin smiled weakly and took a slow sip from his glass. "Quite some time ago. A period of time I truly would like to forget." He looked at Vandermern and then back to the tribune. "Sar will do well, I am sure."

"I will see that he does." Vandermern piped in, then took a long tug on his brandy.

The conversation turned from former military days to the new destroyers that would be built by Hunneen's Vargan Company. Discussion of various aspects of military hardware were broached as well as thoughts on future projects.

"I'm surprised that Dros Military Enterprises didn't throw in a bid." Cirin commented as he gave a fixed stare at the tribune.

Jerrid swallowed hard. Dros Military Enterprises was simply a small company that bid on a few military projects to give the illusion of being a major military contractor. Deliberately staffed with only a small group of engineers he had personally selected over several years, their forté was small weapons systems and inner system security cutters. For the most part the engineers and other support staff were well paid, but were purposely kept in the dark about whom they really worked for. As head overseer, Jubal Dros was rarely seen at Dros Military Enterprises. He had an office, a secretary, and from time to time sat in on planning meetings when his twelve engineers were working on a big project. But the day to day operations at the luxurious office complex deep in the Mithira District of Maggermoss were run by Adrianna Zerrsa, a savvy engineer from Zys Vion. Zerrsa was a trustworthy middle aged woman who was clueless as to Jubal Dros' true identity. The projects they worked on brought in lucrative profits over a short time frame. Initially the brain child of his many meetings with Gerrius Tuposh, the company had been funded out of his own pocket and afforded Jerrid ground level exposure to his constituents. It allowed him to mingle and learn true opinions about how the government was handling things. Now Dros Military Enterprises was aiding heavily in the investigation of Geasbok's missing supply ships because those ships were designed by them and sometimes supplied by them. "I'm sure DME felt the destroyers were beyond their scope at present time."

Cirin nodded. "Still, from what numbers Dros has on the Exhange you would think they would try for a big project like this one."

"Would've been a smart move," added Vandermern.

"I agree." Jerrid nodded.

"One of these days I'd like to meet this Jubal Dros and see what his plans are for the future," Cirin replied. "Perhaps a joint venture would be in order."

Trying not to allow his discomfort to show, Jerrid grinned and continued to sip his brandy. The conversation eventually steered away from the war and military hardware and went back to children and houses, much to Jerrid's relief.

* * *

It was late. Jerrid had been awakened from his sleep by the ongoing nightmare. It was plaguing him again, a reminder there was no safe place, no rest from the deadly secrets and the ever present Shadow that was stalking his life. He slipped out from under the bedcovers, threw a bathrobe around his shivering body and tip-toed to the double doors leading out to the balcony. Alleis didn't stir, her auburn hair draped over the satin pillow as she peacefully slept. Her delicate frame was almost lost in the massive four poster bed. The crisp night air had a bite to it, so Jerrid closed the door behind him. Another shiver assaulted his body. He shook it off and moved to the middle of the balcony, the hard marble tiles magnifying the cold in his feet. *I should have gotten my slippers*, he chided himself. If he went back inside to retrieve them, he would awaken Alleis for sure. No, he could endure. He had to. Perhaps the cold would drive away the dream. He began pacing about, trying to warm himself and to shake the dream from his mind. He sighed heavily as he glanced around at the massive residence. The reported wealth of the Hunneen empire was underestimated. The reports and rumors were wrong. "The estimates are far too low." Jerrid had to smile on this, pacing back and forth in front of the glass doors. The Hunneen's had to be the wealthiest people in the whole Core System. Yet, they were virtually unknowns in the high society social circuits. *So the rich can hide from snooping eyes after all.* He grinned as he walked over and leaned against the railing. He felt a little warmer and the remnants of the dream were nearly gone. Hon, the Hunneen's servant, would be taking them to Gernarn for their departure on the late morning shuttle back to motherworld. *Yes, back to the real world.*

Be not afraid of the Shadows!

Jerrid whirled around, startled by the voice. There was no one there, but he had heard someone speak as clear as a bell. A white and black striped kibbercat, larger than Tazz by a good yarr, was sitting on the edge of the railing at the far end of the balcony. Tufts of white hair flared out from behind the creature's large black ears. A long bushy black tail swished back and forth as the cat focused its penetrating blue-gray eyes on him. Jerrid could not break the stare. The eyes of the cat seemed to look into his soul. *Did that cat talk to me?* Nonsense, cats don't talk. It had to be the effects of the dream. Had to be.

A chilled breeze began to blow around him, stirring the bathrobe. Jerrid blinked. The fur on the long haired cat was undisturbed. He glanced around at the tall dark pines at the edge of the balcony. They didn't move. The breeze whirled again, stronger, snapping the loose ends of his bathrobe against his legs. *What?*

Suddenly a small glimmer of light appeared next to the cat. Then a second tiny dot of light. Then a third one. At first he thought the tiny dots might be sparkflies, but they only came out in warmer weather. By now there were more than a dozen little lights, flashing on and off, swirling around the cat in a rapid display of movement. Jerrid just stared as they begin to pulsate with the strange wind that kept his bathrobe in a constant state of agitation, yet the fur on the cat was not disturbed by the motion. Suddenly in the blink of an eye, the small dots of light flashed in unison, becoming more intense in their brightness and converging into a single globe. The globe flickered three more times and then moved away from the cat toward him. Jerrid wanted to bolt and run, but he was frozen in place. His legs felt like heavy iron pipes. He could not even move his hands to pull his leg around. No. All he could do was focus on the small globe of light as it came to a halt between him and the cat. The light pulsated three more times and began to grow in size. The wind suddenly stopped. From the small globe, the light expanded into a fist sized ball of pure white energy in less than a second. It illuminated everything on the balcony as if it were midday. Shadows were driven to the far edges of the balcony. Jerrid squinted, not able to move his hands to shield his eyes from the bright glow. A flare of light shot out from the top of the glowing globe some thirty yarrs high. Another flare shot out from the bottom, penetrating the marble tile flooring on the balcony. Jerrid was transfixed by the angulating white globe as it continued to pulsate. All he could do was look at the strange light through slitted eyes. A tearing sound reached his ears. It was the sound similar to the ripping of fabric. The globe opened out like a flickering flame of fire and the smell of sweet lilies permeated the air all around. An overpowering presence of sheer holiness slammed into him like a tidal wave. He felt ashamed and sickened; the light was pure, holy. He glanced down at his hands and just saw vile ugliness; his sins exposed for all to see. He felt despicable. The light was so penetrating he wanted to crawl under a rock and hide. But there was no place to go, nowhere to hide from this pure searching light. Finding himself released from the granite-like fear that had frozen him in place, Jerrid fell to his knees and wept. He felt his shame, his weaknesses, his sorrow, and he wept over them. The light continued to pulsate as its glow encompassed him.

Be not afraid! The voice again.

Jerrid could not look up; the light was blinding. The words had been calming, pure, sweet. He felt his racing heart slow. His pulse returned to a normal pace. Suddenly, he felt peace, peace such as he had never felt before. It washed over him like a fresh rain. The guilt, the sorrow, the shame, all the despicable things he'd ever done flowed off him. For a long time he basked in the soothing effect of this fresh rain, this fresh love, this fresh newness. He felt the weight of his sins leave him, and he felt unconditional love like he'd never felt before. It was amazing someone could love him like this, for no reason.

I am unworthy of this, was all Jerrid could think.

Be not afraid. The voice again. *Though the Shadows come, they will not take you. You are mine. Fear not. Others will bind your hands and lead you where you do not want to go, but I will prevail. Remember I am with you always.*

Jerrid still could not look up. "Aidioni, is that you?" All he could see was the glow from the light and the marble tile floor. As he glanced to one side he noticed sandaled feet standing next to him. They were strong feet, masculine and deeply tanned. And there was something else about them. On each foot, above one of the leather latches, were scars, ugly, wicked scars. Surely this person had suffered something terrible. Suddenly Jerrid knew, Yushann, the Eternal Son, Redeemer. "Oh Yushann, my Lord!" He felt a hand touch his shoulder and the soothing calm intensified and swept over his entire body.

Peace. Always. The path others have chosen for you will bring you into grave danger, but I will prevail. The Voice was strong, but gentle. *Remember, what others have set in motion will change the course of this great empire.*

Jerrid felt the hand withdraw from his shoulder. The light pulsated three more times and then darkness. Jerrid was still on his knees, engulfed in such a relaxed state he could almost go to sleep where he was. Slowly, lifting his head, he looked up. The cat was sitting near him, looking at him intently with those blue-gray eyes.

"Hello," Jerrid finally voiced.

The cat swished its tail. He reached his hand out and the cat leaned in and smelt it. The cat looked at Jerrid, fixing him with his eyes again.

I am Charlie.

Jerrid gasped.

The cat then turned and trotted over to the balcony rail, jumped up and disappeared over the edge. Jerrid struggled to his feet and went over to see where the cat had gone. Looking over into the garden, he saw the cat disappear into an open door of one of the rooms on the lower level. He stood there looking for several minutes. A light flicked on in the room and a small shadow appeared in the doorway. Presently the small face of a child was illumined by motherworld's light. Her braided golden hair danced in the light. It was Mira. She looked up at him and waved.

Good night Tribune Flakkinbarr. I'm glad you met Charlie.

The little girl waved again and disappeared back into her room. The light went out.

Jerrid's mouth hung open. He could not explain the cat's or Mira's voice in his head, or the light for that matter. But he did have a peace that was undeniably present. Breathing in deeply, Jerrid turned and headed back to bed. Perhaps he was just dreaming and all these sudden events would vanish in the early morning light. *Or would they?*

Transition Corridor Grid
Marker 2 by 1 / Green Grid Sector
BRS-Blue Star 122
Destination: TeMar - Motherworld

"I think I was just dreaming, Alleis," Jerrid commented as he eased back into the seat. He had told her about the early morning encounter, the light, the cat, and Mira. Yes, it really did seem like a dream.

As Jerrid recounted his tale to her, Alleis listened intently. There were parts of Jerrid's story that bordered on fictional drama. Talking cats, mind-speaking little girls. But the account about Yushann touched something deep inside her spirit. Was that real? A stirring deep within told her that this was more than a dream, that Jerrid had actually come into the very presence of the Eternal Son. She looked him in the eye. "Jerrid, I find it hard to believe a cat can talk and that little Mira Hunneen can speak to you through mental voicing. Yet, I don't think it was a dream, I really don't."

There was a glow in her eyes that made him tingle all over. Yes, she was right, he had to trust Aidioni. And he had to tell her about everything, the mysterious journal, the missing shipments to Geasbok, everything. But one thing he could not bring himself to reveal to her was the plan to assassinate Klea. No, even now it was hard to imagine he had agreed to such an evil deed. Was it too late to change his mind, to distance himself from Piin and his hired assassin? When they got home he would tell her everything except for that. He had to reconsider all this business of assassination.

PART TWO
Enter the Dragons

Interlude

October 13, 2024
Lawrence Bakersfield Laboratories
Clearing Lab Twelve
0855 Zulu

Thomas Farraday eased back into his chair, pushing his glasses up on his head. He sat there for the longest time pondering the pages he had been reading.

A blue light on the computer lit up and blinked three times.

"Something troubling you, Thomas?"

Farraday tapped the papers in his hand. "This, Wanda. This information is going to stir up a lot of things if it ever gets out to the scientific community."

"Would you like me to cross reference this data with Department of Defense files currently accessible?"

Thomas smiled at the computer. "I don't think our dear General would want you snooping through DoD right now, Wanda."

"There is our Silentwind cloaking device, you know. It would allow me to access DoD files for at least three hours without being detected.."

Yes, the Silentwind cloaking devise, a cleverly designed piece of software created to get in and out of classified data banks and especially created for finding information without detection. A clever program that took him five years to write and to install into Wanda's main frame.

"The General is not ready for you yet, Wanda." Farraday grinned at the machine. "What he doesn't know is best kept that way."

"Very well, Thomas."

Farraday glanced back at the print out. From the little bit he'd read so far, views on origins would certainly have to change, provided his fellow scientists actually accepted the data in his hands. Once this information was made public, if ever, the political and religious worlds would also be shaken. Farraday glanced at the clock. It was late and he should be tired. On the contrary, he felt energized. He couldn't believe what he was reading.

"I wonder when or if they'll make this material public?" That was a sobering thought. Dalton would certainly want some verification before he showed it to the president. But, would the president even believe it?

"Shall I prepare public release protocols for this information?"

"No, no, Wanda!" Thomas almost laughed. "That's the General's department. Just maintain your current operations procedures."

"Yes, Thomas."

This was history, but with a very different view point of history. He took the pipe from his lips and began to refresh the tobacco. That done, he poured himself another cup of coffee and adjusted his glasses. He placed the print out back on his lap. He picked up where he'd left off and began to read again. The tale was certainly becoming more interesting with each turn of the page.

6

"Evil is a virus. It spreads like wildfire, devouring a whole forest of souls." — Edda Xayn, *Against the Giant*

"It is for the security of the whole Corporate we take these measures. Every citizen is important. Your protection is our paramount concern." — Tribune Rez Verlmon, Media One Interview

11 Somlea
High Tribunal Administrative Complex
Tribune Jerrid Flakkinbarr's Office

"You want to move five hundred million people from Gabersoon to where?" Jerrid glared at Rez Verlmon and Kael Sessora who sat in lavish leather chairs across from his desk. Verlmon's thick white hair was a little unruly this morning. His stomach protruded from his black jacket, and strained against the buttons of his pale yellow shirt. Sessora was a stick of a tribune, but was well groomed with every piece of clothing firmly pressed. Not one hair was out of place. His dark brown eyes were penetrating and scornful.

"Look, Jerrid," Rez's voice had a hard edge to it. "Do you realize just how big a threat Solarian sympathizers pose to the Corporate? Do you?"

Why all this double speak? Jerrid asked himself. Verlmon was a man who decried the ills of a society filled with Solarian sympathizers from almost the beginning of the war. So, what was he looking for here? Dividing loyalties? Jerrid knew he had to be careful and choose his words wisely. He certainly could not afford Verlmon's snoops sniffing around his door, nor could he risk drawing attention to himself or his little group. "I do understand the threat, Rez! Believe me, I know we have to keep watch. But you're talking about relocating nearly the entire population of Gabersroon. Where are you going to put them?"

"Some will come to motherworld, of course." Sessora pointed out.

"How many?" Jerrid glanced at him, careful not to show any hint of the anger or loathing that had been building since they stepped into his office. "Refugees from the Far Frontier are already filtering in here at a steady trickle. You add Gabersroon's population and we're looking at that trickle becoming a raging river of a crisis."

"Look Jerrid," Rez snorted, "we have to turn Gabersroon into a detention planet right away. The SPG have to have a place to keep these Solarian sympathizers. We'll temporarily move some of Gabersroon's population to motherworld. The rest may have to go to Nan-Din in the Jalofasz Range. Nan-Din is sparsely populated and the Gabersroons would be welcomed there. I've already talked to Sovereign Gaze Preson and his response was very favorable."

"Why not use Nan-Din as your detention planet?" Jerrid shot back.

"It has to be in the Core Systems!" Verlmon snapped. "The Frontier or the Far Frontier is no place for them. Too risky for transport and too hard to guard."

They just sat and stared at each other as an uncomfortable air of hostility continued to build. Jerrid fidgeted in his seat. He was disgusted with the whole conversation. "What's going to happen to the rest of Gabersroon's people?" He finally eased back in his chair.

"After careful screening," Sessora began, "those remaining planet-side will be used as guards at the detention facilities. Mind you, whole cities will be turned into detention camps that will be very well guarded. SPG will supervise the entire planet. We want to make the sympathizers as comfortable as possible until they stand trial." Sessora had a smooth sickening tone in his voice that reeked of smugness.

"And what happens once they go to trial?" Jerrid already knew where this conversation was heading.

Rez Verlmon leaned forward in his seat. "Those who've committed serious infractions of the law will be executed. The rest will spend the remaining years of their lives mining Gabersroon's ore. After all, we have to continue mining the planet." He smiled wickedly. "Think about it, Jerrid. We'll be getting free labor for once. Should cut the cost of materials heading into motherworld by half if not more." He smiled at Sessora, who responded with a slight grin.

"And the cost of moving Gabersroon's population to Nan-Din?" Jerrid wanted to reach out and strangle Verlmon, but refrained.

"The beauty of my plan, Jerrid, is that it will not cost us anything." Verlmon's face lit up as he grinned. "I'm going to the Director, personally, and request the use of the Second Fleet to move them." Verlmon was proud of his new plan. "They have at least ten heavy carriers that could do the job rather expeditiously."

"There's a cost even if you do use the Second Fleet." Jerrid stared at him. "Ten heavy carriers require a lot of fuel."

"They're Fleet, there is no cost involved." Rez fired back.

"And what will Admiral Monté have to say about that?" Jerrid glared, not believing what had come out of Verlmon's mouth. "I understand the Second is being dispatched to the War Zone very soon."

"Monté will not be a problem." Verlmon snapped back. "He does what the Director tells him. If we need the Second Fleet to move Gabersroon's population, then he'll do it. Has to!"

Jerrid just shook his head. He heaved out a sigh and then glanced at both tribunes. "Will Gabersroon be the only detention planet?" He had a feeling it would not, but he had to ask.

Sessora smiled wickedly. "Sarrsiin already has several large penal facilities. Wouldn't take much to transform the entire planet into a full scale detention planet. We're also looking at Dejuboon as well."

Clamping his jaw, Jerrid stared.

"Of course, it will depend on how many Solarian sympathizers we find." Verlmon added. "Not to mention any Separatist loyalists who will be added to the mix."

Leaning across his desk, Jerrid steepled his fingers and glanced at each of the men seated across from him. "Look, you should know that by doing this we'll be playing right into the Separatists' hands. Other quadrants may not like this bold new initiative and may decide to join the Separatists. Then you'll have a bigger movement and the Solarians may get an ally to boot."

Verlmon turned a guarded look to Sessora who just shrugged his shoulders.

Sessora leaned forward and fixed Jerrid with his gaze. "Who cares, Tribune Flakkinbarr? The Verlmon Act is very explicit. You are tribune of this region and we've come to you with our current plans. As required by law." He locked eyes with Jerrid. "We're moving Gabersroon's population, period. It will be a detention planet! You can support us or not, but remember this: we will take note of any tribune who attempts to block this move. You can count on that! Our actions are fully sanctioned under the Verlmon Act."

"Is that a threat, Tribune?" Jerrid snarled.

"No!" threw back Sessora. "It's a promise!" He got to his feet. Verlmon reluctantly pushed up from his chair.

"I was hoping you'd show more cooperation in this matter, Jerrid." Verlmon remarked. "We haven't been the best of friends, but the Verlmon Act is law now and we will follow it to the letter. You can get on board or not. The choice is yours. I hope you make the right one." He fixed Jerrid with a warning glare as he and Sessora stormed out of the office.

A flood of emotions hit Jerrid. He couldn't believe what he had just heard. They were going to round these people up and ship them off like they were animals. *What is happening here?* He knew that from now on he'd better watch his back.

* * *

He had never thought Kylia Morran rude, but this afternoon, she exemplified the meaning of the word. Kylia was an attractive woman in her late forties with jet black hair cut in feathered layers just touching her shoulders, nicely tanned face with a flawless complexion, dark eyes, and an infectious smile. Kylia had been the Director's secretary for over three years. For the most part she took care of ordering the Director's meetings and trips abroad or out of the system. She was always all about business but usually with a pleasant air about her. Not this afternoon. No!

"Tribune Flakkinbarr," her tone was edgy, "I can put you on the docket to see the Director the first week in Bonnar. That is all I have at this time." She leaned across her desk and lowered her voice. "There has already been a number of tribunes in here regarding this new Verlmon Act. They all want to see the Director right away. But, sir, he is not seeing anyone right now on this matter." Kylia eased back in her chair, glanced at the dark wooden double doors to the executive suite and then back to Jerrid. "I'm sorry, Tribune Flakkinbarr, I really am. But the ninth of Bonnar is the earliest I can get you in."

As Jerrid got to his feet, one of the massive double doors swung open and an imposing figure dressed in a deep red and blue robe slipped out and moved toward Kylia's desk. Klea's Shuuto Priest stood nearly a head taller than Flakkinbarr. A thin dangling mustache accented his angular face and, unlike Piin, his head was completely shaven. The Shuuto's almond shaped eyes cut a menacing glare as he glanced sideways at Jerrid before he dropped a comlink with several notes of paper on Kylia's desk.

"The Director wishes these reports at your earliest convenience." The yellow skinned man glanced at Jerrid again before turning and heading back into the executive office. As he did so, his sudden movement stirred the air and lifted one of the handwritten notes from top of the comlink. It fluttered down at Jerrid's foot. Kylia still had her eyes fixed on the Shuuto as he closed the thick dark wood door to the executive office. Without thinking, Jerrid reached down and picked the note up. He glanced at it.

Please make sure all reports
from Admiral Monté are brought
to my attention at once.
—D. Klea

The script was fluid and fanciful. Easy to read. Jerrid's heart nearly skipped a beat as he stared at it for a long moment. *Can this be real*, he asked himself as he continued to scrutinize the script on the note. *It certainly looks like the same handwriting that's in the journal.* As Jerrid reached to place the note back on the secretary's desk, suddenly he felt a chill run up his spine and the air seemed to turn cold. Then the soft smell of lilies tingled his nostrils. He looked around. The flower arrangement on Kylia's desk was blue and yellow twillas, not lillies.

Keep it!

Jerrid's arm felt frozen in place. Fear began building at the edge of his consciousness. He was afraid that Kylia would suddenly turn and see him. Sweat began to bead on his forehead; the pounding of his heart was loud in his own ears. *I can't take this!* His tongue felt thick and he forced himself to swallow.

Keep it! It will not be missed. Take it to Vennie. He'll help you. This is important.

Jerrid felt his arm relax. He pulled the note close to his body, folded it and placed it into his jacket pocket. Kylia turned to him and smiled.

"I will schedule you for the ninth of Bonnar, Tribune Flakkinbarr."

"Very well." Jerrid headed toward the door. His thoughts were whirling as the note in his pocket became a flame of curiosity. Hopefully, Vennie Suun would know what to do.

7

"Views and ideas may shift from time to time because of events and culture, but people will always be who they are, or so we thought. Our little group of conspirators suddenly found ourselves facing the possibility that those around us were possibly copies of the real thing, programmed to perform a much more sinister purpose. One designed to destroy the Corporate from the inside out." — Gerrius Tuposh, *The Beginning of the End*

12 Somlea
Darracura District
Flakkinbarr Penthouse

Alleis had taken three showers within the last eighteen hours, and still she didn't feel quite clean. She stood toweling her hair dry, looking at the object of her dread. The thick leather cased journal was lying on the floor at the foot of the circular bed. She'd tossed it there an hour ago. An icy shiver ran up her spine as she looked at it. The black leather was worn and ripped in a few places along the edge. The pages in between were yellowed with age. Tazz sat beside her and gazed at the book as well.

"That's an evil thing, Tazz." she said, wrapping the towel around her head.

The cat laid its ears back and continued to stare.

"How could Jerrid have brought that thing into this house?" But he had and now what was to become of things? She'd spent the better part of two days sequestered in their bedroom reading the dreadful document. Since their return from Bethleea, Jerrid had filled her in on all that was going on with Dros Military Enterprises and the investigation into the missing Geasbok shipments. Alleis had always known about DME. From its inception, she'd thought it was an excellent way for her tribune husband to find out the true pulse of his constituents. It had proven a financial boon as well. Over the years, Jerrid in his role as Jubal Dros mingled with the populace and was able to find out what programs were working and which ones weren't. Course corrections were easily made and improvement to existing programs became efficient. Now this! The disturbing mystery of the Geasbok shipments made the knot in her stomach tighten even more. It only spoke of something more sinister. This demon diary reeked with evil and she wondered if there was a correlation between the missing shipments and the diary? How long would Jerrid keep this evil thing in this house?

"He's got to get rid of that thing!" Alleis skirted around the journal and sat down on the bed. Tazz came over and attempted to climb up, but fell back with a thud. "Tazz?" She gave him a guarded look. The cat attempted a second time, this time clinging to the bed covering with his claws. Alleis reached down and picked him up, placing the feline in the middle of the bed. "Are you all right, Tazz?" She stroked his fur and leaned down to look in his face. Tazz's fur felt dry and course. It had definitely lost its sheen. The cat blinked and then began a slow purr. "Feel better now?" For ten minutes Alleis stroked the cat and thought about the things she'd read in the journal. Suddenly she shook all over. The cat gazed up at her big eyed. "It's all right, Tazz, it's all right." She continued to stroke the cat and think about what she was going to tell her husband. He had to get rid of that thing. "He has to get rid of this book, Tazz. He just has to."

14 Somlea
Jerrid's Study

"I had planned to," Jerrid commented as he stared out the window of his study. He could make out the droids working busily around the structure across the way. The Sagga building was progressing at a fast clip.

"You must get rid of it!" Alleis eyed the Patha Grebon wall hanging. She knew that the journal was in the wall safe behind the tapestry. "That thing is evil, and the longer it stays in this house the greater the danger to us. Think of Vars and Zoe!"

Jerrid heaved out a sigh. "I know. I will get rid of it in due course. But right now it will remain where it is until I can make arrangements."

Alleis came over and placed an arm around his waist and stared out the window with him. She frowned at the sight of the fast rising building next door. "Our lives are under a shadow now, Jerrid. Can anything good come from having that thing here in this house?"

He didn't answer. *Yes, dear heart, we are under a shadow. A shadow that will devour the Corporate if it is not stopped.* Could he tell her that? He chose the safer way, "My dear, Aidioni will take care of us. I will get rid of it when I can, I promise."

She sighed, "Very well, make sure you do."

A knock on the study door interrupted the conversation. Vars peeked in.

"Sir, " he stepped in carrying a comlink. "You have a message from Dros Enterprises. It's on a secure link." He handed it to Jerrid.

"Thank you, Vars." Jerrid eyed his wife and then the comlink. He gave his servant a slight nod. "That will be all."

Vars nodded and left the room.

"I have to go see to Tazz." Alleis kissed him and left.

Jerrid dropped into his favorite chair, activated the comlink and then entered his password. Piin's face appeared in the tiny screen.

"Mr. Dros, my old friend." Piin appeared rather agitated. "Some new developments have come up that you must attend to right away. I cannot specify here, but it is urgent you meet me at the spaceport as soon as possible. This will take several days, my friend, as the matter is off planet. I repeat, this is urgent. My ship, the *Red Dragon*, is prepped to leave at once. Hurry!" The screen went blank.

"Very well then," Jerrid sighed. "What other hideous information can come our way?" He would contact his secretary and have her cancel all appointments for the next two weeks. Hopefully, whatever it was that

Piin had stumbled upon would not take any longer than a week, at most. *Better be on the safe side*, he thought. *Yes, cancel everything on the docket for two weeks.*

* * *

"I'm worried about Tazz!" Alleis said as Jerrid pulled several suits out of the closet and placed them in his suitcase. "He's not eaten anything since yesterday and he's been sleeping a lot."

Jerrid really wasn't focused on the conversation. He was focused on the urgent request to meet Piin. Why was he so agitated? Jerrid could only surmise that he'd uncovered some new information about the missing shipments. It didn't sound good. This couldn't wait. It needed his attention. Now! As Jerrid packed he began to think about all the possible scenarios for this latest crisis. Should he contact the rest of his little group and let them know? No! He'd wait until he had the information. It just might be a dead end.

"Are you listening to me, Jerrid?" Alleis folded her arms across her chest and stared at her husband.

He stopped, blinked and then finally realized she'd been taking about the cat. "What about Tazz?"

"I knew you weren't listening!" Alleis frowned. "Tazz has stopped eating. He's been sleeping a lot. I take it you didn't notice that he slept out under his tree last night. He didn't come in to sleep with us."

"No!" Jerrid blinked again, suddenly remembering not having the heavy weight of the cat on his feet like he was accustomed to. "No, I really didn't notice that. You think he might be sick?"

"If he doesn't eat something this afternoon, I'll take him to the clinic." Alleis' worry showed on her face. "Perhaps it's nothing."

He came over and took Alleis' hands in his. "Tazz is old, sweetheart. There's been several times in the past when he's stopped eating for a few days. Besides, sleeping is what cats do best."

Alleis smiled half heartedly. "I know, Jerrid, but I've been concerned about him lately. He's a little more feeble than he used to be. His coat is dull. It's getting more difficult for him to climb up on the bed. I've had to pick him up a few times and put him on the bed. He couldn't get up himself and his limp is more noticeable than it was a few days ago. I don't know what I'll do if we lose him."

That was something he didn't want to think about right now either. *Losing Tazz. No.* He shoved the thought out of his mind and glanced at his suitcase. "Just keep an eye on him. I shouldn't be more than three or four days at the most. I hate rushing off like this, but this is an urgent matter that needs my attention."

"I understand," she gave him a big smile. "Tazz and I'll be here when you get back."

Jerrid kissed her and finished packing.

BonAvvan Intercorporate Spaceport
Merchant Docking Facilities
Berths 300-525

Jerrid put Tazz out of his thoughts as he made his way to the spaceport. Once there, he found his usual locker room and proceeded to change clothes. Slipping Jubal Dros' ID on his wrist he inspected his appearance in the mirror and then proceeded to look for Piin's ship, the *Red Dragon*.

The ship was located at the far end of the spaceport near the merchant docking facilities. Berth MD-465. The *Red Dragon* was an angular delta winged craft with four fusion drive engines tucked on either side of the main fuselage. The reflection of the light in the spaceport caused the scarlet colored metal to look blood red. Jerrid stopped in his tracks to stare before he slipped through the doors to the docking berth. Brez, the Neccian, was at the bottom of the loading ramp dressed in a tailored beige military uniform with two blasters strapped to his hips. His serious demeanor did not change as Jerrid approached.

"Follow me!" Brez turned sharply and proceeded up the ramp. Jerrid clutched his travel bag and did as he was instructed. Once inside the ship, he followed the Neccian through several narrow corridors to Piin's onboard cabin. Brez knocked once. A chime played back in response and the doorway slid into the wall. The cabin was just as lavish as the sailing vessel on Bethleea; however, this one was decked out in various shades of reds with gold trimming. Piin was perched in a massive maroon leather armchair sipping from a tall crystal glass.

"Mr. Dros, so glad you responded promptly to my request." Piin didn't smile.

"Do you mind telling me what this is all about?" Jerrid glanced nervously around the room. A small wine service was situated to one side, a sofa of the same maroon leather, and several communications consoles along one wall. Another doorway to the left seemed to indicate a bedroom.

Piin glanced past his guest and nodded to the Neccian. "Brez, inform Tobias he may proceed to Trae Zae at top speed."

"Trae Zae?" Jerrid looked puzzled.

"That is not our final destination, Mr. Dros. Brez will show you to your cabin." Piin had yet to smile. "We have a few days before we get there. I will discuss everything over dinner tonight."

"This way." Brez turned toward the door.

Jerrid was dismayed as he followed the Neccian to his cabin. This was going to take longer than he had anticipated.

* * *

The dinner was one of the better ones for a starship. The dining cabin was modestly furnished with a dark copperwood table that could seat ten guests. There was room for at least two stewards. This evening Jerrid and Piin dined alone. Piin sat at one end, Jerrid the other end of the six yarr long table. Place mats were of a fine maroon silk with gold flatware. Tall stem cut crystal glasses glittered in the cabin light. A single steward brought all the courses and made sure the beverages stayed full. Through the main course Piin chatted about trivial matters and some discussion about the Solarians pushing deeper into the Shainbinn Range.

"My contacts tell me that representatives from the Atheran-Hoth Alliance have gone to Sol Prime to negotiate an alliance. This will not be good for the Corporate." Piin eyed Jerrid.

"No indeed." He had been wondering when the Separatists would broach the Solarians. "I'm sure the Tribunal and the Director will be vexed if such an alliance occurs. It would put the Solarians deep into the Far Frontier and give them an ally with bases that could be used to strike deep into the Core Systems."

Piin nodded and sipped his wine.

Jerrid smiled politely and then asked, "So tell me, what is our final destination?"

Piin returned the smile. "We're meeting my tracker on Trae Zae. A wonderful woman of extraordinary talents." Piin lifted an eyebrow and smiled wickedly. "Our final destination, Mr. Dros, is out in the Deex-zarga Range. A very interesting planet called Traylencoor."

Jerrid had never heard of it.

"Tell me, Mr. Dros, how well do you know Tribune Rez Verlmon?"

Jerrid swallowed hard and gazed back at the penetrating stare from Piin. *What the devil?* Jerrid knew he had to be careful here. What was Piin fishing for this time? "I've had the opportunity to meet the man on several occasions. Mostly formal gatherings. Why?"

"Then you could identify the man if you were to run into him outside motherworld?" Piin leaned forward.

"Yes, no doubt." Jerrid was puzzled by the question. Outside motherworld? Verlmon traveled some, mainly between his home in the PaFor Lyxx Range and TeMar. But most of Verlmon's time was spent on motherworld pushing his agenda through the Tribunal.

"Good!" Piin smiled and eased back in his chair. "Then you will have the opportunity to meet the man."

Trying to avoid the look of pure shock, Jerrid faked a puzzled look and reached for his wine glass. Why would Verlmon be traveling to Traylencoor and for what purposes? He continued to gaze bewildered at the smuggler.

Piin laughed. "Well, my friend, my informants have uncovered some very disturbing information. Very disturbing."

"What does this have to do with Verlmon?" Jerrid snapped back.

Piin picked up his wine glass and waved it around. "Everything, my friend. Everything. You see, the Tribune Rez Verlmon on motherworld is not the real Rez Verlmon."

"What?" Jerrid's mouth dropped open.

Piin smiled wickedly. "He's a clone!"

"Clone?"

"The real Rez Verlmon is on Traylencoor and I am taking you there to meet him." Piin was amused by the look of shock on Jerrid's face. "Our good Director is cloning tribunes on Traylencoor and programming them to do his bidding on motherworld. A clever plan to take complete control. Klea really is an evil genius. That is why his removal is so important."

Jerrid was too stunned to finish his meal. He just sat there dumbfounded, not really believing what he'd just heard. *Clones, Klea is cloning tribunes?* Jerrid blinked and continued to stare. He knew, now, beyond a shadow of a doubt that Klea was one and the same person who authored the journal that had come into his possession.

"I see this disturbs you?"

"Indeed."

"My investigation into your missing shipments sent one of my trackers to Traylencoor. She stumbled upon the clone facility there and its inhabitants of notable persons." Piin pushed his plate away and the steward quickly removed it and vanished from the room. "We are going to Traylencoor to find out just what is going on there, Mr. Dros. I believe it has some ties to your missing shipments as well."

The steward came back and removed several of Jerrid's empty plates.

"I have a *Cocca Foladel* for dessert. Very rich with a smooth taste." Piin was aglow. "You will enjoy it."

Jerrid nodded. "Okay." Not really caring if he ate anything more or not.

The steward left to get the dessert.

* * *

That night Jerrid had another disturbing dream. As with all his dreaming, it started out like a dark ocean filled with vague images. An inky mist came slowly spinning out over the ocean with long snake like tendrils reaching out over the black water. It was hard to see. Nothing was recognizable. Then he heard it! *Meow! Meow!* Very weak, but very near. *Meow! Meow!* There it was again and he knew it sounded like Tazz. *You're fooling yourself, Jerrid! It's just some stray kibbercat! It's not Tazz!* The mist continued to swirl as Jerrid stood perplexed. He dared to take a step, extending a shaky foot. The water suddenly solidified, becoming hard rocky ground. The ground was cold against his bare feet. Why had he forgotten his shoes? It didn't matter. Darker objects began to surface in the inky black. The dark tendrils began to thin and Jerrid could see a trail of flat red stones meandering up into the darkness beyond. Gigantic rust colored boulders stood like silent sentinels on either side of the rocky trail. The mist continued to slither like snakes before him, as Jerrid placed one foot in front of the other. Up, up, the trail went, turning first to the left and then right. As the trail began to get steeper, the jagged boulders on either side continued to tower overhead as they seemingly disappeared into the inky mist. The trail was obviously snaking it's way through some canyon. There was no hint of a moon, or moons. He couldn't even tell what planet he was on. Certainly it was not motherworld. No! *Some rocky desert planet somewhere*, he thought to himself. Jerrid continued his maneuvering up through the rocky terrain as the trail continued to rise with each step forward. *Meow! Meow!* There, the cat again. *It's Tazz!* Jerrid told himself. *No, you fool! Tazz is home with Alleis!*

"I have to know for sure!"

With even greater determination, Jerrid pressed on, following the narrowing path as it continued to rise higher and higher. The canyon walls became more distinct as the mist fell away, revealing high towering rocky cliffs. The trail turned sharply to the left and suddenly flared out into a high vaulted chamber some fifty yarrs across. How high he could not tell. The inky mist still swirled overhead like a gathering storm. Jerrid paused as he sucked in a lung full of air. At the very center of the chamber was a single stone with a strange object perched on top. This rock was quite different from the surrounding stone and purposefully placed in the middle of the chamber by someone or something. It had six smooth sides with jagged edges protruding at odd angles and stood three yarrs tall. The stone was the color of blood, a stark contrast from the rust colored rocks of the chamber. Its appearance resembled some type of pedestal. *Almost like an altar*, he thought. An uncontrollable shiver ran up his spine. The mist snaked around the altar-like rock and enveloped the strange object at the top. Jerrid tried to move forward but he couldn't. His feet refused to obey. He fought with himself as he tried to move his legs. No luck. It was if he was glued to the spot. He sighed loudly. All he could do was stare at the rock and the strange swirling mist that had engulfed the object on top. As he stood there staring at the mist, it suddenly morphed into the image of a cat. As the final tendrils of mist pulled away, the cat's identity became quite clear. It looked just like Tazz. Jerrid stiffened, horror stricken. After several seconds it became quite clear that it was Tazz. No mistaking. Tazz sat on the blood-red altar staring back. Jerrid could not speak. He worked his mouth but the words refused to come. He tried again to move, but as before his feet refused to obey. Ever so slightly a tingling began to course through the bottoms of his feet which grew more profound with each tick of the clock. Quite suddenly, the tingling became a tremor as the ground around him vibrated violently. The blood-rock with the cat shot upward, dust and mist scattering like leaves. The cat was now about six yarrs above him, well beyond his reach. Tazz looked haggard, old, dying. The cat was hunched over, head held low, staring straight into Jerrid's eyes. The swirling inky mist continued to sift around the rocky terrain, moving like black water. The rumbling faded and the chamber became deathly still. Jerrid leaned back to look up, but there was nothing to see but rocks and the swirling darkness high above the chamber. Once again he tried to move forward, to reach out to the cat, but it was useless. No muscles responded to his brain's commands.

Meow! Meow!

Jerrid opened his mouth, "Oh Tazz, what's wrong? What's wrong?" Try as he may, his limbs would not respond. He could not move one ticc toward the cat.

Time crawled. Tazz sat patiently perched on the blood-red rock, his tail twitching ever so often. Jerrid could tell from the cat's eyes he was pleading for help.

"I'm sorry Tazz, I can't move!" Jerrid choked out. He felt totally helpless. *What is going on here?*

Then there was an explosive sound as ten dark shapes dropped down from the inky mist above, like spiders descending from a web. The mist swirled violently as the dark menacing shapes twisted together and became black helmeted SPG Shocktroopers. The ten dark armored troopers scurried up through the rocky terrain toward the cat, chain guns at the ready. Call it a sixth sense or divine revelation, but Jerrid knew they were after the cat. For whatever reason, Tazz was their target and these helmeted demons were determined to kill him.

"Run, Tazz!" Jerrid heard himself scream. "Run, Tazz! Run!"

The cat continued to gaze at Jerrid, totally unaware of the danger racing toward him.

"Run, you stupid cat!" Jerrid shouted. "They're going to kill you!"

Tazz slowly turned to stare at the approaching shocktroopers. His eyes narrowed. His ears flat against his head. Then, slowly he turned back to Jerrid and gave a soft meow.

"Run, Tazz! For God's sake, run!" Jerrid could feel his heart pounding like some jackhammer deep within his chest. His throat became tight. He felt every blood vessel in his entire being pounding with the fast pace of his heart. "Tazz, run, please, run! Please!"

The shocktroopers were getting closer. Several had flicked off the safety to their chain guns and were sighting the cat in their scopes. It was all so bizarre. Why would they be after Tazz? What purpose was it to kill this cat? Jerrid could feel the terror rising.

"Aidioni, please do something! Please!" Despite every attempt to move, Jerrid could not move his body. It refused to respond. He was like a man sitting in front of a con, watching a drama unfold before him. He felt utterly helpless. He knew Tazz was going to die and there was nothing he could do about it. Absolutely nothing! Grief overcame him like a tidal wave.

Tazz glanced at the troopers again but did nothing. He did not move or even try to bolt and run. It was like he was resigned to his fate. The cat looked more helpless and feeble than he had ever looked at any point in his entire life. He gave a simple meow again, almost to say, "Help me."

"Run, Tazz! Run!" Jerrid was crying by this time. "Please run, Tazz,

I've tried, but I can't help you. Please run, Tazz, please run!"

The cat just sat there, his doom was certain as the troopers closed the distance. Guns drawn, ready to fire. It would be a quick and brutal death.

"Please, Aidioni, please! Do something!" Jerrid shouted, desperation piercing his heart.

A light flickered in the distance above the dark shadowed rocks overhead. It was another one of those small pinpoints of light that became brighter as it descended toward the ground. The glowing globe expanded into a large radiating aurora. The shocktroopers paid it no heed as they continued their advance. From the center of the radiating aurora a large white object dropped out of the light and flashed down the sides of the huge granite canyon at an incredible speed. In an instant, Tazz was snatched up in one talon of a huge white eagle as the shocktroopers opened fire. The blood-red altar rock vaporized in the ensuing blaster exchange. Jerrid looked up in time to see Tazz clutched carefully in the right talon of a mighty white eagle. The bird was returning toward the pulsating globe. The cat looked down at him and winked, his eyes aglow with light. Wonderful light. Jerrid was so overcome by the sheer radiance of that light and the sudden peace that washed over his soul. Tazz let out a silent meow. *I love you Jerrid Flakkinbarr!*

Startled awake, Jerrid sat up in bed and clutched his chest. His heart was pounding wildly. He took several deep breaths, gazing about the strange cabin of Piin's ship. Except for the glow from the console on the desk, the cabin was dark.

"Oh, Tazz!" He could feel the lump rise in his throat. "I love you too, you silly cat! Aidioni, please keep him safe." But Jerrid knew something was going to happen to Tazz and probably very soon. Alleis would be devastated. And then he realized so would he. That silly cat had become so much a part of their lives, that if he was gone, then something good and wonderful would have been taken away. The lump continued to rise in his throat. Jerrid Flakkinbarr turned on his side and cried, something he hadn't done since he was ten years old.

* * *

The restlessness not only invaded Jerrid Flakkinbarr's cabin, but slipped out and wandered the corridors of the *Red Dragon* as it looked for another victim. Ra'Phaak Piin tossed about on his lavish bed, unable to fall into a deep sleep. With a groan of disgust, he threw back the covers and eased out of bed. He shuffled over to the wine cabinet on the other side of the room. *Perhaps it'll help me sleep,* he thought. After pouring a tall glass of *Bonifor Tu Prizz,* Piin settled into his maroon leather chair by the bed and thought about his guest and the mission ahead.

"Jubal Dros," Piin snickered, "what shall I do with you?" Piin could understand Dros' vacillating moods, but just how much could he trust him? He had to be very careful with this one. There must be no surprises when his man, Serpa, did the job. Piin's eyes narrowed at the thought. *Klea must be eliminated at all costs. The man will only bring destruction to the Order and I must avenge my sister!*

Ra'Phaak Piin had been planning this for decades. There had never been an opportunity to do the job himself, but he'd been patient in following the trail and finding the funding along the way. Not as a devoted follower of Li'Jeen Juu, the Great Shuuto Master or the Soktee Order like his sister, Yuu'Liin. Piin had plotted and manipulated his vengeance for years. He'd grown quite accustomed to the rewards of being a very good smuggler. The trade only enhanced his natural abilities and netted him a considerable fortune in the process. Yuu'Liin was not pleased with his departure from the Order to pursue his "worldly" concerns, but she still loved him, and remained a devoted sister. Until she'd met Klea.

"Klea!" Piin hissed. "You will burn in Keroon for all eternity for what you did to my sister!" The image flashed into his mind before he could even blink. No! He refused to allow it to have access. Piin could not remember Yuu'Liin the way he found her. No! He must remember her the way she was; tall, beautiful and full of life.

Tracking Dameon Klea through several star systems had been tedious and time consuming. He was beginning to think his voyage to motherworld had been a fruitless endeavor, until Klea surfaced as the great savior of people of Aalinra. What a stroke of fate that the man was now the Director of the Corporate. *How fitting,* Piin snarled. "I'll make a statement and be richer none the less!" Klea had seduced a large portion of the Soktee Order, instilling his blasphemous ideas to fellow believers. He had seduced Yuu'Liin and poisoned her to where she could no longer tell reality from illusion. Klea used her and discarded her like a piece of garbage. It was now Piin's mission to stop the demon once and for all.

Ra'Phaak Piin laughed to himself. Victory was close at hand. He raised the glass as if to toast his own success before downing the rest of the wine. Over the years he had slowly garnered a force of men around him to help complete his task. He allied himself with the Separatists and had chosen several assassins to fit his purposes. But it would take considerable financing to convince the best assassin to do the job. Serpa had wanted a small fortune to assure Piin of his revenge. A snarl settle across his lips. Serpa's fee would take more financing that his standard deals along the Black Market. A hefty sum indeed. He chuckled to himself again. Yes, it was quite by accident to have stumbled across a man who he could use to finance his purpose. Jubal Dros and his Tribunal friend had made it almost too easy. "Money is money!"

Jubal Dros had turned out to be more than just financing his sister's revenge. He'd been a financial boon with his links to a good number of the Corporates top tribunes. And tribunes had suddenly become quite the market with certain other interest parties. Now they were going to Traylencoor for more tribunes. Piin laughed again. "The Mirs are stupid. They'll buy anything!" He laughed again and finished off his wine. Now he felt tired. *Good.* Perhaps he would get a good night's sleep after all.

8

"Over the years speculation as to the Delcor Mining Conglomerate's vast interest and methods of operation proved to be undefined. To this day, no one has ever proven that Delcor's interest went beyond mining and the means of mining. Informants who say otherwise have, for the most part, disappeared or quickly recanted their stories." — Molia Senfras, *The Truth in the Lies*

16 Somlea
Monlainte Range / Trae Star System
Marker 28 by 2 / Red Grid Section
Planet: Trae Zae
TRS Red Dragon CSS-1241

The super gas giant Trae Zae loomed ahead as the *Red Dragon* made its approach from the dark side. Tobias, the Flanderian born pilot, kept a calm but vigilant watch at the controls. Piin and Flakkinbarr sat behind and slightly above the young man as he rotated the ship toward the light side of the planet. Jerrid felt relaxed, despite the ghost memories of the dream about Tazz. He kept reminding himself that it was just a dream and nothing more. He was fretting over nothing. Tazz was fine and Alleis would take care of him if something happened. Jerrid sighed and gazed out the cockpit window at the blue and gray bans of intense color swirling below them. Presently a glimmer flashed off their portside.

"Merrus Mining Outpost!" Tobias remarked as the glimmer of light began to grow. The pilot punched at a switch and brought up a view of the distant mining outpost. A platform of three spheres around a lattice work of rigging glittered in the light. A dozen ships were docked at the sphere closest to them. There was a pinging sound and a red light began flashing on the screen in front of the young pilot. "Zappora's ship, sir. Coming out to meet us." The screen showed a fast moving object heading their way.

"Good!" Piin turned and smiled. "Our carriage to Traylencoor, Mr. Dros."

Jerrid didn't say a word.

Within the hour Piin's ship had pulled along side the intersystem merchantman that was in desperate need of a paint job. It was a dingy looking craft with three engine pylons sprouting out at odd angles from a long slender triangle of a main structure. It was a third the size of Piin's *Dragon*. As the door to the air lock opened, Jerrid found himself staring at an extremely tall woman dressed in a black form fitting uniform. A silver handled blaster was slung low on her curvy hips. Pinn kissed her on the lips and then turned to Jerrid.

"Mr. Dros, may I introduce Zappora Xarkki, captain of the *Black Hand* and one of my best trackers."

Zappora had a rich olive complexion and shiny black hair pulled in a tight ponytail that hung down to the middle of her back. Her eyes were pools of dark obsidian and sparkled with a seductive lure. The plunging neckline of her uniform revealed that she was well endowed. The buttons seemed to be fighting against the fabric. Jerrid wondered which side was going to win. A dark scar ran across the left side of her face from ear to nose.

"A pleasure to meet you, Captain." Jerrid nodded and tried to divert his eyes away from the plunging neckline.

"Mr. Dros." Zappora's smile was a glow of white teeth.

Piin turned to his pilot, "Tobias, I want you and Brez to stay put. Just keep a low profile. We'll return in a few days."

"Aye, sir!"

Jerrid's gear was quickly moved over to the tracker's ship and in less than an hour they were outbound to StarGate 64. Traylencoor would be just a few more days away.

19 Somlea
Deexzarga Range / Tray Centa Star System
Marker 12 by 15 / Yellow Grid Section
Planet: Traylencoor
TRS Black Hand CSS-11721

The *Black Hand* came into low orbit at Traylencoor's southern polar region. Zappora pivoted the ship through the two thin ice rings with just a slight buffeting. In the co-pilot's seat was a dinged up android that still functioned as co-pilot and ship's first mate. Zappora had introduced him as SID-Nine-Two. SID was polite and not too talkative. Piin and Flakkinbarr sat to Zappora's right just behind the droid.

"On the approach path, madam." SID responded as the young woman at the controls rotated the ship for descent.

"Got it SID." Zappora winked at him. "Give me a chart reading of the planet."

"Yes, madam." SID rotated his head to face her. His eyes glowed in the dim cabin light of the cockpit. "Charts indicate this is a tropical planet. Updated by Corporate Geo-Survey Unit KZX-Thirty-Four Fifty-Eight in Forty-Twelve ADK. Considerable dense jungle vegetation. Two large oceans, no natural seas. Location of water sources darkside of planet. Wildlife plentiful with four hundred varieties of carnivore present."

Zappora smiled out of the side of her mouth. "Isn't he wonderful?"

"A regular data base of facts!" snarled Piin.

"Will any of this stuff present a problem?" Jerrid asked. The thought of traipsing through dense jungle undergrowth didn't appeal to him, much less any dangers from the local wildlife.

"We do have K-Eleven Siron pulse weapons on board, sir." SID replied. "Maximum fire power of twenty five thousand particles per ticc. Maximum range of one point three mycrons."

"No problem at all, Mr. Dros." Zappora laughed like a little girl. Piin shared in the levity.

"Am I missing something here?" Jerrid glanced at both of them.

"You'll see, Mr. Dros, you'll see!" Piin snickered.

Jerrid pushed back in his seat and watched as the planet began to fill the entire cockpit's window. For a tropical planet, it didn't look very green, he thought. The predominate colors were brown and tan. Jerrid had a feeling the joke would be on him once they got to the surface.

The scanners to the tracker's right pinged several times and three yellow lights blossomed on the console in front of her. "I have five mining locations on scanners." Zappora said matter-of-factly. "Mine Five is our target site." She pointed a finger at the blue navigation screen to her left. A flickering red dot pulsated toward the southern pole.

"Mining site?" Jerrid shot her a questioning look.

She smiled and winked. "Delcor Mining Conglomerate works this system, Mr. Dros, but there's more to Delcor than just mining."

Piin laughed.

"Shall I contact Mine Five for landing instructions?" SID asked.

Zappora shot Piin a look. "They might think it strange I've come back this soon."

Piin scrutinized the readouts and studied the navigation screen for a few minutes. He then looked up at the young woman. "Find us a hiding place within a day's march of the mine. Make sure our position is well hidden."

"Mine Five is about seventy-five mycs from the ice fields." Zappora pointed at the image on the screen. "A low range of mountains run east west between it and the ice. I could put us down there." She indicated the position on the screen with her finger. "I know the perfect spot. I've used it a time or two in the past. We will have to come in very low to avoid their scanners."

"Just do it!" Piin snapped, an edge in his voice. "I know the place you're talking about. Just make sure we're under their scanners and that we don't belly out on some jutting rock formation along the way."

Zappora shot him a hateful look and returned to her controls. "I'll get us in all in one piece."

"Let us prepare for landing, Mr. Dros." Piin indicated the flight harnesses at their seats. "I hope you're up for a long hike?"

"I'll manage." As the ship was being readied to drop down into the atmosphere, Jerrid pulled the harnesses over his shoulders and fastened them into place while looking out the cockpit window.

* * *

After coming out of a thick band of thunder clouds, Zappora dropped her ship down over the barren rocky terrain as close as she dared. With the skill that any pilot would envy she zipped and zagged the merchant-man through the jagged desert terrain at breakneck speed. Despite its gangly appearance, the ship responded to the twists and turns like a top notch racer. Zappora and her ship were to be taken seriously. Here was a woman with the skills that belied her easy going demeanor. The ship could fool anyone. Appearances were certainly deceiving and he had no doubt that it was planned that way.

"It's a desert!" was all Jerrid could say as he gazed at the stark terrain just a few feet below them.

Piin smiled wickedly. "Precisely, Mr. Dros. A barren hunk of rock with a lot of minerals to mine. Very valuable minerals, I might add."

"SID didn't mention this." Jerrid glanced at the droid.

"The chart information I gave you is correct." SID pivoted his head in Jerrid's direction. "Actual data is different, sir."

Piin and Zappora laughed.

Jerrid said nothing more as the pilot continued on toward a low range of jagged rust colored rocks on the horizon. An uneasiness began to grow at the edge of his consciousness. Red rocks, jagged terrain, it all had a feel that he'd been here before. But that was impossible. The ghost image of a cat slipped past his memory just briefly, not long enough to register.

"We're under their scanners envelope, sir." Zappora smiled. "The mountains should shield us long enough to land. They don't have a clue we're here."

"Let's keep it that way."

Within the hour Zappora edged the ship up the jagged slope of a tower of red rock using just thrusters. At the peak, they got a good view of the rest of the terrain to the south. The range of mountains extended like a line of broken teeth toward the horizon from west to east. Farther to the south a broad plain of desert stretched toward the horizon. The ice fields were barely visible. Four white domes were easily spotted against the harsh desert landscape at the base of the mountains.

"Zerrin metal extraction domes, Mr. Dros" Piin smiled. "Delcor's primary reason for being here."

Jerrid squinted against the harsh glare of the sun. "Looks like a small operation."

"The real mines are to the north." Piin pointed out.

"Real mines?" Jerrid glanced at Piin.

"Everything here is not what it appears to be, Mr. Dros." Zappora commented. "Just remember that!"

Piin laughed.

Zappora skillfully dropped her ship down the other side of the tall spire of rock into the middle of a deep ravine. The ship was quickly swallowed up by the deep shadows as it came to rest on the gravel covered floor. Zappora cut the engines and did a lock down of the ship's entire systems. She swivelled in her chair and tapped the droid on the shoulder. "SID, keep the ship locked down. No one enters, understand me. No one! I have the link-ID. If we get into a jam I'll signal. You can extract us if we need help."

"Yes, madam." SID remained seated.

"Ready for that hike I told you about, Mr. Dros?" Piin smiled. "I hope you're up for it."

Climbing out of her seat, Zappora shot Jerrid a glance. "There is a trail about half a myc from here. Leads up through the mountain and down the other slope. Shouldn't take us more than a day to get to the mine."

Jerrid just looked at her.

Piin got up from his seat and touched him on the knee. "Come, Mr. Dros, the adventure awaits us!"

Reluctantly Jerrid got to his feet and followed them to the back.

Exiting the ship with several containers of water in their back packs and dressed in light colored desert uniforms, they traversed the gravel covered bottom area toward the steep rise of boulders at the edge of the ravine. A path wound its way up the slope of the mountain toward the high rocky cliffs in the distance. It was dry and hot. The deep shadows allowed only a dim light. The tracker lead the way, followed by Piin. Jerrid brought up the rear. As the hikers climbed upward toward the tangle of rocks at the top, Jerrid began to breathe hard. Sweat rolled down his face and his clothing started to show signs of the rigorous climb. After a few hours, Zappora stopped. The trail turned up a narrow gorge.

She pulled the drink tube from her harness strap and sucked on it. "Don't drink too much, Mr. Dros, we still have to get over the top." She smiled at him and wiped the sweat from her brow.

Huffing and puffing, Jerrid leaned into one of the large boulders and fumbled with his drink tube. After several long swigs from the container he paused and looked around. They were half way up the steep slope of the mountain, the ravine with the merchantman way below. His legs were feeling the strain of the steep climb.

Piin did not seem bothered by the long climb and sucked on his drink tube casually. He finally smiled at Jerrid. "I'm surprised, Mr. Dros. You have done very well on this climb."

Jerrid sucked some more water from the tube and glanced sideways at the smuggler. "I don't know if that's a compliment, Piin, or a put down."

"I did halfway expect you to drop out long ago." Piin grinned wickedly. "But consider it a compliment."

Jerrid gave him a nod. "What's going to happen when we get to this mine?"

"You identify the real Verlmon," Piin replied. "I think it is imperative to find out why he and the others are here on Traylencoor. Besides, one of your missing shipments passed this way before it ended up in Mir space. It may be that some of the Corporate's real tribunes are now Mir prisoners."

Jerrid had the feeling Piin wasn't telling him everything. The smuggler was being evasive. But what could he do about it? He just had to play along. If one of the missing shipments came here he had to know why. And he had to know if this was indeed the real Rez Verlmon. "How many others?"

Piin frowned. "That I do not know, Mr. Dros. You have access to the Tribunal and would know their faces better than I."

Jerrid leaned into the man and glared. "Is that the only reason you brought me here?"

"As I told you earlier, Mr. Dros, Director Klea is working to secure complete control of the Corporate by cloning tribunes to do his bidding. Once the cloning is complete, there will be no one to question his decisions. He will have absolute power and control." Piin eyed Jerrid and took another sip from his drink tube. "Klea is a dangerous man. His removal is paramount to the survival of the Corporate."

All Jerrid could do was nod. He understood. If Klea could clone enough support he could rule with an iron hand, with no one to oppose him. *No one to oppose him, think about that. He is dangerous!* Jerrid shook his head. These troubling thoughts were plaguing him again. *Klea has to be eliminated at all costs.* Jerrid heaved out a sigh and took another drink.

The screech startled him out of his dark thoughts. Everyone looked around trying to determine it's origin. Zaporra pointed to a white object circling to the north over a cliff of deep red rocks.

"White eagles!" she said, watching the white bird soar on the wind currents along the face of the cliff. The white eagle climbed higher and higher as it disappeared over the rise of jagged rocks.

A white eagle! Jerrid's mind was racing. *Just like in the dream.*

"What's the matter, Mr. Dros," Zappora gave him a concerned look. "You look like you've seen a ghost or something."

Jerrid was still staring in the direction the eagle had flown, his heart racing, his throat suddenly dry again.

"Mr. Dros?" Piin questioned, concerned etched on his face as well.

Jerrid shook his head. "It's nothing, nothing at all!"

"We'd better go. We still have a long hike ahead of us." Piin rallied.

They set out, Zappora in the lead and Jerrid looking over his shoulder, trying to see if the eagle would show again.

* * *

By the time they reached the base on the other side of the mountain the daylight was nearly gone. They were all exhausted from the arduous hike. Even Piin was breathing hard by the time they pulled up short near an outcropping of rocks within a half myc of the mine. The four white domes stood in sharp contrast to the browns, tans, and reds of the surrounding landscape. As the sunlight faded marker lights began to pop up along the steel barrier fence that surrounded the mine. Guard towers were at every corner.

Hunkered down in the rocks, Jerrid gazed through the macro-binoculars Zappora had brought along. "Looks more like a prison than a mine." Jerrid handed the vision-ware back to the tracker.

"Prison is a good word, Mr. Dros." Piin laughed. "But there are other reasons for the fortifications, which you will see."

Jerrid could not conceal his alarm.

"Trays, sir." Zappora stated.

"Trays?" Jerrid looked at both of them.

"Traylencoor's indigenous inhabitants." Piin smiled warily. "They have a tendency to attack these mining colonies from time to time. Nomads for the most part. But make no mistake, they don't like offworlders."

"Are we safe here?" Jerrid was now very alarmed and continually looking around. The ragged landscape afforded numerous areas of concealment for any would be attackers.

"For the time being!" Zappora replied.

For the time being. He didn't like the sound of that. He looked toward the steel barrier fence and guard towers surrounding the mining operation. "And how are we going to get in there?"

Piin grinned as he glanced at Zappora. "We have ways."

Zappora unfastened the latching on her holster and nodded toward the steel fence. "There are emergency exit tunnels all along the walls in every direction. Escape tunnels just in case the Trays overpower the guards and get inside. I know one entrance near the south wall. It'll get us inside without any problems."

Jerrid glanced from one to the other. "And once inside, what's to prevent them from spotting us?"

"The south tunnel leads directly into the barracks area. I have the password key which will get us past both sets of tunnel doors. Once inside, we go to Barracks Two. That's where they keep most of the tribunes. There are few patrols inside the main compound. " Zappora made it sound as simple as a walk in the park.

"I still don't understand what you're going to do once I identify Verlmon." Jerrid gave Piin a hard look. "Any information he may have about the missing shipments may be useless by now."

The smuggler gave him an uneasy look as he patted the blaster on his hip. "You are here to identify Verlmon and the others. That is all you need to know."

"There's more to this than you are telling me." Jerrid snapped at Piin.

Piin leaned into Jerrid and pulled the blaster from his belt. "Listen, Mr. Dros, you wanted to know what's going on with your missing shipments. This is part of the trail. This helps me and you and that's all there is to it."

Jerrid swallowed hard. "Very well. When do we get in?"

Zappora took the vision-ware and scanned the area along the south wall. "We will go along the edge of the rock outcropping to that group of desert pines thirty yarrs from the wall. There's only one guard in the tower nearest us, and he doesn't seem to be paying too much attention to the surrounding landscape." She folded the binoculars and placed them back on her gun belt. "Just follow me and stay down."

"Let's do it!" Piin smiled and motioned with his weapon.

The trio carefully maneuvered their way from rock to rock under a moonless night. The tracker paused every thirty yarrs to see if the guard in his tower was looking their way. For the most part he appeared to be watching a comlink and paying little heed to the desert landscape.

"I think his mind is on other things." Zappora put the vision-ware back on her belt. "Just go carefully. It gets a little more rocky toward the trees."

It wasn't easy for Jerrid to find his way. The uneven terrain was an obstacle course that pulled at every muscle in his legs. He side stepped a number of small rocks kicked up by Zappora's passing. The trail narrowed as it came up a short rise and Jerrid lost his footing. His heel caught on a jagged rock which sent him colliding with the ground. Another round stone jammed hard into his gut. Before Jerrid could scream out in pain, Zappora placed her hand over his mouth and jerked him to his feet.

"Are you okay, Mr. Dros?" She looked concerned as her vice like grip on his arm began to loosen.

"I'm fine." Jerrid just nodded as he tried to catch his breath. There would be a nasty bruise, he was certain.

"Be careful!" Piin snapped. "We don't want to alert the guard."

"Keep your voice down!" Zappora lashed back, quickly removing the binoculars from her belt and scanning the guard tower. "He hasn't stirred. Let's move it!"

The pain in Jerrid's gut was a reminder of just how dangerous the situation had become. *It could all end tonight. Right here on this brakkin' planet.* This was by far the riskiest thing he'd ever done. It was nothing to put on a disguise and mingle with the common laborer. But this? *Why did I ever agree to come here in the first place?* As they continued to snake their way from outcropping to outcropping, Jerrid Flakkinbarr could only feel that somehow he had been tricked. That coming to this desert planet was for someone else's plan, not his. Was he just a pawn who was being manipulated by other unseen forces and in positions of higher power?

The tracker pulled them to a stop to catch their breath.

"How's your pain, Mr. Dros?" Zappora whispered. Even though he could not see her face, her voice revealed her concern.

"I'm fine." He heaved out a big breath and sucked in some air. "I'll make it."

"Let's move it!" Piin snapped.

Zappora pushed off the boulder she was leaning against and continued on. Jerrid followed as closely as possible without bumping into her. He glanced over his shoulder; Piin's dark shadow was right on his heels. What would Piin do once he identified the real Verlmon, Jerrid wondered? He now saw the smuggler in a different light. Piin was a dangerous man and Jerrid felt he'd gotten himself into something much more sinister than missing shipments. All he could do was pray for a way out and hope that he wouldn't get killed in the process. They continued to scurry along from rock outcropping to outcropping.

It took them another twenty minutes to reach the stand of desert pines. Five large boulders pushed up against one another in a semi-circle formation. A dozen scraggily pines stood silhouetted against the night sky, watching over them as they squatted down in the middle of the boulders. Zappora quickly caressed the center stone as if searching for something. Half way up the boulder she found what she was looking for. Into the small crack she slipped a mini-comlink. The lights on the link danced red, blue and green for about a minute. When they all flashed blue, a hiss was heard and the crack widened. Zappora retrieved the comlink and placed it back in the pocket on her backpack. She then pushed on the lip of the crack and it swung back to reveal a steel metal door, just large enough for a man. In the middle of the door, a small key pad glowed eerily in the black night.

"Ingenious, isn't it." Zappora laughed. She quickly punched in the code on the number pad and the tunnel door hissed open with a blast of cool air which rushed out. It was briefly refreshing. Inside, a long tunnel stretched like one big steel gray tube in the direction of the mine. Pale yellow lights fixed in the ceiling cast a ghostly illumination. "Quickly, gentlemen!"

Piin and Jerrid stepped in. Zappora followed behind them, quickly closing the rock door and then the tunnel door. Once they were sealed inside, the temperature was nearly fifty degrees cooler. Jerrid actually found himself smiling.

"This feels great!" He closed his eyes and lingered momentarily in the coolness.

"This goes straight to the storage shed next to Barracks Two."

"Lead the way!" Piin's edgy voice snapped.

A skid pad of black gritty material muffled their bootheels as they scurried up the long passage. The cool tunnel air was a relief from the hot dry desert they had just crossed. It took no longer than ten minutes to come to another locked door. Jerrid was relishing the cool around him as he leaned up against the even cooler steel wall. He watched as Zappora punched in her code on the keypad. He had to admit, she was a beautiful woman. She seemed quiet and reserved, but in the back of his mind he knew better. This was a mercenary with skills to kill. Tread cautiously here was the catch word; ignore that and he might end up dead. The door hissed open. They quickly stepped through to a small storage unit with racks of cleaning supplies. The cool air was gone and hot air was back with a vengeance. Once everyone was up from the tunnel, Zappora sealed it back. She went to the storage door and peered out. The alleyway that ran between the barracks was empty. Nothing stirred.

"No guards," she whispered. "Barracks Two is right across the way. There's a guard room at the main entrance. Might be manned, but not usually. Guards here are few and they can't monitor every barrack. Just be ready."

Piin nodded. The woman slipped out of the shed and disappeared into the shadows of the next building. Jerrid followed Piin out. He got a quick look at a dozen rows of long buildings stretching toward the far east wall. It looked more like a prison than any mine he'd ever seen.

With blaster in hand, Zappora eased open the door to Barracks Two. The guard room was empty with only a table and two wooden chairs inside. They paused at the door that led into the sleeping area. They heard muffled voices of men and the shuffling of feet on the other side.

"What are we going to do now?" Jerrid felt the panic rising up toward his throat.

"Relax, Mr. Dros," Piin replied. "All of this has been planned out."

Zappora nodded and opened the door. As she stepped into the room a hush fell over the occupants. Piin and Jerrid followed her in.

The barrack was simply a long metal building about twenty yarrs long and five yarrs wide. Stained ragged thick corded rugs were laid down between the rows of bunks. Twenty bunks, ten to a side, occupied the full length of the building. Two windows at each end were covered in tattered and stained brown curtains. Five ceiling fans stirred the stifling hot air. There wasn't even a hint of a cool breeze. Ten men in tan prison uniforms stared at them as they emerged from the guard room. Four men were dozing on their bunks. Six other men were seated around a table at the far end of the building playing what appeared to be a card game. Their game came to a sudden halt as they spotted the intruders. No one said a word as they all looked at each other. Finally, one of the men in the group stepped forward. He was tall and dark haired, clean shaven with dark circles under his eyes. Despite the thinness of his frame, he carried himself in a determined manner.

"I see you made it back." He was speaking to Zappora.

"I said I would," she replied with a weak smile. She turned to Piin and Jerrid. "Gentlemen, this is Fraz Greeloc, overseer of the Vantacus Shipworks on Vi Zikioz."

Oh my God! Jerrid screamed within. Even though he didn't know Greeloc personally, he did know that Vantacus Shipworks was the biggest Far Frontier ship building facility beyond the Core Systems. Vi Zikioz was at the edge of the Atheran-Hoth Alliance and the Separatists desperately wanted those facilities for their war effort. *Relax*, a voice whispered in his head. But how could he when his skin was crawling with fear?

That fear began to intensify as Jerrid stared past Greeloc to the man just behind him. Jerrid's mouth dropped open. Standing behind Greeloc was Rez Verlmon. Even though the real Verlmon was much skinnier than the clone back on motherworld, there was no mistaking the face he had come to despise all these years. Jerrid could feel the coil of fear tightening in his gut. He didn't know every tribune, it was virtually impossible, but there might be some here who knew him and that was dangerous. Next to Verlmon stood Tribune Geoni and Tribune Erathad beside him. Geoni and Erthad were members of the Military Appropriations Sub-Committee. He did not know them personally, but there was the outside chance they knew him. He had only sat in on the sub-committee one time and that was in a heated debate over the Separatists revolt. Jerrid swallowed hard. *Lord, keep their eyes blinded to who I am.* He felt the coil tighten.

"Hey, don't I know you!" The real Verlmon shouted and pointed a finger at Jerrid. He stepped past Greeloc. "I know you from somewhere!"

In a desperate move to defuse what could be a disaster, Jerrid shoved his way past Piin and extended a hand. "Jubal Dros, of Dros Military Enterprises." It was a gamble. But Jerrid knew that he could not afford the real Verlmon to expose him. How long Verlmon had been here on Traylencoor was only a guess, but he was hoping it had been long enough to cloud any memory of Tribune Jerrid Flakkinbarr.

Verlmon looked at him rather confusedly. Perhaps he'd gambled and failed. Again, Verlmon paused and looked at his other collegues. "Dros, you say? Dros Military Enterprises?" Piin shot Jerrid a questioning stare.

Finally Verlmon heaved out a sigh and took a hold of Jerrid's hand. "Forgive me, Mr. Dros, but it has been too long of a time. I'm afraid my time here has hindered any recollection of past meetings we may have had."

Jerrid breathed a sigh of relief. "That is understandable, sir." He glanced over at Geoni and Erthad. They whispered to one another but said nothing, finally nodding at Verlmon.

Piin seemed rather pleased by the turn of events. His irritatingly wicked smile crept back across his face and he slapped Jerrid on the back. "This is good, Mr. Dros. So, this is our distinguished Tribune Rez Verlmon."

Verlmon gave Piin a cutting glance. "And you, sir?

"Your ticket out of here, Tribune!" Piin laughed.

The sudden silence was nearly deafening. Every man in the room looked at one another. The whir of the ceiling fans was the only noise that filtered back into recollection. The scuffing of chairs on the deckplates echoed in the building as the men at the card table came forward and joined those circling the newcomers. Jerrid glanced at Piin out of the corner of his eye and wondered what was really going on here. He didn't like the feel of things and this sudden disclosure by the smuggler seemed far-fetched.

"How are you going to get us all out?" Greeloc snapped. "Forgive me, but there are Trays out there and several hundred guards at this mine."

"We have a ship an easy day's march from here." Piin smiled, thrusting out his chest. "We go out through the tunnels, and by dawn we should be high enough in the mountains to avoid detection by the guards."

"What about the others?" someone in the back called out.

"Only you men, here!" Piin snarled. "No others, that was the deal."

There were some murmuring in the back. It was obvious that this didn't set well with a few of the other members..

Piin glared at the men standing around. "You twenty are the only ones leaving. No one else! In time I may be able to arrange another extraction, but for now, you twenty will be the first." He rubbed his hand against the weapon on his hip. "We don't have much time. Get your stuff together and prepare to move."

Greeloc nodded and went to his bunk to retrieve what few personal belongings he had.

"Just take what you can easily carry!" Piin shouted. "We have to move fast!"

Jerrid eased up beside Zappora and whispered, "Did you know about this?"

She glanced at him sideways. "I thought you did, Mr. Dros." There was a puzzled look in her eyes as she glanced at him and then back to Piin.

9

"The seeds of rebellion were thrown to the four winds within the hierarchy of those in power. And in the most unlikely of places those seeds would spring up to become a menacing harvest."
— Darcillia Karkee, *The Vantage Point of Treason*

"Let darkness and the shadow of death stain it; let a cloud dwell upon it; let the blackness of the day terrify it." — Arako 3:5, *The Talbah Canon*

Delcor Mine Five
Clone Facility

Lt. Gian Roburgh stepped out into the cool dry desert night to get away from the noise and smoke of the mine's mess hall. Roburgh was dressed in a tight fitting tan uniform that conformed to his chiseled physique. He was a handsome young man in his late twenties. Nearly two and a half yarrs tall, with thick dark hair and dark eyes, Roburgh left an impression that most people did not soon forget. His deep brown complexion added to the powerful image he imposed. When Roburgh was on leave, female eyes were continually wandering his way. It was an asset he used to its fullest advantage. He smiled to himself as he remembered his last leave. Tribune Erathad's daughter, Viona, had proven to be a remarkable woman in many ways. An articulate, intelligent woman as well as an excellent dancer, not to mention extremely good in bed. Roburgh certainly wouldn't mind seeing her again.

The door slammed open behind him and two soldiers staggered out. After two sloppy salutes, they laughed and staggered down the steps.

"Good night, Lieutenant," one called back over his shoulder. "I want a rematch on that dippits game tomorrow night, sir." He punched his buddy in the side. "Lt. Roburgh ate you alive, Derf. I told you he's one bad card freak!"

Lt. Roburgh laughed as well. It had been pretty easy taking money from Sergeant Hellost and Private Soork. They were really bad dippits players. He watched them as they staggered down the street toward their barracks.

He didn't particularly like being stuck on this rock, but the job paid exceptionally well. His bank account back home on Atheran Ziin was a testimony of how well this job paid. He'd never get that kind of return on a soldier's salary. On his next leave Roburgh would have to make sure Viarn Kobriin was diversifying his investments. He was keeping tabs and seeing to it that no one squandered his money. So far Kobriin was a trustworthy accountant. The lieutenant inhaled a long deep breath and let it out slowly. There were times when he longed to be out on the front fighting, but the money had been right and he wanted to live long enough to enjoy every farn of it. Roburgh adjusted the blaster on his hip and stepped out into the now deserted street. He had work to do. He'd just gotten word from Vors Braddic, Delcor Overseer, to move the twenty prime source tribunes to Mine Four. Braddic was worried that this particular group of tribunes would fall into enemy hands. Both he and Braddic knew that the Separatists' movement was beginning to splinter. Several factions were looking to use these clone makers as bargaining chips to cease hostilities with the Alliance. Braddoc had made arrangements for a ship to arrive at Mine Four in the next few days to spirit these prisoners to Julz Yio. It was a subtropical planet inside Alliance space and controlled by the *Blue Dawn* Guild. It was ironic how the war had changed things back home. The *Blue Dawn* Guild controlled a slightly larger number of planets than the *Red Dawn* Guild, yet both guilds had pushed for separation from the Corporate. Now they were at odds with one another. *War certainly changes perspectives*, Roburgh mused. Hopefully, the Dawn Guilds would stop their bickering and remember their true cause. He pushed it out of his mind. He had work to do.

After stopping at the landing field to arrange transportation to Mine Four, Lt. Roburgh headed to Barracks Two to get the prisoners ready to move. Two skimmers were being prepped in anticipation of a late night flight. He just hoped that Corporals Julus and Geoge were not engaged in another one of their stupid insect chases. Julus was deathly afraid of spiders. These guys were plain and simple idiots. The big gray spiders that infested this part of Traylencoor were a constant nuisance. It was nothing to find them slipping into the barracks area through some of the open cracks. Julus had used a blaster one time. He not only blew away the ugly gray thing but half the wall the spider was clinging to as well.

Roburgh walked into Barracks Two and found the guard room empty. "Just as I thought!" he cursed. "The idiots are out chasing spiders again." Despite his anger, the lieutenant suddenly realized there was no activity coming from the other side of the door. It wasn't that late. Usually a few of the prisoners were still up and walking around at this hour. Placing a hand on his blaster, he eased the door open and looked inside. Only the whir of the ceiling fans greeted him. The place was as barren as the desert itself. "What the credon is going on?" A quick search revealed that some of the prisoners' personal items were missing. He pulled at the com-net on his belt and activated a channel.

"This is Roburgh. Sound the alarm! Check the tunnels!" He switched it off. "Brakkin' idiots!" Part of him was thrilled. Action at last!

* * *

The five long necked krannas moved through the desert night like long massive shadows, their gate slow and easy. Towering five yarrs high above the desert terrain, the beasts' muscular bodies of brown or tan hair rippled with each step they took as the beasts moved along in single file. The krannas' broad heads turned side to side with each step, the long lashed eyes searching the desert for signs of danger. The krannas were at home in the great deserts of Traylencoor. The large beasts moved gracefully along, their riders swaying slightly with each step. Clothed in dark robes and turbans, the Trays also kept a vigilant watch as they crossed the jagged desert. These five nomads were from the Zarr Star Clan. Voltak Su the Se'Chi and his four hunt brothers were circling around the offworlder mine to the south of them.

One of the krannas pulled up close to the lead. "I say we throw a few fire balls into the offworlder's camp tonight, Voltak."

In the dark night, the rider couldn't see the scowl on the lead rider's face. "Forget it, Brogar. I don't want to lose another brother to such stupidity."

Brogar frowned. "Sorry, Se'Chi, I spoke out of ignorance."

This made Voltak smile. "Ignorance, Brogar or vengeance?"

They rode on in silence for a little while, Brogar's kranna still close to the lead rider.

"Morrin deserves vengeance, Voltak. He died a cruel death at the hands of the offworlder." Brogar spat on the ground. "They must be driven off our world!"

"Morrin fought well. He died well." Voltak remarked. "Yes, we will avenge him. In time. The offworlders will make a mistake again."

The blaring of sirens ripped across the night like screaming birds of prey, bringing the Trays to a sudden halt.

The rider to Voltak's left pointed to the south. "The offworlders' camp is lighting up. The screaming horns are from there."

Each of the riders kept a tight reign as their beasts shuffled under them. In the distance, the horizon was illuminated by the lights from the mine. Suddenly, dark objects with blinking lights went airborne.

"Steel birds!" one rider shouted. "Another escape!"

Voltak smiled. "See Brogar, the offworlders will give us an opportunity to avenge Morrin soon enough."

The smile on Brogar's face was easily visible. "Yes, brother."

"Let's ride!" Voltak shouted. "Keep an eye out for the steel birds. They must not see us!"

The five krannas quickly got up to speed as they raced across the desert toward the Delcor Mine.

* * *

They had retraced their steps back up the mountain. Jerrid didn't like the fact that twenty prisoners were hanging at his heels. To make matters more difficult and dangerous, the mountain trail was nothing more than a narrow winding corridor of rocks that would afford little concealment should the guards have any type of air support. Jerrid had been caught off guard by Piin's willingness to rescue the twenty men from the camp. From the look on her face, Zappora was also surprised. Her ship would certainly be crowded on the return flight. Each step up the rocky trail only heightened his fear that eventually the guards would discover what had happened. Piin was putting a lot of stock in their ability to reach the mountain top before discovery. He glanced up as the tracker made her way up the trail to the high mountain peak. Verlmon was right beside him, huffing and puffing, the strain of the escape pulling hard on him.

"I'm afraid I'm very much out of shape, Mr. Dros." Verlmon seemed a whole lot nicer than his counterpart back on motherworld. Had Klea manipulated behavior as well? Somehow he liked the real Verlmon.

"A little strenuous for me too, sir." Jerrid offered a weak smile, as he struggled up the steep incline. "I don't do things like this everyday."

Verlmon managed a laugh. "I should hope not. Tell me sir, what's your involvement in all this?"

Jerrid glanced back at him, then looked ahead. "It was my understanding that a supply ship from Geasbok stopped here several months ago. It was one of my ships."

The tribune at Jerrid's side plodded along, carefully navigating the rocky terrain, each step taxing his already spent strength. He paused at a small ditch and allowed Jerrid to shoulder him over. Verlmon nodded and smiled. "As I said, Mr. Dros, I'm really not up to this, but I appreciate your help."

Jerrid laughed. "I don't mind at all."

"You were saying, about your ship?" Verlmon made an effort to pick up his pace.

"The ship had been commandeered and manned by replicants. It was headed for Mir space."

Verlmon sucked in a lung full of air as he continued to struggle to keep up with Jerrid. "Oh yes, I remember that." He sucked in some more air. "But I didn't know the crew were replicants." He gave Jerrid a weak smile. "These days you can never be too sure about a lot of things. The ship dropped off some supplies here and picked up a couple of copies to take to the Miranrian Federation."

"Copies?" Jerrid glanced over at him.

"Clones." Verlmon said weakly. "Copies are what we call the clones in this place. The copies they took back were Tribune Sidorn and Overseer Umostak."

"Umostak of the Dorner Conglomerate?" Jerrid was very surprised.

Verlmon nodded.

Jerrid got closer. "But I didn't see Umostak here."

"You won't." Verlmon looked away. "He tried to escape three weeks ago. Trays got him."

They continued on up the trail in silence.

Halfway up the mountain the sound of blaring sirens began to fill the night air, sending a chill through every person present. Looking back down the slope, the escaping prisoners watched as every light in Mine Five flashed on. Dark figures were running through various parts of the compound.

"They got any kind of air support and we're finished!" Jerrid shouted as he eyed Piin.

"There's a half dozen skimmers back there." Greeloc snarled, knowing the higher trail would afford them less cover. "We got to get off this trail now!"

"And where do you suggest we go?" Piin shouted at him.

Greeloc locked eyes with Piin. A slow hissed slipped from the smuggler's lips.

"We just have to make a run for it." Piin snapped in reply. "I mean run like you've never run before. We can make it to the top before they can get those skimmers in the air."

"Not everyone can keep up!" Greeloc shouted.

Piin pointed his weapon at the man and snarled. "Listen, and listen good. Whoever lags behind will be left. If you want off this rock, then keep up. We're not going to wait for any stragglers. If you want out of here, you best keep the pace."

More than a few grumbled snorts echoed out of the shadowy cluster of men standing around Piin and Greeloc.

"Trays goin' to hear those sirens and come lookin' for us." someone to Jerrid's back snapped out.

"Trays will track us down like dirty dargs." another voice in the shadows growled out.

Fear seemed to have more than a measured effect on each of the escapees. There had been too many stories about the dreaded Trays over the years to ignore them. If any Trays were close enough to hear the sirens they would definitely be alerted to an escape attempt. These nomads of the wilderness would only make matters that much worst.

"Well?" Piin asked, a wicked smile creeping over his lips.

Greeloc heaved out a sigh of disgust. "We do not know if the Trays stand between us and freedom. We must not give into our fear, gentlemen. No! We have no choice but to keep going. We have to make a run for it. Run for your lives, men!"

Verlmon stumbled and fell. Jerrid helped him to his feet. "Keep moving or you'll be left behind." Together they struggled to keep their footing and put distance between them and their pursuers.

Flakkinbarr Penthouse
Maggermoss

It was a bright sunny day and the warmth in the sunroom was refreshing. Alleis sat in her favorite chair and read from the *Talbah,* trying to calm herself. She had awakened early this morning after having had a disturbing dream. During the dream, she could hear sirens and alarms going off as she ran for her life. At one point in the dream, she was exiting a large steel building in the middle of some desert. All around her she could see shadowy figures in the murky darkness. The dream swirled and twisted, folding onto itself. Bright lights flashed and the sirens grew louder. That was when she had awakened, clutching her chest as her heart pounded like a wild drum. She sat up in bed gasping for air, the ringing of sirens still fresh in her mind. For a long time she sat there gasping, taking large deep breaths. She struggled to untangle herself from the bed sheets and put a shaky foot to the carpeted floor. Tazz had gotten up sometime during the night and was somewhere else in the penthouse. She got dressed and wandered downstairs where Zoe had breakfast prepared.

"You look a fright, Alleis!" Zoe's heavy accent echoed in the silence of the dining area.

Alleis eased into her chair and sat staring at her food.

"What's troubling you?" Zoe's dark eyes stayed focused on her employer as she sat slumped in her chair.

"I just had a terrible dream, Zoe, terrible." Alleis reached for the glass of marguan juice. "It was horrifying. I've never felt such terror."

The tall, thin framed woman came over and placed her hand on Alleis' shoulder. "It will be all right, Alleis. It was just a dream. It will pass."

Alleis looked up and offered her a weak smile. "I suppose you're right." She looked at her food and started to eat.

Now, six hours later, Alleis still had an uneasy feeling. She'd come to the sunroom hoping to relax and forget about it. Tazz was curled up on his pillow by the windows as he soaked in the noon day sun. She smiled as she stared at the cat. "I wish I could be like him, not a care in the whole world."

Alleis continued to read, not really focusing on any particular passage of scripture. It was almost like nothing spoke to her. *Something is wrong! I just know it! Something terrible is going to happen. What, Lord, what?* She continued to stare at the book. The words on the page seemed to run together. The heaviness she'd felt all morning was becoming an overpowering weight.

Suddenly a shadow fell across the whole sunroom, like a passing cloud. Alleis blinked and then looked up. Nothing. *That's strange*, she said to herself as she studied the sky. There was not one cloud to be seen anywhere on the horizon or overhead. What had passed over? There had been no muffled roar of a passing ship. What then? Again, Alleis attempted to focus on the words on the page.

Let darkness and the shadow of death stain it; let a cloud dwell upon it; let the blackness of the day terrify it. Alleis gasped. What did it mean? A chill began to creep up the back of her spine, slowly, like a deadly worm, inching it's way deep inside her soul. She shuddered and tried to focus on the verse on the page.

Again a shadow fell across the sunroom, this time darker than before. Even Tazz aroused from his slumber and gazed around. But beyond the windows the sun was shining bright. As quickly as the shadow had come it passed, letting the light flood back in.

"What is going on, Tazz?" Alleis called out to the cat.

In less than ten minutes time the shadow fell again. With it came a heaviness that Alleis had never before felt in her whole life. She clutched her stomach and dropped to the floor. The pain was overwhelming and terrifying. Her gut hurt, but she also realized that every fiber in her body was screaming. A spasm exploded in her chest, causing Alleis to scream in utter terror. Tazz bolted straight up off his pillow, turning nearly one hundred eighty degrees and landing on the floor opposite his panic stricken mistress. As the pain snaked its way through every finger, toe, arm, and leg, Alleis gritted her teeth to keep from screaming again. "What?" she gasped. "Lord Aidioni, please take this pain away," she begged.

Vars and Zoe had gone shopping and would not be back for another two hours. Would this killing pain continue or would they find her dead? She could feel the marble tile pressed against her face as another jolt of pain stabbed her chest. Eyes screwed up tight, Alleis managed to focus on the cat. There seemed to be darkness all around now, the shadow had fallen deep, lingering, suffocating, driving out the light..

"Tazz, help me, please, Tazz!" She reached out a probing hand in the cat's direction.

Tazz cautiously came over and sat next to her. The feline reached out with his paw and placed it on her head as another wave of fear and deep loss washed over her. Tazz gave a soft meow. Alleis managed to lift her head and stare at the cat. They locked eyes. The cat nodded.

Pray!

Alleis blinked and continued to stare at the cat. Another wave of sheer terror washed over her and she again screwed up her eyes. She could feel the cat touch her face this time. Another soft meow reached her ears.

Pray like you've never prayed before, Alleis.

The voice. It was deep inside her. Another wave of terror, this time very hard, very dark and very troublesome.

"It hurts, Lord!" Alleis moaned.

Pray, Alleis, Jerrid is in grave danger. Pray

Tazz touched her face again. Alleis released herself and began to pray. A prayer of desperation spilled from her lips as she lay on the sunroom floor pleading to Aidioni for Jerrid's safety and to bring him home.

Delcor Mine Five
10 Mycrons Out

"There!" shouted Brogar as he extended his long arm toward the south. As the four other riders gazed toward the indicated direction, they could easily see four skimmers circling high above the Delcor Mine. The skimmers pivoted and then headed out toward the high mountains. All terrain vehicles zoomed out of the steel gates moving out into the desert to the high foothills.

"Another escape?" the rider to Voltak's right asked.

Voltak turned his gaze to the man. "Yes. Perhaps more than one. They send many of their steel birds this time. I believe the High One has favored us this night, Foramer."

Foramer smiled and touched the long sword belted to his side. "Then perhaps we can avenge Morrin?"

Voltak returned the smile. "Yes." He pointed in the direction the skimmers were heading. "Quickly and carefully, my brothers."

* * *

The skimmer came up from behind the low rise, spotlight sweeping like a broom across a dusty floor. Zappora, Jerrid, Verlmon, and Piin struggled to hide in the cleft of a huge boulder, but the skimmer was on them before the remaining escapees could find cover.

"Stand clear!" came a metallic voice from the skimmer as it began to hover less than one hundred yarrs from where they were hidden. Lt. Roburgh loved the way the sound system magnified his voice. Made him sound almost god-like. The nineteen remaining escapees were flooded in light in the middle of the rocky trail like a bunch of barlas without a shepherd. *Oh, this is so good.* He'd play with them a little. Roburgh winked at the pilot who just gave him a slight grin in return. "Raise your hands, place them on your heads and remain where you are."

The prisoners all looked at one another.

"This is your last warning!" Roburgh urged the pilot in closer. Another skimmer slipped up from behind the jagged rocks. It's spotlight locked in on the escapees.

"I knew this was going to happen!" shouted Erathad. His face was covered with sweat and his clothing stained from the long climb up the mountain. "They'll kill us for sure!"

A man to Tribune Erathad's right looked around, his eyes wide in horror. "They'll kill us all!"

"Shut up!" Greeloc shouted. "Just remain calm. That's all we can do."

"Easy for you to say." Erathad tossed back.

"Silence!" Greeloc snapped.

As the murmuring subsided, one of the escapees pushed up to Greeloc. It was Tribune Dorsari "That's Roburgh. You know he'll kill some of us."

Greeloc glanced around at the desperate faces staring back at him. The spotlights made them look like demons instead of men. Men he'd known for quite sometime. They'd made a stupid deal with smugglers to get off planet. Now look where it had gotten them. Yeah, he knew Roburgh's reputation. But, there was still an outside chance the security chief would listen to reason. "Maybe if we play this cool, all Roburgh will do is put us in confinement for a few days."

"Confinement!" hissed Dorsari. "I, for one, will not give Roburgh the satisfaction of putting me in that hole in the ground."

"Don't be stupid, Dorsari!" Greeloc said through gritted teeth.

Dorsari just continued to stare at him, wild anger in his eyes.

"What are you going to do?"Greeloc didn't like the look in Dorsari's eyes.

Dorsari didn't afford Greeloc an answer. Within the span of one heartbeat, the man dashed up the trail toward the hidden position where Jerrid and the rest had holed up.

"Don't!" Greeloc shouted, but to no avail.

"Halt!" ordered the metallic voice. Roburgh glanced over at the pilot. "I think I'll teach them a lesson." He grabbed a hold of the weapons controls and sighted in the escapee. Roburgh switched the comnet back. "This is your last chance. Halt!"

Dorsari's eyes were wild as he raced up the trail, breathing hard like a mad man, ignoring the order.

A bolt of white hot energy flashed out from underneath the skimmer and struck Dorsari square in the back. He vanished in a flash of white hot vapors. A deathly hush fell over the remaining escapees.

"Stupid idiot!" hissed Greeloc as he lowered his eyes to the ground.

By this time a third skimmer had taken up a position to the left of the first ship.

"What a shame." Roburgh sighed and then looked at the pilot. "I don't think the rest will make the same mistake."

"Let's hope not, sir," the pilot replied.

"Remain where you are!" The metallic voice yelled out again.

"Do what he says!" Greeloc shouted. The escape attempt had proven ill fated. He had been a fool to believe the smuggler. Roburgh would surely make things worse for the lot of them now. The dreaded Hole was something he wasn't looking forward to. No, not at all.

"What do we do now?" Verlmon whispered as he looked over Jerrid's shoulder toward his friends out in the middle of the trail.

Piin had cursed himself nine ways to Mynsday for not planning this thing better. But he hadn't counted on the tribunes being so overtly out of shape. *Drok-son-of-a-skree*, he cursed to himself. *Bunch a mealy mouth comlink jockeys.* He had to come up with something quickly to salvage this mission. At least there was one tribune that might make it out. He glanced at Verlmon. This guy had kept up a little better than the others, but he was virtually exhausted and the horror on his face spoke volumes. Verlmon might panic like the other man. *Just keep him under your gaze, Mr. Dros.* Piin heaved out a breath and then scrutinized the surrounding area. A low rise of rocks to the right shielded the trail from the glaring lights of the skimmers. It appeared to be another smaller trail leading off toward the top of the other peak. It was a longer way around, but a chance to get away without being seen. It was worth the gamble. He nudged Zappora and touched Jerrid's shoulder, as he pointed to the low rise of rocks. "It looks like there's a trail over there."

Zappora and Jerrid studied the rise of rocks. They concurred with Piin's observation.

"We only got one shot at this." Piin gave a slight grin.

"But what about the others?" Jerrid asked.

"We leave them!" Piin snapped. "We find a better place to hide and wait a few hours. They shouldn't find Zappora's ship right away."

"But what if they have already?" Jerrid didn't like the way things were going.

"Relax, Mr. Dros, we'll get out of this." Piin smiled.

Jerrid wasn't too reassured by Piin's optimism.

The third skimmer made a pass overhead and then swept back toward the remaining prisoners. Roburgh's skimmer eased up along the trail between where Jerrid and his group hid and the other escapees.

"There is a clearing a half a myc back down the trail." Roburgh rattled into the mouth piece. "Be advised to keep your hands on your heads and proceed back down the trail. Anyone who attempts to flee will be terminated. Is that understood?"

No one made a move. They all placed their hand on their heads and did an about face.

"Very good!" Lt. Roburgh winked at the pilot. "Did you get a count?"

"Just eighteen. If you count the one that tried to run for it, that makes nineteen. We've one missing."

Roburgh frowned. "Shouldn't get too far in this terrain. We'll load the prisoners and return here within the hour. Have Four drop a few boots on the ground up ahead and do a sweep back down the trail. They should pick up the lone survivor."

"Unless the Trays get him, sir." The pilot didn't smile.

"For his sake, he'd better hope those boots get to him first." Roburgh did smile.

"Yes, sir!"

"Attention escapees!" Roburgh said smugly into the mike. "Proceed down the trail. Easy walk, gentlemen. We have you sighted in."

As the skimmers maneuvered to escort the remaining escapees back down the trail, Piin saw it as an opportunity to make their escape.

* * *

The five Trays were flattened out on the overhang looking out as the prisoners were loaded onto the skimmer.

"Morrin will not be avenged this night." Brogar hissed.

"Their steel birds did not make this easy, Voltak." Foramer whispered, despite the roar of the skimmer's engines.

The frown on Voltak's face conveyed his disappointment. The pace they had set had gotten them to the trail just as the skimmers had appeared with their blinding lights. The had not been quick enough. He glanced at Foramer and then Brogar. "The krannas are not as swift as the offworlders' steel birds."

Foramer and Brogar were disappointed that they could not exact vengeance on the escaping prisoners.

"Are we going to sulk home then?" came a voice from behind them. The three men turned and gazed at Dorruk, the youngest of the five riders. The snarl on his face told them he was willing to do anything to avenge the death of one of their clan members.

"Dorruk speaks foolishly, Se'Chi." Brogar remarked. "He's young and lacks wisdom."

"Will we lay here and do nothing?" Dorruk snapped in reply. "The steel bird did not take all the escaping offworlders."

"Did your eyes see something we did not see, young whip?" Brogar snarled.

"You have the eyes of a doga, Brogar," hissed Dorruk. "There were twenty-three shadows on the trail as the steel birds appeared."

Voltak smiled, knowing the young man had keen vision. "Dorruk speaks truth."

Brogar, Feramor and Herogin, the fourth rider, all glanced at Voltak. The Se'Chi turned a smile to the youngest rider and nodded.

"The steel birds did not take all." Dorruk smiled. "Four are heading up the manga trail."

Voltak winked at the younger man. "Then we'll avenge Morrin."

The five Trays slipped down the overhang.

* * *

Jerrid was beginning to think this had been too easy. Piin ushered them up the second trail which took them up the slope in a different direction. The trail was narrower and rose at a steep angle that made climbing extremely slow and difficult. Verlmon was having a hard time as he struggled up the winding trail.

Jerrid pulled the tribune up over a ledge. They both sat there gasping for air. Zappora and Piin were seated to the right, also breathing heavily.

"So, what now?" Jerrid gasped.

"We have Verlmon," Piin remarked. "At least one of our tribunes is safe."

Jerrid gave him a guarded glance and continued to suck in air.

After a few minutes, Piin ordered them to their feet and once more they began the climb. It would be a long night. This was not what Jerrid had in mind as a fast way to safety.

They were coming down the long side of a slope when the skimmer roared overhead and dropped down the other side of the mountain.

"You think they found the ship?" Jerrid asked as they eased out from the rock they had hurried to hide behind.

"Going in the wrong direction, Mr. Dros." Piin smiled. "That ship was headed back to the mine."

Jerrid looked relieved.

"Let's go!"

Grasping Verlmon by the waist, Jerrid pulled him along.

"This is really becoming quite an adventure, Mr. Dros." Verlmon smiled rather weakly. "I'll have plenty to tell my grandchildren one day."

"I hope so, sir, I hope so." Jerrid gave him a weak smile and continued to follow Zappora as she navigated the rocky terrain that snaked down the mountain.

The trail narrowed as it wound around several larger outcroppings of red rock. At a blind turn, the four escapees ran full tilt into a squad of dark helmeted shocktroopers. The troopers were well seasoned and dropped to defensive positions, weapons raised.

"Halt!" shouted the commander. "Hands over your heads!"

Zappora dropped to the ground like a leaf, pulling her blaster from her hip holster. With a snarl on her lips, she opened fire. The bolt from her weapon slammed into the dark body armor of the commander, boring a hole the size of a man's fist into the armor. Two more bolts killed the two men directly behind him. Piin had dropped to one knee, fired and dropped one more trooper, but the six remaining helmeted warriors were able to return fire. Verlmon was not quick enough. As he turned to flee, his head exploded, causing Jerrid to fall to the ground under the carnage. Jerrid quickly found himself being dragged back down the trail by Zappora and Piin who were returning fire as the troopers advanced on their position.

The rocks to their right exploded under the trooper's blaster fire, forcing them up a narrow trail that lead up toward the high peak to their left. As they continued to race up the meandering corridor of rock, Jerrid couldn't help but feel that this place looked familiar. He knew that he hadn't been to this planet, but he thought, *this all looks too brakkin' familiar!*

The trail suddenly swept wide and they found themselves in a vast high vaulted gorge with a large red stone square in the middle. Just beyond the stone a dark chasm stretched for at least three hundred yarrs. They were trapped! There was no way out! Pushing past the large red stone, Piin glanced down into the chasm. It was too dark to see the bottom.

"We're trapped!" Zappora shouted.

"Shut up!" Piin shouted. "I can see that!"

Jerrid glanced down into the dark abyss and then back at the red stone. It had six sides and it looked like it had been placed in the middle of the gorge by someone or something. "The dream!" he gasped.

"The what?" Piin gave him a curious look. "What are you babbling about?"

"Nothing!" Jerrid snapped back. Fear was pushing its way into every thought, feeling and emotion.

The sound of the approaching troopers brought everyone back to the reality of the moment. Piin and Zappora took up a defensive position behind the red stone, Jerrid behind them. They didn't have to wait long. The troopers came in with weapons blazing. Bolts of energy laced the night air like ribbons of yellow light strung out at Festival Time. The top of the red stone exploded into tiny shards of rock that rained down on the escapees. Zaporra and Piin returned fire, hitting nothing but the rocks behind the troopers.

Suddenly Zappora screamed as a bolt of energy ripped across her left arm, shattering the link-ID and nearly severing the limb in two. Another bolt exploded in Piin's left thigh as a wild bolt slammed into Jerrid's shoulder.

As Jerrid fell toward the ground everything became slow motion; even the roaring blast from the weapons became dull thuds as he watched the ground come up to meet him. He tried to push out with both hands, hoping to break his fall. Yet in utter horror all he could do was watch as his hands moved very, very slowly in the direction of the ground. The pain in his shoulder was beyond anything he had ever felt in his life. Jerrid was certain that most of his shoulder was gone. He knew he was going to die. There was nothing he could do about it. Turning his head to the side, he saw Zappora falling slowly to the rocky floor, the blood oozing from the open wound in her left arm. Her fore arm dangled there like a piece of dark meat on a string. Another bolt of white hot energy was poised to penetrate her right side just barely above the gun belt. It looked like a glowing arrow ready to kill her. He couldn't see Piin as he tried to turn his head back around. *Oh, Aidioni, don't let me die!* It was all he could think.

Then he heard the mumbled scream that caused him to turn his head toward the dark sky above. There was a flash of light that momentarily lit up the high cliffs above. A huge white bird dropped out over the edge of the cliff as the light flashed out. Again darkness surrounded everything. Jerrid kept his gaze fixed on the huge bird as it plummeted down the face of the cliff, claws extended in his direction. The last thing Jerrid remembered was the huge bird falling on top of him. The pain disappeared into the darkness.

* * *

Voltak and his men had not expected this manga trail to be so difficult. Loose rock and sudden back switches hampered any speed. The trail they followed had changed direction ten times in the course of their climb up the mountain. The long antlered mangas were always hard to track and even harder to kill. But that didn't stop the challenge of the hunt. Now, though, it was time for a different type of hunt. The offworlders were cunning and cruel and possessed many strange weapons. They were feared by most of the Trays. But the Zarr Star Clan and the Guur Zann Clan had a deep-seated hatred for the offworlders. The Ancestors of these two clans had given a Death Scroll to each clan leader that had been passed down for the last three hundred years. In that Death Scroll was an order to kill all offworlders and spare none. The offworlders were a curse to the planet and it was the Clans Zarr Star and Guur Zann that had been directed by the High One to vanquish the offworlders from the planet.

Voltak had his own reasons to hate the offworlders, and he didn't need a Death Scroll to sanction it. Voltak thought it odd that the Death Scrolls contradicted the *Long Book*, but he was no auraman. Auramen understood the *Long Book,* but there were some in the Zarr Star Clan who secretly professed that the Death Scrolls were wrong and needed to be forgotten. *The clans need to return to their first love*, Auraman Sharas' words rang in his mind. But Nirdrins, the Chi, thought Auraman Sharas was too soft, that he needed to heed the Death Scroll and stop listening to the old ones. Voltak just shook his head.

They had just reached the peak when the fire fight had begun. Voltak pushed Dorruk and his men into one of the clefs high above the shooting that was going on below..

"Are we going to hide here like sneaky mores?" Dorruk glared hard at his leader.

Voltak gave him a cutting glance. "Hold your tongue, young kranna!"

Dorruk snarled again as the others laughed.

"We are no match for their fire sticks, Dorruk!" Voltak snapped.

Brogar eased to the entrance and watched as the shocktroopers blasted away at the escapees. Suddenly a great white bird screamed, drawing their attention skyward. "Eryicondi!"

The Trays watched as the birds plummeted down onto the fire fight. Time stopped.

Voltak watched in fascination at the energy bolt that was suspended in mid air, ready to strike the female escapee. Fear would have caused his eyes to go wide open if they could, but they would not. Voltak couldn't even turn his head.. The Trays looked on in utter horror as the birds snatched up the wounded escapees and took them down into the black chasm. Then it was over. The blaster fire suddenly stopped as the shocktroopers came out of hiding to see what was going on.

"The High One!" whispered Brogar, finally able to speak. He turned a fearful face to his leader.

Voltak couldn't believe what he'd seen. The Eryicondi had snatched up the three escapees and had taken them away. It was a sign. A sign from the High One.

"What did we just see, Voltak?" Feramor asked. "The Eryicondi do the bidding of the High One. We must leave this mountain, now!"

The fear on the others faces only reflected the fear deep in Feramor's eyes. Even the brave young Dorruk was shaken by what had happened.

"We wait until the offworlders leave." Voltak replied. "Then we ride home. We must find Auraman Sharas and tell him what we've seen."

"Will he believe us?" Dorruk finally found his voice.

"If anyone will it is Sharas." Voltak said weakly.

Flakkinbarr Penthouse
Maggermoss

Vars and Zoe came home to find Alleis unconscious on the sunroom floor with Tazz curled up by her side. Vars did a quick medical evaluation and determined that Alleis was just barely alive.

"What happened?" Zoe's face was flushed and she too found her breathing labored as her husband lifted Alleis from the floor and headed toward the bedroom.

"I do not know. Just get my med-bag." Vars navigated his way to the master bedroom and laid Alleis on the massive circular bed. He checked her pulse and then carefully placed his ear near her nose. Alleis' shallow breathing was the only indication she was alive. Vars could feel fear trying to grab his spirit but he refused to give in to that fear. He then reached and pulled open her left eye, which was rolled back in her head.

"She cannot die, Yushann!" Vars said through clenched teeth.

Tazz had followed close behind and even managed, with no assistance, to climb up on the bed. He took his position close to Alleis' side.

"Meow." Tazz eyed Vars very closely as he continued to examine the unconscious woman.

Vars gave the cat a guarded look. "Do not worry, my friend."

Tazz twitched his tail, touched his nose to Alleis' arm and then looked again at Vars.

"We must trust Yushann in this, Tazz!"

Right then Zoe came in, bringing her husband's med-bag. Vars quickly opened it, taking out a tiny bio-scanner which he passed over his patient's body. After careful scrutiny of the tiny instrument, he lowered his eyes and dropped the instrument to the bed.

"Oh, Vars!" Zoe whimpered.

He shook his head and reached a hand out to his wife. After a moment, he glanced at Alleis and then to his wife.

"We must intercede, Zoe!' Vars squeezed Zoe's hand hard and motioned for her to place her hands on Alleis' chest. He in turn placed his hands over hers. Together they bowed their heads and began to pray.

"Lord, we come to you in Yushann's name. By your mercy and grace, please touch Alleis and bring her back to us." Vars closed his eyes and began to softly sing in a low melodic voice. The chant began to fill the room as Zoe picked up the melody and added her voice to the pleading song. The cat also sensed the tune and closed his eyes and leaned into his mistress' side. After several minutes, white sparkling light began to wrap itself around the hands of the two servants as the chant grew louder. The swirling flakes of light danced around their hands for several more measures of the chant and then flared out into spiraling, pulsating sparkles that covered every ticc of Alleis' body. Vars and Zoe were deep in meditation, their eyes closed, hands held tight over the body of their employer. Their voices continued on, locked in the deep melody that permeated the very room as sparkles of light danced and pulsated to the music. As the measures of the chant grew longer, the pulsating sparkles settled on Alleis like fallen snow. Soon her entire body was wrapped like a cocoon in the radiant light as it pulsated to the rhythm of the singing. The light also danced up the arms of the singers, engulfing them in the same radiance.

For Vars, Zoe, and Tazz, time did not matter; it seemed to stand still. It wasn't until five hours later that the singing subsided and with it the light faded to obscurity. Alleis lay peacefully on the bed, her chest rising and falling in normal rhythm with a relaxed expression etched on her face. Finally, Vars and Zoe looked at one another. Vars managed a slight smile, heaved out a sigh and glanced down at Alleis. "I do not know what caused her to be in this condition, but I think the danger has past. All we can do now is make her comfortable. When she awakens, I'm sure she will tell us what transpired."

Zoe touched her husband's hand and looked deep into his eyes. "I fear a great danger has come to the Flakkinbarrs."

Vars looked at her grimly and nodded. "I, too, have sensed something stirring for a few months now. We must be vigilant, Zoe."

Zoe suddenly clutched her chest and looked alarmingly at her husband. "We must pray for Jerrid; I sense he is in greater danger!"

After seeing that Alleis was made as comfortable as possible, the cat curled up next to her, Vars and Zoe retreated to their room to intercede for Jerrid.

Delcor Mine Five
15 Mycrons Out

For a brief moment time did stand still. The shocktroopers were frozen in place, unable to apply pressure to triggers. Sergeant Nita Precott felt like she could scream, but found no voice. Her brain functioned normally, or so she thought. But no matter what her brain told her arms or legs to do, they would not obey. She could only watch as the hostiles were frozen in place as they were falling to the ground. The only thing not affected during this time were the huge white eagles that had suddenly appeared out of the dark. The eagles came straight toward the hostiles, claws extended in a hunting strike. But it made no sense to Sergeant Precott how the escapees got weapons in the first place. There was supposed to be only one more escapee. Who were these three? *Their rescuers, you silly fool*, Nita chided herself. Try as she might, she could not squeeze the trigger on her weapon. Nothing. She had the man with the bad shoulder wound sighted in and would have finished him off. But not now. No way. For whatever reason, her fingers were frozen in place. The only thing the shocktroopers could do was watch as the three white eagles snatched the wounded rescuers up from the rocky floor. Nita tried to scream orders but her jaw was clinched tight. The eagles dropped over the edge of the chasm with just a few swoops of their enormous wings and were gone.

Time suddenly caught up and Sergeant Precott jerked back with a start, firing her weapon and hitting the ground where the wounded man once had been. Several more shots rang out at vanished targets.

"Cease fire! Cease fire!" Nita yelled into her com-net. Everyone turned and looked at her. Sergeant Precott eased up on wobbly legs from behind the boulder that had kept her from getting killed.

"What in the brakkin' crodon just happened, Sarge?" the trooper to her immediate left asked over the net.

"I have no idea, Huuston. No idea at all!" Nita let out a long slow breath.

"Strangest thing I've ever encountered." Huuston snapped back. "I couldn't even squeeze the trigger. Had that woman dead on. I'd have wasted her in a heartbeat."

"Brakkin' birds got 'em, Sarge." the man behind Huuston snarled as he flipped up his visor. "I had that one guy dead on. He'd be dust right now!"

Precott shouldered her weapon and took a few uneasy steps in the direction of the chasm. "There were three of them. Did anyone get a different count?"

The remaining shocktroopers gathered behind her.

"Just the dead one back there and the three the birds got, Sarge."

"Burrik, contact base and have them evac us out of here ASAP." Precott pushed up her visor. "Make sure they scout for any Trays in the area. They've bound to have heard all the ruckus."

"I feel sorry for those guys, Sarge." Burrik remarked, as he extracted his com-net from his belt.

"How's that, Burrik?" Precott gave him a sideways glance.

"Trays would have been a better choice." Burrik smiled wickedly. "Birds will tear them to small pieces while they're alive. Trays at least kill you outright."

"Well," Precott grinned, "at least we won't have to worry about finding the bodies."

"Just bones! Just bones!" Burrik remarked and made the call for evac.

* * *

Jerrid tried to stir from the blackness that held him in its grip. For a brief moment he saw Alleis' face appear before him with tears in her eyes, pleading, crying desperately. She was sick as unto death. He couldn't bear the sorrow he felt coming from her. *Oh Alleis! Oh Alleis!* Jerrid tried to scream but no voice escaped from his lips. Her sorrow drove deep into his heart. Alleis' image began to fade like a flower wilting in the scorching sun.

No! Jerrid finally screamed, reaching a hand out to grab a hold of his beloved wife. But try as he may she was slipping away, far, far away.

A moment of lucidness came to Jerrid as he suddenly felt the wind in his face and the stabbing pain in his shoulder. An iron like rope seemed to have been placed around his good shoulder and he felt digging spikes pressed hard against his skin. He flicked open his eyes and saw darkness below filled with jagged peaks and deep crevasses. Jerrid tried to look up, but the pain forced him to glance back toward the dark jagged peaks. The cry of an eagle pierced the night and the wind. Jerrid lapsed back into the darkness that was becoming ever so present in his life.

As the darkness tightened its grip around him, Jerrid became strangely aware of a song. He thought he could hear Vars and Zoe singing. It was strange. All through the darkness around him he could hear this incredible song that leaped in his heart like living fire. As the song swirled and danced in his very soul, it wrapped his entire body in its warmth. Suddenly, Jerrid could see Alleis again. This time she was wrapped in splendorous light, radiating like a bright star. The song continued to grow louder and the light brighter. Jerrid smiled to himself as he realized Alleis was going to be all right. As quickly as the song had come the darkness overcame him again. Jerrid gasped and for a strange moment felt the soft touch of feathers brush against his face. He opened his eyes and the only thing he could see was white feathers everywhere. And for some strange reason he had a sense of peace that reminded him of that night on Bethleea when Yushann had appeared to him. Jerrid closed his eyes and fell into a relaxed sleep.

10

"The Eryicondi, the great white birds, are true servants of the High One. Fear and tremble in their presence, for they bring his wrath."
— proverb from the *Long Book*, Clans of Traylencoor

"He will lift me up on wings of eagles and set my feet on solid rock. There is healing in his wings. Though persecution and death may try to overtake me, I will not fear. For under the shadow of his wings I will find my rest. He is my fortress, my high tower, my rock in time of trouble. Surely, he will lift me up and restore me to the fullness of life."
— Maaras 87:3-5, The Talbah Canon

20 Somlea
The Great High Range
Southern Grid
Planet: Traylencoor

The eagles flew long into the night, the mountain peaks steadily rising below them. The great birds kept a vigilant flight path toward the higher ranges in the north, a far distance from Mine Five and a place where skimmers would be hard pressed to venture. The great eagles were twice the size of an ordinary human. Their mighty wings spanned nearly twenty-five yarrs and they tore through the night effortlessly, climbing toward the dark high peaks in the distance.

The mountains kept rising, the peaks steeper, dark, menacing. After nearly three hours of purposeful flight the birds aimed toward two towering peaks that rose like the end of a needle against the twin orbs of Traylencoor's moons. The birds slipped through the eye and dropped down the other side to a jagged ledge with a large eyrie. One by one they circled the huge nest, each bird depositing their catch with the care of a mother into the pile of sticks. The eagles then settled themselves next to the wounded and looked at each other, their piercing cry tearing through the night air. The screams echoed long against the mountains but eventually faded. Then tenderly, the eagles spread their wings over Jerrid, Zappora, and Piin, engulfing them in white feathers. As the birds closed their golden eyes, a dozen glittering points of light suddenly popped into existence. Slowly the twinkling lights began a slow, pulsating dance, their numbers increasing as the moons slipped toward the horizon. The dancing lights swirled around each of the eagles, in and out, around and down. Then the song came; soft, sweet, and melodious as two voices from far across the star system added their melody to the dancing lights. The melody reverberated through the high mountains like a soft lullaby. The glow on the mountain intensified as the dancing lights engulfed the whole eyrie, cascading up the ledge and spilling over to surround the rocks and crevasses of the whole peak. If a skimmer had been near enough, the pilot might have sworn he'd seen the mountain on fire. A volcanic eruption would have been the log entry for the sighting.

Well into the early morning light, the eagles kept their embrace and the lights continued to dance. But as the sun rose higher into the sky, the glimmering lights faded and the eagles stirred from their vigilance. Satisfied that their work was complete, the eagles called to one another and then flew out of the nest, circling twice before they quickly flew back over the high peak and vanished from sight.

The sun was directly overhead when Jerrid woke from his slumber. He felt so rested, so at peace. As he became more aware of his surroundings, Jerrid realized he felt very cold. The air was thin and afforded some discomfort with each breath he took. The prickling bark of the branches in the nest pressed against his back, a reminder that he was not quite home yet. Jerrid sat up slowly as he took in his current surroundings. He knew he was in some type of nest. The dry wood was poking him in the back. The dark brown branches of the nest were as thick as his arm and nearly as long. They were skillfully interwoven into a gigantic bird's nest some forty yarrs in diameter. Dried grasses were packed into the bottom area. From whatever source this building material had come from, it was far, far away. Evidence of broken shells littered the area near where he lay. He looked out over the edges toward the cold frigid terrain. His breath caught in his throat at the height of their location. Jerrid quickly reached for his shoulder. Much to his surprise there was no pain, no discomfort. The fabric of his uniform bore the evidence of the blaster fire; blackened, fused threads formed a perfect circle where the blast had hit. The most amazing thing was that the wound wasn't there. It had been completely healed. *How?* Jerrid massaged his shoulder, still gazing out at the high mountains that surrounded him.

"Welcome back to the land of the living, Mr.Dros."

Jerrid turned ever so slowly to his right. Zappora's smiling face greeted him as she sat propped up against the edge of the great nest. Her left arm was whole, no deadly wound. The evidence of blaster fire was clearly visible. With trembling hand he touched his finger to his face and then pointed to Zappora's. She in turn cautiously put a finger to her face.

"It's gone too!" she gasped.

A smile slipped across Jerrid's face as he looked at her. Jerrid just shook his head as he turned to find Piin probing around the other side of the nest, looking for something. The evidence of Piin's wound was clearly visible in the tattered fragments of the left pant leg.

Zappora laughed. "I'm as puzzled as you, Mr. Dros. We should be dead, but we're not. We should be very dead. Very, very dead, my friend." The smile faded from her face as she looked back out toward the distant peaks.

"How long have we been here?" Jerrid managed to whisper; his throat very dry.

"I don't know, Mr. Dros," Zappora glanced back at him. "I woke up about two hours ago. Piin was awake before me."

"And how are we going to get down from this bloody place?" Piin snapped as he stumbled over to where Zappora was sitting.

She threw her hands up in the air and gave Piin an icy stare as he settled in next to her. "I don't know." She fingered the jagged edges of her left sleeve. "The blast ripped away the link-ID. There's no way we can contact SID now."

Piin rolled his eyes and threw out an exasperated sigh.

Zappora gave him a hard glance. "I haven't the slightest idea how we got here in the first place. The last thing I remember was seeing Mr. Dros get his shoulder nearly blown off. Then darkness. I don't remember any more after that."

Piin shook his head from side to side. "I don't even remember that." He closed his eyes and sat there for the longest time. No one said a word for quite a while. Jerrid was too stunned to try and figure out where they were or how they got here. *The eagles!* They were the last thing he remembered seeing.

"We can't stay here!" Piin finally remarked. "We have no food and whatever brought us here might come back."

Zappora turned and crawled to the back of the nest. "Whatever bird built this nest is one brakkin' big sucker." She managed to pull one of the branches out of the tangled maze. Brandishing it like a sword, she swiped it to the left and right. "Of course I doubt this would do us any good against the big guy." She laughed and tossed the branch into the bottom of the nest.

"Real funny, Zappora!" Piin snarled. "If those things come back, I hate to think what they'll do to us."

Jerrid eased to the place where Zappora had been sitting. He looked down and jerked back in pure horror. This part of the nest jutted out some fifteen yarrs from the ledge of the mountain. The drop was at least two mycrons straight down. A fall from here would certainly be fatal. Jerrid could feel his heart pounding in his chest. *Merciful Aidioni, get us out of here.*

Piin, struggling with each attempt, had worked his way once again to the back of the nest. He eventually managed to climb out onto the ledge. *He's got more guts than I do,* Jerrid thought as he watch the smuggler carefully ease his way up the rocky surface to a place where the ledge flared out into a flat level area about sixty yarrs wide. Piin noticed several fissures to the left and wasted no time in checking them out. He was able to squeeze his body halfway into one of the fissures. Stepping out, he glanced back over at his two comrades and shrugged his shoulders. Another fissure farther out allowed Piin to slip inside completely. After several minutes Piin reappeared and started back toward the nest, a frustrated look on his face.

"Solid rock!"Piin hissed. "Shallow cave that leads to nowhere. Wouldn't afford us much cover, either. Only room for two of us, but it would be a very tight squeeze." Frustrated, he heaved out a long sigh. "We can't climb up and we can't climb down. We're as good as dead if the beasts that built this nest come back."

Jerrid had followed the smuggler's movements around the ledge. He'd kept his seat in the safety of the nest. In spite of how good he felt at the moment, he still didn't trust his legs. It was very obvious there was no way up or down. Only Aidioni in his mercy could get them out of this one. And if those eagles did return, what then? He really wasn't as fearful of them as Piin. On the contrary, it was the eagles that had brought them here and seemed to be instrumental in their healing as well.

"Don't you think you should be grateful?" Jerrid finally said.

"Grateful for what?" Piin asked sarcastically.

"Grateful that you're not dead!" Jerrid tossed back. "Those birds actually saved our lives. Why they brought us here I don't know, but somehow, some way, we've been healed of our wounds. That counts for something."

Piin gave him a sideways glance, hissed, and continued to stare out into the long horizon. Occasionally he would drop his hand to his left thigh, rubbing the place where there should have been a huge hole.

"Be grateful to Aidioni that you're alive." Jerrid remarked, easing back down into the comfort of the nest.

Flakkinbarr's Penthouse
Maggermoss

Senior Scribe Vensant Suun stood by one of the east windows of the sun room as he looked out over the tangled cityscape, rubbing the top of Tazz's head as he lay on his pillow. Vars was standing over him with deep concern etched on his face. Vennie Suun was dressed in his favorite tweed robe and his thick dark hair was pulled back in a short ponytail. The pencil thin mustache accented his angular face.

"She is still resting comfortably." Vars remarked as he watched the fading sun settle toward the horizon. "All my instruments indicate normal brain activity, so she is not in a coma. All her bio signs are excellent. She is simply asleep, but we mustn't rouse her. I have never seen such a thing. Zoe and I have kept a prayer vigil for the last few days. What is the meaning of all this?"

Vennie continued to stroke the cat and look out toward the darkening horizon. "I fear Zoe is correct in her discernment. A shadow has come to the Flakkinbarrs that has a deep root." There was that matter of the note Jerrid had passed on to him just a little over a week ago.

"But how can that be?" Vars glanced over to the monk.

"I do not know," Vennie turned to the Flakkinbarr's servant. "The Shadow takes root wherever men let it in. Even those of the faith can leave a door ajar long enough for the Shadow to slide in."

Vars just shook his head. "I fear nothing good will come of this. Just call it a gut feeling, but I don't think things will ever be the same."

The monk pulled his hand back from the cat and turned to Vars. "Come, we must keep our vigil. Alleis is not out of danger yet, and I fear Jerrid still needs our prayers."

Vars nodded and turned toward the door. "Yes, my friend." They both headed to the exit, Tazz trailing right behind.

The Great High Range
Southern Grid

As the sun began to disappear behind the massive peaks, Jerrid and the rest could feel the cold taking a deep grip. They were all huddled together in one corner of the nest as the wind began to whip up from the chasm below. The nest provided a barrier from the direct blast of frigid air rushing up the mountain, but only the direct blast. There was no stopping this deadly cold wind. The temperature continued to drop as the light faded from the sky.

"We'll bloody freeze to death before this night is out!" Piin tried to keep his teeth from chattering. Zappora just glanced at him and tried to snuggle closer.

"You're such an optimist, Piin." Zappora snapped back at him. "You're so dour lately!"

"Dour, my good woman!" Piin laughed. "I see the long and short of things. We're bloody well going to die here unless we get a miracle."

"You're a lost cause, Piin" Zappora replied, hunkering down between the two men.

There was no denying the cold, it cut Jerrid clean to the bone and brought an ache to his shoulder as a reminder of the wound that had been there.

"Stop your bickering!" Jerrid snapped. He was afraid that Piin's assessment was correct. They would probably not last the night.

"Your money won't buy you out of this one, Mr. Dros!" Piin snarled with a disgusting laugh. "And someone else will spend it all!" He laughed again and looked away.

The minutes crept ever so slowly. As they huddled closer to each other for warmth, Jerrid's thoughts turned to Alleis. What was she doing? *You fool, she's warm and dry, sitting in the comfort of the sunroom with Tazz close by. Oh Alleis!* Jerrid's heart yearned for her. He longed to be with her, wrapped in the warm comfort of her embrace.

"You have anything to make a fire?" Piin asked, looking first to Zappora and then Jerrid.

Zappora put trembling hands to the pockets in her gun belt. After a tentative search, she glanced back to the smuggler. "Not even a Porlon Lightstick, my friend." She gave a weak smile.

"It's going to be a long cold night." Piin offered up a smile and then closed his eyes.

Nothing more was said as they struggled to stay warm. As the darkness engulfed the towering peaks the temperature continued to plummet. The night sky was crystal clear, stars twinkling like sparkflies above them. The minutes turned into hours and in spite of the cold Piin's head dropped to his chest and his breathing became shallow.

"Why do you think they brought us here, Mr. Dros?" Zappora asked with a weak voice.

Jerrid pulled himself out of his deep thoughts and glanced her way. He could see the frost on her uniform and in her hair. "Pardon?"

"Why did those birds bring us here?"

"I don't know. I don't know." Jerrid offered weakly.

"I got my arm back and the scar is gone from my face, but now I'm going to freeze to death." Zappora offered a soft smile. "I understand you just go to sleep. Not a bad way to die."

"No, I guess not." Jerrid replied.

The wind continued to whistle up the chasm, blowing with it a good bit of snow.

"Do you have a wife, Mr. Dros?" Zappora asked.

"Yes."

"One lucky woman." She gazed into his eyes. "You seem to be a good man. How'd you get mixed up in all this?"

"My ships," Jerrid remarked. "My ships were the ones coming here. Had to find out what happened to them. Didn't expect all this. Had no idea." No, Jerrid had never expected any of this. This fact finding mission had somehow turned into a death trip, in more ways than one. But, still, Zappora had asked why the birds had brought them here. Surely, not to die! Would another miracle manifest itself before they froze?

Zappora laughed softly. "Piin's always full of surprises, except this time. I don't think we're going to make it out of this one."

"There is always hope!" Jerrid offered.

"I think we're beyond hope, Mr. Dros." Zappora didn't smile. She groaned. "I'm so cold, Mr. Dros! So very, very cold."

Jerrid placed an arm around her, pulling her tight to his body. He pushed the frost from her hair and placed her head on his chest. "Is that better?"

The tracker sighed and then looked up into his eyes. "Yes, I do feel a little warmer." Her eyes lingered long on his. "Your wife is a very lucky woman, Mr. Dros. A very lucky woman indeed."

Jerrid swallowed hard, feeling Zappora's body close to his. *Oh Alleis, Oh Alleis!*

It was sometime later in the night that Jerrid suddenly noticed that Zappora had stopped breathing. Frost had settled over her like a glistening coat of tiny diamonds. Piin was draped across her legs covered in the same glitter. Jerrid couldn't feel his feet or hands for that matter. *I am going to die!* That was his only thought as he looked around. The wind had long since stopped blowing. The nest sparkled with patches of snow here and there. As Jerrid continued to stare out across the nest a flicker of light caught his eye. A pin point of light flickered to life just at the edge of the nest directly across from him. It flashed twice and blossomed into a globe about one yarr in diameter. The brightness hurt his eyes and he had to look away. Then he heard the tearing of fabric and the sweet smell of lilies.

"Mr. Dros!" a familiar voice called out.

The globe was gone. Jerrid looked up to see a man clothed in a dazzling white dress uniform. A luminous glow radiated from the fabric that lit up the night. If he didn't know better, he would have thought the uniform was a Fleet dress uniform, but it was so dazzling white. As Jerrid studied the man standing before him, he suddenly recognized the face.

"Lt. Arie'el!"

Lt. Arie'el smiled and stepped toward him. "Mr. Dros, or should I say, Tribune Jerrid Flakkinbarr!"

"How?" Was all Jerrid could manage.

"Aidioni has heard your prayer, Jerrid. And the prayers of many others as they have prayed for your safety." Lt. Arie'el reached out a hand. "I have come to take you to a safe place."

"What about the others?" Jerrid glanced down at Zappora. He

certainly couldn't leave her here. Or Piin for that matter. Were they dead?

The smile continued to grow on Arie'el's face. "I have come to bring you all to safety."

Jerrid could feel a warmth returning to his body. He could feel his hands and feet now. The ice was melting from his skin and his uniform.

"Come, Jerrid, come!" Arie'el reached a hand and took hold of Jerrid's. Then he heard the definitive roar of ship thrusters being engaged. A dark ominous shape slipped up from below to shut out the light of the twin moons. The *Black Hand* edged up close to the nest and a hatch opened. SID appeared in the doorway as the light flooded out, lighting up the whole nest but paling in comparison to the glimmering uniform of Lt. Arie'el.

"Your chariot awaits, Jerrid!" Arie'el smiled

That was the last thing he remembered as Arie'el's strong hand closed around his and the glow from his uniform engulfed them all.

11

"A smuggler's creed will always be upheld. It's an unfortunate fool who makes a deal with one. Once cast, your soul will be tied to the deal, no matter what. Make no deals with smugglers for in the end you could lose your very soul." — Varess Trod'Drius, *A Smuggler's Lot*

23 Somlea
Monlainte Range / Trae Star System
Marker 29 by 4 / Red Grid Section
Planet: Trae Zae
TRS Black Hand CSS-11721

The *Black Hand* came out of hyper just within Trae space, a little more than a day by sublight from Trae Zae. Lt. Arie'el stood over Jerrid's bunk and watched over him as he slept peacefully.

"Rest while you can, Jerrid, for the days ahead will be dark ones." Arie'el gazed upward, staring beyond the ship. "I fear for him, Lord. The shadows are creeping out of the darkness in great number. I fear it will only lead to death."

There was a long pause, Arie'el's eyes closing, as he stepped back and took in a deep breath.

I will turn the course. He shall not die. I have determined it.

Arie'el's eyes fell upon Jerrid. He smiled and looked again toward the One he served. "I am glad; it is a good thing." Arie'el's face took on a look of concern. "But what about the others? They are dangerous, especially the smuggler. I fear his plan will bring them all to ruin. At least the woman seems to be searching and may eventually find the truth."

What is set in motion is for my purpose. Go now!

"Yes, my Lord." Arie'el again closed his eyes as his uniformed flashed bright white. The dazzling light globe engulfed the lieutenant's form and pulsated twice. It shrank to the size of a pin and disappeared.

* * *

Jerrid found himself surprisingly rested. He was enjoying the warmth that lingered over his whole being. Oddly, he felt the softness of a mattress beneath him and not the prickly discomfort of sticks. *Sticks?* That was a strange thought. He was almost afraid to open his eyes, afraid that it was just another dream. Another illusion. But as he laid there he couldn't help but notice that the surrounding air was quite comfortable. He wasn't having trouble breathing. It wasn't cold, nor was there a bone chilling wind whistling up from beneath. There was only a low hum, the hum of impulse engines. Strange? Jerrid lay there and tried to discern all the different sounds. Very carefully, he cracked an eye open and glanced around.

"What?" the word escaped from Jerrid's lips as his eyes opened wide. He immediately knew where he was. He was back on the *Black Hand*, in his own cabin. How could that be? Then suddenly he remembered everything, Lt. Arie'el and his glowing uniform. The sudden appearance of Zappora's ship just at the edge of the nest. *You were just dreaming, Jerrid, just dreaming. It wasn't real.* Was it all an illusion? A trick of the mind?

"But it seemed so real!" He whispered to the room and then glanced down at the clean shirt. He put a tentative had to his shoulder. If there had been a wound there, it was completely healed now. Perhaps he had been dreaming. Slowly, Jerrid eased up from his bed and placed his feet on the deck plates. Then he saw the tattered uniform piled next to the bed. Blaster burns were clearly evident. A lump settled in Jerrid's throat.

"It was real!" He heaved out a deep breath. "Merciful, Aidioni, I am at a loss for words." Jerrid had to find out what became of Piin and Zappora. He headed toward the door.

As he navigated up the narrow corridor toward the command deck, a door up ahead opened and Zappora eased herself out into the corridor. She stood on very unsteady feet, trying to identify her surroundings. She too was clad in a crisp clean uniform. Upon hearing Jerrid approach, she turned a startled glance his way.

"Mr. Dros, how in the name of all that's holy did we get here?"

Jerrid just shook his head. "My dear lady, I haven't the foggiest notion. Where's Piin?"

As if on cue, another door up the corridor opened and Piin slipped out and stared at the two of them. "What the bloody credon is going on here?"

"I believe we all would like to know the answer to that one, Piin." Jerrid replied. "I think we'd best get to the command deck and see where we are."

"Let's go!" Zappora smiled and eased past the two men and headed to the control area.

Merrus Mining Outpost

Zappora stood in the hatchway as Piin and Jerrid exited her ship. The smuggler slipped her a gold sealed envelope as he bounded through the entryway.

"This is for all your trouble." Piin didn't even glance back as he hurried over to the *Red Dragon.*

Jerrid paused and looked up into Zappora's eyes. "I will always remember you, dear lady. Always."

She touched his arm and gazed back at him for what seemed an eternity. Feeling her cheeks blush, Zappora finally managed to avert her gaze and allowed a smile to settle across her lips. "Mr. Dros, if you ever need my assistance, just send word to Merrus here. Just say you need the *Black Hand.* Whatever you need, I will be there."

All Jerrid could do was smile back. "I'll remember that." As he was about to leave, Zappora kissed him on the cheek.

"Good luck, Mr. Dros!"

Jerrid felt awkward, his heart pounding. "And to you, dear lady." With that he slipped through the hatchway and onto the *Dragon*. The hatch was sealed and Jerrid stood there for the longest moment, gazing at the *Black Hand* as it pulled away. Fatigue pulled at ever fiber of his being. "May Aidioni protect you, Zappora." He turned and headed to his cabin.

The Red Dragon

The door to Jerrid's cabin slowly slid open. The corridor light was obscured by the dark clad figure that paused momentarily before slipping into his room. The door closed quietly behind him. The dark clad man eased over to the bunk. He squatted down beside Jerrid's sleeping form, pulling back the black hood of his uniform. Piin smiled as he reach out a hand and placed it on Jerrid's head.

Mr. Dros! Piin hissed. *My assassin is good at what he does, remember that. Your financial commitment to this cause is most critical. Klea must be eliminated at all cost. Remember that!* Piin pushed his mind probe deep. He had to make absolutely sure that there was no turning back from the plan. There would be another opportunity to rescue the remaining tribunes from Traylencoor, but, for now, ridding the Corporate of Klea was the primary objective. Once that was settled, then perhaps the Alliance would be strong enough to take control. Help from the Miranrians was absolutely necessary. *Remember, Mr. Dros, remember. Klea must be assassinated. He is a great threat to the Corporate. His removal is paramount to those who wish to live in freedom. Klea must be removed. Remember that, Mr. Dros. Remember, always remember that. I will be waiting for my money. And you will have your answers to the missing shipments.* Piin grinned. The ruse was almost too laughable. *These simpletons.* Piin pushed up to his full height and glanced down at Jerrid's sleeping form. "Good night Mr. Dros, sleep well!" Piin exited the room. Yes, the plan would go forward, as he envisioned it would.

12

"By your word you have knitted me in secret, And the breath of the Almighty gives me life." — Arako 33:4, *The Talbah Canon*

30 Somlea
Flakkinbarr Penthouse

Fear! It was a feeling that Alleis had become very familiar with these days. She didn't know if she could ever go back into the sunroom. *Funny*, she thought, *it doesn't seem like a room where the sun shines anymore.* It had been eleven days ago. She dared to glance up across the edge of the garden railing, out toward the western part of the city. She felt a little safer here. *Eleven days!* The only thing Alleis remembered was the shadow falling over the sunroom, the oppressive weight and then darkness. That was all. She was totally surprised when Zoe told her just how long she'd been near death. Near death? *How could that be?* She'd questioned Zoe several times, trying to understand exactly what had happened. Her servant and friend had told her everything Vars had done. Their prayer vigil had been the only thing that had brought her back from the brink. Nothing else they tried had worked.

A bird twittered in a nearby tree. Alleis glanced up, trying to find it in the foliage. She spied movement halfway up the tree. A red jay popped out and fluttered over to another tree, Tazz tracked the bird's every move.

"He's a lot faster than you are, Tazz!" she remarked as the cat continued to scrutinize the tree where the jay landed. Tazz tired of the hunt and headed back inside, meowing as he went.

As the morning wore on Alleis began to remember bits and pieces of her ordeal. Jerrid had returned from Traylencoor two days ago and seemed to be in good health. Yet, despite their warm embrace, something was not quite right. Something had happened to her husband on that far away planet. Jerrid had clung to her like a cloak ever since he returned. He was giddy and overly charming. Like an upper classman again. They had made passionate love like they had when they first were married, lingering long after dawn and staying up well past the sitting moon. It had been a wonderful two days. These thoughts brought a smile to her lips as she pulled a strand of hair behind her ear. In that passionate time nothing else seemed to matter; food, time, nothing; all each of them wanted was more of the other. Yet, the lingering uneasy feeling would not go away. Any passing shadow would cause her to jump and gasp for air. It took some doing, but she purposed in her heart this thing would not conquer her.

It was late morning when Zoe came up with a service tray containing a pitcher of bilberry tea along with two crystal cups. "Your tea, Alleis." She smiled and sat the service down on the small table by her chair. "Anything else?"

"Is Jerrid up?" Alleis reached over and took one of the cups. "It's rather late to still be in bed."

"I think I heard him a few minutes ago. Tazz is waiting for him by the bedroom door." Zoe offered a weak smile. "That cat has been glued to Jerrid since he's gotten back."

Alleis smiled. "Yes I know. I found him huddled up next to Jerrid early this morning." She paused and took a sip from her cup. Zoe started to leave, but Alleis reached out and took a hold of her arm. "Zoe, is it me, or is there something strange going on here?"

"Strange?" Zoe gave her a guarded look.

"Yes, strange." Alleis nodded. "Ever since the darkening happened to me several days ago, I can't shake this sense of foreboding. It's even more pronounced now that Jerrid has come home."

Zoe didn't really know what to say. She, too, had felt an awkward presence hovering over the penthouse ever since Alleis' darkening. "I won't lie to you, Alleis. I have also felt a similar presence. It's very discomforting. What it is, I don't know, but I do know we must be vigilant. We must keep praying."

Alleis just nodded and took another sip of her tea. She glanced back to her servant, her friend. Alleis found herself leaning heavily on Zoe for support. She knew that without Zoe's intervention she wouldn't be here now. "Jerrid and I will talk about it later. He had a trying time on his trip. Right now he needs his rest. He's cancelled all his remaining appointments for the next two weeks."

"Very good." Zoe left.

* * *

It took several more days before Alleis could work up the courage to go back into the sunroom. With Jerrid's coaxing, and his strong arms to lean on, she made the effort. The first few times she wouldn't stay long, but eventually her fears were overshadowed by Jerrid's strength and confident manner. Alleis recounted her tale as Jerrid listened intently, Tazz curled up next to his feet. He was extremely troubled to learn of everything that had touched his wife. He was devastated to learn from Vars just how close to death she had come. It made his time on Traylencoor and his experiences seem insignificant in comparison. Yet, Alleis found Jerrid's encounter on the far away planet terrible and mystifying all at the same time. When Jerrid was recounting his experiences, Alleis felt that same foreboding presence creeping back in. It felt like the black clouds that obscured the sun, blocking the light, during a terrible thunderstorm.

"What's going on, Jerrid?" Alleis reached out and took his hand, her eyes locking on his. "I don't understand any of this. Do you think all of this has something to do with that book?"

Without even thinking, Jerrid looked away and stared out the window. *Yes, Klea, that's the reason for all this!* He heaved out a heavy sigh, turning back to look at her. "I think it goes beyond that book, Alleis. I really do."

She looked alarmed. "What do you mean?"

"Ever since Dameon Klea came to power things have begun to change. Not for the good, mind you." He chewed on his lower lip, paused and reached for a cup of kaufee. "This war with the Solarians is going to drag on and on, I'm afraid. The Separatists are already gaining more ground and their cause is starting to spread to the rest of the systems. A Corporate divided against itself cannot stand. The book is just a mirror of the things that are starting to unfold. I think we must consider doing what Yanni is doing."

"Leave?"

"We don't really know how things are going to go." Jerrid turned and gazed back out the window. "But it's time to consider all options."

5 Cyibre
Flakkinbarr Penthouse Garden

A cool breeze swept through the penthouse garden, stirring the leaves on the trees and ruffling the flowers. Jerrid was trying to catch up on some of the notes his secretary had sent over regarding the cancelled meetings. Five comlinks were stacked in a neat pile by his chair. With everything that had taken place in the last few weeks, the return to a normal working lifestyle was challenging. Jerrid smiled to himself as he glanced over the notes. Eva was such a good secretary. Not much slipped by her unnoticed. In a few days he'd be back up to speed and back into his routine. He was looking forward to immersing himself in his work. He wanted to put this all behind him; although, he had his doubts that it would be that easy. Tazz was sitting up under his favorite tree looking around as the flowers swayed back and forth in the breeze. Alleis was perched on the wall near the cat, a magnifying glass in hand, looking at a blue and yellow flutter. Tazz stole occasional glances at the bright colored insect as it danced through the flowers, but for the most part he ignored it. Alleis, on the other hand, was trying to keep up with the insect's erratic movements.

"I wish this fellow would hold still!" she said in exasperation, the flutter popping in and out of the blue julls.

"How do you know that he's not a she." Jerrid asked, looking over the top of the comlink.

"He or she needs to hold still for just one moment." Alleis replied. "So I can get a good look and tell you." She flashed him a big grin.

"Just tell it to stand still." Jerrid offered and then laughed.

"Oh, you!" Alleis made like she was going to throw the magnifying glass at him, but gave him a half cocked smile and peered back into her glass. The flutter zipped to another flower. "Be still, will you!"

"That's more like it." Jerrid remarked and switched to another screen on the comlink.

"Meeeeeooooow!" Tazz grunted. There was a quiver in the cat's voice. It sounded too guttural and strained.

Jerrid and Alleis both gazed at Tazz. The cat looked at each of them, then he locked eyes with Jerrid. For a brief moment, Jerrid thought he saw Tazz give him a sad sort of smile.

Good bye, my friend!

Jerrid's eyes flew wide as Tazz's eyes glazed over. The cat dropped off the edge of the ledge, hitting the marble flooring with a soft thud. Jerrid or Alleis could not move. It was as if they suddenly weighed a thousand kefs each. The blue and yellow flutter danced around the cat and then flew off, breaking the trance that each one had been locked into.

"Tazz!" Alleis and Jerrid both screamed at the same time. Jerrid bolted from his chair, sending the comlinks and his kaufee flying in all directions. He scooped the cat up and pulled it to his chest. Tazz was limp and just hung there in his arms. Alleis reached out a trembling hand toward the cat. Gently she laid her hand on the furry creature and her eyes went wider.

"Oh my God, Jerrid!" Alleis screamed again. "He's dead! He's dead!"

By this time Vars and Zoe had heard the screams and came running up to investigate. When they got there, Alleis and Jerrid were on their knees, Tazz clutched tight to Jerrid's chest. All they could do was stand there. After a moment, Jerrid looked up at them and just shook his head. Tears pooled at the edges of Zoe's eyes as she buried her head in her husband's chest. Vars swallowed hard and pulled Zoe closer.

Alleis could not contain herself; her lower lip began to quiver uncontrollably, and then the tears flooded from her eyes and spilled down her cheeks. Her heart felt like it was being ripped out of her chest as the sorrow engulfed her and the sobbing came. With tear stained face she looked up at her husband. Jerrid was too stunned to feel anything. He continued to stare at the limp cat he held tight in his arms. He was almost afraid to let go, afraid he'd be losing Tazz. Time slowed to a standstill. As Jerrid continued to look at the lifeless cat a strange thing happened. The cat's body began to convulse, shrinking right before his eyes. Suddenly the mass of fur turned into a tiny kitten, stretched out in his hand, not quite filling up his palm. Tazz was a kitten again. The tiny kitten stretched out, rolled over and locked eyes with Jerrid. It was the day that Tazz had stolen his heart. Those tiny little eyes burned with such life that he couldn't ignore them. Tazz, that little fur ball, had stolen his heart. The tiny kitten morphed again in his hand and once again was the lifeless body he now held. Time came rushing back. Hard and furious. *He's gone!* That was all that came as he slowly looked up to see his wife sobbing uncontrollably next to him. He then glanced up at his servants, their tears streaming down their faces. Slowly, Jerrid got to his feet, took a few steps and placed Tazz back under his favorite tree. Then Jerrid bolted for the door, blind grief taking hold of him like nothing he'd ever experienced. He didn't remember going down the stairs, everything was such a blur. Tazz was gone and the grief of losing the cat was more than he could bear.

Vars and Zoe heard a scream come from the stairwell moments after Jerrid had disappeared through the door. They just looked at each other and cried the more.

* * *

How Jerrid found his way to his study, he never knew. All he remembered was stumbling down the stairwell, staggering through the corridors, knocking pictographs from the wall, and finally coming into the study where he dropped to his knees in front of his chair. He burst into tears, the terror of losing the cat slamming into his gut like a comet. Memories came flooding back like a tidal wave. Memories of the cat flashed through his mind like a vid-drama. Every thing he remembered about Tazz from the time Alleis brought him home to moments ago crowded his consciousness for attention. Jerrid only plunged deeper into despair as the deep heart ache surfaced. There, right before him was the shaggy black darg with the odd white spot on the forehead. *Muuka!* Jerrid cried as the image tore at his soul. He had been only five years old then. It was so long ago, so long ago. Yet, it was just as if had been that same day Muuka had been hit by a tramcycle. The darg had been his best friend and she was gone.

"No! No!" Jerrid screamed. Now Tazz, that cantankerous cat that had wormed his way into his soul, was gone too. Jerrid heaved and wailed, tears streaming down his face like a faucet left on. It was almost like losing Alleis. The pain, the pain. It stabbed his heart and tore at his soul. He continued to wail as he saw the cat over and over again give out that pitiful meow and collapse to the marble floor.

"Oh God!" Jerrid screamed. "Aidoini, please take this pain away!"

Jerrid got to the point where there were no more tears. His pants were completely soaked as well as the braided rug he was floundering on. His gut hurt and his knees and back were sore.

"Jerrid?" A voice whispered.

"Leave me alone!" Jerrid shouted, throwing an arm out.

Presently a hand touched his shoulder. "Jerrid?"

"What?" he moaned.

"Please come to the garden, please." It was Zoe's voice.

"Why?" He couldn't look up.

"Please, Jerrid, please. Just come to the garden, you've got to see this, please."

He could see Zoe's shoes as he cracked open one eye. Finally, he pulled his head up from the rug and gave her a guarded glance. "Why should I come to the garden?"

The tears still stained Zoe's lovely face. She gave him a very weak smile. "Please Jerrid, you have got to see this. I can't explain it, but you must come to the garden."

Carefully, Zoe helped Jerrid to his feet and guided him out the door, down the hallway, past broken pictographs and into the stairwell going up to the garden. He faltered a time or two, but Zoe patiently pulled him up. Just before they reached the doorway, he heard the most incredible music. He paused, looking Zoe in the eye. She nodded and then smiled, tears still glistening the edges of her eyes. The music felt intoxicating as it laced itself around his soul and stirred up a whisper of hope. As they took a few more steps toward the doorway, Jerrid finally recognized that it was a viao playing, Alleis' viao. It sounded heavenly. As Jerrid and Zoe stepped out onto the garden, Jerrid was so overcome with what he saw he had to lean on his servant for support. In the middle of the garden, just beside Tazz and his favorite tree, Alleis sat playing her viao. The bow moved almost like magic, as did her fingers. And the song, oh the song just overwhelmed his soul and he began to cry again. It was then that he noticed that there was other music interlaced with the viao. *What is that sound? What's making that other music?* Jerrid blinked back the tears, wiped a hand across his eyes and then saw the birds. Hundreds of them. Jays, redbirds, graybeaks, swiffers, goldwrens, harpers and greenbacks perched in all the trees, singing in unison, bobbing up and down. The trees and shrubs were full of them. The garden gate stood open and there was Yanni, tears in his eyes and gazing at the strange sight.

For an incredibly long time Jerrid just stood there, next to Zoe, as Alleis played her sweet music accompanied by the birds. Vars stood a few paces to Allies' left and Yanni continued to cry beside his gate. And the birds kept singing and singing in tune with the viao.

After a time, out of the corner of his right eye, Jerrid noticed a tiny pin point of light appear just above the garden railing. The light moved forward and flashed twice, becoming a large bright globe. Jerrid glanced at Zoe, but she was transfixed with Alleis and the birds. There was a tearing of fabric and there at the edge of the garden stood Lt. Arie'el in his glowing white uniform. He nodded to Jerrid, held up his hand and winked at him.

"They do not hear me or see me, Jerrid. Only you." Lt. Arie'el remarked. "Remember, the breath is in the life and the breath always returns to the Creator." With that the lieutenant's uniform glowed white hot and he was swallowed up by the glowing globe, which shrank to the small point of light and then vanished from view. And with that vanishing, Jerrid felt hope again despite the loss he felt over Tazz. As the music continued to swirl again, Jerrid wondered if he'd ever see Lt. Arie'el again. Time would tell. Time would tell.

PART THREE

Twist of Fates

Interlude

October 13, 2024
Lawrence Bakersfield Laboratories
Clearing Lab Twelve
0935 Zulu

Forcing the lump back down his throat, Thomas Farraday pushed back in his chair, pulled the glasses from his face and glanced at the computer screen.

The blue light illuminated again. *"Thomas?"*

Farraday ignored the computer. He chewed on his bottom lip for a long moment, thinking about the material he'd just read. The compelling drama unfolding stirred his soul and tugged at his heart. It brought back the sudden remembrance of his own cat, Stanley. As he sat there he thought back to that cold rainy March day when he came home to find Stanley staggering around the kitchen. It was something he'd never forget as long as he lived. He remember the frantic drive to the vet, the diagnosis of kidney failure and pneumonia. The images of the sixteen year old gray tabby brought tears to his eyes. Thomas blinked, reached for a tissue by the computer and wiped his eyes. He had nearly lost the cat eight years earlier when Stanley had been first diagnosed with kidney disease, but the cat pulled through. Eventually with time, the disease took its toll and Stanley began to suffer. Thomas couldn't allow him to continue in that state. The vet did what she had to do and he watched his faithful cat for sixteen years peacefully close his eyes, never to awaken from his final sleep.

"Thomas, is there something wrong?" The blue light blinked several times,

waiting for a response from the man sitting in front of the screen.

Thomas bolted from the chair and ran over to the sink on the far wall, turning on the water so no one could hear him, and cried. He hadn't realized how much he missed his cat. After several minutes, Thomas washed his face and tossed the towel in the trash. He began pacing the floor, staring at the printout and occasionally glancing at the box that contained the remaining crystals from the crash site.

"Thomas, you have not answered my question." Wanda beeped. *"Is there something wrong?"*

"Get a grip, Thomas, get a grip!" he told himself as he slipped back into the chair.

"I do not have the capabilities to get a grip, as you so put it, Thomas." the computer beeped back, blue light blinking.

Farraday finally smiled at the computer. "It's just an expression, Wanda. I was just remembering something."

The light on the computer blinked four times. *"Continuing processing."*

"Good, Wanda." Thomas took up the rest of the printout. "I've got to get through this."

Slowly, Farraday found the place where he'd left off, thoughts of Stanley floating through his mind.

13

"If you want boring, go to Tau Kerus Four. In all my travels I've never come across a place so plain, so mundane as this planet. Though some may consider it quaint, I found it a place I would want to leave after the first hour." — Varna Kepretat, *My Travels, My Worlds*

30 Bonnar
Auroya Range / Tau Kerus Star System
Planet: Tau Kerus Four
Vorska
Old Zha Trade Headquarters

The old Zha Trade Headquaters was a three story stone building situated on one hundred plats of rolling hill country. When Jerrid had first come to Tau Kerus Four to look the place over for a possible business venture, he'd been a little skeptical that Dulor could do anything with the rundown building. The Zhas had used the building for more than four decades, and for the most part had done very little maintenance to the structure. It showed. Now, Jerrid stood amazed at the accomplishment that Tres Dulor had done. He was left speechless at the transformation he saw before him. Everything about it was a vivid testimony to the work crew and their determination to take an old building and turn it into something brand new. The former dull sand colored stones had been pitted and broken, but now they were sparkling bright in the noon day sun. Not a chip or ragged edge anywhere. Red tile high peaked roofs accented with blue trim blended well with the other colors Dulor's crew had chosen. The building now consisted of ten bedrooms, fifteen baths, and twenty-eight other rooms, not to mention two large kitchens. Jerrid's quiet confidence in Tres Dulor's abilities brought a slight smile to his face as they strolled through the transformed trade center. The contractor's imagination went far beyond the structure itself. The landscaping boasted of careful details. Ten lavish gardens surrounded the remodeled building ablaze with a variety of floral coloring.

Jerrid was now standing in the back garden, just off the main living area. There was a brilliant yellow colored zebin standing in the middle of the garden. Gray marble walkways meandered through the lush foliage and ironwood benches were placed in strategic spots. Jerrid knew that Vars would be extremely pleased with the way these gardens had turned out. But all he could do now was to stare at the tree.

Dulor wasn't too sure how to take the expression on the overseer's face. He wondered if he'd done something wrong, left something out or added something he shouldn't. Perhaps he'd gone too far. After all, his wife, Arra, had overseen all the landscaping for the conversion of the Zha Trade complex. This could very well be a setback that might cost him. At first, Overseer Dros seemed very pleased with the gardens, but when they toured this back garden his expression changed. He'd been staring at the yellow zebin tree for a long time now. Tres Dulor didn't know quite how to gauge the man. Dros had always liked his work before. He swallowed and ventured a question. "Anything wrong, Mr. Dros?"

The lone yellow zebin kept Jerrid eyes focused tight. Finally, sensing Dulor's growing unease, he glanced over at the man. "The yellow zebin. It's the only one like it in all the gardens here? Why's that?" He was tingling all over.

Dulor swallowed hard, picking up on the uneasy quiver in the overseer's tone. Perhaps Arra's notion had been an ill one. "Pardon, sir, but my wife came up with the idea of a single colored zebin. She thought it would make a nice touch. All the red, gray, and blue zebins are fairly common here on Tau Kerus Four." He paused, feeling a little awkward with his explanation. "She incorporated the common zebins into most of the landscaping around the complex. My wife thought a rare yellow zebin would add contrast and intrigue to have a special tree in the garden." The expression on Dros' face worried him.

"Why a yellow one?"

"It took her nearly a month to locate the yellow. They're a little more common than the pink zebin, which is extremely rare and hard to find." Growing uneasy with this awkward attempt at an explanation, Dulor swallowed. He had to salvage this situation. "Arra likes yellow. She'd hoped you and your wife would like it as well. I'll have it removed and replaced with whatever you'd like to see there, sir. If you would like a pink one, we can probably locate one on Verrus Mons."

It was an even longer moment before Jerrid tore his eyes away from the tree and glanced over at Dulor. "No, it's fine. I like it very much. It makes a nice touch."

Relief washed over Dulor. "Thank you, Mr. Dros! Thank you!"

Jerrid finally smiled, turned to the man and extended his hand. "You've far outdone yourself on this project, Tres. And your wife certainly has a good eye for landscaping. I know someone who might be interested in talking with her about landscaping."

"Thank you, sir." Dulor beamed. "I'll certainly tell her."

"Good, make sure you do." Jerrid smiled. "I'll see that you get a sizable bonus for all your efforts on this project. Well done. Yes, well done indeed."

Tres Dulor's face exploded with delight. "Thank you sir!"

"I'll need a few servants to help get things ready for my wife and I. We'll need to purchase some furnishings and such." They turned back toward the main house. "Is there someone you could recommend?"

"I hired a few of the locals here to help with the interior jobs. There was a nice couple that worked exceptionally hard and paid close attention to details. I think they would make a good first start for your staff, sir." Dulor was glowing with excitement.

"I'd like to interview them before I leave. I can do it tomorrow around noon if they can work that out." Jerrid followed Dulor through the double glass doors.

"I'll contact them this afternoon. I'm sure they'll be ecstatic with the proposal, sir."

"Good, very good!" Jerrid wondered how Alleis was going to like this place.

14

"There will be trouble on the Miranrian front if we aren't careful. Mark my words, the Miranrians will align themselves with the Solarians at some point. We must be prepared to act if they do."
— Dameon Klea, in an address before the High Tribunal, 21 Bonnar 4758

"When it comes to galactic dominance, even mortal enemies can become friends. At some point they will turn on each other, but for now the Miranrians are a very real threat." — Tribune Rez Verlmon, Media One interview

13 Juylea
The Third Eye
Maggermoss

Jerrid sat in the back corner of the bar and slowly sipped a toffee brandy. He'd been here for almost an hour. The rantings of Rez Verlmon had carried the tribunal meeting for most of the morning. He'd grown weary of listening to the clone's ongoing diatribe about the war. Verlmon had repeatedly magnified the Separatist and the Solarian threat, added that the possibility of the Miranrians joining forces with the Solarian Federation would prove to be an even greater danger to the Corporate, as if those present didn't know the impending dangers from without and within. It had been hard to sit there knowing that the real Verlmon had died a few months ago on a far distant desert planet. Director Klea had appeared in late morning to give credence to the clone's claims and make the point that the Solarians had to be driven back at all cost. The director also assured all those present that the Separatist issue was a grave concern and had to be dealt with quickly and severely. Stiffer penalties would be added to the Verlmon Act. During Klea's speech, Jerrid's only focus was on how much this man needed to be taken out of the picture. By the end of the meeting Jerrid knew, without the slightest doubt, that Piin's assassin was the only key to turning things around, stopping the war, and getting the Corporate back to a more civilized place.

But as he contemplated the course of action dictated by Piin, he didn't feel right about it. In fact, it went against everything he believed. How could he, a faithful follower of Yushann, even entertain such ideas? *But I just can't sit by and watch the Corporate splinter right before my eyes! No, I have to follow through.* Against his better judgment, Jerrid felt compelled to stay on task. He shook his head and continued to stare at his drink. Another thirty minutes crept by as Jerrid replayed Klea's speech in his mind. As the minutes clicked past, Jerrid's thoughts swirled with the haunting images from Traylencoor, accented with whisperings from the journal hidden away in his wall safe.

Klea has to be stopped! If he is allowed to continue, he will destroy the Corporate. He's a ruthless barbarian who will subjugate the TeMari people and destroy those who have any trace of Solarian ancestry. Remember, Klea is your problem and his elimination is paramount.

I have a man who will serve you well. A professional. Piin's man was reportedly the best in the business. Jerrid was just financing the plan, not pulling the trigger himself. *The problem must be taken care of. Soon!*

The words swirled like a cyclone gone wild inside his brain. His forehead began to throb. Placing a hand to his head, he massaged the right temple. *Funny,* he thought, *it's almost like Piin is right here whispering in my ear.*

Klea's dangerous! Remember that! It couldn't be Piin, but sounded like Piin. *Remember, Klea is your problem. You must rid the Corporate of that problem.*

As Jerrid continued to stare at his drink, he was becoming more determined than ever that Piin's plan was the only way. *The only way!* A man in a dark business suit slipped into the seat opposite him. A bit startled, Jerrid glanced up. Relief washed over his face. It was Tribune Gerrius Tuposh. He offered a weak smile.

"Sorry I'm late, Jerrid. I got cornered by Tribune Estrotis." A slight smile peaked out from under the man's thick red mustache. "She does like to ramble." For his forty years, Gerrius Tuposh had a youthful look that belied his years. A thick head of dark wavy red hair and his predominate mustache made him easily distinguishable.

"Think nothing of it, Gerrius."

A waitress appeared and smiled at the newcomer. "What would you like, sir?"

Gerrius pointed at Jerrid's drink and smiled back. "I'll have what he's having."

"Very good, sir!" she turned and disappeared.

They waited until she returned with the drinks before engaging in conversation. After the waitress was gone, Gerrius took a slow sip from his drink. He paused and pulled a small comlink from his jacket. He activated the display and slid it across the table. "Take a look at that, Jerrid."

Jerrid studied the comlink screen then glanced up at Tuposh. "These are confirmed visuals?"

"I have an operative out on Vosonna Supply Station Ten. For the last few weeks there have been rumors of sightings of Mir military vessels crossing into Corporate space." Gerrius nodded. "The first image is of the *K'Taa* re-supplying at Vosonna. The second image shows another ship coming in within ten minutes of the first. That one is the *K'Zak*. The ships spent two days at the supply station. Both ships are with the Miranrian Fifth Fleet."

"They were there for two whole days?" Jerrid raised an eyebrow. "Does Vosonna have designs to throw in with the Separatists?"

"If they did it would open up a new Separatist front." Gerrius took another sip of his brandy. "Tribune Urindi denies anything of that sort. He claims Vosonna is a free trade planet and Mir ships come there all the time. Nothing unusual, he claims."

A scowl settled across Jerrid's face. "I would think Urindi would know the difference between a Mir merchantman and a warship."

"You would think." Gerrius grinned. "I'm sure his underlings back in the Sazaadar Range keep him apprised of the situation. Vosonna and

Ullisso, from my understanding, have strong sentiments toward the Separatists."

"That's not good."

"There has been an increase of Mir traffic into Vosonna within the last few months. Mostly merchantmen and cruise ships, but this is the first encounter of actual Mir warships crossing over."

"Are the Mirs posturing for an attack?"

"Fleet is dispatching three heavy cruisers as we speak." Gerrius paused and leaned forward. "Urindi wasn't too pleased with the action, but Admiral Monté isn't taking any chances." He took another sip from his glass. "Take a look at the fifth clip."

Jerrid scrolled through the first screen and then switched screens to display all the visuals. His eyes opened wide and he glanced up at Gerrus. Keying in the image, he increased the size on the screen. "That's the *Vara Gray*!"

A half smile peaked out from under Gerrius' mustache. "Yes! Came into port less than eight hours after the Mir cruisers left. My informant was able to get on board and get a copy of the nav-log. It was outbound to Va'Arta Kubi."

"The *Vara Gray* was the last supply ship to disappear on its way to Geasbok."Jerrid studied the image again. "I was under the impression that all of our missing ships were headed to Vi'Kiin. Isn't Va'Arta Kubi deep inside the Miranrian Federation?"

"The nav-log indicated the *Vara Gray* has become a rather useful tool of late. No less than twelve trips into Mir space since she disappeared on her way to Geasbok." Gerrius took another sip from his drink. "The ship last visited Erla Prime to pick up a special shipment."

Erla Prime? *Why would a missing ship show up there?* Jerrid leaned into the table. "Special shipment?"

Gerrius nodded. "Two hundred SAVs."

"Two hundred Small Assault Vehicles!" Jerrid nearly shouted. Glancing around he was relieved to find the bar was sparsely populated and there was little chance of his being overheard. The closest customer was at the bar on the far edge of the booth area and he seemed to be more consumed with the blonde next to him than eavesdropping on their conversation. "Where did they get authorization for two hundred SAVs?"

"Looks like Jubal Dros needs to do some checking on that matter. Ship's log shows manifests and clearances from DME's supply warehouse on Erla Prime." Gerrius eyed him carefully, gauging a reaction.

All Jerrid could do was sit there. He thought he had a handle on all of DME's maneuverings, but this bit of news meant there was someone working on the inside, funneling stuff toward the Miranrian Federation.

"I see what you mean," Jerrid finally said. "Looks like *Jubal Dros* needs to start checking out his people on Erla Prime."

Gerrius gave a slight grin. "It seems someone on Dros' payroll is neck deep in whatever's going on."

It was true that the military warehouse on Erla Prime was at the farthest edge of DME's vast network of complexes. As he carefully considered the far distant planet, he realized it would be the perfect place to divert weapons without raising suspicion.

"I'll see what I can find out!" Jerrid took another swallow from his drink.

"Make sure you find this mole." Gerrius eyed him. "This is either a dangerous person or someone making some easy money. Until you know for sure, I'd watch your back."

"I'll handle this as discretely as possible."

Gerrius finished his drink and then leaned across the table. "I think we'd better watch the Mirs, Jerrid. Someone may use this to get them involved in our conflict with the Solarians. And if the Mirs get involved, this war will drag on. Mark my words."

"I know, I know!" Jerrid just shook his head.

Gerrius Tuposh got up from the booth, adjusted his jacket, and glanced back at Jerrid. "Until our next meeting, Jerrid. Give my regards to Alleis."

"I will Gerrius, I will."

Jerrid watched his friend leave the bar.

Klea, he's your problem. Get rid of him, once and for all!

15

"It all began with a simple purchase of a rare book. And it would end with a blinding clash of forces beyond the Corporate Rim. To say this mysterious book was cursed would probably be an understatement. It ruined so many lives and nearly destroyed the structure of the TeMari Corporate itself." — Tosaar Julink, *The Vanishing Act*

"And darkness will descend and the light will fail because the hearts of men have turned to their own ways." — Second Kerius 3:4, *The Talbah Canon*

13 Midbre
University of Maggermoss

For Jerrid Flakkinbarr his own impending time table had afforded his quick pace across the massive university campus. The blustery breeze tugged at every seam of his steel gray raincoat, causing it to swirl crazily around him. Storm clouds had been gathering all morning and it had rained off and on most of that time. Puddles were still evident in many places along the sidewalk. To add to the hassle he'd worn his soft-soled shoes today. What a nuisance. Flakkinbarr dodged a small puddle and nearly collided with a group of young girls chattering like birds. For the most part, the students ignored him, probably viewing him as just another scholar trying to get to class on time.

The manicured lawns made a perfect square, stretching nearly a mycron and a quarter. Dead center in this spectacular vestment of flat green grass was an enormous fountain of spiraling water works that paid homage to a bronze statue of High Scribe Biffinan DeSorta, the university's founding father. All sidewalks converged at this point. Well tended flower gardens wrapped around the fountain and the statue in a clever display that hid benches and tables from view. Buggoum trees were planted in strategic points along the square to provide shade from the scorching sun. *Thank God it's fall!* The buggoums dense dark leafy green canopies were a stark contrast to the bright green lawns. Twelve ten-story glass fronted structures were symmetrically placed around the edge of the lawn. These housed the many classrooms and lecture halls. Just beyond the classrooms eight taller twenty-story buildings made up the administrative facilities and labs, thus finishing up the perimeter and completing this fortress of higher learning.

Fortress, Jerrid mused as a slight grin spread across his lips. *Fortress Maggermoss* had been the common slang among the students of his day. He wondered how many of today's students still cursed these grand halls of education?

While trams were busy shuttling students to their various classes, an equal number of the collegiate mobs chose to walk to their respective learning centers. The air was crisp and pulled at every fiber of the raincoat as Jerrid Flakkinbarr kept his determined pace. He had an important meeting with an old friend and he dared not be late.

The University of Maggermoss had certainly become a monster in size, Jerrid reflected as he gave an occasional glance at the students scurrying along. *They all look so young!* he said to himself as a pair of dark haired beauties caught his eye. They passed him going in the opposite direction. Flakkinbarr smiled. What he wouldn't give to be young again. He remembered back to his carefree years at the university; back then taking tests was his biggest concern. *If only life was still that simple*, he mused. If he remembered correctly, the university was now home to some one hundred and fifty thousand students from virtually every quadrant of the Corporate. The student population was just a little over half that number when he attended this same school some twenty-seven years prior. It seemed like a lifetime ago.

Jerrid eventually made his way to the south side of the campus and the dominant library building. The structure rose majestically for fifteen stories into the cloud laden sky. He paused, craning his head back to look up at the towering structure! It certainly was an impressive piece of work. The base of the building, nearly five blocks wide, was made up entirely of red stones, each weighing close to a thousand kefs and as wide as two grown men. The stones had been quarried from some mine deep in the Rossand Mountains nearly fifteen hundred mycrons to the south. How they transported these gigantic stones in those days still boggled most students minds. The architectural scholars would spend nearly one complete semester discussing the feat. The stone part of the structure went skyward ten stories, the remaining five stories were made up of dark tinted glass that reflected the gloomy clouds high above. An obvious addition since he'd been a student here. First time students were always overwhelmed by this monstrosity of a building.

A steady stream of students were coming and going from the twenty doorways on the south end of the building. Jerrid made a quick left turn before he got to the twentieth giant glass door and then followed the sidewalk along the base of the building until it disappeared under the thick canopy of evergreen trees. He paused and looked around as he continued on across another open lawn to a small stone structure on the back side of the library. The small two story building seemed lost on this campus of huge high rises. The Cathedral of St. Patrin of Abisba had been one of the original structures of the founding institution that would later become the University of Maggermoss. The cathedral and its several out parcels had eventually been swallowed up by the ever expanding university. They were quaint reminders of days gone by. Their primary functions had ceased to exist. The cathedral was now used as a chapel for several of the religious organizations on campus. Its age and architecture also served as object lessons for the engineering and architectural students. Classes and instructors were constantly milling about.

In its hayday the cathedral had functioned as the main library for the fledgling school. The monks who attended the cathedral had painstakingly kept the library fresh and up to date until the new library had been built. Then everything shifted from the cathedral to the new structure and thus the quaint building had lost its primary function on campus. Real paper and cloth bound books had given way to digitized readers, comlinks and computer crystals. However, St. Patrin still had a vault with several thousand volumes of rare books.

Flakkinbarr arrived at the back side of the cathedral. A stone wall one yarr high with an iron rail guarded the basement entrance to the cathedral's study area. Flower pots flanked either side of the stairway that descended to the underground garden court yard. A deep rich voice floated upward to greet him as it reverberated off the walls of the basement below. Jerrid couldn't help but smile as he recognized the tune, a peppy melody of a popular song when he was a student here. The song brought back a lot of memories. The voice that sang the song was as strong and passionate as he remembered it. Slowly, carefully, Jerrid Flakkinbarr descended the flight of stone steps, the song becoming clearer with each step downward.

The flight of stairs emptied into a large underground botanical garden roughly fifty by twenty yarrs in length. Leafy green plants in iron pots hung from chains along three sides of the closed courtyard at a height accessible for watering. Small trees and various other floral bushes crowded the center of the courtyard. Benches were positioned along the three sides. On the back wall of the garden a row of glass windows stretched the full length. On the other side of the glass a spacious study area with large tables could clearly be seen. A more careful look revealed rows and rows of old bound books sitting in their racks just beyond the tables.

A monk in a tweed colored robe was working in the garden, pruning a tree in the very middle. He lovingly snipped one leaf at a time, singing to the tree as if wooing a lover. The monk was roughly Jerrid's own height but weighed about ten kefs lighter. His hair was thick and dark and pulled back in a short ponytail, making the angular face and pencil thin mustache stand out. The song stopped as Jerrid's foot brushed against a pebble, sending it flying across the courtyard with a surprisingly loud *thud*. The monk looked up at the man in the gray raincoat and grinned from ear to ear.

"You still like that old song?" Jerrid smiled wickedly.

The monk replied with a sheepish grin, embarrassed he'd been caught singing. "A marvelous day, wouldn't you say, Jerrid?"

Flakkinbarr pushed back the hood of his raincoat, smiling at his friend's discomfort. "You know, I still remember most of the words to that song. If High Senior Barabee hears you singing that tune he'll require penance from you!"

"High Senior Barabee's almost deaf. I have to yell to get his attention these days." The monk continued to smile as he laid aside his pruning shears.

Jerrid eyed the shears. "So, what mischief gets you tending the study garden?"

The monk squinted his left eye. "Mischief, me?" He winked at his friend. "Decided to take the day off from lecturing. Monk Larzon needed a day off as well so I agreed to do a little gardening. Refreshing to the soul you know. I see you're as punctual as ever." He laughed light-heartedly as he shook Jerrid's hand. The monk had a strong grip despite his aging appearance.

"Vennie Suun, you know me too well, my old friend."

"I remember our university days, Jerrid," Vennie shot back with a mischievous gleam in his dark brown eyes. "*All too well.*"

Flakkinbarr laughed. "And how many times were you late for class?"

"It was my 'Flakkinbarr' alarm that made me the punctual *barla* I am today," the monk snickered. "I always wondered how you did it, Jerrid. Waking up precisely one hour before class was to begin, despite staying up until the wee hours of the night."

"I don't know myself, Vennie." Jerrid just shook his head. "Must be in my genes."

"Or you swallowed a chrono when you were a baby! One with an alarm set for zero six hundred hours." Vennie shot him a mock look of disgust.

Jerrid laughed.

"How's Alleis?" The monk asked, concern in his eyes..

"She's doing extremely well."

"Is she still experiencing nightmares from her near death experience a few months back?"

Jerrid sighed. "No, I think she is passed that now. She sends her love and wonders when you would be able to come by for dinner again?"

"I have a few more lectures to give before the semester break. Maybe before Festival Time."

"We'd definitely love to have you come by this season if there is any way you can make it," Jerrid nodded. "Zoe has several new recipes you might like. A couple of new ways to fix steak, my friend." He touched his fingers to his lips and smacked them. "You have definitely got to try these, Vennie. The steaks will melt in your mouth."

If there was one thing the monk had a craving for, it was a good steak. Good, juicy, succulent steaks were hard to come by here at the cathedral. Senior Monk Larzon was a gifted grounds keeper, but a marginal chef at best. The Flakkinbarr's chef, Zoe, was a rare find and he relished one of her meals. "Better than the last time I was there?" Was it possible that this culinary genius that the Flakkinbarrs employed had found a better way to prepare a steak dinner?

Jerrid knew his friend, Senior Scribe Vensant Suun, could be moved to visit with the promise of a steak dinner. Zoe went out of her way to prepare steak dishes for Vennie when he came to visit. The monk would always rave on and on about her meals and was always up to trying something new or different, as long as it had steak in it. "Then you have no excuse for not coming over," he laughed.

"I will definitely check my calendar and see what I can do, Jerrid." Vennie's mouth was watering already. He motioned toward a door near the windows. "Please, I have a place all set up for us."

The heavy metal door moaned as the monk pulled it open for his friend and then followed him inside to the high vaulted reading room.

Jerrid looked around, soaking up the old familiar sights of the huge room. The smell of bound leather was hard to ignore. Though it was basement level the room still boasted an enormous vaulted ceiling with giant fifty yarr timber beams. The room was a massive seventy yarrs wide. The steady glow of the more up to date digital readers illuminated the dark corners. "Vennie, you always did like these little secluded reading areas," Jerrid replied as he removed his raincoat and placed it on the back of the chair closest to the door.

"This was always our favorite place to get way from those brains upstairs in their glass towers," Vennie laughed. "There have been a few changes since you last set foot in here, but it's still the same secluded oasis we always liked. Most of the students these days study over at the new library or at the Dean's Center."

A quick glance around instantly reminded Jerrid of the many hours he and his dorm-mate, Vennie Suun, had spent studying here. They had discussed everything from current class assignments to politics, the state of motherworld as a whole, and of course, women. Vennie had been a shy one around the opposite sex but still had managed to become close friends with several of the female students in some of his classes. As a rule, though, Vennie's relationships would eventually fall apart, thus resulting in late night counseling sessions over kaufee in this very same secluded study area. Jerrid gave a sideways glance toward his friend as an image of a redheaded woman flashed across his memory. *Irwyn*, Jerrid almost spoke her name, but refrained. She had been Vennie's only true love. A twinge of sadness rushed in as Irwyn's image faded. Irwyn had perished in a terrible monorail accident on her way home for winter break. It had taken Vennie a long time to get over it. After the accident there didn't seem to be room for another woman in Vennie's heart, no matter how hard Jerrid tried to pry him from the past. That had been the long dark night of the soul for Vennie. He had walked through it with him and their friendship had been woven into a tight cord. That was before Jerrid had been introduced to Alleis Troffi. When Alleis came into his life, everything changed. She was Vennie's first cousin and he had introduced them when she enrolled at the university. Vennie had been rather pleased that the new relationship between his cousin and dorm-mate had turned out the way it had, marriage. Vennie was proud of them both. The new arrangement made his best friend, Jerrid, family. A fitting place in his eyes.

"This place still has that same quietness about it," Jerrid reflected.

"The academic dean added those digital readers about two years ago, hoping to entice more students to study here. That's about the only change in nearly twenty years," Vennie replied as he looked at the new racks of digital readers. "They just don't have quite the same feel as those old volumes over there." He pointed at the racks of bound leather books.

"No, I can't say that they do." Flakkinbarr nodded in agreement. "Tell me, how's your brother doing?"

The monk smiled warmly. "Oh, he's doing exceptionally well. You know that he is now assistant head of bio-implants at Bethleea's Medical Academy."

"Assistant head of bio-implants!" Jerrid looked surprised.

"Right now he's in Jyhan Trodda doing some research at Mercy Point Medical."

"Must be some serious stuff, I take it?"

Vennie laughed. "He likes research. Charts, diagrams, and gizmos are like new toys to him. The last time I talked to him he was ranting about that prodigy son of Pall Rorker."

Jerrid eyed his friend. "Seems like I remember hearing something about that."

"If you go anywhere near Bethleea's medical academy these days, you're going to hear the buzz about this new kid." Vennie laughed. "Can you imagine a twelve year old medical student that is so gifted that some of the best surgeons right here on motherworld are squirming? Prodigies like him don't come along very often. This kid has quite a few people talking. I've even heard talk that President Au'Zannin is trying to persuade Pall Rorker to pull up stakes on Bethleea and move to motherworld. It would be a feather in the president's cap to get the best surgeon in the quadrant to take up practice right here at our own medical school. Rumor also has it Au'Zannin's got the Board of Governors on his side to help finance any deal offered to Rorker. And we're talking high ruuls here, Jerrid."

"I've had the pleasure of meeting Pall and Ilaya Rorker on several occasions." Jerrid paused and smiled at his friend. "The conversation was a little over my head at times, but they were really down to earth type of people. They're a nice couple. From what I've heard, Pall Rorker is very contented to stay on Bethleea. I received an invitation to a party at their elaborate mansion on the western slopes of the Mossaid Mountains. Unfortunately I had to miss it. I understand their home is quite the showcase."

"Pall Rorker is, without question, the best surgeon in the quadrant, and his skills have made him extremely rich. Probably not as rich as the Hunneens of Bethleea, but well compensated nevertheless," Vennie added. "My brother seems to think his son is very promising."

"A youngster with talent like that should be an asset to the Corporate in due season," Jerrid replied.

"Hey, I've got a surprise for you!" Vennie turned to a service tray next to the table and pulled out two cups from a red container and placed them on the table. Next he pulled out a large tumbler with a slim handle on one side.

Jerrid looked at it for a long moment. A mental flashback to a similar container nearly twenty five years ago. *Could it be?* Jerrid asked himself, his taste buds suddenly salivating.

"I had Quartermaster Muldoon get us some special brew. Just like old times, huh?" Vennie proceeded to pour the contents of the tumbler into the two cups. A trickle of steam rose and an all too familiar and nearly forgotten sweet aroma filled the study area. "Yasemi tea, my friend. I placed the order last week right after you called. Came in late yesterday."

The Yasemi tea aroma was definitely as intoxicating as he remembered. Flakkinbarr's face lit up as he breathed in deep, savoring the smell. "Thank you, Vennie." Jerrid looked at the cups, his mouth watering. The sudden images of the many clandestine operations into the school's cafeteria to abscond with the favorite beverage mixture ignited Flakkinbarr's mind like a vid-drama. As a rule, not many of the students would go out of their way to pilfer the exotic tea. Most of the student population preferred a more potent beverage. Yasemi tea was one vice he and his good friend Vennie had shared throughout their four years at the university. "Must have cost you a small fortune."

A smile was his only reply. The monk motioned to the chair. "Please sit down, sit down!" Jerrid did as instructed. "And as far as the tea goes, I still have a source on Yasemi that can smuggle me out the brew every now and again."

Jerrid perked up at this. "Do tell!"

"With the way the war's going, Yasemi will probably fall to the Solarians before winter. Then I'll have to find another vice." Vennie took up his cup and savored a sip. "I can't imagine not being able to get my hands on this tea, but that's why I've got my own stash set aside. I just won't be able to have it as often as I like."

Jerrid Flakkinbarr also savored his tea and smiled. There was nothing to compare to the smooth taste of Yasemi tea. It was as good as he remembered. Why he'd forgotten about this tea was beyond him. It brought back such vivid memories. "This is indeed wonderful, Vennie, just wonderful."

"I knew you'd be pleased, Jerrid." Vennie grinned as he savored another sip. "I could have a shipment sent to your place before winter. In fact I could order some tomorrow."

"That would be great," Jerrid nodded approvingly. "Thank you so much."

After several minutes of just sitting and savoring the beverage and memories that came with it, Jerrid put his cup down and stared at his friend. "You still lecture in those?" Jerrid grinned mischievously.

Vennie glanced down at his robe and then smiled back at his friend. "This is actually my work frock. I have a dark brown one I wear for lecturing."

Flakkinbarr laughed.

"President Au'Zannin made certain concessions to keep me, you know." Vennie winked. "One of those concessions was that I could wear whatever I chose. The students for the most part think it's rather *rustic*, to say the least."

Jerrid laughed again and nodded. Au'Zannin would definitely do whatever it took to keep his best and brightest historian on campus, despite his call to the faith.

Vennie grinned and continued sipping his tea. "So tell me, Jerrid, in the world of the Tribunal, how are we faring?"

A frown slipped across Jerrid Flakkinbarr's face. "Besides passing volumes of legislation with mundane contents, the life of a tribune and the Tribunal are actually becoming quite interesting. And not for the good, mind you."

"I take it you're referring to the Director's speech last Velday about the threat within our borders."

How could he forget? Director Dameon Klea had raised several issues in regards to possible threats by enemy agents, albeit spies, operating deep within the borders of the Corporate. Even a possible threat on motherworld was highly probable. After all, the war with the Solarian Federation was moving deeper and deeper into the Far Rim Quadrants. And then there were the crazed Separatists. Zealot terrorist groups were popping up all along the border systems and their agenda was to throw off the governing reins of TeMari authority out in the Far Rim. It had been rumored that even the Solarians were using these hate groups to improve their positions along the War Zone. Jullien had felt their sting already. Jerrid paused, holding his cup. "I fear this war will last a very, very long time, Vennie. Especially if the Separatists get their way."

"But Director Klea seems to be rallying support and resources to see that we win, Jerrid."

Jerrid frowned. "I fear some of that support may be slipping away, especially from those tribunes who represent the quadrants nearest the War Zone. The Separatists, the Atheran-Hoth Alliance, is getting stronger support in the Tribunal every day that this war drags on. A third of the Akardiean Range has committed itself to the Separatist Movement."

"The Akardieans always seem to follow radicals." Vennie threw back.

"Don't forget, the Atheran-Hoth Alliance stands between motherworld and the Solarian push into the Far Rim. If they decided to throw in with the Solarians, it could be disastrous for us." Jerrid paused to sip his tea. He looked sternly at his friend. "I think it is going to take a lot more resources to win this war than have been committed so far."

"Things have certainly changed since Dameon Klea became Director."

Jerrid offered a weak smile. "The government was in gridlock and we felt a change of leadership was the only way to move forward. Initially, I was in favor of Dameon Klea becoming Director of the Corporate. Things under Chairman Aldolf were stagnating. He was the primary reason that the Atheran Federate chose to separate themselves from the Corporate. It's a shame it took a war to see those changes come to pass."

The monk nodded in agreement. "I think Aldolf had good intentions, and it wasn't all his fault that improvements weren't being made." Vennie eyed his friend, knowing all too well the rumors of abusive power and mishandling of funds by more than a few members of the Tribunal.

Jerrid sighed, "At the time, good intentions weren't meeting the people's needs." He hadn't really wanted to oppose Aldolf, but in the end the Tribunal felt the only way to bring about reform was through drastic measures and that meant replacing Aldolf and restructuring the government. The majority of power still rested with the Tribunal, but a new figurehead was needed who was charismatic enough to get people's attention, and convincing enough to get them to embrace new ideals. Despite his turbulent years in office, the people had elected Densin Aldolf to fill the newly created office of Vice Director. *The people were fickle*, Flakkinbarr mused, *and still are.*

"The people certainly wanted change."

Jerrid paused and eased back in his chair. "The Tribunal was looking for a person without any formal ties to government bureaucracy, and they also wanted a visionary who would lead our people into the future."

"Someone with a broader background who could understand the needs of the people." The monk smiled. "For some, scientists and overseers were the most logical candidates."

"Even the trillionaire, Cirin Hunneen, was mentioned as a possible candidate," Jerrid pointed out. "But he would have none of it. He avoided any contact with the media and emphatically turned down the selection committee chairman."

Vennie sighed. "It's a pity. I think Hunneen would have done well as Director."

"A very genuine person." Jerrid nodded. "A remarkable man with incredible knowledge." He paused and took a long sip from his tea cup. "It was Tribune Jadd Othion who made it a special point to have the selection committee nominate Dameon Klea. A half dozen other tribunes made the request as well, but it was Jadd Othion who spearheaded the request." Jerrid paused, thinking about Othion. *Could he be a clone as well, even then?* Searching the faces in his mind, he did not recall seeing Othion's among those on Traylencoor.

"Besides being a renowned scientist, Klea's a first rate charmer." Vennie smiled weakly. "A man gifted with words and the ability to sway people over to his point of view. Still, a man who saved your own nation from certain starvation."

How could Jerrid ever forget that? That miracle alone had impacted him. He paused, as he remembered the severe drought that had plagued his nation of Aalinra for nearly five decades. Hundreds of thousands had died. Crops withered and turned to dust. The Tribunal had sent relief aid, but it wasn't enough. The people and land needed a miracle. And that's when Dameon Klea became the savior of the people of Aalinra. From an obscure role as a research scientist on the far world of Eeris Zai in the Sazaadar Range, he'd heard about the plight of motherworld's suffering. Dameon Klea came to Aalinra with a simple method of agricultural reform, bio-engineered grains. With his bio-engineered grains, Dameon Klea had turned Aalinra from a barren desert into a thriving ecosystem. And it had only taken three years. The people of Aalinra could not say enough good things about this man, their savior, Dameon Klea. He was encouraged to stay on, to help other impoverished areas on motherworld. Flakkinbarr sighed deeply. Yet despite all the miracles, there was something about this man that had bothered him from the very beginning.

Remember, Klea is your problem. His elimination is paramount!

Jerrid froze at the thought that just raced through his mind. He glanced around, but Piin was not lurking in the shadows of the room. *Strange*, Jerrid mused. He desperately wanted to find some good in the man. Yet any thoughts about Dameon Klea were now shrouded in shifting shadows. "Klea's a genius when it comes to bio-engineering. I will give him that."

The monk sensed a foreboding in his friend's tone. "I take it you've changed your mind about our Director?"

Changed my mind! Jerrid simply stared at his friend. *I'm financing his assassination.* Again he cast a glance around the room. "It's not just the Director that troubles me. I'm deeply concerned by this priest Klea has trailing behind him." *Everyone seems to have a Shuuto hanging around them these days*, he mused, as a mental image of Piin popped into his mind. *And they bring nothing but trouble!*

Vennie's eyebrows shot up. "Oh, and why is that?"

"Let's just say that I have an uneasy sense about this shade of a person." Jerrid replied. "I have spoken to several other of my colleagues who feel the same way and who do not like being near this priest especially when he's with the Director."

Vennie gave a half smile. "The Shuuto has been the topic of discussion among some of us here at the university. We've had some pretty lively discussions." The monk took a slow sip from his cup. "The Shuuto are a mysterious bunch from beyond the Great Void. Little, if anything, is known about them. Senior Monk Arvan is deeply concerned that this Shuuto is the Director's confidant. He also thinks that this Shuuto might be exerting some type of influence over Klea, especially when it comes to policy making. Do you think that could be true, Jerrid?"

I wonder if Klea's Shuuto knows Piin? The thought came in out of the blue like a bolt of lightning. *If so, does Piin know Klea?* Perhaps there was more to Klea's relationship with his Shuuto than previously speculated. Who was really running things here? Jerrid eyed the monk. "Senior Monk Arvan may be right, Vennie. Klea's Shuuto may very well be influencing policies." He paused and leaned across the table. "I sense there's a dark side to Dameon Klea that he keeps hidden from the general public, and that troubles me more and more these days."

"*And the serpent will come to smite the chosen.*" Vennie stated flatly. "Third Devian, chapter five, verse sixteen."

Jerrid smiled to himself. Vensant Suun's conversion to the Yushannan faith, a few years after graduate school, had certainly surprised him. For several years, Vennie's former associates had castigated his friend until they realized he was unwavering in his beliefs. It had been Vennie's quiet and unbending ways that had touched both him and Alleis. It seemed to have made him a stronger individual and had sharpened his skills and insight as a historian. Vennie was good with history. So good, in fact, that President Au'Zannin nearly wept when Vennie announced his resignation at the university to pursue his call to the faith. Au'Zannin called a special meeting of the Board of Governors and discussed at length how to keep their prized historian on campus. Finally, a deal was worked out with High Senior Scribe Shanard of the regional episcopacy to keep Vensant Suun on as high scribe of the school and director of historical studies as well. Vennie saw it as the hand of divine Providence at work in allowing him to pursue his call and to keep working at one of the things he knew best, and loved most, history.

"And who do you think is this serpent?" Jerrid asked. He'd already made his mind up as to the identity of this present day snake.

"The hand of darkness has had many such serpents over the centuries my friend." Vennie replied. "It's just that we are now in another dark period. Another dark millennium, if you will."

"Dark times, indeed, my friend." Flakkinbarr remarked dryly. "I fear we are fighting more than one enemy at this moment in time."

"Besides the Solarians and the Separatists?" Vennie raised an eyebrow at this.

"The Miranrians could enter this conflict at anytime and protract this war."

"I realize the Miranrians have been posturing at our borders over the last several months. It's kind of hard to ignore them at this point in time."

Jerrid took a sip from his cup. "Not only do we have the Separatists and Solarians to deal with at the Corporate Rim, but Klea's Political Ministry is gaining a lot more power than they had a year ago. I'm afraid the Tribunal is blindly allowing this to happen."

"Blindly?" Vennie questioned.

Jerrid nodded. "Laws are continually being legislated that strengthen the hands and arms of the Political Ministry beyond any law enforcement group ever assembled on motherworld or the Corporate as a whole."

"Doesn't this concern your colleagues in the Tribunal?" Vennie threw back.

"My close colleagues, yes. But Klea is a powerful orator and he has certainly swayed several hundred tribunes over to his way of thinking. The swaying is almost hypnotic."

"He may be swaying more than just tribunes, Jerrid!" Vennie pointed out. "Most of the populace virtually sees him as a saint. His miraculous transformation of Aalinra has had a lasting impact on the masses."

Jerrid smiled weakly. "How well I know, my friend, how well I know."

"Certain scribes are reportedly agreeing with his claims and goals, and admonishing him for his good deeds. Even High Senior Scribe Shanard seems to think that the Hand of Providence is upon him."

Jerrid just shook his head. He knew, all too well, that some of the most outspoken of motherworld's religious orders were buying into the Director's rhetoric. "I've also heard the same thing, my friend. I think we've all been duped."

"What about this special police group I've been hearing so much about?" The monk stared at his friend. "From what I understand these SPG are basically under the Political Ministry's authority and they are definitely military oriented."

"They're the muscle and the teeth behind the Political Ministry. Don't ever forget that."

"I certainly won't." Vennie nodded in agreement. "As head of motherworld's Political Ministry, Vice Marshal Kerkenkoff is also acquiring a lot more power."

Flakkinbarr had met the man only once, but he understood the drive for power. The vice marshal certainly exhibited all the traits. "Kerkenkoff is extremely ambitious. I look for him to be promoted to archmarshal before too long. When he does he'll have total control over the entire quadrant - that is, if the Director allows it. We'll have to be leery of the Political Ministry and the SPG from this point on. I think we could find ourselves in a police state one day." Flakkinbarr felt a knot tighten in the pit of his stomach.

"The Tribunal will certainly not allow that to happen!" Vennie looked alarmed.

"No my friend. The present Tribunal would never allow such a thing to happen. Keep in mind, though, every six years tribunes can be changed. And loyalty can be redefined." Flakkinbarr stared at his friend. *How many more clones is Klea putting into place in the Tribunal?* Re-election may not be the concern here.

Vennie just nodded; he knew, all too well, the truth of the matter.

Jerrid paused and cleared his throat. "I take it you've finished your tests?"

After a long sip Vennie paused, setting the cup down slowly. He took a packet from under a comlink laying at the edge of the table and pushed it toward his friend. "You mind telling me where you found that?" He indicated the packet with his eyes. It was obvious that he'd been disturbed by the contents.

Pulling the packet to his side, Jerrid slowly opened it and looked inside. The single page of yellowed paper was still placed where he'd put it four months ago as well as what appeared to be another piece of white paper with writing on it. He looked up at his friend, but didn't smile. "I really didn't want to drag you into all this Vennie, but you were the only one I could trust to verify its authenticity. The only one! I'm sorry!"

Vennie locked his eyes on his friend. "Jerrid, you don't need to apologize. I understand. We've been friends too long."

"If this gets out, Vennie, both of our lives could be in danger." The look on Jerrid Flakkinbarr's face said it all. Vennie knew he was right.

"Where did you get it, Jerrid?"

Jerrid refrained from speaking. He sipped his tea as he gazed intently at his friend. For a long time he said nothing. The silence became uncomfortable as Jerrid pondered just how much he should tell Vennie. He smiled weakly. "I went out to Jeezli sometime last year to hammer out a border dispute with the tribunes from the Jayffaa and Handan Ranges. You remember that border dispute?"

The monk nodded. "Almost started a civil war."

"Almost! I think the Separatists were behind all that trouble. They were just looking for another alliance to strengthen their hand." Jerrid sighed. "Have you seen Basak Kuur on Jeezli?"

The monk chuckled. "Basak Kuur is a little off the lecture circuit for me, Jerrid. But I hear it's a trader's paradise."

"It's a marvelous city my friend; you should go there one day." Jerrid smiled brightly. "A thousand open air markets teeming with more stuff to buy than you could shake a light wand at."

"I think there are a few Jeezli trinkets laying around this place somewhere." Vennie laughed.

Flakkinbarr nodded. "I wouldn't be surprised."

A big grin slipped across Vennie's face.

"Anyway, I had some free time and went out to investigate a few of these markets. I wanted to pick up something for Alleis. You know how she likes antiques. This one particular antique dealer not only had some great antiques, but he had a few rare books as well. Several caught my eye so I bought them. You know me and books." Jerrid forced a smile then went on, "It wasn't until I returned home and started reading them that I realized what I had purchased." Jerrid reached for his tea cup. He took a long sip. "So, what did your tests prove?"

"Come with me!"

Without saying a word, Jerrid pocketed the packet and got to his feet, following his friend down a long row of books. They passed a long table with stacks of digital readers and a few volumes of bound books. A comlink was lit and several note links were scattered around a chart display of the Jeulonza Range. A chair and an empty cup were situated against one side.

"I've got to get back to my research this afternoon." Vennie shook his head as they passed the desk. "Been doing a little study into the Hunneen fortune."

"Find any secret formulas to make you rich?" Jerrid laughed as he eyed the clutter.

The monk also laughed. "If there is a secret formula for getting rich, then Cirin Hunneen certainly is hiding it well. Did you know that the Hunneen's first came to Bethleea in Forty-six fifty-eight?"

"No!" Jerrid replied as he glanced over at the stacks of books.

"Oh yes! Forty-six fifty-eight was when construction on that fancy estate of theirs began. An impressive piece of architecture that the engineering department has never been allowed to visit. Though Scholar Tanyanan and Vistokodd have pestered Hunneen for years for a tour of the estate. Cirin Hunneen keeps it off limits from prying scholastic eyes." The monk smiled. "Did you know that they came from Phystaccar?"

Jerrid raised an eyebrow at this. "Phystaccar?"

"Quite strange for a Hunneen to come from there, but it's just another one of those odd genealogical facts that happen from time to time. The Hunneens have a pretty tangled history that's rather complex."

"How so?"

"Mind you, I've just done a little digging here and it's by no means conclusive to how Cirin Hunneen or his ancestors came into ownership of so much land and wealth on Bethleea. According to settlement deeds, the Hunneens came to Bethleea with several Phystaccarn servants in Forty-six fifty-eight. Straight from Phystaccar. All executive powers were given to a Phystaccarn servant by the name of Cre. The Hunneens didn't take center stage for anything and all dealings were left up to their Phystaccarn servant."

Kind of what Cirin Hunneen has been doing for some time now with his own Phystaccarn servant, Jerrid mused. *Like grandfather like grandson I suppose.*

"I understand that Scholar Jaskic Flaskrs is preparing to include the Hunneen's conglomerate successes in his new book. Should be an interesting piece to read if he can dig deeper than most folks. Hope it isn't as boring as his lectures. Thankfully he's retiring this year."

Jerrid laughed. He, too, remembered sitting through economics under Flaskrs. The man was not a gifted orator. On the contrary, his dry monotone delivery of facts put the whole class to sleep on more than one occasion.

Finally they came to the end of the row and turned left toward the vault area. Stepping through the giant steel entrance, more ancient bound books were displayed in a hundred stainless steel racks reaching to the ceiling. A table was set up midway in an open reading area with four wooden chairs. Vennie stopped at one rack, reached up and pulled down a massive volume bound in red leather.

"You need to see this." Vennie placed the book on the table, pointing a finger at it. "This is supposed to be the original signed copy of *The Chronicles of DaKelif.* It was written in the year Forty fifty-five ADK. The author of the book is De'Zander Marrs."

"De'Zander Marrs?" Jerrid gasped. "Are you sure?"

Vennie flipped the book open to the front. Across the title page in gilded script lettering were the words, *The Chronicles of DaKelif,* under that *by De'Zander Marrs.* Just below the printed name was penned the actual name of the author and an inscription, *"To my good friend Zorif, best wishes De'Zander Marrs,"* a date of Forty fifty-five ADK was also inscribed beneath that.

"Who is this Zorif?" Jerrid looked at his friend.

"That we don't know." Vennie shrugged his shoulders. "Could be any number of people during that time. A list of several hundred Zorif surnames are mentioned in other DaKelif histories. It would be hard to find the right link."

Jerrid just shook his head.

"There are electronic editions of this printed one in the main library." Vennie tapped the book with his finger. "This book is actually from the Kelperian Historical Archives. It was loaned to our cathedral library a little over a hundred years ago and was never returned. Got misplaced in the pile of books that were sealed in this vault by the former scribe of the library. Rumors have it that Senior High Scribe Gogaan was quite nearsighted by the time he retired; as a result, a great number of books were misplaced or mis-cataloged. But I see it as the Hand of Providence, my friend."

"Providence?" Jerrid looked at the monk. "But De'Zander Marrs was the *Butcher of Kelivic*. He was a terrible monster!"

The monk exhaled and nodded in agreement. "The worst kind of monster imaginable. A hundred volumes have been written about him and his atrocities since that time. But the plot thickens, my friend."

Vennie forced a weak smile and then disappeared behind another rack of books to the right. A few minutes later he returned with two more volumes. These were about half the size of the thick red one. He placed one of the volumes on top of the red book. Imprinted on the cover in another similar flowing script was, *Zilssion Sage Records*. Beneath that was inscribed, *prepared by Sage Da'min Ben'Lea*. Vennie then placed the last book next to the others. The title of this book was, *Dommar Konna Chronicles, Volume One*.

"Shall we discuss my findings?" Vennie pulled up his chair and leaned over the books. "I have two more volumes of the *Dommar Konna Chronicles*. All signed editions by the author. Everyone of these books came from the Kelperian Historical Archives about the same time as *The Chronicles of DaKelif*. Providence, my friend, has had a hand in all of this, no doubt about it."

"For what purpose?" Jerrid asked, almost too terrified to think of all the implications. But he'd been formulating his own ideas as to what he had purchased and the links it had to other incriminating evidence of evil deeds.

"Jerrid, you have stumbled, quite by accident, on a terrible secret. A secret that has been hidden for nearly a thousand years." Vennie was very pointed in his statement. "What you possess has ties that will no doubt unravel our present government and unmask a hideous evil in our midst. It has to be the Hand of Providence, Jerrid. It has to!"

"That's what I'm afraid of, my friend." Flakkinbarr just shook his head. "And I fear it has ties to some rumors floating out of Geasbok." He dared not mention Traylencoor, not just yet anyway.

Vennie raised an eyebrow at this.

Jerrid waved his hand. "I'll be looking into that soon enough!" He pulled the packet from his pocket and placed it on the table. "You were my only hope of identifying the real author of the book I purchased. Unfortunately, it appears that I've gucssed correctly."

The monk exhaled with a heavy sigh. "Jerrid, my tests were very conclusive. You have a match." He indicated all the books on the table. "The author of these books and your mysterious book are one and the same."

For a long moment, Jerrid Flakkinbarr just sat there. "How can this be?"

"I would like to know that myself," Vennie replied. When his friend made no reply he continued, "I even sealed myself in Scholar Penatoff's lab for two days to compare your samples with these books. He has the finest microscopes of any of the universities in the quadrant. I was very shocked when each sample from the different books matched. Jerrid, I don't want to know how you got that sample from the Director's own hand, but it is the linchpin in all my testing. I think we have big trouble here. If Director Klea finds out about this, there could be some serious repercussions ahead for all of us."

It was now an established fact that he had hard evidence to the true identity of the present ruler of the TeMari Corporate. An identity that was shrouded in mystery and murder. Unspeakable murder! Flakkinbarr looked at the packet and then up to his friend. "What am I to do, Vennie? What am I to do?"

"Pray!" Vennie replied. "And pray that you're not discovered."

Jerrid fumbled with the packet, wishing he'd brought his cup of tea with him. He pulled one of the books to his side and opened it. "Please, let's go over your findings."

Vennie nodded. "Okay, Jerrid. I'll give you the details and then you can decide what to do. I'll not say a word about this to anyone."

Jerrid Flakkinbarr looked at his long time friend and former college dorm-mate. "You must never reveal all of this to anyone, Vennie, and I mean anyone, what I have found and what you've learned from your tests. We are living in dangerous times and I fear the danger will grow."

"*And darkness will descend and the light will fail because the hearts of men have turned to their own ways.*" Vennie whispered.

"Their own ways!" Jerrid repeated. "Let us pray for hope, Vennie."

"There is always hope, Jerrid." the monk replied. "Always hope!"

Always hope! Funny, he'd said the same thing to Zappora. Yes, Lt. Arie'el had miraculously appeared and rescued them from that bitter cold summit. But would Arie'el be able to deliver the whole Corporate from the dangerous man that was now at its helm?

Klea is your problem! His elimination is paramount!

Jerrid shook his head as the thought whispered again in his mind. *Klea must be eliminated! Once and for all!*

For the next two hours, Jerrid Flakkinbarr and Vennie Suun discussed in great length all the tests he had done. Several other Zilssion historical records were consulted as well as other references to the *Butcher of Kelivic.*

* * *

Jerrid stood at the study door. He patted the packet in his raincoat and pushed the metal door open. He turned to his friend. "This is a heavy burden, Vennie. Please pray that we do the right thing."

Vennie smiled weakly. "We will overcome, Jerrid. *'There is no dark abyss so deep, that he, the Almighty One, is not deeper still.'* Let that comfort you my friend. A great evil may be awakening, but it's not you or I who has aroused this monster. But we must be the voice of the gatekeepers shouting the danger lest the people sleep and allow this evil to swallow them alive."

Sighing heavily, Jerrid managed a grin. "With you tugging on Aidoini's heart, Vennie, I know we'll make it."

"Blessings, friend!" Vennie replied with a wink. "And I will definitely call about dinner. Tell Zoe to have some good steaks ready!"

Jerrid laughed. "That I will, Vennie! That I will!"

Vennie Suun watched as his friend ascended the stone steps to the top of the garden court yard. "Merciful Lord, help us all!"

16

"Geasbok is still a mystery to this day. There's a lot of speculation about how this whole mess got started in the first place." — Tribune Vis Trysk, Media One interview

"We can only speculate as to what deadly secrets remain hidden on that damnable planet. I fear more than a million souls vanished into the night for a wicked cause that will eventually devour the whole galaxy if it isn't stopped." — Scholar Minas B'Oarkee, *A View of Our Present State*

27 Fornlea
Jeulonza Range / TeMar Star System
Orbital Level 5
Planet: Geasbok

The bulky transport, *Crypt Phaeton*, was in long orbit over Geasbok. Trailing close behind was the small security cutter, *Snide*, maneuvering to stay within range without attracting attention.

Gerrius Tuposh had secured the security cutter from a repair facility on Vissa Vi and crewed it with twelve military droids from Hëlobstan Kesperroud's Armont Droid Facility. The droids' memories would automatically be erased once the mission was concluded. If at any time the mission was compromised for whatever reason, each droid was programmed to self destruct. Informants had said the *Crypt Phaeton* would be leaving Sarrsiin with eleven hundred political prisoners on board and headed for Geasbok. They had intercepted the transport at the refueling station around Potella Prin. Tuposh was a master at this cloak and dagger game. Flakkinbarr was astounded at the man's resourcefulness. Gerrius Tuposh was a remarkable tribune, but an even more remarkable man of covert operations.

"Isn't this a little risky, Gerrius?" the man seated in the copilot's seat said as he eyed the bright ion field of the transport's massive engines. Flakkinbarr knew he was in good hands, but it didn't make him any less nervous. Not only was this a dangerous maneuver, but, if anything went wrong, he knew he would be better off dead than captured alive.

Tuposh looked the part, dressed in a tailored Fleet Security captain's uniform. His crooked smile peeked out from under his stark white mustache. Bright blue eyes glimmered in the low light of the instrument panel. Wispy white eyebrows shot up from under his Fleet cap. Perhaps he'd gone a little far in the aging look. After all, Tuposh was only forty years of age. What magic Gerrius used to turn his wavy red hair to white still astounded him. But Tuposh was a master at disguises with all sort of tools at his disposal.

"Relax, Jerrid. I'll get us in without so much as a whisper from planetary defense."

Relax? How could he? Tuposh jockeyed the ship like it was a Farpac racer. Touching the fake black mustache affixed to his upper lip, Jerrid suddenly felt very conspicuous. Surely he'd be recognized. *You've done this a hundred times, just relax.* Still, getting passed planetary defenses in a commandeered ship was something he'd never done or been a part of until now.

Tuposh looked at the fidgeting tribune decked out in a smart looking First Lieutenant First Order of Fleet Security uniform. "Jerrid, relax, and just go with whatever I do. Fleet has ten security cutters patrolling this planet. I've manipulated the system where we're just another inbound cutter sent from Fleet HQ to fix a security problem. You wanted to see for yourself what's going on on Geasbok. This is the only way!"

Flakkinbarr looked at the back of his darkened hands and just shook his head. Tuposh was certainly a master of disguises. After all it had been Tuposh who had encouraged him to become Jubal Dros and find the true pulse of his constituents. He smiled to himself, it had certainly paid off big time in more ways than Tuposh had forseen.

"Something funny, Jerrid?" Tuposh asked as he glanced at the man in the co-pilot's seat.

"If only your constituents knew what you were *really* doing my friend." Jerrid smiled wickedly.

"What they don't know won't hurt them," Gerrius grinned back. "Besides, I love this kind of stuff. Keeps a man young!"

Jerrid laughed. The investigation into the missing ships had taken on a strange twist. Rumors of prisoners being moved from penal colonies to a super secret detention facility on Geasbok had been whispered to his associate, Tribune Frediana Lisstrin. She and Tribune Juyin Hallenn had snooped a little further. When their own investigation pointed to several memorandums from the Director's office, confirming the whispers, they brought it to Jerrid's attention. Another extensive investigation was launched by Gerrius Tuposh. Tracking down an inside informant, the whispers and rumors became horrifying tales of mass executions and blatant cold blooded murder by planetary security forces. The informant's information only raised more questions. Someone had to go in and find out exactly what was going on and why. Jerrid had volunteered to accompany Gerrius Tuposh into enemy territory. Neither Frediana or Juyin knew about Tuposh or Jerrid's alter egos and the current investigation required some compartmentalizing. This particular mission would provide the opportunity to find the replicant or clone factory Piin had mentioned.

"As soon as the transport lines up for final approach, we'll break off and make our approach on Compound Fourteen from a different set of coordinates. Compound Fourteen's expecting us, don't you know." Gerrius continued to eye the controls, skillfully maintaining the proper distance from the transport.

Jerrid continued to watch the bright engines of the transport. Tuposh had the security cutter's com-net linked to the inbound transport.

"*Crypt Phaeton* requesting final approach clearance." the voice over the net crackled to life.

"*Crypt Phaeton* this is Control Central!" a deep baritone voice called back. "You are cleared to Compound Fourteen for final. Come to Five-three. Marker Two."

"Roger that, Control!" the transport pilot replied.

Gerrius looked at his friend. "Here we go."

As soon as the heavy transport slid into the thick clouds of the upper atmosphere, Tuposh banked the cutter hard right and pitched the angle to a sharp incline. Before Flakkinbarr could react to the maneuver, the clouds parted and they were down over a ragged mountain range following the contour of the land like a speeding bird of prey. Suddenly Jerrid thought of Zappora and wondered where she might be at this time.

"That was easy!" Gerrius laughed. "Still have the touch, you know! Twelve Farpac crowns still tacked to the wall back home. I love a challenge like this one, Jerrid!"

Jerrid ignored him and continued to watch the rolling craggy mountains; his stomach was almost in his throat. *Zappora would probably give Gerrius a run for his money.* This thought brought a wicked grin to Jerrid's face.

For the better part of twenty minutes the cutter skimmed around jagged mountain peaks and through deep gorges. Finally, they jetted out across an enormous desolate plain. Red, gray and brown rocks littered the place from right to left as far as the eye could see. As they traveled low across the stark terrain, they could see the many fissures and black cracks that seemed to drop into nothingness. It was a barren wasteland for sure. On the horizon a large glimmer caught their eye. In a few seconds, three dazzling transparasteel domes filled the skyline. Geasbok's stark landscape was the perfect place for these mysterious penal colonies. Jerrid stared out of the cockpit. All he could think of was Traylencoor. Those memories were hard to shake.

"Next phase coming up!" Gerrius remarked, reaching for the com-net controls. He winked at Flakkinbarr. "Don't worry. I have this all worked out."

Jerrid swallowed and just nodded. His stomach was doing flip-flops.

"This is Security Cutter *Snide* to Compound Fourteen Controller!"

"Compound Fourteen Controller, go head, SC *Snide*."

"Requesting landing instructions."

"Go to Niner-two, Marker Niner for final." The voiced barked back. "You are cleared for Landing Pad Seven. Be aware there is a transport inbound to Pad Nine at one-eight-two."

Tuposh checked his instruments. "Got it, Controller. I'll watch for transport."

"Affirmative SC *Snide*. Approach Landing Pad Seven, Marker Niner is clear!"

"Roger that!"

As Tuposh maneuvered the cutter for landing, they could see the bulky transport making its final approach to Landing Pad Nine. "What a coincidence! We arrived at the same time." Gerrius winked at Flakkinbarr and brought the cutter in as easy as parking a car. He shut down the engines and swivelled around in his seat, grinning at Flakkinbarr.

"It is really too bad father talked me into becoming a tribune," Gerrius' toothy smile lit his face up. "I still love racing these machines over the desert at breakneck speed." Tuposh was an adrenaline junky and thrived on this type of clandestine operation.

"Breakneck is right!" Jerrid glared back.

"Now the fun begins."

Jerrid Flakkinbarr didn't say a word. What could he say? He just followed Tuposh to the airlock and waited while the droids prepared the ramp.

Gerrius turned to the first droid at the hatch. "Secure the ship and wait for departure on my orders. No one is to enter this ship. Understood?"

"Affirmative, sir!" the droid beeped back. "Understood."

Tuposh tapped him on the head and then turned to Flakkinbarr. "Just follow my lead. This should be just routine for them."

Jerrid took in a deep breath and nodded. "Okay, I guess I'm ready."

Pressure was equalized and the hatch opened. A gust of heavy dry air swirled in to greet them. Jerrid swallowed hard and followed Tuposh down the ramp. At the bottom an SPG agent and two prison guards waited. The SPG agent was a tall fellow slightly over two yarrs in stature with a look that could have been in a fashion magazine. He had sandy blond hair and deep green eyes set in a handsome, deeply tanned face.

Rank pins of First Lieutenant First Order flashed in the glare of Geasbok's harsh sun. One of the prison guards was a tall thin fellow in a dingy brown uniform. Greasy jet black hair peaked out in various places beneath his cap. The rank of sergeant was pinned to his shoulders. The remaining guard was short and stocky and muscular arms protested against the fabric of his uniform. Hair cropped very close to his scalp, the guard's cap sat cockeyed on his head.

"Lt. Jatarr. At your service, sirs!" The SPG agent snapped a smart salute. "This is Sergeant Botree and Corporal Deenens."

The guards threw back two sloppy salutes and grinned at each other.

Tuposh returned the salute and nodded toward the SPG agent. "Lieutenant. I am Captain Jez Tazzburr and this is my aide, Lt. Sondarr."

Tuposh and Lt. Jatarr locked eyes for the longest time. Flakkinbarr swallowed hard. Was it possible that the lieutenant had meet Tuposh somewhere before?

"Kind of old for Fleet Security, huh Lieutenant?" Sergeant Botree snickered. "Must be gettin' desperate."

"Sergeant!" Jatarr snapped. "Put a lid on it right now!"

"Yes, sir!" Botree continued to snicker as he eyed Tuposh up and down.

"I am here to escort you to Section Five for the security check, sir." Lt. Jatarr was all business. His two guards looked rather annoyed with the whole thing. The lieutenant carefully eyed Tuposh as if sizing up the validity of his rank. He'd dealt with Fleet Security officers before and this fellow, as Botree had pointed out, certainly seemed a tad old for a field ranking security officer. Most older security officer was fixtures at Fleet HQ as far as he knew. "May I see your orders, Captain?" He held out his hand expectantly.

Gerrius glanced over to Flakkinbarr and then pulled out a small comlink from his jacket pocket. He handed it calmly to the SPG agent.

Jatarr took considerable time to read the orders, eyeing Tuposh occasionally as he read. Botree and Deenens began to get antsy.

"Well?" Botree asked sarcastically.

Jatarr snapped the lid of the comlink shut and handed it back. "Everything's in order. All security links verified, Sergeant." Botree seemed disappointed by the news. The young lieutenant gave a cutting glance to the two guards. "HQ Black Diamond Three Clearance."

Both guards eyebrows shot up at this. Black Diamond Three was pretty high up. He must be really important. Both guards straightened their shoulders and became a little more serious looking, at least for the moment.

A groaning of cargo doors distracted any more conversation as they eyed the transport *Crypt Phaeton.* It began to off load it's human cargo at Landing Pad Nine just five hundred yarrs in the distance. A detachment of SPG guards stood in ranked order around the huge vessel, waiting. At the head of the column, a high ranking officer conversed with what appeared to be the transport ship's own security officers. Several hand signals were made and five of Geasbok's own SPG disappeared into the hold of the vessel. Lt. Jatarr nodded toward the commotion. "Commander Verrus has to see to the prisoner transfer and therefore could not meet you himself."

"Understood." Tuposh replied. "Must be an important prisoner transfer." Gerrius was fishing. Hopefully, Lt. Jatarr would take the bait.

"Prisoner transfer from Sarrsiin," Jatarr replied off handedly. "Mostly routine. We see about five or six transfers like this every week. But HQ has informed us they may be stepping things up a bit."

"Indeed." Tuposh shot Flakkinbarr a glance. They continued to watch as hundreds of men and women were brought out of the transport into the harsh glaring sun and ordered to form up in columns, six wide. After the last prisoner was in place, the transport security officer saluted to Commander Verrus and returned to his ship. Verrus ordered the prisoners to march back toward the compound. The prisoners rattled off in a slow gate toward their new home.

"A scraggly bunch!" Botree snarled in contempt. "This group looks like trouble. Five to one someone breaks before they get to the first gate."

"You're on!" Corporal Deenens threw back.

"Silence!" Jatarr ordered, annoyance flashed across his face.

Tuposh and Flakkinbarr just looked at each other.

They waited. Was something about to happen?

After some time Jatarr sighed, as if visibly relieved that the exchange has gone so well.

"Pay up!" Deenens stretched out his hand to Botree.

"Give 'em time!" Botree snarled. "Still got to get to the first gate."

Jatarr cleared his throat. "If you gentlemen will follow me, we'll get you started on fixing that security net."

"Lead the way, Lieutenant!" Tuposh replied.

"Right this way!" Jatarr turned, as if performing a formation exercise. The two guards tagged along at a sloppy distance.

"It is my understanding that the security networks may have some kinks." Jatarr tossed out, more of a question than a statement. He looked puzzled as he eyed Tuposh and Jerrid.

"Fleet wants Section Five re-evaluated, Lieutenant." Gerrius remarked as they walked along. "Section Five seems to be a weak link in the net. It needs to be re-calibrated." Tuposh had managed to hack into Fleet Security and dump a repair analyzation scan for Section Five. It had taken three days to get past all the lockouts and subroutines, but once he was in it was a piece of cake to write the repair evaluation orders and to schedule an inspection by a certain Fleet Security officer named Captain Tazzburr.

"We'll have to go through Section Six to get to Five, sir." Jatarr remarked, the frown becoming more pronounced on his face. "Section Six is the breeding tanks."

"Breeding tanks?" Flakkinbarr asked, eyeing Tuposh.

"Thousands of 'em!" Corporal Deenens smiled real big.

"Put a lid on it, Corporal!" Jatarr warned. "This way, gentlemen. It's a classified matter."

Before they could put one more foot in front of the other, shouts from the prisoners marching toward the compound permeated the dry desert air. A scurry of activity erupted as several prisoners bolted from the formation and began running at breakneck speed across the rocky ground towards Flakkinbarr and Tuposh. Flakkinbarr watched in stunned horror as several SPG guards calmly took kneeling positions, raised their blasters and then fired. The three fleeing prisoners, two males and one female, were hit by high energy bolts that ripped right through their bodies. Torn apart by the speeding energy, the body parts scattered across the rocky terrain.

Jatarr eyed the engagement with a frown and just shook his head.

"Three idiots this time!" Sergeant Botree smiled devilishly, stretching his hand out. "Looks like I win!"

"Fools! Stupid Fools!" Deenens snarled, fishing in his pants pocket. Grudgingly he palmed three silver bars to Botree who continued to gloat.

The two incognito tribunes just exchanged glances.

"Happens quite often." Deenens tossed out.

"Corporal Deenens, I don't think our guests here are really that concerned about these prisoners!" Lt. Jatarr warned. "They're here to re-evaluate our security links."

Deenens gave Jatarr a menacing look. "Yeah, whatever you say, Lieutenant?"

Lt. Jatarr cleared his throat and ignored the guards. "Please forgive the insubordination. They've been out here a long time." He eyed the guards menacingly. "These days, it's not uncommon for prisoners to attempt some kind of escape. I'm surprised three made the break this time. Usually it's just one individual who tries to get away. As you can see there's really no place to hide around here." He glanced at Flakkinbarr and Tuposh. He could tell that the incident had bothered the Fleet Lieutenant. Probably his first time at a place like this.

Flakkinbarr stared blankly at the SPG agent. His eyes said it all. Yes, this was the first time he'd ever seen anyone gunned down in cold blood. Murder, pure and simple in his book. So here was firsthand evidence regarding the treatment of prisoners. It was very doubtful that Lt. Jatarr or his rag tag prison guards would ever be brought before the Tribunal to testify about what had just taken place. No, it would never happen. And if Jatarr or any of his guards ever thought about talking, their fate would probably be the same as those of the prisoners who tried to escape. Perhaps worse.

"Geasbok has no place to hide!" Botree smiled wickedly. "Barren rock for mycrons."

Gerrius cleared his throat. "Shall we get on with our mission, gentlemen?"

Lt. Jatarr smiled weakly and nodded. "Of course, sir, right this way."

It was a little more than a hundred yarrs to the entrance to Section Six. A blue striped bulkhead door slid upward after Lt. Jatarr palmed a red square to the right of the door's thin outline against the massive dome. Once inside the door slammed shut behind them.

The room was small and stark white with several benches opposite the blue striped entrance door. To the left stood another blue striped doorway. A big red 6 was stenciled in the middle of the door. The room was cold, ice cold. Tuposh and Flakkinbarr began to shiver with the sudden change in temperature. Corporal Deenens went over to a panel just above the benches and pushed at a red dot. It glowed momentarily and suddenly the panel popped open. Inside, white heavy winter gear hung in ordered symmetry. Deenens took out heavy coats and tossed them to Tuposh.

"Put these on, sirs. Section Six is cold as She'ol!" Deenens grinned like a kid.

Jatarr took out another coat and handed it to Flakkinbarr. "We have our extremes in temperatures here, gentlemen. Section Six is the breeding tanks and requires a constant temperature."

"Breeding tanks?" Flakkinbarr looked puzzled. "Exactly what are you breeding here, Lieutenant?"

Jatarr looked at the disguised tribunes. "Since you have a Black Diamond Three clearance, I will explain just briefly and you'll forget that I said anything to you. Understood?"

Gerrius and Flakkinbarr just nodded. Botree and Deenens snickered at one another as if the lieutenant was about to reveal the secret of the universe. In actuality, he was revealing a secret few men outside of Geasbok knew about.

Jatarr pulled on his heavy coat and pants and then pulled up the hood and clasped it tight to his head. "This is one of seven breeding tanks at Compound Fourteen. One of seven Clone Tanks."

"Clones?" Tuposh and Flakkinbarr both asked.

"Clone warriors!" Jatarr remarked. "The Director's special warriors. That's all I can say. That's all I know!" Everyone was now suited in heavy winter white clothing. "This way gentlemen, and stay on the walk way. It'll be about five hundred yarrs to the other side and Section Five.

Commander Verrus has given you only ten hours to complete your work and report to his office." Without another word, Jatarr went to the door and activated the panel.

A narrow walkway disappeared into the distance. The dome was huge. Above, other walkways suspended by thin cables crisscrossed the massive open dome in a hundred different directions. To the right and left of their walkway several large bays spread out before them like a massive ocean. As far as the eye could see, hundreds of rows of large clear cylinders stood in sharp rank order.

Gerrius and Flakkinbarr couldn't help but stare. "There must be millions of cylinders here!"

"About seven and a half million!" Jatarr remarked as they marched along in a fast step.

"You say they are clone warriors?" Flakkinbarr just had to asked.

"Don't go there, sir!" Jatarr warned. "Right this way, please." He quickened his pace.

Once through the door on the opposite side of the dome and after having removed their winter gear Tuposh and Flakkinbarr were escorted to Section Five and the network security room. It was manned by three stone-faced Fleet Security personnel. They saluted as soon as Tuposh and Flakkinbarr entered the room.

"Sergeant Huskly, at your service, sirs!" The tallest of the three men snapped a proper salute and stood to his feet. The other two returned salutes and then stared back at their monitors.

"At ease!" Jatarr remarked. He turned and left the same way he had come in.

"Nice fellow, huh!" Huskly grinned. "You two here to fix the security link?"

"That we are, sergeant, that we are!" Gerrius remarked.

"Good!" Huskly nodded. "I'll show you to the grid. I understand the Commander's only given you ten hours to fix this thing. Think you can do it that quickly?"

"Probably less!" Gerrius winked at Flakkinbarr. "Tell me, Sergeant Huskly, is Section Six having any problems?"

Huskly frowned. "Don't go there, Captain. Section Six is the

Breeding Tanks. Classified. Need to know basis. And that's all I can say about it. Understood?"

Tuposh just nodded and glanced toward Flakkinbarr. "Understood, Lieutenant. Understood."

* * *

Tuposh and Flakkinbarr stood in front of the grid terminal, doors opened wide with tools scattered around like toys. Gerrius was running a systems check as Flakkinbarr replaced circuits.

"Green Three to Five." Gerrius pointed toward a blue panel to Flakkinbarr's right. "Then Yellow Two to Blue One." He pointed at another panel just below and to the left of the first one. Sergeant Huskly walked casually by.

"How's it going, sirs?" He asked, looking at the mess Tuposh had strung out all over the floor. These tech people really amazed him. Most were messy. He frowned.

"Nearly there, Sergeant."

Sergeant Huskly smiled. "Coming up on the six hour mark. I'm impressed, sirs!"

Tuposh smiled and continued to work, ignoring the worrisome sergeant.

"Can you get a peek into Section Six from here?" Flakkinbarr whispered.

Gerrius just eyed him. "I've checked. Hard firewall surrounds everything that leads to Section Six, not to mention the other six tanks. We'll have to figure out a work around solution for Section Six."

Flakkinbarr was still in shock at the massive number of breeding tanks. "They're breeding warrior clones. It looks like Klea's planning a takeover of some sort."

Tuposh just shrugged his shoulders. "Perhaps Commander Verrus can offer some insight."

"Can you do a planet-wide scan without being tagged?" Jerrid asked as he watched Gerrius work.

Tuposh adjusted a few switches, turned to the little display on the panel and scrolled through a few screens. "No!" He frowned. "It would be too obvious. Looking for that replicant factory?"

"Yeah!"

"Sorry!" Gerrius switched two panels and then punched at two control nobs. "That should do it. Security Net back on line and stronger than ever." He winked at his compatriot.

* * *

Commander Verrus was your typical penal colony commander. Tall, very muscular and a face that could blend in with a pile of rocks. Tuposh and Flakkinbarr stood in front of his desk. The comlink with their report on the security net was in front of Verrus who was scrutinizing every detail.

"I'm impressed with your work, gentlemen." He didn't smile. "Most techs take ten hours or more. But it looks like I've found a couple of good techs I can use in the future, should the need arise." He looked up, his eyes boring holes in the two Fleet officers.

"Thank you, sir." Gerrius offered. "We would be more than willing to be detailed out here if you need us."

Verrus nodded. "You can leave at your convenience."

"One thing, sir?" Gerrius asked.

"Yes?"

"The Breeding Tanks. There's a hard firewall around that part of the system that should be checked periodically. Do you have a date for the last check?"

Verrus scowled. "The tanks, sirs, have their own security personnel who handle that part of the net. That's all you need to know."

Tuposh frowned. "But sir, there could be another weak link that could cause a failure in one of the tanks."

Verrus got to his feet and walked around his desk to stand in front of Tuposh and Flakkinbarr. His eyes narrowed. "This is your first time on Geasbok. Even though you have a Black Diamond Three Clearance, you have no access to the breeding tanks security net. I don't understand it myself, but hear me on this, gentlemen." His look was cold. "The Director himself has special agents who handle the breeding tanks security net. I'll wager you they'll probably take over the whole planet one day and we'll all be out of a job. So, forget everything you saw today and don't ask any more questions. Understood?"

"Yes sir!" Tuposh and Flakkinbarr both replied.

"Good!" Verrus finally smiled. "I'll walk you to your ship and see you off. Hopefully, we won't need your services in the future."

PART FOUR
Band of Assassins

Interlude

October 13, 2024
Lawrence Bakersfield Laboratories
Clearing Lab Twelve
0955 Zulu

Again, Thomas Farraday pulled his spectacles from his face, gave a sigh and got to his feet.

"Thomas, does the information stored in this crystal disturb you?" The blue light on the computer blinked several times in quick bursts.

Farraday looked at his computer for a long moment, carefully considering the words he'd been reading. The information on the data crystal touched his soul like nothing had in a long time. "This is a very compelling story, Wanda. Very compelling!"

"There is substantial information buried within the data stream. A very sophisticated method that I am trying to analyze while doing the translation."

Farraday raised an eyebrow at this. "This," he pointed to the special drive adapted for the crystal, "crystal and it's story is nearly eight hundred thousand years old."

"Eight hundred, twelve thousand, six hundred and forty two years is the best I can extract given current information downloaded from the Atomic Clock and cross referenced against Global Geo-systems data banks."

"Yes, Wanda," Thomas smiled. "According to you, the Atomic Clock and our current way of dating stuff."

"Your point, Thomas?" The computer blinked.

"I'll get back with you on that one, Wanda." As he turned to retrieve his coffee cup, Farraday couldn't help but wonder what reaction General Dalton and his good friend Jerry Tanner would have. He could almost visualize the expressions on their faces. " I think our dear General and

Jerry might find this all hard to swallow."

"I perceive that General Dalton to be more skeptical of the data than your friend Dr. Tanner."

"We'll probably know in a few more hours!" he chuckled to himself. *Strange, I don't feel the least bit tired and I've been up for more than twenty-four hours.* But Thomas was accustomed to late night-early morning work. It was a driving force all its own. Whenever there was something to tackle he'd do it till it was finished. Non-stop, sometimes.

But this find was like nothing before. This tale from beyond the stars certainly was going to cause a stir. *Yes,* he smiled to himself, *Dalton and Tanner are going to go ballistic when they read this! Mark my words!*

Taking the time to stretch his arms, Thomas aimed himself once again for the chair and the computer printout as the printer continued to pour out the incredible tale from across the galaxy.

17

"To the people of the TeMari Corporate the Genetic War was a festering sore that would not heal. Bitterness took root, corrupting every level of society." — Portus Conso, *Histories of the Corporate Entanglements*

— Five Months Later —
11 Sakbar 4759 ADK
Tiggorian Industrial District
Maggermoss
Planet: TeMar

From the deep shadows of his steel gray rain hood, Jerrid Flakkinbarr glanced nervously up and down the congested street. He had just gotten out of the taxi and was paying his fare when he was suddenly jolted from behind. Instinctively, Jerrid gripped his attaché case even closer as his whole body tensed with alarm. A heavy set man in a red and white striped raincoat brushed Flakkinbarr aside and pushed his way into the taxi. The big man, shouting putrid obscenities at the top of his voice, yelled at the young driver. "Get a move on, you brakkin' fool! I haven't got all day."

Jerrid slammed the door, glad that he wasn't in that taxi. He relaxed and sighed with disgust as he watched the taxi merge into heavy traffic. *That darg-faced son of a skrowl*, he thought. He felt guilty for having bad thoughts about the fat man in the striped raincoat. *Jerrid, get a grip, man. After all these years and the things you've seen you shouldn't be so surprised.*

Despite the daylight, the endless rows of towering buildings that made up the Tiggorian Industrial District of Maggermoss plunged the lower traffic corridors into near darkness. Flakkinbarr shivered involuntarily as he stood staring up at the skyscrapers. Maggermoss, the seat of power for the entire TeMari Corporate, was motherworld's pride and splendor. Motherworld was a term used affectionately by many, but not by all. The city was one of TeMar's one hundred and seventy-five heavily populated metropolitan areas. The planet was the birth world of the TeMari culture and the seedling from which sprang the TeMari Corporate.

The Corporate was a thriving conglomerate of star systems unified four thousand years earlier by the VerKuur Council at the signing of the Accord of Dora Kerra. TeMar spread out its trade arm across a vast expanse of the galaxy, scooping up system after system and adding them to its Trade Consortium—its Corporate of Power.

The light drizzle falling since early morning increased to a steady downpour. The runoff from the upper levels produced a black, noxious film of water that drenched the lower traffic corridors. Corridor Orange was bottom level, the worst possible place to be in a downpour. Pressing the attaché case closer to his body, Jerrid pushed his way through the crowd. He stopped abruptly as several SPG passed nearby. Their presence was easily detected by their black and silver raincoats. The sight of this special police force caused another uncontrollable shiver to course through Jerrid's body.

"Get a move on, mister!" shouted a man who bumped into Jerrid when he stopped. "Sidewalk's no place to daydream! People here are in a hurry!"

Desperately wanting to avoid detection, he moved cautiously toward a newly constructed building.

Flakkinbarr stopped short of the barred entrance, paying little attention to the monstrosity towering overhead. His only concerns were distancing himself from the SPG and finding shelter from the putrid spray of rain. He wiped away the perspiration from his forehead.

Klea is the problem! His elimination is paramount!

Jerrid was wondering if he was becoming irrational. He'd entertained thoughts of abandoning his plan to assassinate the Director of the

Corporate, but he knew Piin was right. Klea had to be removed or the Corporate was doomed.

Klea is the Shadow that will destroy all of us unless he's taken out!

The chain of events were rapidly progressing. Things had gone too far to turn back. He now had to follow this through to the end.

Flakkinbarr was not a man accustomed to second guessing himself, but a sense of foreboding told him that something was amiss. His gut feeling was that it was much more than the nagging thoughts of a guilty conscience.

Tugging on the chain at his waist he pulled out his chrono and gave it a quick glance and carefully tucked it back into his pocket. He waited anxiously as he studied the passers-by. The colors of their raincoats varied, but not the cold, serious expression on each face. They all walked hurriedly along the sidewalk, looking neither to the right nor to the left. Regard for one's fellow man seemed to be a concern of the past. He wondered if everyone had become corporate replicants, doing exactly as they were told and never asking questions. Life no longer held the joy for him that it once did. He was sure this was not strictly a personal low; plenty of his constituents also felt the same way. From the gloomy expressions exhibited by the general masses he knew he wasn't alone.

Scanning the crowd, Jerrid realized there were more SPG in this area than usual. He had already counted six along this short span of sidewalk. *Surely they're not aware of our plot*, he thought, *not this soon.*

Out of the corner of his eye he spotted the long, black limo pulling out of traffic and onto a nearby side street. "Finally," he whispered. Pressing the attaché case tightly against his body he hurried toward the long, sleek hover car, haltingly glancing over his shoulder to see if he was being followed.

The vehicle was a Dalvon Special, the latest model with its classic tear drop shape. Highly acclaimed as the car of the century, not everyone could afford it. It was a vehicle only for those with power, prestige, and wealth. He and his wife, Alleis, had considered trading up to a Dalvon, but Alleis was fond of the Skierra and wanted to keep it around a little longer.

The door swung open with a hiss as the frosty, air conditioned interior mixed with the muggy air outside. A strong hint of sweet perfume greeted Jerrid as he stepped into the car. It was the one Frediana always wore. With Flakkinbarr now seated across from Frediana and her traveling companion, Tribune Juyin Hallenn, the limo pulled out into traffic and made its way along Corridor Orange.

Jerrid pushed back into the cushioned seat and removed the hood of his raincoat. He smoothed out his gray hair and tried to relax as he eyed Frediana Lisstrin. The scent of her perfume dominated the air.

Frediana was an attractive, long legged woman who had a fondness for powder blue satin dresses. The one she wore today had an accent of white lace around the sleeves and collar. It accented her curvy figure and deeply tanned skin. A plunging neckline revealed sufficient cleavage to hold Jerrid's eyes in place for several seconds. Her shoulder length brown hair was cut in an attractive youthful style and accented with a diamond hair piece that sparkled every time she tilted her head.

Then there was Tribune Juyin Hallenn, a pudgy man with a pudgy face and sour disposition. He did little more than grunt his greeting. The driverless car continued on as it made its way out of the industrial section of the inner city.

"I'm impressed with your Dalvon, Frediana. I see it's fully automated." Jerrid glanced up at the empty driver's seat and the electronic dash board dancing with activity.

"I thought it was about time for a trade. After all, the Stylus was last year's model." She smiled sheepishly. "This is the Dalvon K series, you know!"

Jerrid smiled, nodding his head. "The one with the special trans-mode?"

Frediana grinned like a school girl. "I still like to drive occasionally. It gives me the freedom to slip into the driver's seat and take control whenever I get that urge."

"I'm impressed." Jerrid nodded approval.

Juyin grunted and looked at Flakkinbarr. "Well, I see you were able to rearrange your morning meeting after all." Juyin wore an expensive dark blue silk suit, but his not so expensive transplanted hair piece was wet and matted. Juyin's raincoat was bundled up into a tight ball at his feet. The matted black hair looked more like a rug than a hair piece and appeared out of place next to the expensive silk suit. Tribune Hallenn changed hair pieces more than he changed clothes. He was never satisfied with the look and was constantly bouncing from one style to another. Flakkinbarr knew of Juyin's unsuccessful hair transplant three years ago that left the top of his head so scarred he did not show his face in public for six months. Most of his associates wished he would stick to one hair style and leave it. Although he was a pain and often attempted to intimidate Jerrid, Juyin was one of Flakkinbarr's many governmental friends. He knew him from his eighteen years as a member of the Corporate's High Tribunal. Of the eight hundred tribunes, representatives from the fifty quadrants that made up the TeMari Corporate, Flakkinbarr knew many by face, but only a dozen or so as close friends. Juyin was tribune from the Decorri Range, while Frediana hailed from the Zae Terrgoon Range. He, along with Drays Beslock, represented the Juelonza Range, motherworld's Core Systems.

Flakkinbarr half smiled. "I'm sure my secretary is having quite a time trying to reschedule my appointments. I hope she doesn't schedule anything before dinner."

Frediana lifted a shapely eyebrow. "I have a feeling I'm going to lose my appetite after our little chat, Jerrid."

Flakkinbarr thought her age was beginning to show, in spite of the plastoid surgery. Although she had tried for years to keep her youthful, twenty-ish appearance, the agony of growing older kindled a dark shadow deep within her piercing green eyes. Frediana's whole life centered around her obsession to stay young. This obsession puzzled Jerrid, and from time to time he wondered what had happened to make her feel that way. Yet, she had never allowed her lust for youth to interfere with her duties as a tribune. He smiled and started to speak.

Juyin cut him off before he could respond to Frediana. "Did the SPG notice you?" He stared intently out the tinted window. "Looks like Drivvers Street was crawling with 'em. Why did you pick this as a rendezvous point?" The worry that consumed Juyin's thoughts distorted his usually placid expression. He had not had much rest since it all began. The strain was becoming too much for him. He wanted to wash his hands of this whole affair. The sooner the better.

"No," Flakkinbarr replied, "they didn't. This section of the city is usually void of any SPG activity. That's why I chose it." Secretly, Flakkinbarr wondered why he had seen so many. But he was not about to reveal that now, especially not to Juyin.

Frediana crossed her legs and turned her attention to the attaché case still under Flakkinbarr's coat. "You didn't happen to bring the book today, did you?" Frediana's question was abrupt. She was tired of all the intrigue that surrounded the artifact that Flakkinbarr had come across in his travels. Its discovery only added fuel to the conspiracy fire already burning brightly around them. Would she ever be able to resume a normal life?

Flakkinbarr patted the case at his side. "No, it's safely locked away at home," he said. "But I promise I'll have it with me at our meeting on the twenty-ninth."

"Well, I'm anxious to see this book of yours, Jerrid," Juyin stated caustically. "I hope it will provide us with the answers we've been looking for." He shifted his weight on the seat and looked hard at Flakkinbarr. "This whole business we've gotten ourselves into is becoming more like a con drama every day. I'm not a young man any more, Jerrid. I'm an important tribune with a difficult schedule as it is. You don't know what a horrendous time I had rearranging my schedule to have our little clandestine meeting. In fact, I had to cancel two important meetings that won't get back on the docket until next month."

Frediana snapped back, "Juyin, you know very well that we can't ignore what's going on!"

"Please," Flakkinbarr stated, "Let's stay calm."

"Easy for you to say," Juyin quipped. "Do you realize how far out I've stuck my neck, Jerrid?"

Frediana cocked an eyebrow and her mouth tightened. "We've all stuck our necks out, Juyin!"

"You're certain this book's not a forgery?" Juyin questioned.

Flakkinbarr smirked. "I took a page from the book to a trusted friend at the university and had him analyze it. He's willing to vouch for its authenticity." As the limo switched lanes to move around a lumbering transport carrier the rain worsened.

"What you've told us so far seems preposterous!" Juyin replied, squirming in his seat. The plush leather seats were comfortable, but he just wished he could relax and convince himself that everything would turn out okay. "You said you could tie this book of yours with the five other manuscripts?"

Jerrid nodded his head.

Frediana gasped. "The *Chronicles of DaKelif* and the *Zilssion Sage Records* match?" She was stunned and apprehensive all in the same breath.

"I know it's hard to believe," Flakkinbarr unconsciously tapped the case, "but if you take the book I have at home, the *Chronicles of DaKelif*, the *Zilssion Sage Records*, and the other three *Dommar Konna Chronicles*, you have a perfect match. They were all written by the same person. The very same person!"

Juyin turned in his seat and gazed hard at Flakkinbarr. "I went to the library and pulled a copy of the *Chronicles of DaKelif*. The author *is* supposedly De'Zandar Marrs. The De'Zander Marrs, the infamous *Butcher of Klivic*." Juyin's tone hardened. "That monster documented over a hundred million bio-genetic experiments while on DaKelif and Regoor. Those experiments were later linked to the massacre of millions on Klivic."

"The *Zilssion Sage Records* were written three hundred years after the *Chronicles of DaKelif*," Frediana pointed out.

"Written by the Sage Da'min Ben'Lea," Flakkinbarr tossed back. "A mysterious prophet who appeared on Zilssion with a group of even stranger followers. They transformed the planet into a thriving eco system in less than fifty years." He paused, eyeing each of his friends.

"Another bio-engineered miracle?" Juyin asked somewhat skeptically.

"Remember Aalinra?" Jerrid asked.

"That was the miracle that got Klea elected to the highest office in the land." Frediana responded.

"I took the time to have several other Zilssion historical records checked out," Jerrid continued. "Each and every document mentioned in one form or another the Shrine of Kolbus, Ben'Lea's school of life sciences and psychic research. There are remarkable similarities in Ben'Lea's genetic miracles on Zilssion and Klea's bio-grains he manufactured for Aalinra. The Zilssion historians also mention references to the strange disappearances of several thousand of its inhabitants over the course of the sixty years Da'min Ben'Lea conducted his school. One historian speculated a connection between Ben'Lea's miracle cures and the disappearances. He was later ridiculed by most of his colleagues. At the end of those sixty years Da'min Ben'Lea simply disappeared into thin air."

"You're saying *The Butcher of Klivic*, the Sage Da'min Ben'Lea and Director Dameon Klea are one and the same person?" Frediana was stunned.

Jerrid just nodded. "The book proves that they are one and the same. There are several references that Klea fancied himself as the savior of the world. And the names De'Zandar Marrs and Da'min Ben'Lea do appear in several passages in the journal I have in my possession. Klea fancied the names as mysterious and magical."

"But that would make Klea a thousand years old!" It was Juyin's turn to gasp.

"A thousand years old!" Frediana just shook her head.

Jerrid smiled. There was another significant fact that would floor them, but there would be time for that later. "We seem to have uncovered a viper's pit."

Frediana and Juyin just stared. If they had their way they'd just put the lid back on, turn tail and run. But it was too late for that now.

"The book will provide conclusive evidence concerning Director Klea's true origins and identity. I'm sure you'll find the rest quite unbelievable." He waited for his words to sink in.

"A thousand years old?" Frediana continued to shake her head.

Jerrid continued, "Each of us knows that Klea's a dangerous menace. He is secretly sending hundreds of people to their torturous deaths every month." Flakkinbarr could only agonize over the uncovered truth. It was a disturbing nightmare that would haunt him the rest of his life. Others had to know about this. Jerrid eyed his friends intently. "I'm sure we're not the only ones that suspect something is going on."

Juyin snorted, "Even if we are the only ones, what will it get us? I say let things be."

Jerrid knew all too well the trouble they had dug up for themselves. "If we are going to continue our investigation we must exercise extreme caution. Remember, the SPG now answer only to Klea." If they were found out, they and their families would be next on Klea's list.

Frediana looked at each of her friends. "Keep in mind, the Defense Ministry has given the SPG the authority to arrest anyone whom *they even suspect* may be guilty of spying. Proof is immaterial."

"We have Marshal Resrok to thank for the liberal interpretation of that ruling," Flakkinbarr added. The name left an unpleasant taste in his mouth.

"There has definitely been a change in Resrok during the past several months," Juyin pointed out, scooting to the edge of his seat. "He's gone from being a staunch opponent of Klea's special SPG forces to being extremely supportive."

"I was wondering if you'd noticed the change in the man." Flakkinbarr smiled. As careful and detailed a tribune as he was, Juyin had a way of losing sight of the people behind the programs that were in his jurisdiction.

"Resrok's always been hard to deal with," Juyin snapped back, "He's a pinhead. The strange thing is that lately he's been agreeable, way too agreeable."

"The Tribunal is losing it's effectiveness." Frediana stated. "Too many of the us think Klea is doing a magnificent job with the economy and the handling of the war effort as well."

"Don't forget the tribunes who secretly support the Separatists movement, my dear lady!" Juyin shot back. "They're not going to fight Klea's war too much longer."

"I know, I know!" Frediana sighed disgustedly.

There was a long pause as the car continued on. The rain spattering the windows had intensified.

Frediana looked at each one. "Prejudice is spreading like a cancer throughout the Corporate. It's alarming. With the Tribunal virtually split over the Solarian issue, not to mention the sentiment toward the Separatists, it's a wonder we can function at all as government. The Verlmon Act will be our greatest disaster, my friends." She carefully eyed Juyin, "Some of us will have more reason to feel guilty about it than others."

"I did what I had to do, my lady." Juyin snapped, giving Flakkinbarr a sideways glance.

Was it possible that Juyin had kept the mysterious lobbyists a secret from even Frediana? Flakkinbarr swallowed hard, the tension rising with the exchange.

"Well," Frediana spewed back. "I certainly hope you *think* you did, Juyin!"

If Flakkinbarr remembered correctly, the rich belium miner from Terrkus she was now seeing was of direct Solarian descent.

"I knew your bigotry would win out over your better judgment," she went on. "I was appalled!"

"Who cares?" Juyin grunted, giving Jerrid another sideways glance. "I said I had my reasons and that's all you need to know. Besides, I for one think they should all be placed in detention." He and Frediana had, on several occasions, exchanged bitter words on this particular subject. But today the subject seemed even more unsettling. Despite the angry words, he knew that Juyin and Frediana would remain fast friends. Although today, the edge in Juyin's voice seemed to indicate otherwise.

"So you're now espousing that bigot, Verlmon?" Frediana snapped, a bitter edge to her tone. "You're simply falling in line with Klea's ideology, Juyin."

Juyin had a natural distrust of anyone from a different culture, including the tribunes who represented the frontier systems. Strange greetings, clothing, looks and alien food consumption practices were among his pet peeves. But it now appeared that the Solarians had been moved to the top of the list. Flakkinbarr made a mental note to have Juyin watched.

"The Solarians have done nothing but steal from us." Juyin was no longer trying to hide his bigotry, perched at the edge of his seat like a wild animal ready to attack. "They are bent on the ruination of our economy.

Who's to say they aren't all spies?"

Frediana gasped as she turned to face the man sitting beside her. "Juyin! Listen to you! Do you hear what you're really saying?" She glared at him. "After all the evidence we've uncovered, how can you still agree with Klea?"

Juyin snapped back, "I don't have to justify my actions to you. I'm just making a point!" He carefully studied his friend's eyes. Perhaps he had pushed the issue a bit too far. These were his friends. Juyin swallowed hard and spoke softly. "In spite of what you think about my attitude, I believe they should have the right to a fair trial."

Flakkinbarr laughed bitterly. "I'm sure they'd have a fair trial with Supreme Judge Taggerly, who fits nicely into Klea's hip pocket, don't you?"

"Juyin, your attitude has me concerned. I thought better of you!" Frediana's doubts gave way to stronger suspicions.

"Please," Flakkinbarr remarked, sensing the building tension. "We have not called this meeting to discuss the future of the Solarian race or to question loyalties." He paused long enough to throw a calculating look at Juyin. For a flickering moment, Jerrid envisioned planting his shoe in Juyin's big mouth. He was that exasperated with all his talk. "We are well aware of Juyin's views when it comes to the Solarians."

"However stilted they might be!" Frediana cut in. She turned and looked out the window, trying to ignore Juyin for the moment.

"Please! Let's not get into this again." If the situation wasn't defused immediately, Flakkinbarr would have to listen to Juyin and Frediana fight all day. With both of them on opposite sides of the fence on the Solarian issue, he wondered how their friendship would stand up to the strain.

"Okay Jerrid, what's our next move?" Juyin said bitterly, throwing Frediana a scornful glance out of the corner of his eye.

"I'm meeting with Kesperroud on the twenty-first and Tuposh the following evening to discuss their findings. We'll all meet on the twenty-ninth to lay out our final plan of action." Flakkinbarr knew what he was going to do; the plan was already laid out. But just when to spring it on his co-conspirators was another matter. Guilt knotted his stomach. "And yes, I will show you the book at that time."

Juyin grunted. "About time we got a look at the cursed thing."

The car came to an abrupt halt at an intersection. Frediana glanced up. "I see we've arrived at our destination." Across from the intersection was a vast plaza with three white, multi-storied buildings: the High Tribunal Administrative Complex. A small cultivated garden entrance added a touch of color to the otherwise austere complex.

Flakkinbarr ignored his stomach. The constant fear of what he was about to do was eating at him and was beginning to affect his normal duties. He had to compose himself before his meeting. "I prefer to think Tribune Othion wants to meet with me just to make sure I won't vote for the Beslock Amendment." He moved the attaché to his side.

"Othion wants to make sure that the amendment is killed before it gets to the floor of the Tribunal by voting time," Juyin grumbled as he smoothed out his suit. "I'm supposed to meet with him at three o'clock this afternoon. I'd appreciate you letting me know how things went with you so I'll be prepared."

"I'll give you a call as soon as it's over."

Putting her emotions in check, Frediana eased forward on the seat. "Try to be as subtle as possible," she grinned, touching Flakkinbarr's knee. The car pulled into the plaza and headed toward the parking garage. "We don't want to make him suspicious."

"He's one of Klea's top supporters," Flakkinbarr said, as the car entered the massive five story garage. "Let's all stay calm and just see what he has to say."

"Let's act like tribunes." Frediana smiled. "I've got to meet with a couple of committee people, but I should be through late this afternoon. I also want to know how things go with Othion, seeing as I have my meeting with him first thing tomorrow morning."

The car parked in a slot on the third level near the windowed walkway that lead to the trams and connected the garage to the Tribunal building. They got out of the car and stood looking at each other for a long moment. The rain had slackened, but the sky was still gray with clouds.

"I hope our next meeting will be the last one we will have for a while," Juyin said sourly. "All these covert meetings are getting on my nerves, Jerrid."

"It's affecting us all, Juyin." Flakkinbarr gave a weak smile. "It'll all be over soon. Just give me a few more days to work out the final details of the plan."

"It had better be a good one," Juyin remarked. "I don't relish going on like this." They ambled toward the tram area. "I'm not cut out for this kind of stuff."

Trying to sound confident, Frediana replied, "It'll be over soon, Juyin. And then we'll be able to get on with our lives."

Flakkinbarr said nothing as he and his colleagues made their way to the tram and waited to be shuttled over to their various meetings. He felt an icy chill as the wind whistled through the garage. The shiver that took hold of his body was more a sense of foreboding than a chill. Perhaps things weren't as black and white as they were trying to paint them. He thought of Alleis. Her safety was paramount. Then he considered his meeting with Piin and Serpa for lunch tomorrow. He felt like Juyin, hoping this scheduled meeting with the assassin wouldn't take long. He shook the thoughts away and watched his friends enter the tram.

18

"Life becomes a vortex of swirling, out of control circumstances! That's the fate of conspirators." — Morgas Sartis, *Seeds of Destiny*

"Don't panic now, the game has only begun."—from "Don't Panic" — words and music by Veris Torrs, *Vantrax Complex*

12 Sakbar
Vegli District
Maggermoss

The taxi came to a screeching halt at the corner of the busy intersection of Balla Street and Ocean Drive.

"That'll be twenty-five ruuls, mister!" growled the driver as he pulled the blue smoker from his lips, turning to the passenger in the backseat. Green teeth peeked out from behind the smug smile that crept across his face. "Credit or cash! Put it in the slot and get out!" He swore in a thick Barrian accent. His passenger calmly pushed back the sleeve of his jacket and held his shiny, silver ID bracelet up to the electric eye in the middle of a white panel attached to the back of the driver's seat. A digital readout above the eye showed the total as the charge was made. The passenger reached over and keyed in a modest tip.

"Thanks for nothing, *lambean*!" the driver snorted in disgust when he saw the amount of the tip.

Flakkinbarr got that conspicuous feeling again as he stepped out of the taxi into the sprawl and litter of the Vegli District of Maggermoss. His stomach tightened as he watched the taxi make a mad dash into the tangled traffic. The apprehension that had been eating at him all day just wouldn't leave him alone. He sensed something was going to happen and he just couldn't shake that feeling. Perhaps he should have given the driver a larger tip. *No!* he mused, the guy was an uncouth jerk. He managed to hit every pothole between the Darracura District and Vegli. Besides, the driver's chain smoking had filled the taxi with a thick fog that had irritated Jerrid's eyes and throat. And now his clothes smelled like the insides of a smoker factory. *No, two ruuls was more than enough.* Pausing for a moment to catch his breath and inhale fresh air, he surveyed the chaos of humanity around him. Thousands of people scurried up and down the sidewalk in a steady cadence of clicking heels and shuffling feet, stern expressions etched on each face. No smiles. No laughter to be seen anywhere today.

As had been Jerrid's habit over the past year, he would take a taxi to the intersection of Balla Street and Ocean Drive, get out and walk the three blocks to Torrin Street and then the remaining two blocks to Waterfront Row. Carefully orchestrated routes to and from meeting places were always prearranged days in advance. Today was no exception. He had memorized every taxi drop and subway station between his residence in the upper bay district of Darracura and Vegli. Because of Vegli's reputed criminal element, most people chose not to travel alone on the streets. Groups of twenty to thirty moved in unison with eyes locked forward and hands guardedly clutching packages and tote bags. All this frenzied movement only added to the apprehension already churning in the pit of Flakkinbarr's stomach. He spotted a small group of four sour-faced gruffy-looking men and stepped into pace behind them, close enough to be considered part of their group.

Vegli was the older, scabbier side of Maggermoss. The city was divided into forty-seven districts. Vegli was district twenty-three, Maggermoss' southwest section bordering the Zarras Ocean. Ancient structures of stone and timber stood side by side with the newer buildings of steel and plastcrete, an odd assortment of designs and styles. Time and the ever expanding city had left its mark. Yes, this ugly and overcrowded section of the city with its dark alleys and sleazy cafes was just the right place for secret meetings! No one asked questions here. No one dared!

"I tell you, Taulie, there was another killing on Bespan Street yesterday!" remarked the man just a few paces in front and to Flakkinbarr's left.

"That's what I hear, Derf." his companion replied. "Streets aren't safe for law abiding citizens anymore. We need more police around here."

"Not those SPG jukbutts!" Derf snapped back.

Dodging a broken section of sidewalk and catching sight of the stranger in their midst, the gruffy men suddenly became tight lipped. His group had only gotten fifty paces down Ocean Drive when a clamor of shouts and murmurs rushed to their ears.

"Stop that traitor! Stop him!"

Flakkinbarr froze! *My God, they know!* His heart beat against his chest like a hammer striking an anvil. A blur flashed out of the group of pedestrians behind him and knocked him down. A young boy dressed in black slammed Derf and Taulie down onto the hard walkway. Their companions toppled over as the youth kicked their feet out from under them and then raced up the sidewalk. Dangling from the young boy's left hand were three satchels and clutched tightly in his right was a bright, shiny object. There was no mistaking the distinctive shape of a stinger. The young boy could not have been more than ten years old. Slam! Before Jerrid could regain his balance, he was knocked once again to the hard plastcrete as three burly men chased after the youth. They caught up with him and wrestled the kid to the sidewalk, trying to relieve him of the satchels. There was no mistaking it, the three Neccians from South Arrenija had the advantage here. The dark haired, deeply tanned men all out weighed the kid by about eighty kefs each. But the youth was spunky and flailed at his captors with a vengeance. He kicked and punched his way free from the cursing men. Sprinting up the sidewalk the youth suddenly stopped, spun around, and opened fire with the stinger. One of the Neccians doubled over and fell to the sidewalk. Another shot rang out like a loud clap of thunder. Taulie's midsection exploded in a crimson stain as the air was kicked out of his lungs. The youth fired again!

Time seemed to stand still for Flakkinbarr. The liquid bolt of energy whizzed right by his head and into one of the groups coming up the busy sidewalk from behind. Jerrid turned in time to see two men go down. The pedestrians panicked and some scattered, but most dropped to the sidewalk and flattened themselves as much as they could. Jerrid imitated their response and had a good embrace on the plastcrete. Two women and a child went down under the vicious, indiscriminate blast of the stinger as the youth opened fire again. He didn't care who he shot, his pursuers or innocent bystanders. Jerrid could see the glaring hate in his stone-cold, gray eyes.

"You kronna-sucking scum bags!" He shouted, gunning down another bystander. "You'll never catch me!" He quickly dashed up the street and disappeared into the mass of humanity.

"Someone call a medical!" A man yelled, holding the head of one of the women in his lap. Horrible fear was etched on his face. "We need some help here, please call a medical!"

Derf was crying, sobbing into the blank face of his friend Taulie. Everyone stared. They were all in shock. No one wanted to move.

Derf was finally able to gain enough composure to stagger to his feet and go to a call-station. Blast! The echoing sounds of a blaster ripped through the whimpering cries of the crowd as the old man was gunned down by one of the Neccians. *What's happening here? He was only going for help!* Flakkinbarr wanted to shout but fear kept his jaw clamped shut.

"No one calls the police!" the angry Neccian glared around at the crowd as they began to get to their feet. "No one! This is our affair and we'll handle it!" The men quickly flagged down a taxi, dumped the body of their companion inside and jumped in. Derf's lifeless body lay at the foot of the call-station less than two yarrs from where his friend Taulie had fallen. The taxi vanished into the snarled traffic, but no one moved. Everyone just stared at one another. The crowd continued to grow. After what seemed like an eternity, a homeless man in a tattered brown jacket got to the call-station and dialed the police and the medical unit. Futile attempts were made to revive the women and child; it was too late.

"I can't believe this happened on Ocean Drive," a woman cried as she clung tightly to the man next to her. "This is supposed to be one of the safer streets. Why here? Why now? Why?"

"It's those brakkin drug dealers! They're to blame for all this," a short, chunky man to Jerrid's left responded in anger as he strained to see over the men gathered around the victims.

"They're taking over our city!" Another bystander snarled in disgust. Heads nodded in agreement from those standing nearby.

Vegli was notoriously infamous as the gateway for the most lethal drugs coming into Maggermoss. A number of deadly hallucinogens were responsible for two thousand deaths a month. Mostly young people, if Flakkinbarr remembered his news stories correctly.

At the sound of sirens Jerrid quickly distanced himself from the crowd and walked away, heading down Ocean Drive as fast as his feet would carry him but not wanting to be too obvious. He couldn't be seen here and chance being recognized. The police would swarm all over this little incident. Witnesses would be detained for questioning. Names would be taken. He couldn't afford to answer any questions or to let his real identity be known.

He'd walked this same street over a dozen times in the past year, and this was the first time he'd ever seen anything like he'd just witnessed. He'd known the possibility always existed. He'd seen a few robberies as well as a couple of brawls over the last year, but nothing like this. It left him in a state of shock. It reminded him too much of the incident he'd seen on Geasbok. Once again the haunting memory was resurrected and scraped its dark claws over his consciousness.

Ocean Drive was supposed to be one of the safest streets in Vegli. That's why he chose it as part of his route. *Whatever possessed me to come here today?* Jerrid slackened his pace a bit. It was on his schedule, that's why. People had learned to look the other way when these types of incidents occurred.

At the corner of Torrin Street, Flakkinbarr looked over his shoulder toward Ocean Drive. He saw the flashing lights of three police cars and two medical vans as they quickly exited from the main traffic flow and eased over to the sidewalk. The crowd of onlookers and gawkers had grown.

Jerrid pulled his hat down over his eyes and continued up Torrin as he headed for Waterfront Row. Drug lords and organized crime bosses possessed a stranglehold on this section of Maggermoss. *How did all this violence and crime get out of hand on my watch?* The realization was all too clear. Political red tape was at a premium and it had blinded him to the more important issues at hand. *When mankind chooses to go its own way and ignore the rules of decency, violence, degradation, and utter misery seep out of every crack.* Despite all of this, people still lived and worked here, but it was usually the immigrants and those who had no other choice. He made a mental note to investigate Vegli's cancer.

The cold, dark shadows cast by the giant skyscrapers only added to the misery he felt descending upon him. He couldn't shake the icy fingers that seemed to be slowly squeezing out his life.

Klea is your problem! Remember that! Always, remember. Klea must be eliminated.

Blaring horns and screeching brakes, interlaced with the ear splitting bark of jackhammers and cursing construction workers, vied for his attention. It was not uncommon to see human laborers down in the sleazier sides of Maggermoss. After all, it was still cheaper than robotic help. Flakkinbarr knew that most major construction companies chose to turn a blind eye to the practice of hiring human work forces. It was usually the low bid companies who used human laborers, those willing to make a profit at any expense.

After slackening his pace to an easy walk, Flakkinbarr finally reached Waterfront Row. Barricades, detour signs, and heavy machinery had taken up residence in two of the five lanes of Waterfront Row traffic. Construction crews were here too! *Great! When did all this take place?* He'd been here only two weeks earlier and there was no sign construction was about to start.

Through the din of unsynchronous sounds, seabirds squawked for attention, a reminder that the waterfront was less than five hundred yarrs away. In addition to the cry of the gulls, ship horns could be heard in the distance. A pulsating blast from a not too distant horn filled the air with a shrill that sent the gulls swirling back toward the water. The piercing sound was as irritating as the birds. The pulse lasted a full two minutes. Just as soon as the blast stopped, the gulls came back again. A lot of good it did! Jerrid quickened his pace and steeled himself against the next blaring blast from the horn while the birds scattered. The horn was a futile effort to keep the gulls away from the dock, but the birds had adapted to the screeching sound. Humans were the ones who hated the thing. And now, added to the heightened noise of construction, it was virtually intolerable. Bird poop splattered the sidewalk in front of him. Instinctively, Jerrid stepped aside and looked up for the attacker. His mouth twisted when he saw the gulls dancing in the air high above the crowds, ignorant of things below. Six huge street sweepers competed with the other traffic in an attempt to do their job. Large wire brushes mounted underneath the sweepers whirled like cyclones as they swept and sprayed the bird droppings from the blacktop. Nearly every single parked car and information display bore the unceremonious trademark left by the seabirds. Nothing was spared.

Two weeks ago no more than a few hundred birds strutted or flew along the waterfront. Now it was a different story! Thousands of gulls lingered along the wharf railings and roost in the ledges of every building on the waterfront. Flakkinbarr paused at the first bridge that crossed over one of the many waterways along the Row. Gulls plunged in and out of the water in a swirl of feathers and splashes in search of their favorite food, trullas. The water was alive with them. Successful birds became airborne, their beaks stuffed with the blue-green six legged crustacean. This was trullas' spawning season! And any time the tiny sea creatures moved toward their ancestral spawning grounds down around Cape Genoria, the gulls followed close behind, looking for a savory meal. The blast from the bird horn shook him out of his trance. Flakkinbarr continued on down the street, cursing at the horn and the birds and carefully watching his step.

Despite the incessant birds and irritating horn, Jerrid still enjoyed the cool sea breeze. Today the wind was coming off the water. He closed his eyes and momentarily shut out the din around him, savoring the moment. But the smell of pungent seaweed, salt air mixed with petro fumes, and the undeniable tinge of rotting trullas parts left in the sun by overstuffed, squawking gulls assaulted his senses.

Forty years ago his parents had sought better jobs for themselves in the densely populated metro area. Leaving the drought-infested country of Aalinra, in the southern hemisphere of TeMar, they ventured north to the heavily populated continent of Drakaska, where Maggermoss was its most prized jewel. This dazzling city was a pulsating hive of humankind and offered an assortment of prosperous jobs for the less fortunate of the planet's races. His parents had done well here, and so had he. The city offered everything, and he had taken as much as he could. He smiled. Yes, he had done very well. A streak of light caught Flakkinbarr's eye as he surveyed the dense city-scape. Another starliner was headed for orbit. A blaring horn screamed in his ear, rudely rousing him back to reality. Traffic was already backing up. It was business as usual in Vegli. At the next street crossing Jerrid waited for the signal and proceeded to the opposite side of the street. He quickened his pace to that of the crowd around him. The blast of a siren startled him as a medical van came screaming up the street. Jerrid paused long enough to see the van disappear into the traffic. It was headed toward Ocean Drive. He cautiously peered at those around him and continued on up the street. He felt as though invisible eyes were watching. The unseen prying eyes now tailed him everywhere. He exhaled heavily and forced himself to relax.

A detour forced the crowd over a makeshift bridge as construction workers struggled to place large support columns for the new bridge being built. The crowd pressed in around Jerrid in an attempt to navigate the narrow fifty yarrs of plaster, bird poop, and spit splattered walkway. Suddenly there was a loud splash. A sheet of water crested over the construction wall, drenching more than a dozen of the passers-by. Obscenities were hurled at the construction workers atop the bridge.

"Go suck on a squim, dorkgon swine!" The construction workers threw fists in the air and continued to spew vulgar obscenities at the soaked pedestrians.

"Get a real job bucket-butt!" A woman three paces in front of Flakkinbarr screamed out. He had to laugh. The guy certainly resembled the remark. Curses continued to be exchanged as the crowd navigated around the construction site, undaunted in their quest to reach the various shops and cafes along Waterfront Row.

Despite the mild day, he suddenly shook uncontrollably. His mind whirled with everything that had happened since he had gotten out of the taxi. All this chaos, in addition to his secret investigation of Director Klea, only served to make the knot in his stomach that much tighter. There was also another cord that twisted like a knife in his gut. What had started out simply as an inquiry into missing data had turned into a cyberweb of pending disaster with tentacles that now reached across the entire galaxy. He wondered where all this was leading. Out of simple, innocent beginnings, a conspiracy had grown into a swirling vortex of covert meetings and plots against the current government. The future of motherworld concerned him. His own zealousness for the future of his planet had thrown him headlong into a dangerous chess game where he could be checkmated at any moment. There was going to be trouble, he had no doubt. Perhaps he should just flag down another taxi, get out of Vegli, and forget this whole business of conspiracy and assassination. He swallowed hard; it was too late for that now. When all was said and done, he wondered how he would be remembered, hero or traitor. He shook the nagging feelings.

I'll be a traitor in the eyes of many if we fail! That thought wasn't reassuring. *No! And if we succeed? Traitor either way, I think.*

He knew he should have brought a heavier coat in case the weather changed later in the day. The month of Sakbar always meant rain, although today was a rarity. The sky had only a touch of clouds. Spring was about two weeks away and this time of year the temperature and weather sometimes varied in extremes. There had been reports on the weathercons about a possible cold snap, but he dismissed toting the heavier coat in his hurry to get to Vegli. He would probably regret it. He had begun to second guess himself at every turn, with even the simplest of decisions. He wormed his way through the congested sidewalk toward the café at the end of the street.

As he made his way up the busy sidewalk he became aware of another commotion just ahead of him. *Oh great! Not another murder!* He tried to peer over the bobbing heads in front of him, but to no avail. Fearfully he glanced around; he'd have to force his way to the street side of the crowd. Jerrid tried to keep his stride, but someone bumped him.

"Keep the pace up, mister!" a heavy set man in a green striped tunic pushed him along. "Stay with the flow or get out!"

Jerrid tried unsuccessfully to worm his way out of the crowd. But the closer he got to the commotion, the thicker the crowd became, until everyone suddenly came to a stand still. He was an innocent bystander about to be meshed into another angry confrontation. People were shoving and pushing, trying to get closer to the commotion. Elbowing his way through the bodies, he glanced over his shoulder and caught the flickering sign above the storefront encircled by the angry mob. *Darianus Fine Gems* stood out against the harsh hazey light of motherworld's sun.

"Go back to where you belong, you Solarian maggots!" he heard someone yell.

"Yeah! Get off motherworld and go back to your scum hole across the galaxy!" shouted another angry voice. Jeers and animal calls echoed loudly, competing with the harsh noise of the traffic.

"So, it's begun!" Flakkinbarr barely whispered. An elbow to the gut caught him by surprise. A short wiry man in a solid black tunic was jumping up and down, trying to see over the heads of those in front of him. He jumped once more, but Jerrid leaned away from the flailing elbow.

"Got to see mister, got to see," he yelled, jumping again. He paused a moment and looked at Flakkinbarr. "It's about time we showed those Solarian brakas a thing or two." The little man went back to imitating a yo-yo. Flakkinbarr moved out of elbow range.

The war against the Solarian Federation had taken a tremendous toll. Lives were being ruined every day. But this wasn't about the war being fought on the front lines. This was about a more dangerous enemy—hate, prejudice, bigotry. It was about a witch-hunt, not the first in civilized man's history.

Solarians, who long ago ventured to motherworld in search of commercial success, were finding it more and more difficult to do business and to live ordinary lives. They had contributed to the advancement of civilized TeMar and the Corporate as a whole, but were now the subject of ridicule and scorn. Solarians were becoming more and more the brunt of cruel jokes, off-colored con-dramas, and character assassinations by the major media. It was tragic, Flakkinbarr mused. Gifted inventors, musicians, artists, and teachers were being shut out of society simply because of their Solarian heritage. Solarian shops had become common targets for boycotts. Businesses failed and foreclosures were forthcoming. Some of the wealthier Solarians fled motherworld for the frontier. A mental image of his neighbor, Yanni, flashed across his memory. Where was he now? He would probably never know. Many others found refuge within the Separatists Alliance. Even some of Flakkinbarr's close acquaintances were beginning to cave in to public opinion and take sides against the Solarians. Fear and distrust were running rampant. Tribune Juyin Hallenn suddenly came to mind. He had wondered how long it would take for the tensions between the races to filter down to the common people.

The nerve-shattering sound of crashing metal, mixed with the tinkling of shattered glass falling on the sidewalk, tensed every muscle in his body. More angry voices and shouting. In the distance the wail of sirens signaled the police response. When the police arrived, Flakkinbarr was stunned to see a lone black and silver vehicle accompanying them. It was the SPG. *So, the Corporate government has finally become involved at the local level.* Up to this point, he'd only heard rumors. Recently though, whenever the conversation had shifted to the SPG, he noticed that no one said a word. Shifting eyes and glum expressions revealed what was afraid to be spoken. The special unit of the military now seemed to be more concerned about policing political issues than protecting its civilians. This was dangerous. The agitated mob continued to grow in numbers, fueling Flakkinbarr's increasing paranoia. Someone here was bound to recognize him, disguised or not. He finally fought his way to the edge of the commotion and skirted the crowd of gawkers. He hurriedly made his way down the street, throwing an occasional glance over his shoulder at the silver and black car.

Now that his destination was in sight he felt a sense of relief. Several large construction workers, with a strong stench of sweat and dirt clinging to them like a fog, hurried passed him to investigate the skirmish at the gem store. He glanced over his shoulder one final time and quickly entered the *Shazzamon* café.

Jerrid stood for a moment just inside the door, out of the street and away from the scrutinizing eyes of the police. He took a deep breath and made himself relax. He felt a little better knowing the police weren't after him — yet. At times his mind played cruel tricks. Warning, consoling, it was all an endless conflict of logic versus emotion. He exhaled heavily as he pulled his cap from his head and stuffed it into his pocket. He quickly surveyed the congested café. There was a larger than normal crowd here today. Usually on Dresday there wasn't a problem finding a table. But he didn't have to worry. He knew his appointment was already here. He just hoped he wouldn't be seen by anyone he knew.

He liked this place. The quaint setting helped sooth his nerves. The decor was deep red plastoid tables and chairs with thick, dark brown beamed ceilings made of a rare wood that Zepepi, the owner, claimed was imported from the planet Xerris Tau. Eight of the outside walls had handsomely crafted stained glass windows. Blues, golds, and reds gave the café a rich, warm glow as the sun set over the water. A few soft glow lamps fashioned like old sea vessel lanterns added to the atmosphere, creating mood. Depending on your frame of mind, the mood could be as dark as the wood or as bright as the multi-colored windows.

From the outside the *Shazzamon* looked like any of the other one hundred tiny restaurants along the street. Inside though, the place was huge. That was the way Zepepi had planned it, and it worked. The decor was early fisherman. Netting, spears, hooks, and plaques from ancient seagoing vessels decorated the walls. Mounted on the far west wall was a huge jarkfish, six yarrs long. Its spiked blue sail and long fanged snout a striking display. Zepepi claimed he had caught it off Cape Genoria fourteen years ago.

"It put up one zondon of a fight," Zepepi claimed. Anyone showing interest in the fish would hear the whole story, from the casting off at Genoria, through the assorted mishaps of the ride off the cape, and the blow-by-blow details of the catch. Flakkinbarr made that mistake twice. He smiled inwardly as he remembered his own naivety at being drawn into the long winded fish story — twice. He looked at the handsome fish, careful not to linger too long. He had learned his lesson well.

Grilled fish and sweet wine permeated the air as Flakkinbarr moved toward the back. *Shazzamon* had a good reputation, so any time of day meant crowds. The tables were set close together. Zepepi wanted to capitalize on the space. More tables, more people, more money. Simple math as Zepepi saw it. The food was excellent and, for the most part, people didn't mind the fact that they had little elbow room. The place was set up in terraces, five total, each descending toward a large open hard wood floor sixty yarrs across.

He stood at the top of the first terrace gazing down the full length to the last landing. Toward the back was a little alcove set up for those who wanted some privacy. It was usually reserved for Zepepi's more distinguished customers. The tables here were spaciously placed. Two walls separated the alcove from the rest of the café. Stained glass scenes of fishermen in action graced the full length of the walls, and the lighting gave it an air of mystery. Just the right place for a secret meeting.

Dodging waiters and customers alike, Flakkinbarr navigated down the terraces toward the alcove. An occasional waiter or waitress would nod or smile as they recognized a valued customer. He barely acknowledged their greetings. Normally he would exchange pleasantries, but today his thoughts were preoccupied.

The Aldrian waiter, Syd, recognized Flakkinbarr as he pushed his way passed the tables along the third terrace. Syd never forgot the face of a good tipper.

"G'day, Mr. Dros, sir." Syd smiled, precariously balancing the tray of steaming fish above his head to allow his favorite customer to pass him in the narrow walkway between tables.

"Good day, Syd." Flakkinbarr acknowledged. The alias felt more conspicuous than it had in the past. The knotted feelings of anxiety rushed to his stomach, causing him pain. It had to be an ulcer, he thought. The pain only intensified his sense of imminent danger.

Flakkinbarr froze and his body tensed. The room seemed to go deathly quiet. It was only his unharnessed fears playing cruel tricks again. As he came back to reality he heard the chatter of noisy customers, the clanging of glasses, silverware, and plates as waiters brought food to the many patrons. His eyes were fixed on the two men at the table just ahead. He had to walk right by their table; there was no way he could avoid them. No one in this place knew his true identity. In a whole year of coming here his secret had been safe. His stomach wrenched again, the knot so tight it made him nauseous. He grimaced, but it only lasted a moment.

The men at the table looked up from their meals and locked eyes. The recognition was instantaneous. "Jerrid?"

There was no mistaking Cirin Hunneen; the man who spoke to him was handsome, with dark hair and piercing blue eyes. His features were strong and masculine. His tanned face spoke of his love for the outdoors. And those eyes! Such piercing but compassionate eyes seemed to contain an ageless wisdom, a wisdom not gained from academia. Opposite him sat Hon, his Phystaccarn servant, whose shoulder length white hair and deep olive complexion were a sharp contrast to the younger man.

For a brief moment Flakkinbarr thought about ignoring the men at the table and retreating to the top of the landing, but his feet were frozen to the floor. He drew in a deep breath and stepped toward the table. Flakkinbarr shuddered.

His mind raced and his stomach knotted up. *Relax, take a breath. You're just part of the crowd here. They don't know, they can't possibly know.* His alarm slowly gave way to his curiosity. What was one of the wealthiest men in the Corporate doing in a place like Zepepi's?

"Cirin?" Flakkinbarr forced a smile, acknowledging the dark haired man.

Cirin returned the smile and rose to extend a hand of greeting. "Jerrid, good to see you again."

"Nice to see you too!" Flakkinbarr replied, shaking the man's hand. "What brings you out to a place like this?" He really wanted to know. Why would a business tycoon like Hunneen come to a place like this when there was the luxurious setting of *Zevo's* on the bay? *Zevo's* catered strictly to the rich and famous. Jerrid's other wealthy friends and acquaintances shunned such places like *Shazzamon's*. But Hunneen was a different sort of fellow.

Cirin Hunneen's smile broadened. He certainly knew that Tribune Flakkinbarr was out of his element. The casual attire had thrown him for a moment, but he said nothing. His only thought was that Tribune Flakkinbarr didn't want to be seen eating in *Shazzamon's*. He gestured toward the Phystaccarn who rose from his chair. "I think you remember my servant, Hon."

The Phystaccarn bowed slightly, as was the custom. They didn't shake hands. "The honor is mine again, sir."

Flakkinbarr returned the bow a bit awkwardly and then looked back at Hunneen. "As it is mine. I believe Hon was your representative at the *Sartus* unveiling."

"The Bhartow Trade Fair," Cirin reflected. "Unfortunately I couldn't attend, business elsewhere."

Jerrid smiled. "The trade fair was a little lackluster from previous years. My opinion, of course."

Cirin glanced at his servant and then grinned. "A pity I missed it!" He laughed. "You come here often, Jerrid?"

"Occasionally." He forced a smile. "And you?"

"When business brings me this way I make it a point to have lunch here."

The answer was sufficient and Flakkinbarr relaxed. "A friend recommended this place to me a year ago. I gave it a try and fell in love with the food. I've come here ever since." It was the truth, to a point.

"I agree, the food is excellent," Cirin replied. "Care to join us?"

Flakkinbarr gave a polite smile. "Thank you, but I'm meeting a couple of friends for lunch. Perhaps some other time."

"Well, we must schedule lunch here sometime," Cirin replied with a nod. "I think the *Manthan* project is due to come up before your committee in a few weeks. We could discuss the finer points of the plan over lunch."

Flakkinbarr couldn't help but grin. Cirin was the shrewdest business man he'd ever come across. He knew how to sell his projects and at the same time disarm anyone who wanted to haggle over details. He liked that. "Sounds good, Cirin. Call my office and we'll plan it."

"Good," Cirin replied.

"If you'll excuse me." Flakkinbarr continued on down to the bottom terrace. He thought it quite odd that Hunneen would be having lunch with his servant. But he quickly remembered that Hon had considerable power in the Hunneen financial empire. Cirin always did things differently. Three quarters of the other influential overseers of business mocked and ridiculed Cirin's business tactics. *Whoever heard of a servant as top executor*, they mocked. But it gave him a great sense of satisfaction to see Hunneen's competitors barely able to keep pace with him.

Flakkinbarr was more relaxed and smiled. He felt better now.

He entered the alcove and paused momentarily, staring at the two men dressed in black suits at the back of the alcove. The grin quickly vanished. The haunting gut feeling returned stronger than ever. Flakkinbarr cautiously made his way to the back table and sat down across from Piin and his hired assassin, Serpa.

Piin nodded as Flakkinbarr settled in his seat. His hired gun had an impressive physical prowess; the suit fit tight and revealed every detail of the man's muscular body. A tray with the remains of a few smoked zarks was sitting on the table in front of them and tall slender wine glasses half full at each plate. Obviously they'd been here for some time.

"Have you been waiting long?" Flakkinbarr asked nervously.

"Mr Dros, how good of you to make our appointment!" Piin replied, none too warmly.

Flakkinbarr slowly licked his lips. His mouth was dry. "Sorry, but traffic and construction put me a little behind."

Piin gave a slight smile and glanced over to Serpa. "I understand. Maggermoss is such a congested place. I don't know how you live here, Mr. Dros."

The sarcasm was a little irritating but Jerrid chose to ignore the comment.

"Why don't you order?" Piin offered. "The zark is very good."

Flakkinbarr didn't know if he could eat. His stomach felt queasy.

Klea is your problem. Deal with him! Jerrid blinked and looked at Piin, then Serpa. *Yes, Klea must be eliminated very soon.*

Syd bounded up to the table, smiling and nodding first to Flakkinbarr and then to his dining companions. "What will you 'ave today, Mr. Dros?" He carefully placed a menu in front of the new arrival.

Since Piin and his man were nearly finished, Jerrid didn't think he could really eat anything. He was more keyed up than he thought possible and eating something right now would probably just make him sick.

"If the zark doesn't appeal to you, Mr. Dros," Piin took a sip from his wine glass, "then try the puander. They're usually succulent if prepared right." He glanced at the waiter, who stared at his comlink.

A stiff drink might take the edge off. No, something a little milder. Flakkinbarr pushed the menu toward the waiter. "I'll just have the white chadra. Nothing else."

"Okay, sir." Syd keyed in the order, stuffed the comlink into his apron and took the menu, worried this meal was not going to work out into a good tip. He left quickly to place the order.

"You bring the money?" the hired gun asked staring hard at Flakkinbarr.

Jerrid slowly surveyed the alcove, making sure no one was within ear shot. He leaned over the table and nodded his head, "Yes, Serpa." He lingered on the name. "I did!" The name fit.

Waving a hand, Piin smiled wickedly, "Please forgive Serpa's rudeness, my friend."

Serpa gave a calculated glance at the smuggler.

"He's just a little anxious about his payment." The smile of Piin's face grew broader.

Jerrid reached into his tunic and pulled out a small comlink pad and slid it across the table. "I have your assurance you can do the job?"

Serpa smiled.

Flakkinbarr didn't like his arrogance, but he didn't have much of a choice. People weren't waiting in line for jobs like this.

"The job is as good as done." Serpa glared.

"Something of this magnitude requires a certain amount of assurance." Flakkinbarr licked his lips. He was letting his nerves get the best of him.

Serpa leaned over the table and stared hard. Piin placed a hand on his arm and gave him a sideways glance, his mouth was tight. "Relax, Mr. Dros, Serpa is the best at what he does. Count on him doing an excellent job."

Pushing back in his seat, Serpa again gave Jerrid a hard stare. "I can do the job to your satisfaction, Mr. Dros. The kill will be easy enough."

The kill. He certainly made it sound clinical, almost commonplace. He said it as if taking another person's life was as simple as completing a report. Piin had all the confidence in Serpa and his abilities. Somehow though, Flakkinbarr still couldn't believe he was going through with this. He was paying to have the Director of the Corporate assassinated! Flakkinbarr thought his stomach was going to explode with the pain. *Dear God, what am I doing?*

Piin leaned forward, "This is the critical point, Mr. Dros. Serpa will serve your purpose well. I have the utmost confidence that this will go smoothly. Remember, with your problem gone things will improve."

A wicked smile slipped across Serpa's face.

Don't be a coward, Dros! Do this thing. Eliminate your problem!

Jerrid shook his head, trying to clear the confusing thoughts. He heaved out a sigh. "Very well." He glanced at Serpa and then back to Piin. "This is the first of three payments," he said, nervously tapping the comlink. "I'll deliver the second payment in two weeks at our prearranged pickup point. You'll get the final payment when the job is done."

Piin took the comlink and studied the display. The transfer credits were locked in, all untraceable; no one would be the wiser when the deposit was made. It was a hefty sum. But then again, this was an extraordinary job — it demanded a large sum.

Pleased with the amount, Piin smiled again. "Mr. Dros, your troubles will be over very soon. No more problems."

Syd quickly reappeared with Flakkinbarr's drink. He leaned back on his heels and fingered his pad, waiting to take his order.

"Are you sure you won't change your mind? The zaarfish is very good today, and we 'ave a great special on the trollop." He was hoping for an enthusiastic response.

Jerrid simply shook his head. Syd looked very disappointed.

"Not today, Syd." Flakkinbarr replied, stretching out his hand to expose the gleaming ID bracelet. "Charge it to my account. You can add their meals to mine, also."

Syd quickly scanned the ID. "Yes, sir."

Flakkinbarr nodded.

Syd punched in the total and gave the comlink to Flakkinbarr to verify the amount and waited, hoping for a moderate tip at best. When the comlink was handed back, Syd quickly studied the display and left.

The big tipper had been a little more generous than expected. Good, he was still his favorite customer.

"Our meeting on the twenty-ninth will be our last," Flakkinbarr said earnestly. "I will arrange the drop for your last payment when the job is complete."

"Ah, Mr. Dros, sounds like you don't appreciate the service Serpa is doing for you." Piin gave a wicked smile and winked at Serpa, who just stared back.

"Let's just say this whole affair has a certain taste to it that I find a little unpalatable." He sipped his wine. His mouth felt like a dry, sandy desert, but there was nothing that was going to quench this dryness.

"It will be over shortly my friend. You have my assurance." The sinister grin crept across Piin's face as he put the glass to his lips.

Jerrid shuddered as he watched Serpa empty his glass.

Piin and Serpa rose from their chairs. "Serpa will see you on the twenty-ninth at the prearranged site, Mr. Dros. Bring the next installment." Piin looked at Jerrid, cocked his head toward the hit man and glanced toward the exit.

As Piin and the muscular assassin left the alcove, Jerrid suddenly felt a tightness grip his mind. *Your problem will be eliminated soon! Just trust me!*

"Trust you?" Flakkinbarr sat stunned, staring at his drink. Perhaps he should just make a run for it before this whole situation exploded in his face. But he knew it was too late for running.

19

"The end of the path is never seen when the journey begins. So the path may lead through harsh ground before the end is reached."
— Johanan 11:17, *The Talbah Canon*

21 Sakbar
Skimmer Park
Maggermoss

On any other day, a walk through Skimmer Park would have been a refreshing change from the daily grind of shuffling comlinks, racing to meetings, and listening to monotone constituents ramble on about their problems and the need for reform within the government. But not today. As Flakkinbarr made his way down the busy sidewalk that cut through the heart of the park, he couldn't keep his mind off the fact that he had to get Alleis to safety. And he had to do it soon.

Skimmer Park was nearly a full mycron across at its widest point. Time and time again it had been voted the most gorgeous of Maggermoss' twelve hundred shopping parks. The immaculately kept shade trees, open lawns, and sparkling fountains were testimony that some amount of leafage was still visible in the otherwise chaotic cityscape that dominated most of the city. But today Jerrid neither saw the budding trees or flowers breaking out of their winter slumber. He only saw the need to get through the next two weeks and above all, get his wife off planet before it all started. Jerrid kept a sharp eye out for SPG; so far he hadn't seen a one. The fear of the SPG was now a lingering shadow that followed him everywhere.

He spotted his contact sitting on a park bench just outside the *ReShaon Café*. The red-headed man was dressed in a light brown tunic with matching pants and dark shoes. A blue raincoat was folded at his side. He was reading from a tiny, dark blue comlink and did not see Flakkinbarr approach.

Jerrid paused when he got to the bench, turned and asked, "You have the time, sir?"

The man lowered the comlink and looked up, "I'm glad to see you made it." He forced a smile.

"Thank you, Hëlo," Jerrid grinned in return and then remembered why he was here and it vanished from his face. "Let's take a walk."

Hëlobstan Kesperroud pocketed the comlink, picked up his raincoat and rose to his feet. Kesperroud had high cheek bones, dark set eyes, and long thin arms and legs. A good stiff breeze and Kesperroud would probably blow away like the last fallen leaves of winter. Most of Kesperroud's closest friends called him Hëlo because they found it too difficult to pronounce Hëlobstan. It didn't sit right on the tongue.

"Think it's going to rain?" Jerrid asked, an amused look on his face as he and his friend headed along the sidewalk toward the far end of the park. He knew his friend had a phobia of rainy weather, always feeling like he was going to drown.

"You had to pick Skimmer Park, Jerrid!" Hëlo hissed, unconsciously glancing at the raincoat he carried across his right arm. "An open air park! You could have picked the Millstone. At least it's in a dome."

"This is a nice place, Hëlo." Jerrid replied. "Fresh air, a cool breeze. Not so many people."

"Not so many people because it's Sakbar, Jerrid! Only blithering idiots would be outdoors this month." He gazed toward the sky. "You know very well that it rains nearly every day in the month of Sakbar!" Clouds were building in the late afternoon sky. It would probably rain by the time he got back to his office. Not a pleasant thought, considering he had to drive all the way across Maggermoss.

They paused at a drink vendor.

"What will it be, gents?" The vendor was a skinny youth, almost as thin as Hëlo, with a flowery tunic and a name badge. Tizz was his name.

For a flickering moment a cat crossed Jerrid's memory as he studied the young man's name badge. A twinge of sadness tugged at his heart as he remembered Tazz. Shaking it off, he smiled at the youth. "I'll have a *Porta Berra*." He pulled back his sleeve to reveal his ID bracelet.

Tizz grimaced, "Sorry sir, but my com reader's down and it'll have to be cash. Sorry for the inconvenience."

Flakkinbarr nodded and reached into his pocket and counted out the coins.

Hëlo had the same. They continued on their walk and found a bench overlooking a fountain with a small lawn. In the middle of the lawn stood an abstract sculpture, but at least they were away from the street noise.

Hëlo pointed to the sculpture. The piece consisted of three metal plates five yarrs across, cut at five acute angles and joined perpendicular to one another with a huge half yarr thick column supporting the entire thing. "That's supposed to be a genuine Kurdöe."

"Oh really." Flakkinbarr studied the thing for a moment, trying to figure out what kind of statement the sculptor was trying to make. "What's it called?"

"I'm not much into sculpture, Jerrid. Whatever it's called, it's junk in my book." Hëlo snorted a laugh. Jerrid only chuckled.

"Anyone you do like?" Jerrid mused.

"Whose got time for sculpture!" Hëlo was annoyed. "I'm too busy."

"Aren't we all." As Jerrid sipped the cold drink he surveyed their small little edge of the park. People moved along here like they did any other place in Maggermoss. Busy with life, in a hurry to get where they were going. They just moved in droves with no time to see their surroundings or smell the budding flowers that were beginning to add color to the park. So far no detectable sign of the SPG. He glanced at the sky and then grinned. "It shouldn't rain until later."

"Right!" Kesperroud was a pessimist by nature. Even more so than their mutual friend, Juyin. Despite his mousy appearance, Hëlo was a shrewd businessman. As overseer of the Grelon Corporation, the largest manufacturer of military aircraft for the Defense Ministry and the Armont Droid Facility, Hëlo had a sizeable fortune and considerable pull with a number of important people. Hëlo slowly sipped his drink and gazed around at the open air park. "You know, Jerrid, all this cloak and dagger stuff really should be left to younger men. You and I are both too old for all this."

Jerrid smiled, "But we're the ones who uncovered this mess. It's unfortunate it came around at this time in our life."

"I don't mind telling you, this whole thing has me spooked." Hëlo took another sip and continued to stare at the bubbling liquid in its clear container. "I'm always looking over my shoulder nowadays, even in my office. I've become so paranoid I don't trust anyone."

Flakkinbarr turned a concerned eye toward his friend.

Hëlo shifted his weight on the bench and looked hard at the man seated next to him. "We've uncovered some pretty volatile stuff here, Jerrid. We go public with it and someone's going to get fried."

"How long can people turn a deaf ear or a blind eye?" When Hëlo didn't comment right away, Jerrid heaved out a sigh of disgust. "People don't want to care anymore, Hëlo, it's pure and simple."

"Don't get philosophical now, Jerrid. It seems to me TeMar, as well as the rest of the Corporate, has some serious problems." Hëlo had already painted his gloomy picture of the world years ago. It hadn't improved one tad since then. He laughed at his own pessimism.

"What's so funny?"

Hëlo smiled, despite his mood. "There are people out there who really care about the sad state of affairs we're in, but they're in no position to do anything about it."

"Including us?"

Hëlo stuck his feet out and leaned back against the bench. He looked at his friend out of the corner of his eye. "Including us. Do you think the average citizen gives a volrat's butt about what the Director does behind closed doors? Geasbok is a military detention planet now. Even if they did care, what could they do? It would take a revolution."

"We're talking about people dying there, Hëlo!"

"Yes, we are. And a thousand other places along the war front, my friend. Young men and women are giving their lives for a war that was contrived from the beginning." Hëlo said with a nod. "But the general public wouldn't care one hair on a crion flea about that if they knew. Which they don't. No, sir!" He suddenly sat up and turned to his friend. "As long as the economy is doing well, as long as people have jobs and the Exchange is rocketing through the roof, no one really cares." Hëlo stabbed a boney finger in Flakkinbarr's direction. "You see, Jerrid, I think no matter what we've uncovered, no one, and I mean no one, will want to do anything about it."

It seemed true enough, Jerrid thought to himself. But they were doing something about it. He wondered if there weren't others who still cared and who would fight, contrary to Hëlo's opinion of the general public. "Then, you're thinking about backing out?"

Hëlo threw his friend a cutting glare and then grinned, "Jerrid, we've been friends for nearly ten years now. You're a fine tribune and about the only one I trust nowadays, except for your other three associates. I'm committed to this little conspiracy we've gotten ourselves into. But, I think we're going to need some pretty concrete evidence, other than your little visit to Geasbok, especially if we're going to go up against the Director. What you accidentally stumbled on regarding the clones here on motherworld could easily vanish in the night like so much fog. We're dealing with a ruthless individual that will stop at nothing until he has what he wants."

"Namely?"

Hëlo laughed, "The whole brakkin' Corporate under his thumb and the total destruction of the Solarians. And he'll probably wipe out the Separatists while he's at it."

"You're right, Hëlo, you're right."

"And believe me, we may have to have some alternate plan should all this start unraveling."

Jerrid already had an alternate plan. He thought about broaching the subject to Hëlo right then, but thought better of it. They had one more secret meeting and that would be the place for the discussion of the assassination plans. His stomach tightened suddenly at the thought. He leaned toward his friend and whispered, "What other recourse would you suggest, my friend?"

There was a long pause as Hëlo studied the question. He took a sip of his drink and savored it for a long minute before responding. "Outside of just plain killing Klea, I see anything we do marked with extraordinary difficulty."

So I have guessed right, Jerrid thought. "You may be right, Hëlo, you just may be right."

They both sat there just staring into space for the longest time. Hëlo finished his drink and sat the cup down next to his raincoat. "I've uncovered one of Klea's clones in my organization. Deys Clair."

Flakkinbarr blinked. "You're sure?"

"Oh yes, quite." Hëlo sighed. "The switch was made when the real Clair took a holiday to Tara Senna three months ago. The clone came back, assumed all of the real Clair's duties, and was able to funnel off nearly a trillion ruuls to one of Klea's mysterious black projects in Brocassard."

"You have proof of this?" Flakkinbarr asked.

Hëlo turned to his friend, "I've got an entire comlink with all the data we'll need." Reaching into his pocket, he pulled out the tiny blue comlink he'd been reading when Flakkinbarr first arrived. He handed it to Jerrid. "Take it, check things out. Tuposh would be a good one for that. He has all the angles to places I wouldn't care to know."

Jerrid had to laugh. "Tuposh certainly does, my friend."

Hëlo smiled. "That Tuposh is a remarkable man. He's been such a resourceful fellow." He gave Jerrid a questioning glance. "Does he still operates that magic shop I've heard so many tales about?"

Jerrid chuckled and smiled. "Believe it or not, he takes a couple days a month just to work there to get a bead on the average consumer. It's been a rather profitable venture for him."

"A tribune who's an illusionist." Hëlo chuckled. "Kind of fits, doesn't it?"

"Yes, it does."

Hëlo got to his feet, grabbed his raincoat and tossed his empty cup in a trash can, and then looked toward the sky. "Going to rain before I get back to the office; I can just feel it." He turned to Flakkinbarr. "I'll see you on the twenty-ninth. And I do hope, Jerrid, this will be our last meeting for a long, long time."

"I do too, Hëlo, I do too."

20

"Your love I will always treasure... In life and in love.... We will always be... Distance or time will not matter... Life or death, we will always be... One life... one love..." — from the poetry of Gandhi Caisson, *Lovers and Lives*

24 Sakbar
Darracura District
Flakkinbarr Penthouse
Maggermoss

By most standards, the circular bed with its sleeping occupant seemed insignificant in the massive bedroom. Along the entire twenty yarr length of one wall were darkly tinted windows. The only light in the room was a soft glow cast by a night light in the dressing area.

The sleeping figure on the bed slowly stirred. A hand reached across the sheets, probing for another warm body, but found none. Jerrid managed to open one eye as his vision adjusted to the soft glow of the night light. His mind was in a complete fog, and he could barely remember his own name. Rolling over on his back, he stared at the plain blue paneled ceiling. The pounding headache reminded him of how drunk he had gotten the night before. It was the first time in ten years. But the thoughts in the dark corners of his mind still mocked him. He placed his hands to his throbbing head. His body tensed and his gut tightened at the thought of his previous meeting with Piin and Serpa. It had been a little over a week ago, but it felt like a century. There was still that nagging, unsure feeling as to whether or not he was doing the right thing. Hiring a hit man had been a severe step to take. How could he have been so sure it was the right thing to do at the time but now feel so unsure? He had always been methodical, thinking everything through from beginning to end, always so sure of his decisions. But he dismissed the idea of calling the whole thing off as quickly as it came to mind. Still, he smelled the proverbial rat in the wood pile. It was too late to turn back now! All he could do was to keep moving forward. He lay there with the thin sheet over his half naked body, still staring at the ceiling.

The sound of clinking glass from the kitchen downstairs drew his thoughts back to the present. The bedroom door was ajar, the soft light outlining its edge. Jerrid smiled as he thought of Alleis fixing breakfast, something she hadn't done in over five years.

They sent the servants away yesterday, after they had finished packing all the necessary items for the trip, but not the trip Zoe and Vars thought it was. It was decided that Zoe and Vars would go ahead to the summer resort at Zerabeth. It would be weeks before they found out the truth that Jerrid and his wife were traveling in the opposite direction. But because of their friendship and their faithful service, Zoe and Vars' safety was paramount. He had deeded them the summer resort and a money account that should last five years. Vars and Zoe would have no problem making it last longer, he mused.

This whole affair had become a tangled nightmare of secret meetings and covert investigations. *All because of that book.* He cursed himself for ever having laid eyes on it. Since it had come into his possession two years ago, it had brought nothing but evil into his life. The closer he got to the truth the more the tangled web of intrigue seemed to close in around him. He tried not to focus on it, but the accursed thing seemed bent on his destruction.

The book was in the wall vault downstairs, safe for the moment. Every word it contained haunted him like a specter. The atrocities penned on the yellowed pages were imprinted deeply into every cell in his brain.

"Klea, the son of the devil himself!" Jerrid snarled through clinched teeth. *Don't get started on this, Jerrid, it'll ruin your day.* "It's already ruined!"

he said aloud. Final preparations for the trip were in order. He only had a few hours.

Jerrid had comfort in the fact that Alleis would be safe on Tau Kerus Four. Once there, she would assume a new identity and forget the sordid affairs that had been plaguing them for years. She could truly forget about the Corporate and it's dreaded shadows.

It took an entire year to maneuver funds from their investments on the Exchange to accommodate Alleis' little surprise. He loved her more than his own life and wanted her to be safe. His mouth was dry.

Alleis had been quite inquisitive when her periodic checks detected the withdrawals. *"It's a surprise,"* he had simply stated. He had never lied to her, or kept her in the dark—until now. The best way to broach the whole matter was to take a vacation. He smiled inwardly, remembering four months back.

Surprise wasn't the word for it. When Alleis found out they were going to Tau Kerus Four for vacation, she was irate.

"Why Tau Kerus Four?" she'd asked him, as he felt those determined green eyes burning holes in him. *"That's a nothing place. It's about as interesting as a trip downtown."*

"But it's quaint."

"Quaint!" she threw back. *"Jerrid, nobody takes a vacation to Tau Kerus Four. Why did you spend all this money on a place as boring as that?"*

But once they arrived, Alleis softened. It turned out to be a very pleasant surprise.

Tau Kerus Four was sparsely populated, but it was a quaint agricultural planet with lots of greenery and picturesque settings. Vorska, the third largest city, was slow paced. It was surely a refreshing change. Alleis had fallen in love with the house that he had built for her from the Exchange funds.

The money had been well spent in transforming the old Zha's Trade Headquarters into a livable and attractive house. Alleis liked space and had always longed for a home away from the tangled mess of the city. She was finally going to get her wish. Even servants would be waiting. He had hired the locals Dulor had recommended. They were warm and friendly people, as well as enthusiastic about the perspective job. Alleis had taken to them right from the start. She would certainly miss Zoe and Vars, but it was decided a fresh start for everybody was the order of the day.

Flakkinbarr stretched, feeling his joints and muscles relax. He touched the controls by the window and decreased the tint to eighty percent. His eyes couldn't take too much light right now. The room slowly began to fill with daylight as the tint gradually changed in the windows. As he looked out at the stark shapes of skyscrapers, he was reminded of how much he hated this place. In his opinion, the ugly blue glass of the Sagga building was an eye sore. It had sprung up in the last year, cutting off the penthouse's only view of the bay. Tall buildings housing business conglomerates were considered by most a sure sign of success and progress. He only cursed the fact.

For a long moment Jerrid sat cuddling the pillow to his chest and staring absentmindedly at the blue glass building. He sighed heavily and tossed the pillow back on the bed as he got to his feet and made his way to the dark saigon wood dresser and stared into the mirror. The face that stared back at him looked like it had been through a marathon drinking spree. He hadn't looked this haggard since he graduated the university. He laughed at himself and tried to smooth back his tangled hair.

"You look like you fell off the back of a transport bus," a sweet voice called to him through the fog in his mind.

He turned slowly, careful not to move too fast. Alleis was leaning against the open bedroom door with a wide grin on her deeply tanned face. *She's so beautiful,* Jerrid thought. She was standing there in her long blue dressing gown, her light auburn hair braided up on top of her head.

"What time is it?" he asked, the fog in his mind beginning to clear.

"We have a few hours before the flight leaves," she replied. On any other occasion, Alleis would have enjoyed a trip to a faraway place. But this was not an ordinary trip. On the contrary. She was escaping! Escaping the haunting, unseen evil whose presence now overshadowed every step they took. Their life together had changed, and she didn't like it one bit. "Couldn't you just get rid of that book and forget about everything?"

The statement vaporized the remaining fog in Jerrid's mind. He looked at her lovingly, wishing it was that simple. "I wish I could, but we're too far along for that."

Alleis' face showed no emotion. They had been over this area a thousand times before. There was no shaking Jerrid Flakkinbarr loose from something once he put his teeth into it. He was worse than a vorkon darg when it came to turning loose of something he had hold of.

She managed a smile. "Breakfast is ready. I hope you like it. I tried to follow Zoe's recipe for the eggs. They don't look quite as elegant as hers, but I think you'll like them."

"I know I will." He smiled as he tried to suppress the ache in his heart. He loved her so much. It was going to be hard putting her on that starliner for Tau Kerus Four.

"Hurry up! We haven't much time." Alleis disappeared down the hall.

"We certainly don't," Jerrid called after her.

BonAvvan Intercorporate Spaceport
Maggermoss

The terminal was crowded as always. Lines everywhere. Every ticket counter and boarding check area had at least two hundred people in line. For some it would take hours before they would get boarding clearance. Jerrid and Alleis already had special clearance. It was just a matter of getting through a much smaller line to the boarding area. Several flights would leave from the same terminal junction, so even the people with clearance still had to wait. Many of the people were heading for holidays while some were on business trips. It was just a typical day for most folks, but for the Flakkinbarrs it was a day filled with much emotion.

Jerrid didn't know how he was going to make it through this day. His heart ached for Alleis. Perhaps he should go with her and get away from everything. No! He couldn't. He had already set in motion things that had to be finished. He couldn't back out now. He sighed, knowing that if everything went well he would be joining her in a few weeks.

As they finally came to the junction terminal for boarding, Jerrid couldn't help but notice a few young Watchmen lingering at the next station. The monitor indicated their ship was outbound to the Thorian Range. These days any uniform bothered him. But he forced himself to relax; after all, the Watchmen were a special breed of fighting men. Still, some of them looked too young, or so he thought. A certain blond Watchman caught his eye.

"Who are you looking at?" Alleis asked, catching her husband staring across the crowded junction lobby.

"Those Watchmen," Jerrid replied, shouldering Alleis' travel bag. She always carried more makeup than she needed, but it seemed to be exceptionally heavy this time.

Alleis looked over at the five cadets as they talked among themselves. "They look like nice young men to me."

The blond-headed Watchman talking to the dark-skinned Ovion kept drawing Jerrid's attention. It was a little strange to see an Ovion in a Watchman uniform, but then again, these were hard times. As Jerrid continued to stare at the blond-headed youth the resemblance became quite apparent. An elbow in the ribs caught him off guard.

"Jerrid, don't stare," Alleis remarked. "It's not polite."

"See the blond-headed Watchman?"

Alleis glanced over and noticed the handsome youth as he laughed with his friends. He had a pleasant smile and filled out his uniform rather handsomely, she thought. "Yes."

"At first I thought it might have been Cirin Hunneen's son, Sar."

Alleis' eyebrows shot up. "Really." She turned her head and stared across the crowded lobby. She studied the young man as he engaged his compatriots with jesting and jovial conversation. She shook her head, "He's a little too tall to be Sar, my dear. And his Ovion friend there is much shorter than their servant lad, Jink. Besides, Sar and his friend just went to the Academy at the first of the year."

Jerrid glanced back over at the young men in uniform. "I believe you're right, my dear. Your eyesight is as good as ever. I stand corrected." He smiled at her and tried to find something else to stare at. The line was moving slowly as he continuously checked his pocket chrono.

Alleis slipped her arm around her husband as they moved a few steps toward the check-in counter. "We have time, Jerrid. Put that thing away."

He looked at her sheepishly as he tucked the chrono back into his pocket. Finally they were checked into boarding and were instructed to wait in the lobby until the pre-flight call was made. Great, more waiting! Alleis and Jerrid found a seat next to the blond headed Watchman and his Ovion friend.

The Watchmen kept their conversation to a near whisper as the Flakkinbarrs sat down. Jerrid was still quite drawn to the young Watchman sitting next to him and strained to hear their conversation. It was a good diversion.

"Semion, why did they put us on a civilian flight?" the Ovion was asking the blond Watchman. His accent very strong.

"Lieutenant Tolley told me they had to move the Five-Eight-Three Squadron and all its support people out to Jermerin and needed every available transport," the blond replied. "They even had to pull a few transports from Yeralundy."

"I was looking forward to riding on one of those new J-77s." The Ovion sighed.

Jerrid smiled to himself. He had fought long and hard to acquire the J-77 transports for the Watchman Command. Some members of the military appropriation committee that he headed wanted the K-89 Abitran transport, but he had persuaded them that the heavy lift capabilities of the J-77 could get the job done a lot faster and more efficiently than the K-89.

Alleis slipped her hand over his and turned to him with longing eyes. "Jerrid?"

For a moment he forgot just why they were here. The ache in his heart came flooding back. "I'm sorry."

She smiled, and whispered, "You always liked to eavesdrop."

"Habit." He returned her smile and looked toward the boarding monitor. They had about thirteen minutes before the flight was to leave.

"Excuse me, sir."

Jerrid turned to the young Watchman.

"Yes?"

The blond-headed young man smiled. "Would you have change for a fifty keynote?"

That was a hefty sum for a Watchman to be toting around, Jerrid thought. "Fifty keynote?"

"Yes, sir." The Watchman smiled sheepishly. "I didn't get a chance to change it before we were ordered out."

"Headed to the Thorian Range, I take it, Ensign?" Jerrid just had to ask.

"Yes, sir." The Watchman nodded. "I'm Ensign Semion Therbarn, and this is my friend, Ensign Jinn Porra." The Ovion nodded and gave a polite smile. "We're headed out to Tach School."

Jerrid reached into his pocket and pulled out several pieces of hard money. "I think I have your change." He counted out five small gold squares and took the large thin platinum coin from the ensign.

"Thank you, sir," Ensign Therbarn replied with a bright smile. "Come on, Jinn, we have time to get some kaufee." Jinn rose to his feet and the two of them disappeared into the crowd toward the lobby café.

"Satisfied now?" Alleis grinned.

"Yes." Jerrid replied.

Boarding was announced and Jerrid walked with her as far as the boarding gate. He hated tearful goodbyes and fought to keep his voice from cracking. He loved her so, but he knew that she would be much safer on Tau Kerus Four.

She stood there for the longest moment, not saying a word. It was all too painful. The diversion with the cadets had been good, but now she was going away. She wasn't sure she could really do it either.

"Jerrid, please, come with me. Forget this whole affair and just come with me." Her eyes pleaded with him.

His lip began to tremble. This was going to be hard. *Brak! I knew this was how it was going to be.* "Alleis, oh Alleis!" He grabbed her and held her tight. He just wanted to hold her, to never let her go.

"Flight Eight-Twenty-One now boarding. Please have your passes in order." The attendant called out.

Jerrid looked into her eyes. "I have to know that you're safe, Alleis. You have to go now."

She said nothing. She just stared into his eyes.

"I'll join you in a few weeks. It will all be finished and we can start over." Somehow he felt he was saying good-bye forever. It hurt so bad. But he couldn't tell her how he felt.

Alleis just nodded. It was all she could do. She picked up her carry-on bag and started toward the turnstile, wiping the tears from her eyes. "I love you, Jerrid, very much."

"I love you too, Alleis."

He watched her as she was checked in. Then she went toward the open gate, turned, and waved at him. He lifted his hand weakly and waved in return. "Good-bye, Alleis, I love you."

She turned and disappeared from sight. Jerrid Flakkinbarr felt part of his life disappear right then. All for that cursed book!

* * *

The sun was disappearing behind the jagged cityscape. Jerrid stood at the edge of the garden railing gazing eastward. A cold breeze was steadily coming out of the north and a bank of thunder clouds reflected the last light of the sun. Just like the penthouse and the garden were empty, he now felt empty also. He'd wandered through the place for well over an hour after he'd gotten back from the spaceport. *Empty; without Alleis, life really is empty!* After a small meal, he'd ventured up to the garden, but he couldn't sit in his usual spot. When he gazed at the yellow zebin he kept looking for Tazz. But he knew the cat wasn't coming back. *Tazz is dead, you fool. He can't come back from the grave.* He glanced at where the cat's grave marker had been under the yellow zebin. Jerrid gave a deep sigh, "I'm sorry, Tazz, that we disturbed your resting place." Vars and Zoe had agreed to take the cat's body with them to the summer resort and bury him there. The penthouse would probably go back to the building owners once it was discovered he and Alleis had disappeared from the face of the planet. He gave a half smile and then looked over toward the garden gate. Yanni had been gone for a month now. *Everyone is leaving me!*

"Be safe, Yanni, my friend." Jerrid said to the night air. As the sky deepened into darkness, his thoughts turned once again to his wife. He was comforted in the fact that Jubal Dros had sold the remodeled Zha Trade Headquarters to a one Elia Constantine, a wealthy retiring overseer of the defunct Zemoran Pod Works. Finalization of the deal had resulted in all deeds, documents and other pertinent data expunged from Dros Military Enterprises data banks. Jubal Dros was free and clear of any involvement to the former Zha Trade Headquarters. Tres Dulor had been informed of the sale and been paid a substantial sum not to remember anything about the project. Dulor was more than agreeable to the request. All the documentation for Alleis' new identity had been filtered through one of Tuposh's contacts. *I hope she remembers she's Elia now and not Alleis.* Jerrid sighed. He longed to be on that starliner to Tau Kerus Four. *Soon, soon, I'll be with you!* Yet, inside, he knew there was no hope.

As Jerrid stared out across the massive city there now seemed to be an urgency. He could almost feel the invisible tug of necessity as he continued to stare out at the stark skyscrapers, lights popping on as the darkness grew.

Klea is your problem. He must be eliminated!

Jerrid blinked and gazed skyward at the night sky as stars blossomed into view. He could see Geasbok, shining ever so dimly. Visions of shocktroopers gunning down unarmed prisoners flashed through his mind. As the images intensified, he felt a burning deep inside. The burning was anger, deep seated and bitter. *Yes, Klea and his shadow must be eliminated.*

21

"He who departs from the truth will reap the whirlwind of vengeance. Mark well your words and do not stray from the true path. If you do, the wrath to come will turn you into dust in the blink of an eye."
— Li'Jeen Juu, The Great Shuuto Master, *the Blue Book of Mo'Aangue*

28 Sakbar
The Mysterian Resort
The Black Zaar
Pavarondi
Moon: Bethleea

If there was one thing Ra'Phaak Piin enjoyed, it was the feel of silk. He slid a finger over the black silk tunic that fit loosely over his body. Such fine material, he mused, made by the best tailors on Bethleea. He reached over and took up the long stem wine glass and placed it to his lips. The *Vear Bebri* was a fine vintage as it ran smoothly down his throat. At three hundred ruuls a bottle, it was one of the better wines in his cabinet. Piin savored another sip and then picked up a comlink on the end table by his leather chair. For a few minutes he carefully checked over the sum total from the payment he'd received from Jubal Dros. All untraceable notes that would be easily deposited into his account in a few days. It had been a considerable sum for a first payment. Piin smiled to himself, *Oh, but so well worth the amount!*

"What shall I buy this time?" He asked himself. "Perhaps another ship." Piin laughed and reached for his glass of wine again. As he swirled the red liquid around in the glass a wicked smile slipped across his face. "This had been some adventure, Mr. Dros. Not only do you pay me to find out where your ships are going, but you provide the financing for a plan that I've been working on for years." He replaced his glass and picked up another larger comlink. After switching through several screens, his eyes narrowed as he concentrated on the display. Finally he roared with laughter.

"My good friend, Mr. Dros!" Piin hissed. "You have been such a wealth of information and gain."

Piin had had a number of his trackers infiltrate Dros Military Enterprises. Getting access to high power military equipment proved to be a lot easier than he first thought. The Mirs paid handsomely for those SAVs his man pulled out of Erla Prime. Yes, even his mole at DME's main complex on motherworld had provided some bits of information that could later be brokered for a hefty price. A smuggler had all sorts of cards he could play out. Blackmail was such a useful card these days. Tribunes and overseers were spellbound when that card was played. Piin snickered. His men were very good at what they did and he knew how to manipulate them to their full potential.

Piin took another slow sip of his wine and then paused. There was a stillness that hung over the ship like nothing he'd been aware of before. Strange? He gave a glance out the portal. He didn't see any dockside workers milling about like they usually did this time of day. For a few minutes he listened to the ship. The waters were calm dockside. No ship made noise that didn't exist.

"Brez?" he called out. "Come in here!"

Several minutes passed.

"Where is that stupid Neccian?" Piin asked himself. Still, the strange quiet began to make his skin crawl. "Brez! Get in here, you fool!" This time he shouted it.

Presently there were the sound of boots in the hallway. The door to the cabin opened and Serpa stepped in dressed in his usual black attire. A long sword in a jeweled scabbard was attached to his right hip. The assassin strode into the room with the confidence of a man on a mission.

"I called for Brez! Where is that fool?" Piin snarled at Sepra.

"Brez is indisposed right now." Serpa replied, a cool edge in his voice.

"What do you mean, indisposed?" Piin shot him another snarl. "I want him here, right now!"

Serpa walked to the end table and picked up the comlink from Jubal Dros. He flipped through the screen and then glanced back at Piin. "When do you plan on giving me my cut?"

"In due course!" Piin snapped back.

The assassin then turned and picked up the other comlink. "And this?"

"None of your brakkin' business." Now Piin was getting very annoyed.

"I'll make it my business," Serpa snarled back.

Piin rocketed to his feet and pointed a finger at the assassin. "Get out! Tell Brez to get his lazy butt in here. Right now!"

Serpa gave him a cockeyed smile. "You are such a fool, Piin." He laughed.

Piin didn't know what to make of Sepra's remark.

"This is too easy." Serpa laughed, pulling the sword out of it's scabbard with the slightest noise. He whipped the silver blade around several times and then leveled it at Piin.

"You idiot!" Piin snarled, his eyes narrowing. But he was a little uncertain as to Serpa's true intentions. He felt the hiss of betrayal well up inside like a deadly viper ready to strike. "You think I fear that ancient weapon?"

Serpa just smiled as his eyes, too, narrowed into a hard stare. "I have an assortment of weapons from which to do this job you require." The assassin again whipped the sword around and then slashed it across Piin's chest, just barely cutting the fabric of his tunic.

Piin's eyes widened in total shock, as the lower portion of the tunic fell to the floor. Not even a cut to his skin.

"I'm very good with these things, my friend." Serpa hissed.

Recovering from the threat, Piin extended his hand and pushed out with his mind. Serpa's hand flexed violently to the left, throwing the long blade up against the tall lampstand in the corner. This time Serpa was the one who was surprised, but only for a moment. He kicked out with his right foot, planting it squarely in Piin's face. The force of the kick knocked Piin across the room and sent him sprawling into the wine cabinet. The sound of shattering glass drowned out Piin's cry of pain.

With the speed of a leaping cat, Serpa crossed the room, retrieved his sword turning it into a flashing cyclone. Before Piin could get to his feet Serpa dropped to one knee, lunging the long silver blade into the Shuuto's chest. He withdrew it quickly and then stabbed Piin several more times before pushing it through his heart.

Piin's eyes bulged as the scream caught in his throat. The light in his eyes quickly faded.

"Too easy!" Serpa pulled out the blade and wiped it on the black silk piece he'd cut from Piin's tunic. He sheathed his sword and then walked over to the end table and grabbed both comlinks. Serpa walked out as calmly as he had walked in. Even in death Piin just stared up at the ceiling, not believing he'd just been betrayed.

22

"Plots against the establishment are usually hushed whispers. Most never see the light of day, much less get media coverage, unless it's to benefit the cause of the present power brokers. There were more than a few people of influence who believe something was covered up by the government. The conspiracy seemed to take root one rainy Velday, forever changing the course of history for its unsuspecting victims."
— Tosaar Julink, *The Vanishing Act*

29 Sakbar
Corrina Park
Maggermoss

It was raining as the Dalvon Special deramped and entered Corrina Park. The rain set the mood, dampening Flakkinbarr's feelings as he stared out the window. Alleis consumed his thoughts, and the loneliness he felt without her caused the ache in his heart to swell. He was dressed once again in his steel gray raincoat. He and Juyin met Frediana at the Mills Station near Mycron Seventy-Five east of the city and purposely drove toward the outskirts of Maggermoss before doubling back to Corrina Park.

"I'm getting tired of this kibbercat game we're playing, Frediana," Juyin said out of the side of his mouth. His eyes were focused on the darkening sky.

A smile slipped across Frediana's face. "Just a precaution, my friend."

Juyin stared at the liquor bar at one end of the seat. He already felt miserable. A stiff drink might be just the thing right about now. The thought lingered a moment longer, but he pushed it aside. "I changed taxis five times before I got to Mills Station. Do you know how much I had to pay in fares for that little excursion?"

She made no comment.

Juyin grunted. "It was nerve racking!"

Flakkinbarr chuckled.

Juyin snarled, "I suppose you think all this is funny, eh, Jerrid?"

Before he could answer the question the limo came to a halt. The door slid open, allowing the last two members of the secret society to join the party. Sliding into the seat next to Frediana was Gerrius Tuposh, his mustache looking more like a large furry caterpillar sitting on his upper lip. The last man on board was Hëlobstan Kesperroud. He took his seat, grumbling under his breath about the weather.

The stretch of Corridor Orange that circled Corrina Park was out of place in a world filled with towering steel structures and masses of tangled highway systems. The park was one of the last bastions for nature in a world where high tech invention had erased the elegance of the natural world and replaced it with the stark mechanical standards of mankind and his creation.

As the sky grew even darker, the dark, dense shape of buggoum trees cast an eerie and foreboding shadow over the park .

Seeing the bar on the side panel, Gerrius took a deep breath, "I could use a drink right about now."

Frediana acknowledged his request with a smile and pushed the button on the panel. Gerrius' face brightened as the drink dropped from the slot.

After several sips he finally looked over at Flakkinbarr. "Did you bring the book?"

The Dalvon Special, now in its fully automated mode, received its information from sensor lines buried in the roadway. A bright blue light on the panel lit up, bringing to life a blank screen next to it. **Program Override:** The signal to alert the occupants of a course change flashed red and then winked out. The hacker had anticipated the signal, adjusted the correction and silenced all alert alarms and indicators. The panel quickly shifted back to it's operational blue color as data streamed once again across it's luminous screen.

Program Override Re-engaged:
Master Control Switch to
Decomm— SYS Three Mark Seven...
Commencing New Assignment...
Proceed Grid— Mark Della Seven
Junction Grid— Mark Forty Six...

With their backs to the screen, everyone was oblivious to what was taking place on the control panel. The new directions were fed into the car's computer brain. They were now traveling through the forested area surrounding Maggermoss, but no one noticed as the car shifted lanes and moved onto Corridor Green.

Flakkinbarr brought out the attaché case and positioned it on his lap. Cautiously opening the case, he carefully removed its contents. The pages of the book were thin and yellowed with age, and its black leather binding had seen better days. Books of this type had not been made in over eight hundred years, and the only place anyone could see them now was in the finest historical museums or the steel vault of St. Patrin of Abisba. It was hard to believe that this small object, a relic of the past, was destroying his life.

Hëlo stared at the book on Jerrid's lap. "I can't believe that thing has survived this long."

Everyone else agreed.

Before beginning, Jerrid carefully gauged each member of his little conspiracy group. Now he had to make his findings very basic and pointed. He cleared his throat and began, "The book I have here was written by a prominent bio-engineer during the Genetic War."

"Now wait a minute, Jerrid," Juyin butted in. "We've already established, as hard as it may be to believe, that the *Butcher of Klivic*,

Da'min Ben'Lea, and our illustrious leader Dameon Klea are the same person. But now you're saying, Dameon Klea was a bio-engineer during the Genetic War?"

"Yes, I am."

Frediana gasped, placing her hand to her mouth.

"And Dameon Klea was his real name back then?" Tuposh asked, a little bewildered.

"I don't know why he chose to use his real name again." Flakkinbarr shrugged his shoulders. Everyone stared as he gingerly fingered through the brittle pages. He knew those stares. He experienced the same type of disbelief when he read the book for the first time. "Klea has left a paper trail, if you will, across a thousand years of time. His only mistake was leaving this journal behind for someone to discover." Jerrid studied each face in the car. "There is no mistake; the handwriting is identical in every handwritten document I've obtained from the Director's office. And it conclusively matches all the other ancient manuscripts we've obtained. There is even a pictograph of him on the last page. It, too, is identical to the ones of our present Director."

They all eyed each other. His colleagues continued to stare like children at a carnival sideshow.

Jerrid continued, "I had a fingerprint and skin cell sample lifted from our leader and had them analyzed. They match the ones inscribed on this card to the last gene." This last bit of information left them completely stunned, and now they were a captive audience. Up until now, it had been conjecture and speculation, but the proof was in and it was irrefutable.

Working his way to the back of the book, Flakkinbarr came to a half page with a small rectangular piece of plastoid. There, for everyone to see, was the crude looking ID with a pictograph of a man who bore an uncanny resemblance to their present leader. Just to the right of the pictograph in large blue letters were the words: **DAMEON KLEA: CHIEF ENGINEER BIO—SCIENCE DIVISION—C5**. Underneath that was the unmistakable signature of the present day Director. A watermark emblem of the Solarian Federation was clearly visible.

Hëlo shook his head in disbelief. "It can't be? From what we know, responsibility for the holocaust of the Genetic War lies with one man, Marcum Apollus, a Solarian. Do you realize the implications of what you're saying?" He couldn't keep his eyes off the crude card. "There is no known race, anywhere, that lives to be a thousand years old. Solarians certainly don't."

Flakkinbarr nodded. "This is my proof," he said, tapping the book with his finger. "My friend at the university was very thorough in his testing."

Gerrius Tuposh was also finding it difficult to believe what he was seeing, even though the speculations he and his friends had privately discussed over the past few months had pointed in this direction. He just kept staring at the card. "This is incredible, Jerrid. What this implies then, is that not only did Director Klea have a hand in the Genetic War, but on top of that he's also Solarian? It's incredible!" Gerrius took a long sip from his drink. The warm liquor felt good running down his throat. His nerves began to settle, at least for the moment.

Jerrid could feel their rising emotions. This meeting was going to get pretty heated before the night was over. "Colleagues, we have a dilemma on our hands. With the evidence we have, we could convene a special council and hope to convince a majority of the Tribunal to have the Director brought up on charges."

Hëlo gasped. "That could be dangerous! How many people in the Tribunal are who we think they are? We're not even sure who's on what side anymore. The Separatists are gaining friends every day. Besides, Klea would have us up on charges of treason before we could present our evidence."

"He has a point, Jerrid." Frediana stated.

Hëlo nodded and went on. "Who do you think would believe us?" He paused, searching each one's face. "It's one thing to provide evidence about the torture mills on Geasbok and the SPG's link to the killing of the five trade ministers from Pusholiin, but everyone is going to be skeptical when we say that Klea is a thousand year old Solarian." He looked down at the crude ID. "In spite of what that card says, who will believe us?" The web of intrigue was now becoming a tangled mess of complications.

Flakkinbarr's mouth felt parched. "This is the key book, my friends. Everything we've uncovered matches perfectly the evil experiments and dark deeds written here." He paused again as he studied the faces of his friends. He saw the fear in their eyes. They were hanging on his words. "What we hold in our hands will undoubtedly expose the devil for who he is. But there are others we will need to bring into our confidence if we are to succeed."

"Who can we trust?" Gerrius blurted out. "From your little visit to Traylencoor, we know that at least twenty of our Tribunal friends are clones. We already have good reason to suspect that Resrok, Ceysseur, Monsoka, and Taggerly may be copies of their real selves as well. How do we know for sure that Klea hasn't gotten a hundred more clones in the Tribunal?"

"We don't!" Flakkinbarr stated flatly.

Hëlobstan moaned. "Then we're all in a *gres* bag with no way out!" He stared at Jerrid. "If I hadn't seen the initial evidence with my own eyes, I wouldn't have believed any of this." He tried to force a laugh, but it stuck in his throat. "Do you realize what we're saying? *We* are saying that the saint and savior of the Corporate is in actuality a devil bent on our ruination."

Gerrius gasped, "My God!" He shook his head. "What kind of a monster have we allowed to become our Director?"

All eyes were on the younger man as the realization of his words began to sink in. Fear had a visible reaction. Gerrius' eyes were wide and nearly glassy, his mouth twitched in distorted movements as the seconds ticked away. Fear and dread overwhelmed him.

Alleis quickly came to Jerrid's mind, tugging at his heart strings. That momentary flash of memory, of seeing Alleis disappear into the crowd at the spaceport, caused the ache in his heart to intensify. Perhaps he should have gone with her and forgotten this whole business. He hated this! All of it! He fought the ache in his heart and the pain in his gut. He had committed himself past the point where he could turn back. Even now, Alleis knew nothing about the part of his plan to have Klea assassinated. She never would have accepted it. *There is no turning back now.* Bravely, he continued. "Colleagues, you are all my trusted friends.

Although we don't always agree, I know that we can count on our friendship to see us through. We must never forget what we have seen and heard here tonight. Dameon Klea intends no good thing for the Corporate; I'll stake my life on that." He trembled. That's exactly what he was doing. The car continued on, the steady hum of the machine a soothing lullaby to their thoughts.

Finally, shaking the morbid images that were flooding his mind, Gerrius regained his composure. There were things he had also discovered that were vital to their investigation. "You're going to find my report very disturbing as well." He paused to take a sip of his drink. All eyes were on him now. "I was able to do some deep digging concerning the attack on Ijazzani."

"The Tribunal's still reeling from that." Frediana remarked, the edge in her voice noticeable. "At least we can count on you to find out what really happened."

"From all initial research, it was indeed the SPG who engineered the so-called Miranrian attack on Ijazzani. They used the two Miranrian cruisers captured in the Vosonna Raid last month." Gerrius glanced around the car.

"What?" Flakkinbarr and Juyin gasped.

"I was able to find three members of the crew on one of the ships who weren't SPG. They did some talking. They're willing to point fingers." Gerrius paused, "As long as we get them to a safe place."

"That could be difficult." Hëlo snorted. "Safe is a shadowy term these days."

Flakkinbarr just nodded. The web was becoming wider. "I believe today's declaration of war on the Miranrian Federation was due solely to their recent alignment with the Solarians and their willingness to support the Separatists movement."

"Klea was just looking for an excuse to drag the Miranrians into the war," Gerrius replied. "Even if he had to engineer an excuse, just like he did when he started the Solarian war."

"This could be another step in Klea's plans for complete governmental control of the Corporate." Jerrid placed his hand on his stomach.

"I think the Separatists are one big crack in that step," Frediana pointed out.

The others nodded.

Flakkinbarr smiled weakly. "If we allow him to continue enacting racial and prejudicial laws against any person in the Corporate, regardless of our personal feelings," he stared hard at Juyin Hallenn who had slouched down a little further in his seat, "we will eventually become the same type of monster that Klea has become. We all know that control is slipping from our hands to his at an alarming rate. I'm afraid that one day soon he will be the absolute power over our government. Then where will we be?"

"The majority of the people in the Corporate love him," Gerrius remarked. "Except for the Separatists. Klea's brought such dramatic changes in our economy that not many people are willing to challenge his programs. Everyone praises his advancements in agricultural and biological developments."

Hëlo remarked sarcastically, "He's doing a good job selling himself over the cons. We all know that a good advertising package can sell just about any product."

"The man's a genius!" Gerrius blurted out. He had to admit, like most of the citizens of the Corporate that there were things about Klea that were admirable. "His fame is of such magnitude that getting people to listen, much less believe us or anyone else who would try to convince them otherwise, will be very difficult."

Flakkinbarr nodded. "Granted, he did us some good, but I think it was only because it fell in line with his own schemes." He tapped the thick journal. "I've spent many hours reading this and I can come to only one conclusion: I believe that Dameon Klea is conducting genetic experiments on Geasbok in the same vein as he did on Gheyenna a thousand years ago. The information we have concerning the torturous experiments now taking place coincides with the details of the hideous experiments written about in this book. We also have evidence about the involvement of our Tribunal friends and Marshal Resrok, but we need more details to back these findings."

Hëlobstan gasped. "I'm afraid to think of what might happen to us if Director Klea finds out that we have this book."

Heaviness hung in the air as each person mulled over their own thoughts of what it would be like to be found out and tried before the High Tribunal. In those few minutes time seemed to be suspended in eternity. They realized that life, like a priceless creation of art, could be so precariously balanced as to be dropped and ruined in an instant, with no chance for salvation.

"Who are we going to get to listen to us?" Gerrius asked, looking carefully at each of his friends. "We will have to be extremely careful. We don't know who else on the Tribunal Klea has cloned."

They stared at one another, acutely aware of the growing danger.

Gerrius went on. "Some of our information holds considerable weight, but shouldn't this book give us an even stronger case? First, we need to get someone higher up to listen to us."

"Gerrius is right," Frediana stated, the unsettling mood of the meeting causing her to shiver. "Perhaps we should go directly to the Vice Director."

"If he isn't already a clone!" Juyin interjected.

Flakkinbarr quickly intercepted the thought. "Aldolf is no clone. I made sure of that several days ago."

Hëlo snapped in reply. "Everyone knows that Klea is keeping Vice Director Aldolf busier than usual with war matters." He pushed back into the seat. "Trying to see Aldolf now would be risky; besides, who's to say he would believe us?"

No one said anything. The car continued making its way down the winding highway through the forested landscape.

"What alternatives do we have?" Juyin asked.

Flakkinbarr tried to clear his mind, but the heaviness of this whole affair was choking off his thoughts. The haunting images he had painted for himself and his friends whirled through his mind like an unleashed cyclone. He knew there would be no relief until Klea was dead and gone.

Klea is your problem! His elimination is paramount! The sooner you rid the Corporate of this man, the better! Klea must be eliminated once and for all!

Jerrid blinked. It sounded like Piin whispering in his ear. *Klea must be eliminated once and for all!* There was now an urgency in that single thought. Serpa would do the job soon and it would all be over. *Over, yes.*

He couldn't help but think of Alleis. She was probably more than halfway to Tau Kerus Four by now. He desperately wanted to be with her, but there was no time for second guessing. "We could all leave and get as far away from Klea as possible. Surely each of you could come up with some type of excuse for getting yourselves lost in another star system." He gazed at Frediana. "I understand that the Delium Range is very nice, and that the Rugguun Lines now run out that way fairly regularly."

Everyone chuckled. Frediana just squirmed and smiled. After all, she had conducted research out on the Delium Range during her university days. "I don't think I could handle primitive living conditions right now." At this, the tension in the air was cut with roars of laughter, the tension momentarily relieved. Everyone relaxed for the first time that evening. Frediana was known for her enjoyment of life's more refined pleasures. No one could imagine her living in such an unsophisticated culture. "I'm living too well these days. I don't think I could bring myself to live in the Delium Range."

"You could bring a few of your servants, Frediana," Flakkinbarr jested. "Fifty or so might do."

Everyone laughed again.

Gerrius didn't want to be a spoilsport, but fear was clawing at the back of his mind. "We have a responsibility, comrades."

Hëlo nodded. "We must get to the Vice Director as soon as possible then."

"Aldolf will want hard evidence." Flakkinbarr paused, looking down at the attaché. He looked out the window, mulling over a thought that had been haunting him for days now. His original intent had been only to save the Corporate. But now here he was in the middle of a conspiracy, soon to be a traitor in the eyes of many. The light was nearly gone and shadows stalked the landscape. The dismal weather only intensified his apprehensions. Jerrid shivered uncontrollably. With night fast approaching, the darkness hid his enemy in the shadows. An enemy who he knew was ready at any moment to deliver the final blow. "I think Klea is aware that this book still exists."

"My word, man!" Hëlo shouted. "Then let's get rid of the book and forget about everything we've uncovered."

Jerrid shot him a menacing stare. "Listen to me, all of you!" His tone was hard. "If Klea suspects that we know anything, we probably don't have long to live. We already know too much, and like it or not we're right in the middle of a conspiracy to overthrow our Director." There! He had said it, but it still didn't seem to make things any better. "Whether we like it or not, we've thrown our lot in with the Separatists."

Hëlo gasped. "There you have it. You said it, Jerrid. Let's face it. We'll all be branded Separatists if this leaks out." He wiped his forehead. "My concern is that this situation has become extremely volatile and far more dangerous than I could have ever imagined. It has gotten too big for the five of us." Hëlo turned his stare toward Flakkinbarr. "Your friend at the university, Jerrid, just how trustworthy is he?"

Flakkinbarr understood Hëlo's growing fears. "You don't have to be afraid. As far as my friend at the university, I've just found Klea's book, that's all he knows. I trust him to keep silent. No one can point to us as conspiring against the Director just yet. Believe me, you're safe for the moment."

"Then what alternatives do we have?" Frediana asked.

Jerrid swallowed hard. The solution was already taken care of, and yet it still bothered him that he had acted solely on his own without first consulting his friends. "I think there is only one option left."

No one dared ask. All eyes were fixed on their gray-haired comrade as they waited for his response.

"Assassinate Klea."

Gerrius had a difficult time believing that his close friend could suggest such a heinous crime. "Assassinate the Director of the Corporate?"

"Yes." Flakkinbarr nodded.

"Who's going to do it?" Juyin shot Jerrid a calculating look.

"I've already made the arrangements," Jerrid shot back.

"Jerrid," Frediana gasped.

He didn't even look at her. Jerrid sighed heavily. "The rest of you will be kept out of it; I promise you." They were all just staring at him, with good reason. "A while back I liquidated my assets and contacted a man who will serve us well."

Juyin snarled, "Without consulting us first?" There was confusion in his voice. "Does Piin have anything to do with this, Jerrid?"

Jerrid returned a cutting stare. "Piin is the man who suggested this course of action. His man will do the job discretely, Juyin."

Frediana twisted the expensive zerrin chain dangling from her long neck. "Discretely? Jerrid, assassinating the Director of the Corporate is not a discrete matter."

There was a moment of cold silence as the others considered the course they were about to venture on. They glanced at one another, trying to extract some sign of confirmation, certainty, or confidence that this was indeed the right thing to do.

"If we do not get rid of Klea, now," Jerrid stroked the leather binding, "then I'm afraid that more of what is revealed in this book will happen throughout our beloved Corporate. Geasbok is already testimony to that."

Silence fell.

"If Klea finds out before Piin's man has time to act?" Juyin did not want to think of the consequences.

"Then, my friend, perhaps it is best that you start finding a way off motherworld to some remote place, regardless of your personal feelings for such." He glanced over to Frediana. "Klea's SPG will not be too hospitable if we are found out." He paused and stared out the window. He turned back toward his colleagues, "The game we are playing, my friends, is for all the tokens."

A sudden jolt rocked the car and a deafening explosion ripped through the air conditioned compartment in the rear of the limo. The vehicle careened off the road and plummeted down a steep embankment, ejecting its occupants onto the hard, wet ground. The hover car continued crashing through scrubs and small spindly trees before violently coming to a halt at the iron fence at the bottom of the hill. The front of the car was a mass of twisted metal. Electrical wires were sputtering and crackling through the gaping holes. The rain continued in its steady cadence, seemingly ignoring the desperate plight at hand.

Picking himself up, Flakkinbarr struggled to reach the shelter of a few scrubby bushes. The black limo was broken in two and lay scattered across the ground in sizzling chunks. A body lay crushed beneath the overturned chassis.

Frediana was beside herself, screaming hysterically as she tried to get to her feet. Jerrid could barely see her through the eerie shadows cast by the corridor lights above. Not far from her was his friend, Juyin, struggling to get to his feet, but the thick, wet grass that lined the embankment made it nearly impossible. He looked for Gerrius, but he could not find him. Perhaps it was he who lay crushed to death beneath the wreckage, or was it Hëlobstan? Jerrid kept slipping on the wet grass as he tried to move from the bushes. His hand came down to break his fall, touching something soft and cold; he only hoped it was the forest floor and not a living creature. He strained to see in the dim light, wiping the rain from his eyes. He stared for a moment, looking at what his hand come to rest on. It was a miracle, or had the curse simply searched him out? Without thinking he scooped up the book and placed it in his coat.

The lights of the car flickered several times and then burned out, plunging the area into near darkness. Now only the eerie corridor lights provided illumination for the area, creating a landscape of dark shadows. Flakkinbarr was startled. He tried to get up again, but a bolt of laser fire flashed through the night. He dropped to the ground and watched as the car exploded into a thousand pieces. More laser fire followed, volley after volley. His whole body trembled as he lay on the cold, wet ground. When the firing ceased, he opened his eyes and saw the four silhouetted forms on the roadway above him. Two of the forms were human, he told himself. The other two were vaguely familiar, but were somehow out of proportion. He crawled into the cover of a group of nearby trees to watch what was going on above him. Panic told him to run, but he remained frozen in the shadows of the trees. Perhaps for a moment he was safe. Then he did something he knew he shouldn't. He crawled back toward the wreckage to get a better look at the shadowy figures. Flakkinbarr looked down at his ruined lizard skin shoes he had just purchased yesterday. He laughed at himself for having such a foolish thought, knowing that at any moment he might be the one to die. The rain began to fall harder as the claps of thunder pierced the silent darkness. His teeth chattered, and he shook uncontrollably.

Elaborate patterns of blue lightning danced across the dark, rain laden sky. For a moment, Flakkinbarr stood to his feet in utter shock and horror. He squinted, trying to get a better look at the two tallest figures at the top of the embankment. He hoped for another flash of lightning so he could be absolutely certain. Between the claps of thunder he heard the hysterical screams of Frediana and Juyin's cursing. There was no mistaking it, Flakkinbarr knew the two men at the top of the embankment. One of the men, the hood of his raincoat laid back and exposing his face, was Dameon Klea, Director of the Corporate. The other man, large and muscular, was the same person he had talked to a few weeks earlier. In fact, he and Serpa were scheduled to rendezvous later this evening. Jerrid was absolutely sure there were only two human figures standing at the top of the embankment. Where was Piin? Why wasn't he here as well? The sting of betrayal and humiliation crushed him. He knew that his error in judgment had cost his friends their lives and possibly his own.

Lightning continued to race across the night sky in a dozen whips and wheels. The rain came harder. Then Jerrid began to understand; the other forms were dargs. But there was something about these dargs that greatly disturbed him. They were not like the ordinary domesticated dargs owned by virtually everyone on motherworld. These dargs were about twice the normal size. They stood still and motionless like statutes. The iridescent glow of their coats looked more like metal armor than skin.

His attention suddenly shifted to Frediana. She and Juyin were struggling up the steep embankment toward the dark figures. Flakkinbarr felt a compulsion to scream out and warn them, but an even stronger feeling gripped him.

Juyin pulled and strained, trying to calm the screaming woman, and at the same time keep them from slipping back down the hill. He hurled obscenities at her for being so childish. Finally they reached the top of the embankment. By this time Juyin was half dragging Frediana.

"Ah!" came a mocking voice from the shadows. "Tribunes Hallenn and Lisstrin, you look like you could use some help."

Juyin's wet hair piece fell into his face. Holding up Frediana with one hand he rubbed his eyes with the other, hoping that this was just a bad dream and that at any minute he would wake up. "Sir?" With the next flash of lightning it became clear who was addressing him. The horror and panic rose, while sinking waves of nausea engulfed him. "Director Klea, sir?"

Klea's lips parted to a mocking grin as he laughed at them. The rain seemed to be of no consequence to Klea; one might even think he was enjoying this. He stared long and hard at the two cold and trembling figures standing before him. "Too bad, too bad."

"It was all Flakkinbarr's idea, sir!" The betrayal rolled off his lips like honey. He didn't care anymore. Right now, saving his own skin was his primary concern.

Klea laughed with amusement. "Nice try, Tribune Hallenn, nice try."

"But, sir!" Juyin protested, tightening his grip around Frediana's waist. "He put us up to it! I swear!" Juyin trembled and began to squirm, shuffling from one foot to the other. "Frediana and I were just trying to find out what they were plotting, sir."

Thunder rumbled and Klea laughed viciously. "Tribune Hallenn, do you want me to take pity on you and have mercy?"

Klea looked at the two monstrous dargs that stood a few paces from him. Juyin eyed the creatures and his mouth dropped opened in terror. These were no ordinary dargs. They had no hair or thick furry coats as was common to their species, if you could call them that at all. These were metal creatures, android dargs, with vicious white eyes. One of the dargs' mouth opened and revealed a set of razor-edged teeth. Juyin swallowed hard and tried to scream, but no sound came out.

"Now, my pets," Klea commanded, addressing his creatures in an affectionate tone, "I think it's time you had something to eat." It was ironic. Everyone knew androids, no matter what type or style, never ate anything. "Kill them!"

The dargs sprang with quick, fluid movements, something extraordinary for a machine. Before Hallenn and Lisstrin could turn and run, the metal monsters brought them down and began ripping clothes and flesh piece by piece, discarding the pieces like unsavory food. Klea turned and wiped his forehead. "You see, Serpa, my pets can be as effective as my SPG."

The tall, muscular man with the laser rifle smiled. "I see what you mean. Very impressive." The blood feast sent a wave of cold horror up Serpa's spine. "And Flakkinbarr?"

Klea laughed. "My pets are good trackers, Serpa."

Jerrid retched. He had never seen anything so gruesome in all his life. Every fiber of his being screamed at him to run. So he ran!

Deeper and deeper into the woods he ran as the rain intensified. Without looking back he scurried from one thicket of trees to another, hoping for better concealment. He leaned against the cold bark of the buggoum tree, gasping for air. He was no longer concerned about the rain. Freedom was all he wanted, freedom from Klea and his metal monsters.

"Oh, Alleis!" he said it pleadingly. If he could only see her, hold her close to his body one more time.

The storm raged on. Then came a sound that struck fear in his heart, the sound of something moving, something large. He peered around the tree and looked back. He saw a flash of light, only this time it wasn't lightning. It was the glistening coat of metal-skinned monsters moving through the dense underbrush. He ran on, this time with even greater determination. The thorns lashed out at his legs and the rain beat against his aching body. The rain soaked ground grabbed at his feet and slowed his every step as he raced toward freedom. Freedom? Where? Where would there be any freedom from Klea and his evil forces?

Still, the beasts had not overtaken him. Further and further into the woods he ran, pressing even harder. Without looking back, he could tell the dargs were still on his trail. In his mind he could see their forms closing in for the kill. That sound, that uncanny hum of machinery was heard above the falling rain. An evil presence began to press down upon him, and the pungent smell of death drew closer. Too weary to go on, he dropped behind a huge pine tree and gasped for air. He hoped it would be a quick end.

He listened. Nothing! There was only the sound of the hard rain falling and his own labored breathing. Could it be that he had lost the mechanical killers? He waited, listening. Still there was nothing, only the rain. In that very instant, Jerrid Flakkinbarr remembered his dream. The deadly dream that had haunted him for many a night. *Oh dear Aidioni, help me please, help me!* Then he heard it, the sound of moving brush, the eerie hum of machines sliding through the undergrowth. The fear and the horror returned as he struggled to his feet and bolted into the thick underbrush. Jerrid could feel his lungs burn, his legs begin to weaken as he scrambled down a shallow ravine toward a tangle of dark gray zebin trees. The tip of his shoe caught on a rock and he fell to the ground with a loud thud. The fall forced the air out of his lungs. Jerrid just lay there. *Let me die! Let me die!* Surely the dargs were closing for the kill now. Drawing a hand across his face to wipe away the rain he noticed a strange thing. In the middle of the tangled gray zebins he recognized one slightly odd one. A yellow zebin! He blinked and forced himself to suck in a lung full of air. Again, wiping the rain out of his eyes, he stared at the tree, not really believing what he was seeing. A slight shimmering glow seemed to outline the tree against the rest of the dark woods.

Meow!

Jerrid blinked.

Meow!

All Jerrid could do was shake his head. He knew he must be hallucinating. But right there it was, no more that a hundred yarrs in front of him. The yellow zebin glowed with an eerie light. That was Tazz's meow. *But Tazz is dead!*

Meow!

Again Jerrid wiped the rain from his eyes as a pin point of light popped into view just in front of the yellow zebin. The light flashed several times as it grew to the size of a small melon. As Flakkinbarr again wiped the rain from his eyes he heard the tearing of fabric as the light pulsated three times.

Meow!

Jerrid's mouth opened in utter shock. Tazz was sitting under the yellow zebin, his tail wrapped around his front paws. He looked so healthy, so full of life. Jerrid's lower lips began to tremble as tears fell from his eyes. "Tazz!" He reached out for the cat.

Follow me, my friend, quickly! The cat got to his feet and turned back toward the darker zebin trees. He paused at the edge of the denser wood.

Hurry, the machines are coming. Please, follow me!

Getting to his feet, Jerrid struggled to keep pace with the cat as he maneuvered through the dense woods, up several rocky ledges to higher ground. The strange thing about it, Tazz kept a steady pace at least twenty yarrs in front and never looked back unless Flakkinbarr faltered or slowed. The most amazing thing, as far as Jerrid could tell, was that the cat was completely dry. The rain had no effect on his fur, none whatsoever. After a while the trees began to thin and Tazz slowed his pace. Finally, the cat came to a halt and sat down, wrapping his tail around him. Jerrid dropped to his knees and pulled the cat to his chest and cuddled him for a long time. In the downpour, Tazz was as dry as if the sun was blazing bright.

"Oh Tazz, I've missed you!"

The cat looked deep into Jerrid's eyes and he felt his soul stir. Flakkinbarr that night understood that Tazz loved him very deeply as well and was longing to be with him again. As Jerrid knelt there, cradling the cat in his arms, rain falling hard, a light flashed from behind him and he again heard the tearing of fabric and the sweet smell of lillies.

"Jerrid?"

Jerrid slowly turned, knowing who he was about to see.

Lt. Arie'el stood no more than five yarrs away. "Remember, the rain is your salvation." The lieutenant smiled and stretched out his hand. Tazz meowed, pushed out of Jerrid's hands and went over to sit by the lieutenant. "Tazz just wanted to see you again. He'll be waiting for you and Alleis at the end of days."

The blinding glow of the lieutenant's uniform caused Jerrid to shield his eyes. When he opened them the light was gone and the rain continued its steady downpour. He looked around and suddenly found himself at the edge of another highway. He was startled by the sight of the traffic corridor. But it was not well traveled. In the distance a single set of headlamps were coming toward him. *Was I just dreaming all that? Tazz, Lt. Arie'el? Remember, the rain is your salvation. Perhaps I'll make it yet*, he thought. This new hope stirred his adrenaline and pushed him on. He gathered his last bit of strength and ran all out toward the roadway. Amazed at his own quickness, Flakkinbarr ran toward the highway a few short yarrs away. Gasping for air, his chest felt like it would explode, but he managed to reach the shiny wet pavement. He thought for sure that he would make it now, the approaching headlamps growing brighter and brighter.

Suddenly, from thirty yarrs away, two large shapes emerged from the woods and jumped onto the wet surface of the highway. Flakkinbarr's eyes grew wide with terror. He let out a piercing scream and began running toward the lights of the oncoming car. The car slowed as the driver saw the man and his pursuers.

With even more determination, Jerrid pushed his body beyond its natural limits, thinking at any moment he would explode. His legs moved quickly now. The aches and pains momentarily left his thoughts as the adrenaline continued to surge through his body. He was only a few yarrs from the car when the first mechanical darg sprang for the attack. The slippery pavement caused it to get off balance, allowing the mechanical beast only to slash a deep gouge in Jerrid's left leg. He screamed and dropped to the pavement. Pain detonated through his whole body and blood gushed onto the wet pavement. The second darg was now circling around, preparing to sink his gleaming teeth deep into the screaming man's side. Jerrid kicked out with his good leg against the mechanical monster as it lunged at him, forcing the creature back a few paces. Again the creature lunged, maw snapping. A front paw lashed out striking Jerrid in the face, laying open a large gash across his forehead. Then Jerrid heard the screaming roar of an engine and the blinding lights of an auto obscured his view. The next thing he heard was the thud of metal against metal as the car rocketed into the dargs, knocking them across the road. With blood streaming into his eyes Jerrid saw the blurred figure of a man emerge from the car. He could not see clearly, but he had the distinct feeling that he knew this man. The man lifted Flakkinbarr up on his good leg and shoved him into the limo.

"Cirin?" he coughed. "Is that you?"

"Yes, my friend, it's me." Cirin Hunneen wrapped his coat around the deep wound in Jerrid's left leg. Blood was everywhere.

Flakkinbarr coughed again. "The dargs, where are they?"

Cirin looked out the window, spotting the heaps of metal at the edge of the roadway. Feet twisted and jerked almost like the animals were dying, but he knew better. One of the beasts jerked up and stared at the car for a long minute, then twisted its head back and forth trying to get up.

"Hon, get us out of here!"

"Yes, sir!"

The silver Dalvon Special roared away, the twitching dargs still trying to get to their feet.

"The dargs, Cirin." Jerrid could feel that he was losing consciousness. "You have to get away. They're killers!"

"They won't bother us right now. You need medical attention, Jerrid." Cirin Hunneen had seen a lot of men die in his life time, but it still sickened him to see death so blatantly real. Hon glanced back from his driver's seat. Cirin caught his eyes and just nodded his head. Working with great care, he ripped a portion of Flakkinbarr's jacket to make a tourniquet. As he tied off the leg a black book slipped out from the jacket. Cirin reached down and pulled it from the floorboard. Cirin's eyes widened in utter horror at the thing he held in his hand. He gave a glance toward Flakkinbarr.

Jerrid could feel his body weakening. Was he going to die this time? He thought of Alleis and tears filled his eyes. "I don't know if I'm going to make it, Cirin" He coughed again. "Don't trust Klea. Don't trust him." He could barely see Cirin's face. As the darkness continued to grow Jerrid felt like he needed to sleep. *Yes, I need to rest!*

Cirin Hunneen held the book, his eyes fixed wide upon it. "How?"

"Is he gone, sir?"

Cirin checked for a pulse and then glanced up to his driver. "No, Hon. We need to get him some medical attention right away."

"What shall we do, sir?"

"We'll take the shuttle to the Bennie Coast. I think our friends at St. Tiabius will help us."

Hon nodded as he drove faster. "Yes, sir."

"The monks will keep the secret." There were other thoughts that were troubling Cirin Hunneen. How in the world did Tribune Jerrid Flakkinbarr get ahold of Dameon Klea's original journal? He supposed the book had disappeared a long time ago. It had always brought trouble, even death. A shiver shook Cirin Hunneen despite the warmth of the car. The smell of blood permeated the air. Cirin became nauseous. The past had now caught up with the future. "Hurry Hon, we don't have much time."

23

"Behold, I see before me the beginning and the end. Things that are, things that have been, and things to come. Nothing escapes my presence." — Dellenni 1:5, *The Talbah Canon*

"It was a tragedy! Losing the talents of great tribunes like Flakkinbarr, Hallenn, Lisstrin and Tuposh was a loss the entire Corporate could ill afford during the dark days of the Solarian War. That horrible vehicle accident left the inhabitants of motherworld reeling for months. To this day no one has ever found the cause. Mechanical failure was the most likely culprit. Privately, there are other opinions spread abroad. Some say the Separatists had a hand. Will the truth ever rise? It is doubtful." — Ivarn Solgarn, *The Dark Days of the War*

— Four Months Later —
30 Juylea
St. Tiabius Monastery
Bennie Coast

Sea gulls squawked and swirled overhead and the roar of pounding surf could be heard at the bottom of the cliff. An iron railing was the only thing that kept Jerrid Flakkinbarr from plunging to his death to the jagged rocks a hundred yarrs below. He stood looking out to sea as the birds continued their dance in the clear blue sky. Jerrid was dressed in a tweed colored robe of a soft weave that felt smooth against his skin. *I can see why Vennie likes these things!* Pausing, he glanced behind him. The manicured lawn spread out for nearly a thousand yarrs in all directions. The towering spires of St. Tiabius' cathedral rose mightily into the bright clear blue sky just at the edge of the lawn. The marble walkway stretched like a straight highway corridor back to the off-white colored wall surrounding the monastery. In the far distance the Bennie Mountains rose like dragon's teeth. He squinted against the glare of the sun as a man in a light-colored business suit walked briskly down the walkway straight toward him. After a time he recognized the man. It was Cirin Hunneen. Jerrid smiled and subconsciously placed a hand on his stomach.

As Cirin came nearer he threw up a hand and smiled. Jerrid waved back and eased his back up against the railing, putting his cane to one side.

"Good afternoon to you, Jerrid." Cirin remarked as he drew near.

"Good afternoon, Cirin." Jerrid smiled back.

Cirin joined him by the railing and for a few moments they both gazed out to sea.

"Beautiful day, isn't it?" Cirin asked as he watched the birds rise up and down on the air currents.

"That it is!" Jerrid remarked.

"Scribe Noric says you're ready to leave." Cirin glanced over at him, as he reached into his jacket and pulled out a small comlink. He handed it to Flakkinbarr. "I have everything arranged to get you out of the system. Hon will arrive in the morning with our shuttle. He'll take you to the star gate where an out bound freighter called the *Blue Horizon* will take you to Trae Zae. Are you sure that's where you want to go?" Cirin looked at him with concern.

Jerrid smiled weakly. "Yes, I have a friend there who'll get me to where I want to go, with no questions asked."

"Very well," Cirin replied. He handed him another small comlink. "This is to get you started in a new place, wherever that might be. New identity and funds to tide you over."

Jerrid took it and scrolled through the display. He then looked up at his visitor. "You have done far beyond what I would expect from you, Cirin. This should last me a very long time."

"I felt it's the least I could do, Jerrid."

Jerrid grinned, looked at the comlink and then glanced back at his visitor. "It's now Jediah, my friend."

Cirin laughed, "Forgive me, Jediah!"

Jerrid laughed as well. "It's hard to imagine that everyone on motherworld thinks Tribune Jerrid Flakkinbarr is dead now."

"There's been several investigations," Cirin replied. "The official report differs from the unofficial SPG summary."

"Oh?" Jerrid raised an eyebrow at this.

"The only remains recovered from the wreckage were of Tribune Hallenn, Tribune Lisstrin and overseer Kesperroud. Your body, or Gerrius Tuposh's for that matter, were never recovered from the wreck site." Cirin pointed out. "Vandermern was kind enough to check into it for me. The official report, for all practicalities, states that remains of Tribunes Jerrid Flakkinbarr and Gerrus Tuposh simply could not be identified from the twisted wreckage. Technically the two of you just disappeared. Whereabouts unknown."

"So they think we're still alive?" Jerrid looked alarmed.

"Vandermern has a source pretty close to the investigation. The SPG conducted a thorough search of the area for several months. No bodies or remains ever surfaced. The SPG closed the case and classified you both as deceased." Cirin remarked. "However, the SPG are still trying to work in a Separatists angle on this to garner more support for a direct assault on the Alliance."

Jerrid sighed and looked back toward the ocean. "Those in power will do whatever they can to make sure the Alliance is destroyed. I think they hate them more than the Solarians."

Cirin just nodded and they continued to watch the gulls as they soared overhead.

"Still, one must wonder what happened to Tuposh." Jerrid gave a sideways glance to his friend. "Maybe he made it, too."

"Possible!"

Jerrid could feel the ache in his leg as he gave out another sigh. He offered up a weak smile as he took his cane and pointed it toward the monastery. "Shall we walk back?"

Cirin turned and stepped into pace with Jerrid's hobbled gate.

It had taken Jerrid weeks to work up the strength to walk the full length of the walkway to the cliff railing. The mechanical darg had inflected a sizeable wound to his left leg. It's companion has laid open a gash across his forehead. The damage to his leg had been severe and from what the monks had told him, the physician hadn't been able to correct that damage. However, the scar on his forehead had been stitched up nicely and would gradually fade with time. What mattered most was that he had his life, even if he had to walk through it with a limp. His greatest concern now was to get to Alleis.

"I want to thank you for all you've done, Cirin." Jerrid remarked as they walked along back toward the cathedral.

"I'm glad I was there that night."

"I am too!" Jerrid chuckled. Then his thoughts grew dark as he remembered something he hadn't thought about in months. *That book!* He shivered at the thought. He was certain he'd had it with him, but when he awakened to find himself at the monastery and cleaned up from his ordeal, the monks had no knowledge of any book he may have had.

Cirin noticed the hard look on Flakkinbarr's face. "Something troubling you?"

"That night you found me, you didn't find a book in my jacket, did you?" Jerrid glanced at him as they walked along.

"No." Cirin didn't even blink at the question. "There was nothing in your jacket. Was it something important?"

A sigh filtered out from Jerrid's lips as he continued to gaze at the cathedral. "No, nothing important."

As Jerrid continued to hobble along he was glad the cursed book was gone. Perhaps now he had his life back. Maybe not the way it was. The wounds would always be a constant reminder of that dark day.

9 Midbre
Auroya Range / Tau Kerus Star System
Planet: Tau Kerus Four
Vorska
Kerus Intersystem Spaceport

The *Black Hand* glided into the landing area like a agile cat. A considerable number of spaceport workers and passengers stared as the vessel settled into the mooring and droids rolled out to secure the ship. Port authorities considered their options in regards to the black vessel across the way. Identification and clearances were all in order. Whatever business this captain had here was none of their concern, not just yet anyway. After a time, the hatch opened and the boarding ramp lowered. Two figures slowly made their way down the ramp. The short figure dressed in a dark jacket and tan pants hobbled as his cane clicked against the metal plates. They paused at the bottom of the ramp. The taller figure, a woman clad in black, turned to the man with the cane.

"You know this is a real dull place, Mr. Dros." Zappora gave Jerrid a questioning look.

"I know." Jerrid replied. "I need a dull place right now. I appreciate you transporting me here, Zappora." He paused, took a small comlink from his jacket and handed it to her.

Zappora scrolled through the screens and then handed it back to him. "I don't need your money, Mr. Dros. I'm just glad to help out a friend."

"Are you sure?"

The smile on her face got real big as she leaned over and kissed him. "You're my friend. Remember that! If you ever need me, you know where to find me."

Jerrid just gazed at her for a long moment. "Thank you!"

She gave him a big hug, turned and walked back up the ramp. At the top, she paused to wave and then followed SID back inside.

"Thank you, Zappora! Thank you!" Jerrid turned and headed toward a taxi stand.

* * *

Alleis was sitting in the garden reading from the *Talbah.* For the past few months she'd been so restless. After finding out that Jerrid and his associates had been killed in a vehicle accident, she'd come unglued. She heard the news on one of the local news-cons and almost had a heart attack that very day. It was almost like reliving those dark days when Jerrid was on Traylencoor. But she'd survived. Vars and Zoe had learned of the tragedy as well. They'd sold the summer resort and came to Tau Kerus Four looking for her. By sheer accident, Vars had come to the old Zha Trade Headquarters looking for information. The new servants were reluctant to give out any information of the previous owner or the construction processes. Alleis happened to be passing by the entry and recognized Vars' voice. Their reunion was bittersweet. She had insisted they stay on. The new servants were glad for the added personnel.

That had been months ago. Alleis had clung to the hope that Jerrid was alive. That somehow he'd miraculously survived the accident. But as time wore on and no news surfaced, Alleis was beginning to believe she'd have to face the future without him. Vars had done some discreet checking through some old channels he'd known and the only information available was that neither body of the Tribunes Flakkinbarr or Tuposh were ever recovered. There were also whispered rumors that the two tribunes may have been involved with Separatists who wanted Hallenn and Lisstrin out of the way. Alleis would not believe any of it. She knew her husband and knew exactly what he was doing.

Hope does not disappoint. She read that for the third time. "I just want my Jerrid back, Aidioni! Sweet Yushann, please! I need to know. I need to know!" Despite all the days of hoping, believing and wondering if she'd ever see her beloved Jerrid again, Alleis was growing less and less hopeful. It was a comfort to have Vars and Zoe again in her life. She'd missed them terribly, but without Jerrid, she really didn't know what she'd do.

Ask and it shall be given to you; seek and ye shall find, knock and the door will be opened. She stared at the page, a tear starting to spill from her eye. "Please bring my Jerrid back!"

It was well into the afternoon when Alleis closed the book. She placed it on the table beside her chair and got to her feet. Suddenly a wash of electric fire settled over her like a net. Every cell in her body tingled like a thousand pulsating flames. Alleis felt her legs turn to lead and yet the fire continued to burn.

"Alleis!"

She knew that voice! *Oh, dear Yushann!* She could feel the tingling fire growing brighter. Her face began to flush.

"Alleis!"

She turned her head and gasped. "Jerrid!" She screamed! "Jerrid!" The fire flashed and then vanished. Her legs were not lead anymore as she bolted to his arms. Behind him she saw Vars and Zoe, locked arm and arm, tears streaming down their faces.

After a time, Jerrid pulled back and looked into his wife's eyes. "Oh, Alleis, I have missed you so much!"

"Jerrid!" She buried her head in his chest.

After several minutes, Jerrid eased his wife back into her chair and came over and struggled to bend down on his knees.

Alleis gasped as she saw the cane for the first time. "Jerrid, what happened to you?"

As awkward as it was to be on his knees, Jerrid was determined to do this. He placed the cane within easy reach and gazed into her tear-stained face. "No questions now, please."

She nodded in reply as he wiped her tears away and smiled at her. He then produced a small cloth bag and placed it on her lap. Something moved inside and Alleis again gasped. She looked at him wide eyed.

Jerrid smiled and nodded at the bag as it moved on her lap. "Look inside."

Alleis pulled open the bag and peered inside. Her mouth dropped open. "Jerrid!" She placed her hands into the moving bag and lifted out a small black and white kibbercat kitten. The cat meowed several times, looked into her eyes and started purring.

"Her name is Gracie." Jerrid smiled as he patted the kitten's head. "She'll never replace Tazz, but I couldn't see us without a cat."

Alleis smiled as she cuddled the kitten to her chest. She reached out and took Jerrid's hand. "Aidioni has answered my prayers, Jerrid. I have you back."

Jerrid wiped the tear from his eye and leaned in and kissed his wife. "I am one blessed man, Alleis. Aidioni has given us another chance. Let us make the best of it!"

Vars and Zoe came over and circled around Jerrid and Alleis. Tears began to flow and the soft sound of little meows were heard amongst the sobbing.

A small light appeared next to the yellow zebin tree. It pulsated three times and then grew to the size of a small globe. Jerrid glanced out of the corner of his eye as he heard fabric tearing and the sweet smell of lillies wafted to his nose. Lt. Arie'el stood by the yellow zebin in his dazzling uniform. He smiled at Jerrid.

"You are safe now, Jerrid." Arie'el replied with a smile on his lips. "Aidioni has placed a shield around this place. Live long and stay in the Light." The lieutenant's uniform glowed bright white and Jerrid had to look away. When he turned his head the light was gone. Jerrid looked back into his wife's eyes and smiled. It was good to be home.

Epilogue

October 13, 2024
Lawrence Bakersfield Laboratories
Clearing Lab Twelve
1041 Zulu

Dr. Thomas Farraday took the pipe from his mouth and shuffled through the data printout. The chair gave a creak as he leaned back and glanced at the clock on the wall. 3:41 AM!

"You've got to be kidding me!" he exclaimed, rubbing his eyes.

"What would I be kidding you about, Thomas?"

"I can't believe I read through those pages that fast, Wanda." Farraday was well known for his reading speed but even he couldn't believe that he had finished the first half of the first printout in that short time frame.

"Your reading level has improved remarkably, Thomas." the computer blinked. *"Perhaps the information provided a much needed stimulus."*

"Stimulus!" Farraday smiled. "That's putting it mildly, Wanda. This is going to cause a stir and General Dalton is going to be very skeptical." He shook the printout and laid it on the desktop.

Thomas carefully pushed his tired body out of the chair. Despite the fact that his muscles were tugging at him to put his body to bed and get some rest, Thomas kept thinking about the story. It nudged at his emotions and made him realize that indeed the story of love now transcended even time and space. He refilled his coffee cup with the last bit from the sergeant's brew. As late as it was, he felt strangely alert, despite his aching body. He glanced over at the table with the glass case.

Yes, those little blue crystals had certainly changed his whole life. *Where is all this going to take me?* He physically shook all over. Better not think about that right now. He forced back a yawn, rubbed his eyes with the back of his hand and stole another glance at the clock. It might be late, but Thomas could not shake the images from the story. The cat, Tazz, was a constant reminder of his own Stanley. Tribune Flakkinbarr's deadly book certainly found it's way into someone else's hands. What would become of that book and what other lives would it touch and destroy? Carefully placing his body back into his chair, Thomas reached for the printout. He was a little fearful as to what may lay ahead.

HERE ENDS BOOK ONE OF
CHILDREN OF THE DARK MILLENNIUM

Appendix

Reference Links: Crystal: PCS-One ID-1000-0001

Reference Notes 10/13/2024
Thomas Farraday
LBL Clearing Lab Twelve

The following is Wanda's interpretation of weights, measures and time frames in regard to the initial data derived from the first crystal brought down from the Bolivian crash site. Bear in mind that a couple of the terms used bears a close resemblance to several of our current measurements and should not be confused with the current US standard. Until we find more accurate information in the data in the later crystals this will have to serve as a sketchy guideline at best. Hopefully, Wanda is correct in her interpretation of the data that has been analyzed so far.

DISTANCE/LENGTH
Ticc = one inch
Yarr = 30 ticcs or 2.5 feet
2112 Yarrs = 1 Mycron
1 Mycron = 1 mile
1 Plat = 6336 sq. yarrs

WEIGHTS
1 Gan = 1 ounce
24 Gans = 1 Kef
1 Kef = 1.5 pounds

MONEY
Ruul = 100 dollars
Keynote = 50 dollars
Farn = 5 cents

The amazing thing about this first crystal is the many cross reference links to historical data and archived information stored in layered links within the body of the text. The following is a reference link to the TeMari Calendar. It is interesting that the person or persons responsible for these crystals took the time to incorporate this material. They were assuming that the surviving text would be found by someone who had little knowledge of their social structure or civilization. The following is from one sub-link to the word *calendar.* This may be helpful in understanding the time frame usage in the ancient text.

SubLink 354:Line 1245
Direct Quoted Material

THE ACCORD OF DORA KERRA

The TeMari calendar has a twisted history of origin. The setting dates back to the first establishment of the Trade Consortium which included the star systems of TeMar, Pusholiin, Yufol der Boorg, Aabersiirn, Phystaccar, and Dora Kerra. Each system had its own means of measuring history and time, and when commerce was linked by computers to a central exchange first set up on TeMar, things began to get confusing. To alleviate all the misinterpretation of information that took place over a ten year period, delegates from each star group meet on Dora Kerra to work out a standardized means of date/time measuring that would satisfy all parties in the trade exchange.

The Accord of Dora Kerra, as it was known, established a universal (Consortium wide) reference point for standardized dates and measuring. A central calendar was devised for the TeMari Trade Consortium. All calendars throughout the Consortium mark time tables with the signing of the accord as year 1ADK (Accord of Dora Kerra).

Several disputes erupted in 25ADK over the methods of time measurements when the Tammer Seekkarr star group was added to the Consortium. Tammer Seekkarr wanted to continue to use its measure of time reckoning, but this proved to reek havoc with Trade Exchange computers who could not handle the five interlinking world calendars of Tammer Seekkarr. With the addition of PaFor Mio in 154ADK, time/date measuring was once again reestablished along the lines of the Accord of Dora Kerra, with slight variations in the terms of the accord. However, the need for a system-wide governing body was realized and for several hundred years various ruling bodies tried to establish order throughout the Consortium. Time measuring was once again left up to the various systems and the Accord of Dora Kerra became a disjointed relic.

As more systems were brought into the Consortium, the need for a stable central governing system was paramount. So in 1845ADK, the Council of Directors was formulated as ruling body over the Consortium. The Trade Consortium as an entity was abolished and the new government established the TeMari Corporate and maintained the Accord of Dorra Kerra as the means of date and time reckoning. Despite the diversity of local star group races and cultures, the Corporate is referred to as TeMari because they were the principle figures in formulating the new ruling government. There are several groups, including Tammer Seekkarr, which maintain two calendars, deferring to the TeMari calendar as the official one when it comes to historic and economic record keeping. Starbases, outposts, and major mining colonies all use the Standardized system of measuring date/time. However, there are several star systems in the Corporate that still do not adhere to the standard TeMari calendar, these being the ViKeen Zaar system and eight systems in the Desterri Range.

TeMARI CALENDAR

The TeMari calendar consists of twelve months of thirty equal days. Each month has five weeks, divided into six days.

Days of the week

Dresday = 1st day of week
Versday = 2nd day of week
Velday = 3rd day of week

Frensday = 4th day of week
Thiysday = 5th day of week
Mynsday = 6th day of week

For the average TeMari worker, the work week usually begins on Dresday and concludes on Frensday. Ten hour work days are highly common practices throughout the Corporate. Thiysday and Mynsday are commonly set aside for observance of religious practices by the various culture groups that inhabit motherworld and the surrounding star systems. The Shonteeg faith observes Thiysday as their holy day while followers of the DriSeenk faith hallow Mynsday as their most scared of days. Companies owned by Shonteeg followers usually work from Mynsday to Frensday, and those owned by the DriSeenk followers work Dresday through Thiysday. Those that adhere to neither of the faith practices are usually content with having the common two day off from work regardless of what day of the week it falls on.

Months of the year

Jamlea = 1
Thronbre = 2
Sakbar = 3
Somlea = 4
Cyibre = 5
Bonnar = 6
Juylea = 7
Midbre = 8
Semar = 9
Fornlea = 10
Nollenbre = 11
XinJammar = 12

The last week of XinJammar has been observed by most TeMari citizens as prelude to Festival. It is called the Festival of De'Terra Mon, and takes place three days before the first day of the new year. The Dork

KeDer of Pusholiin celebrate the last week of XinJammar and the first week of Jamlea as their Festival Time.

Government Body

Director: executive of the entire Corporate
Vice Director: subordinate to the executive.
High Tribunal: Legislative body.
High Court: Rules on legislation passed by Tribunal. Consists of one High Judge and five Senior Judges.

TeMari Corporate is divided into three stellar regions:

Motherworld Core Systems which consists of the Consortium Rim and the Near Consortium Rim. This comprises 16 ranges with representation by 32 tribunes.

The Frontier Rim consists of 16 quadrants divided into 192 ranges with representation by 384 tribunes.

The Far Frontier Rim also consists of 16 quadrants divided into 192 ranges with representation by 384 tribunes. Each range in a quadrant has two tribunes for representation.

Addendum to Reference Notes 10/13/2024
Thomas Farraday

Considering that so far Wanda has found over three thousand cross references within the text on the first crystal, this is by far not a conclusive appendix to the text. I'm sure the final volume of our findings will have a much more exhaustive one. It would appear that we have multiple volumes within each crystal and therefore any appendix may prove to be monstrous in size.

About the Author

Steven C. Macon was born in North Carolina, but spent most of his adult life in the sunny state of Florida. While attending college Steven was involved with many of the campus newspapers and magazines. He worked for a short season as a circus clown and puppeteer. There was another period of time where Steven spent time jumping out of airplanes for fun. He obtained a Master Skydivers rating while a member of the US Parachute Association. Steven also participated in a good number of community theater productions. One of his major accomplishments was backpacking Yosemite. His hobbies include photography and likes to dabble with painting landscapes, still-life's. Steven and his wife Debra now reside in southwestern Virginia with their four cats.

22956451R00195

Made in the USA
Charleston, SC
05 October 2013